In the Realm of the Dead

by

Rod Hacking

In memory of our beloved

Elizabeth (Lizzie) Gussman

The Body in the Mortuary

Henry Morley was a permanent night sister and did not like to be spoken of as a charge nurse, and his staff never thought of him as anything other than sister. It troubled no one that he was a self-evident old queen and it troubled him not at all that everyone knew it, and indeed he enjoyed being able to be as camp as he chose. What he knew and everyone else did, and why no one ever laughed at him, was that he was outstanding at his job. The staff enjoyed his willingness to self-mock, but there was no other member of staff, except perhaps the Medical Director who enjoyed more esteem. This regard had also been recognised in the award of an CBE for his work as a mobile medic in Tanzania, travelling across the land on foot with his medicine chest on his back, although Henry made light of it and never mentioned it. To the fore of his mind, however, were two boys, his adopted 'sons' as he called them, back in Africa, and to whom he sent all the money he earned.

He liked night duty for several reasons. The first was that it meant working with black West Indian women auxiliary nurses, who reminded him of his years in Africa and sometimes he would forget where he was and hand medication to a nurse when they were doing the drug round in the middle of the night with an instruction in Kiswahili. Night Duty also provided him with a little time to read when he took his rest, and in the Summer months it was usually light by 4 am and the world outside quiet.

The Hospice had fifty-five beds, mostly occupied by patients in the last stages of cancers of various kinds. The pattern of each night was constant. Henry arrived before the rest of the night staff to receive the reports from the three wards on each patient. Keeping his paperwork up-to-date was essential. Once the night staff arrived there was a drug round which he had to administer on each ward, unless there was a staff nurse on duty to share it with him. Tonight S/N Kathy Haddon was working on the Norfolk Ward, and he knew he could rely on her.

At about 2-00am he had to complete a security round, checking doors and windows, and ending appropriately in the mortuary in the basement. It was supposed to be done by two members of staff but often there were not enough nurses available for him to be accompanied and he did it alone. On this night he took with him Nurse Hanrahan who talked incessantly and provided him with information about every aspect of her life, and that meant *every* aspect, to his amazement about which she showed no trace of embarrassment. Perhaps, knowing him to be gay, she felt quite safe sharing the intimate details of her married life. Normally the security round took him no more than 20 minutes, but with Nurse Hanrahan it might easily double in length, and which according to her, seemed to happen to her husband too!

At night they didn't use the lift unless they had to transfer a departed patient to the basement. The stairs from the ground floor to the mortuary below were few and his first act was to turn on the lights. They then entered the room very occasionally used for post-mortems with a metal bed in the middle. It also doubled with appropriate modification, as a bed for relatives to view their departed family member. One night Henry had entered the room to find a former patient lying on the bed, having been forgotten by the day staff who should have returned it to one of the fridges in the room beyond. As he was alone on this night, he had to move the body by himself and of course, having been left out for some hours, the body was thawing. Eventually he had to summon help. Reporting this as the day staff returned, it quickly became evident that the culprit was none other the sister on Suffolk Ward who went bright red when informed. Still, no harm was done.

Henry passed through the first room to the fridges beyond.

Nurse Hanrahan was chatting nineteen to the dozen behind him. He checked his list, expecting six residents, each with a card on the door bearing their name. He then had to open each door, including the empty ones just to be certain. The doors were large and heavy, each concealing space for three occupants, and four doors altogether. Nurse Hanrahan had seen death often enough not to be fazed by any of this.

When Henry opened the third door he was surprised to find an extra corpse occupying the bottom shelf. There had been no card on the door and no paperwork given to him as he had come on duty.

'Nurse Hanrahan,' he said, 'Could you please count the number of bodies we have here tonight?'

She opened the doors in turn, and then turned to Henry.

'Seven, Mr Morley.'

'Yes, seven, and there should be six. What do you make of that?'

'Probably a mistake on the ward. Someone forgot to fill in a card for the door and it might have been too late to let the office know.'

'Yes, that's it I'm sure, but still I ought to have a closer look and see if I recognise him.'

People were put into the fridge feet first so the tray did not require much manoeuvring. Henry pulled back the cloths over the face.'

'Oh,' he said, 'I rather suspect we may need some help.'

'Why?' said Nurse Hanrahan, somewhat intrigued.

'In the first place, I don't recognise him at all, then it's clear he hasn't been dead all that long, and third because on the whole here, we're not given to shooting someone from close range through the forehead.'

'O my God, Mr Morley. Are you being serious?'

'Come and see for yourself.'

Nurse Hanrahan came forward.

'H'm, I think you're right. What do we do now?'

'First and foremost we have our living patients to consider, so you and I need to be back on the wards. However we need to summon someone to take charge of all that is going to happen here over the next few hours. That means the Medical Director, I suppose, but the best person to take charge would be her PA, Lizzie. We also need at least two of the Reception Staff, and whoever was on duty last thing.'

'That was Tommy and he was complaining that he was on by himself.'

'Then I suppose I had better call the police though they might take some convincing that we've found a body in the mortuary.'

They both laughed, failing to be struck by the incongruity of their mirth.

'Ok, my darling, you go back upstairs and call Staff Nurse Haddon. You can tell her why but ask her, unless otherwise occupied with a patient, to join me in Matron's Office as soon as possible. Stress the urgency.'

'I will.'

She left, and Henry turned to the man with the hole in his head.

'And what am I going to do with you?'

'In the end he pushed the tray back in and closed the door. The police would presumably need to take him away.

Martin Peabody had a number of marriages behind him, and although the woman lying asleep next to him was married, she wasn't married to him. Such things were far from unknown among police officers, especially among senior men and junior women. They were on a parallel rota meaning that they did their night shift on the same week. She assumed he had arranged it that way, he knew it was a sheer accident, and if and when he became tired of her, or when she began to cling, he would arrange to have the rota changed. For now it suited him, though, if he did but know it, she had unspoken doubts.

Just before 3:00 their phones rang more or less simultaneously.

'Sorry to disturb you, guv, but this really is an odd one. Do you know the Hospice in Forest Hill?'

'I've driven past. Isn't is a hospital for the dying?'

'Yeah. Well, the nurses have to do a security round during the night and in the mortuary discovered something unusual – a body that shouldn't have been there, with a bullet hole in his forehead.'

Next to him, Ellie had received much the same message and was already getting into her clothes.

'Ok, I'm on my way. Could you let DS Ellie Middlewood know? She's on tonight and I'll need to get her to serve as site manager.'

'I think it's already been done, guv.'

'Good and we shall have to annoy Doc Smithers by waking him up though as it's in a mortuary, he will at least be at home. SOCOS too'

'Guv.'

Ellie was about to leave but came over and gave him a kiss.

'I'll see you there,' she said with a smile.

The noise of vehicles arriving could quite easily have awakened the dead let alone the still living on the wards, some of whom had left their beds to find out what all the fuss was about. Henry was not minded to disclose any details and encouraged everyone back to bed as he prepared for the 5:00 drug round. Not all patients needed something at this hour but he reckoned that if he let slip what had happened two floors below them, they all probably would.

On arrival, Ellie was taken downstairs by a constable and shown the body still in situ. She visited mortuaries often enough not to be perturbed by what she saw.

'I don't like these places,' said the young officer.

'Oh, I don't know,' said Ellie. 'This one's nice and sweet; I've been in worse.'

By the time they had returned upstairs to Reception, Martin had arrived and was talking to the pathologist. Seeing Ellie, Martin asked her to oversee all comings and goings, and to work out a way in which getting the body in could have been done.'

'Yes, boss,' she said.

'You, constable,' she said to the officer with whom she had been downstairs, 'can take Dr Smithers and DCI Peabody down to the mortuary.'

'Gee thanks, Sarge,' he replied.

'Do you know this is the place in South London where more people die than in any other, and here I am, senior pathologist for the Met south of the river, and I've never been before. Odd, don't you think?'

'I've lived in London all my life and never been to the Tower of London.'

'That's nothing, guv,' said the police officer leading them, 'I live 50 yards from a public convenience and I've never pissed there.'

How the three of them managed the remaining steps they never knew.

The officer, who on his third visit was feeling confident, opened the door and pulled the tray out a little and then stood back, allowing the pathologist and DCI Peabody access.

'Get my photographers down here, please, constable, before we move him. We'll get him out on to the fork-lift before removing the rest of the white sheets he's wrapped in, but the first thing I've noticed is that whoever wrapped him did so exactly as you would expect a nurse to do so performing a last office. Look at the other bodies and you'll see what I mean.'

Martin could see at once what the doctor meant though he was a little confused about the term the doctor had used.

'I thought only a priest could do the last rites, not a nurse.'

'You're correct about that, but I'm talking about what is known as the "last office", used to denote what nurses do to prepare a body for the mortuary. Which usually includes wrapping it in a sheet in a certain way, as this one has been,'

Meanwhile the doctor's team had arrived and were obeying their boss in every regard, capturing the scene. Eventually the tray was pulled out completely onto the fork-lift and the doctor began undoing the sheet.

'Jesus,' said the pathologist as the body was revealed. Below them on the tray was a man wearing a purple shirt with a pectoral cross, and a little lower, body parts of some kind lay on his groin area.

'I would say we have here the body of a murdered bishop

whose balls have been cut off. I would guess that he was a bishop of the Church of England, given catholic bishops don't on the whole wear purple shirts like that. He has a Bishop's ring on his right hand, but no wedding ring on the other though that doesn't mean anything. You will need to disturb the residents of Lambeth Palace to get someone to identify him.'

'Er guys,' said Martin to the photographers and constable, 'only we five know about the testicles. It must remain that way for now and if it leaks we shan't have many suspects.'

'I'll wrap him again, Martin and then we can take him up in the lift.'

'How old do you think he is?'

'He's been in a fridge for some hours and I've no idea how long he was dead before that so I can't really say. Your man from Lambeth will have the details.'

'And what about the cutting off of his balls? Was that done before or after death?'

'Come on, Martin, I know a mortuary is my natural domain but I need to be in my own to be able to answer your questions, but once I get him there, everything will be apparent. The only that strikes me as unusual about that, is that professional killers who cut bits off, tend to cut off the whole works and ram them in the mouth.'

The mortuary team had come down the stairs and waited to be summoned. Both the doctor and Martin knew that these two men were utterly reliable and just got on with what they had to do and mostly gave little consideration to what they were handling, having seen in their time all sorts of unpleasant things. For them it was another job and they were professionals, though even they thought this somewhat bizarre.

Upstairs Ellie had been working hard interviewing the key people – those who had found the body, and the one person who had seen a van park by the back door and assumed it was an undertaker come to collect. Delivery was not the norm! Martin ascended the stairs before the body emerged from the lift and was taken into an awaiting vehicle and on its way to Lewisham

Hospital.

'Anything?' Martin asked Ellie.

'Nothing of special interest. A normal check on the contents of the mortuary during a security round after 2 o'clock by a delightfully camp man calling himself the night sister and a somewhat garrulous West Indian nurse from Brixton. Checking behind each door they found a body that shouldn't have been there.'

'When would the last check have been made?'

'Two patients died yesterday and the second went off the ward downstairs at about 3 pm. Nobody would have gone in after that.'

'Visitors, friends of the deceased?'

'Two families are due this morning at about 10:00.'

'Well, hopefully SOCOS will have finished and gone by then. I think you and I should go and have a talk with the Medical Director though I very much doubt she'll have much to offer.'

'That woman over there organising everyone and everything may be of more use. She's the Director's PA and took charge when she got here.'

'What did she have to say?'

'She said there was a CCTV round the side, but that it showed nothing other than two pairs of feet carrying what looks like a coffin. It shows neither face nor the number plate of the vehicle.'

'Of course not – that would make it far too easy for us. Come on, let's go upstairs and talk to the boss, and don't forget she's an extremely highly-regarded woman – the pioneer of terminal care across the world.'

A knock on the door was opened by the Medical Director herself. She had a big smile on her face and turned and poured Martin and Ellie some coffee. They took the seats she pointed to.

'You will have some questions, I imagine. It sounds like something out of Agatha Christie: a body in the mortuary.'

'Tell me, doctor, is this a Church of England foundation?'

'Not at all. We are under the NHS completely and none of the denominations or any of the religions play any part in running the place. Our chaplains are inter-denominational and all have other jobs which pay their wages. I have to say I wasn't expecting that as your first question.'

'Ah well, you see, doctor, though we would prefer you to keep this to yourself for the time being, the body we found in the mortuary is that of what we think may be a Church of England Bishop who has been both murdered and mutilated.'

The Medical Director raised her eyebrows.

'We receive visits from such people all the time, the great and the good you know, more trouble than they are worth much of the time, but we haven't had any such visit from a bishop for quite some time. Was there any identification on the body?'

'No. His pockets were empty but a post-mortem might turn something up.'

'The van that left a few minutes ago, did that contain the body?'

'Yes. Heading for Lewisham.'

A shame. I probably would have recognised him. I am often used by the Church in various ways and I've got to know some of the people in purple. I suspect you will need to get help from Lambeth.'

'Doctor,' asked Ellie in a puzzled tone, 'you seemed to show no reaction when Inspector Peabody told you about what has been found.'

'Oh, I would have expected you two to understand that. I have been a doctor for a long time and when I worked in Guy's Hospital saw most things and one or two more besides. Now I head an institution in which approximately 650 people die every year. Of course any man's death diminishes me, because I am involved in mankind, as the poet said, but now I'm never shocked, and I would imagine and hope indeed, that it is the same for you, or else however could you do your job?'

'I *am* shocked by the fact that this is the first time I've attended a murder scene and had John Donne quoted at me.' laughed Ellie.

'Look, come when you need to, but if possible try not to disrupt the work of the place – the staff and patients. Finally, I imagine you both dressed rapidly in the dark when you were called in the night and it's just possible that might account for the fact that you're both wearing the same odd socks. I just mention it.'

Ellie blushed at once as Martin quickly rose and shook the doctor's hand.

'Wonderful to meet you doctor. Oh but wait a moment. I took a photo on my phone of the face of the dead man. There is a bullet wound, but is there any chance you could put a name to the face?'

He took out his phone and found the photograph and showed it to her. She held it for a moment and than handed it back.

'Peter Sherriff, sometime Bishop of Kennington. He's retired but still functions or, at least he did. You will still need a formal identification of course, but there's no doubt in my mind. You will get everything you need from Lambeth Palace, but let me wish you good luck with that.'

'Where did he live?' asked Ellie.

'In a vicarage by Clapham Common, I believe, but once again you can find out what you need from Lambeth I imagine.'

'I shall need a full list of all those you have employed here in the last ten years.'

'Yes, of course, as I am assuming you think there must be some sort of inside aspect to this, someone who knew the ropes.'

'Yes, that seems likely,' said Martin.

'Pam, can you do that?'

'I'll do it straight away,' came a voice from the intercom on the desk.

'Is your intercom permanently live?' asked Ellie.

'Whilst Pam is in her office it is. In this day and age I regret to say it has become something of necessity to make sure there is a witness to everything I say and hear.'

'Everything?', asked Ellie.

'Everything,' replied the voice, 'and as you leave you can readjust your socks.'

Martin ignored what he had just heard.

'I'm afraid your mortuary will have to stay out of bounds to all but the Scene of Crime Officers until they have completed their precise and in depth examination. It's almost impossible for someone to enter a room and not leave something of themselves behind.'

'How long will that take?'

'As long as it takes, doctor, I'm afraid. In the meantime you can either make use of a spare room on the ward or arrange for a funeral director to come at once. The bodies already in there cannot be moved until the team have finished, but they will inform you when they have done.'

'It will be a nuisance.'

'Alas, so is the brutal murder and mutilation of a bishop.'

The mystery voice sounded again.

'Inspector, a man calling himself Superintendent Charnley has just arrived asking for you both and is in Reception.'

'We'll come.' said Ellie rising. 'Thank you doctor. You do amazing work here and I'm just so sorry that this happened here, but we'll try and leave you having caused minimum havoc.'

They met the voice in the adjacent room.

'I've printed the list of names but as you may want to cross check it, I've put them onto a USB memory stick. Call me if you need to go further back than ten years.'

'Thank you,' said Martin whose mood had perked up since leaving the doctor.

'Socks!' said Pam before they left, and both grinned sheepishly, her own face remaining straight.

Downstairs, Chief Superintendent 'Dirty Dave' Charnley, was sitting chatting to a cleaning lady in her uniform who looked rather fetching. Catching sight of Martin and Ellie, he whispered something to her at which she laughed and moved off.

'I'm told that at the top of these stairs there is an empty room we can use, so let's go there.'

It was room where visitors could relax but at this time of the morning there were none, and they sat together by the windows overlooking a tennis court.

'So, tell me all about it.'

'Someone in the course of a visit to the mortuary in the middle of the night, a normal part of procedure, spotted an extra resident. We were called and found that he was a bishop in his purple shirt and suit wearing the traditional cross and ring of his office. Less traditional was the presence of his testicles lying on his body and a bullet hole in his forehead. A lot of people come here to end their lives suffering from cancer, but this man most certainly did not. At the moment we only have a partial recognition from the medical director who thinks he is called Peter Sherriff, a retired Church of England Bishop. She suggests we make contact with someone at Lambeth Palace who might be able to give a formal identification and provide us with some information about him. We don't know whether he is married or has a family or anything until we can know for certain who it is, but she warned us that getting information from that source might not be easy. Scene of crime officers are still at work. All we know is that a vehicle reversed to the back door last night and everyone assumed it was an undertaker coming to collect a body which is what normally happens, but it looks as if this one was making a delivery. They were short in reception last night and no one thought to check on what was happening or collect the document that would have been handed in by an undertaker.'

Have you not heard?' said Charnley, 'Bobby Edwards, my most able deputy, paid a visit last night to watch his team, Millwall football club, and found himself trying to prevent a fight getting out of hand between the home team fans and those from Fulham. Unfortunately, he met a bottle full on in the face and one that had already been broken, so he will be in Guys Hospital for some time to come, having plastic surgery which can only come as a comfort to the rest of us.'

'No, I hadn't heard.'

'It's his own bloody silly fault for supporting that lot of thugs, and I mean by that the players. Anyway, it means that you two will have to act up and take this on yourselves. It sounds to me like it must be a local job with inside help but it's your task to find out who and why. You've both been on during the night, so I want you to go home now and get some sleep until you're back at the factory by 1:30. Either I will or, if I get nowhere, I'll ask the commissioner, to get in touch with Lambeth and I'll arrange for a car to pick someone up who can do a formal identity and you will meet them at the mortuary at 2 o'clock. Under no circumstances allow yourself to be manipulated by whoever it is you see, and that includes the Archbishop of Canterbury himself, if it is him. I will also get you updated warrant cards for your new temporary status but from experience do not mention when interviewing anyone the word "acting".'

Charnley stood.

'I'll see you both later, now get off to bed – alone.'

They watched him leave the room and make his way down the stairs.

'Well, Superintendent,' asked Ellie, 'what do you think he meant by that?'

'We may call him Dirty Dave, but he is very sharp indeed.'

Lambeth Palace

A short sleep in the middle of the day can often leave you feeling far worse than having none. Ellie's husband, Ted, was working from home and so was able to wake her up with some food before she had to return to work. He was very proud of her new position.

'That is absolutely brilliant,' he had said when she had called him before she set off for home.'

'It's only temporary but I'm very much hoping they might forget that and let me stay an inspector.'

As she dressed she gazed at her socks and laughed.

'Why are you laughing?' asked Ted.

'Oh just at all that has happened this morning. It's been very strange indeed, quite unlike anything I've known in the job, and believe you me, there's been some very funny things over the years.'

As she drove back to work, Ellie thought about how much she liked Ted. He was a nice man. But equally she knew she didn't love him and never had. She had a lot of time for Martin too, and though they were having a sort of affair, or more of a fling really, she knew that inside it was not what she was wanting, even if at this moment in time she had no idea what it might be.

Martin lived alone although it wasn't for lack of trying and he had to rely on his phone to wake him up in time for him to have a shower and to get dressed ready to start again. He too looked at his socks in wonder. That medical director certainly had very sharp eyes and the more he thought about the work that they did there, the more he was impressed with her even though at the time he had felt irritation.

His phone rang and it was Ellie.

'Go straight to the mortuary, Martin. The boss has already arranged a car for someone to meet us there earlier than he said. It's another Bishop, a woman for a change, and is apparently called the Bishop at Lambeth, which means she is number two to the Archbishop who is in Africa and who we can therefore rule out as the murderer.'

'Pity that, but we'll see what we can manage. Are you going to be there?'

'Don't you mean "Are you going to be there, Inspector?"'

'Oh God you're going to be unbearable from now on, or is it, even more unbearable?'

Martin parked outside the mortuary entrance in such a way as to cause any ambulance to be blocked but he didn't care. He could see Ellie already talking.

'Bishop, this is my boss, Superintendent Peabody.'

If he was hoping for some kind of glamour puss in a vicar's outfit he was disappointed. She was plain and non-descript, in a dark suit wearing a purple shirt with a cross just as the earlier Bishop had been. She shook his hand and made ready for what they had to do. He thought that she was probably in her early 50s and he wondered if she had ever had to do this before.

'I am Helen Bradley. I used to be a bishop in the Midlands and have either been rewarded or punished by my present position as number two to the Archbishop. I hope I can help you with this identification. It's going to be a huge shock for the church, whoever it is, assuming that it is actually a bishop and not someone dressed up to look like one. Anyway, I'm in your hands.'

Ellie open the door and as always the first thing that hit them was the ghastly smell of the formaldehyde used to preserve the bodies. The pathologist was waiting for them.

'Good afternoon Bishop,' he said, 'I very much hope we can get this over with quickly. Many people do find the smell intolerable though it's quite necessary for what we do. Please follow me into this room here. The body will be on the other side of the glass. If you wish to go nearer that can be arranged but I wouldn't recommend it if you can make a positive identification without having to do so.'

The four of them entered the viewing room and through the glass they could see the shape of a body under a sheet and at a nod of the head by the pathologist, one of his assistants pulled back of the sheet from the face. Martin noticed immediately that the bullet hole in the middle of the forehead had been obscured.

'Bishop Bradley, do you recognise this person as someone you know and can make a positive identification? '

'Yes. It's Bishop Peter Sherriff without a doubt.'

'Thank you for that,' said Ellie. 'There is a form which you will need to sign confirming what you have just said. After that we can let you return to your place of work, but I'm afraid we shall need to come and join you there because we have a lot of questions.'

'I'm not sure that will be possible today,' replied the Bishop. 'You will need to be in touch with my secretary and make an appointment and I can then begin to answer your questions.'

'Yes, I'm sure you're very busy,' said Martin, 'but I think you should ring your secretary and tell her, and trust me this is not a polite request, to cancel all your engagements and appointments for the rest of the day, because you will be talking to us on the matter of the murder of one of your colleagues. I repeat, this is not a request, it is an instruction.'

'I certainly have no wish to argue with you in a place such as this, superintendent, but I take my orders from the Archbishop of Canterbury and no one else.'

'I gather his grace is in Africa. How is he going to react to the knowledge that his deputy has refused to help the police in their enquiries into a murder, and is therefore facing possible arrest?'

'I was a solicitor before I took holy orders and I therefore have some knowledge of criminal law, and I know full well that you have nothing for which you can arrest me. I am perfectly happy to answer all your questions but at a time when I can have legal representation and that will not be possible until tomorrow.'

'I'm sorry Bishop, but you're out of date. I require you to answer questions in relation to a murder. I will arrange legal representation for you under the terms of the Police and Criminal Evidence Act 1984. I can also determine where that shall be, and I determine it will be in Lambeth Palace. The inspector and myself will follow your car there. If you wish to arrange for a lawyer of your own choice to meet us there, that is entirely up to you. If you refuse to cooperate in any way, Lewisham police station is less than half a mile away, so it's up to you.'

The Bishop left them and went out to the car that had brought her, closely followed by Ellie and they set off together. Martin stayed behind to talk to the pathologist.

'How on earth, when you spoke to me earlier, did you intuit that dealing with Lambeth would be a difficult thing?'

'Because like all institutions they shut up shop when you approach. They adore secrecy because they think it's the same as power. They're no different from the Masons.'

'I'm grateful for the warning. Now, is there anything from the post-mortem I need to know?'

'The bullet was a .22LR, pretty common, and fired I would say from close to. I'm sure he would have been screaming because everything suggests he, she or they cut off his testicles while he was still alive. Perhaps he thought they would leave him then, but no. What is interesting however, is what we found on his back when we were undressing him. It was a playing card, the Ace of Spades, which had been hammered into his spine with a short nail. I can't say whether he was dead or alive at this moment but I fear the latter.'

'We shall need to check it for prints and DNA.'

'I have it in an evidence bag for you in my office. Finally, for now at least, there is considerable evidence that he took part in homosexual activity, judging from the state of his anus.'

Martin set off for the Thames, and passing St Thomas's Hospital, pulled in on the left outside the Palace Gate, ignoring the yellow lines and No Parking signs, as had Ellie before him. She was waiting for him and he informed her of what the pathologist had discovered and of the content of an interesting phone call he had received shortly before arriving.

'Let's see what the woman bishop has to tell us. Phrases like "getting blood from a stone" come to mind,' said Martin.

A huge medieval gate had an electric bell which greatly amused Ellie, and it was opened by someone who had the appearance of a typical flunkey.

'Yes?'

'Don't piss me about. You know who we are and who we have come to see, so take us.'

The man said nothing but turned and led them across a yard and pointed to some steps. At the top there was a corridor with doors with fancy titles of various kinds – a real bureaucracy.

'Hardly Jesus and his disciples, is it?' said Martin.

Ahead was a man waiting for them, unsmiling and far from warm in his welcome.

'This way, please.'

He turned a corner and led them into a large and comfortable office with the words "Bishop at Lambeth" on the door though the said person was absent.

'The Bishop will be here presently. We are extremely busy here and we would appreciate it if you could not take up too much of her time.'

'Would you indeed?' said Ellie.

'Who are you?' asked Martin.

'Gordon Allen, Chief of Staff and Strategy.'

'I can't recall where such titles can be found in the Bible,' said Martin.

The man did not reply.

Eventually, the bishop arrived and sat behind her imposing desk.

'Sorry to keep you waiting.'

'First of all, please accept our thanks for coming to Lewisham and identifying the body of your former colleague,' said Ellie, ensuring a pleasant beginning. 'What can you tell us about him?'

'Peter had been a suffragan bishop, an assistant bishop, if you like, in the diocese of Southwark, which means most of South

London. He was not married and before that had been a highly successful vicar of a North London parish, and when the Bishop of Southwark was looking for a new suffragan, Peter more or less chose himself because of the esteem with which he was held.'

'Perhaps you can account, then, for how it is that such a man enjoying great esteem should find himself lying dead in the mortuary of The Hospice in Forest Hill this morning with a bullet through his forehead and his testicles cut off and lying on top of him.'

The bishop was visibly shocked.

'I didn't see bullet hole,' was all she said.

'Dr Smithers is a professional and made sure of that. You were there to identify not discover the cause of death. The post-mortem also revealed considerable damage to his anus indicating the likelihood of him having taken part in homosexual activity,' added Martin.

'I'm not at all sure what to say.'

'You could start by telling us what you know of the extent of this man's homosexual involvement.'

'I have no idea.'

'You're the Bishop at Lambeth, standing in for the Archbishop of Canterbury a great deal of the time, and you expect us to believe that. We don't. So I would like you to bring Peter Sherriff's Blue file.'

It was the turn of Gordon Allen to speak.

'I'm afraid that is not possible. They are completely confidential and cannot be seen even by the clergy themselves. The Archbishop himself has never seen his own file.'

'So who sees that one? God, I suppose,' said Ellie.

'No, it is in the possession of the Bishop of London.'

Martin turned away from Allen back to the bishop.'

'You have a lovely view from your window, Helen. Whereabouts do you live?'

'My husband is a surgeon at the Charing Cross Hospital, and we have a flat nearby.'

'And I know it's an odd question given your profession but

what do you do on Sundays?'

She smiled.

'I mostly travel around bishop-ing, which means doing confirmations and things like that, trying to support the clergy and especially women clergy.'

Ellie recognised the signs and prepared to turn into bad cop.

'Bishop, were you aware that Peter Sherriff was a practising homosexual?'

There was a momentary hesitation.

'Well, let's say it doesn't altogether surprise me.'

'It's for that reason that we must ask you to produce his blue file.'

'As Gordon has pointed out, that is not possible.'

Ellie made a big thing of consulting her watch.

'I was hauled out of bed more than twelve hours ago to be greeted by an horrific sight of a man who showed every indication that he was the victim of a vicious homosexual assault and murder and I need to pursue every possibility if we are to discover who did this ghastly thing. If you insist on obstructing us, we shall keep you both here until a court order arrives from Horseferry Magistrates Court just across the river, which will compel you to act as I request, as I'm sure you are well aware even from the very short time you were an articled clerk and not the solicitor you informed us of earlier, and I wonder if the experience you had all those years ago is contained in your own blue file.'

'Thank you, Inspector, that's enough,' said Martin, the good cop. 'I won't have you making insinuations about the bishop's past as I'm sure, you, Helen, would not wish it either. You do see why it is important for us to have even temporary access to the file. I can assure you that there will be no need for it to leave this room, if that is your wish.'

'I'm not sure why the Inspector wishes to bring up any matter relating to the time before I was ordained other than to attempt to intimidate me and in any case all that was a long time ago and not related to the matter in hand.'

'You chose to lie to us,' said Ellie, 'and all we have done is to check on your statement that you are a solicitor, as if it is so it would help us a great deal not to have to explain every aspect of the law to you. As it is, we discovered that recognising aspects of the law was not your strength when you chose to have a sexual relationship with a defendant, resulting in the case being thrown out, and of course you being thrown out with it.'

'I'm sorry, Helen, I instructed the Inspector not to mention this in the presence of any one else. You were not a vicar at the time and I hope, Mr Allen, you will be able to use that to help you forget what you have heard.'

'Of course,' said Gordon. 'It has nothing to with any aspect with Helen's subsequent superb ministry in the Church. With your agreement, Helen, I will go and fetch the blue file. If these officers can compel us to do so with a court order, we might as well do so now.'

The bishop nodded.

'I will come with you, Mr Allen,' said Ellie. 'I would hate any of the contents to slip out.'

They both stood and left.

'I don't think I like your Inspector, Superintendent.'

'I know what you mean. I often call her Jack, after a Jack Russell terrier. She has incredible tenacity and goes where angels fear to tread.'

'Did she really need to say what she did?'

'She would probably say in her own defence that she wouldn't have done so had you not lied. But before they return, let's deal with your other lie.'

'My other lie?'

'About the extent of Sherriff's homosexual activity.'

'His church was known to be a place where gay men gathered after the Sunday evening service in particular. He maintained that if gay men found a spiritual home there and a relationship with God, he could hardly object but I suspected it was actually a place in which men could pick up one another for their evening entertainment, though I don't think Peter involved himself in that. He wasn't stupid and I think he was probably discrete.'

'When he was made a bishop, did those in authority not know

that he was gay?'

'You will need to look in the blue file but I suspect he will have given an undertaking that he was a non-practising gay man. He was very convincing when he chose to be, I suspect. He was also a quite brilliant organist and has given recitals on both sides of the Atlantic to great acclaim. He even played at the Proms about ten years ago.'

Ellie and Mr Allen entered the room at that moment, Ellie engrossed in the file.

'This makes interesting reading, guv. Apparently an accusation has been made that Sherriff took part in an organised sexual assault of choirboys in a vicarage in Bedfordshire. This accusation was made no more than two years ago and seems to have been either ignored or deliberately suppressed here in this building by someone.'

'Inspector, surely the police know or should know, having made a catastrophic series of errors of judgement in the Carl Beech affair, that an accusation may be made for all sorts of reasons. In the matter of Peter Sherriff, we sent someone to meet with the accuser who is himself a retired priest who's own personal life has been far from straightforward. This alleged victim could not provide the names of any others, witnesses, or victims, and on discussion with the Safeguarding Officer at Church House, the decision was made to take it no further.'

'So you're the police now, are you?' asked Ellie rhetorically.

'Who has access to these files?' asked Martin.

'Only Gordon. I don't, nor the Archbishop.'

Martin turned towards Mr Allen.

'Are you able to give me categorical assurance, such as might be asked of you, and indeed probably will be asked of you, in a court of law, that the content of this file is entirely as you received it initially and that at no times have any papers been removed by yourself or anyone else?'

'I wasn't in my present position when Bishop Sherriff retired and his file would have come here. But in my time as Chief of Staff, I have removed nothing and inserted only what is there.'

Martin turned back to the bishop.

'If you are willing, I should like to take this file with me, but only if you are willing. Otherwise, I will ask the Inspector to photograph all the contents and she will return in the morning with a court order and remove it.'

'Your choice is one Mr Hobson would be proud of, Superintendent.'

'I will make sure it's returned as soon as possible.'

With the big gates closed behind them, Martin and Ellie looked at one another.

'I'm not sure that lady entirely took to me,' said Ellie with a grin.

'The complainant lives in Devon, but I think we need to go and see him. I'll call him on the way back to the factory. You head off home, but we may have to stay away for a night when we go west.'

'Ok. By the way, congratulations on your promotion.'

'And yours.'

Yarcombe

Arriving back at the station in Lewisham, Martin was met by members of the team who had spent most of the day at The Hospice.

'The reception staff more or less said that because they were understaffed especially after 5:00 pm it was quite common for the paperwork with the undertakers to be simply overlooked.' The speaker was Detective Sergeant Bob Flack, someone with a nose for crime but a weakness for alcohol. 'They didn't worry about this and simply ticked the official Hospice paperwork. As they said, it was surely impossible that someone would want to pinch a body, let alone put one in.'

'Did you pass this on to anyone, such as the tigress upstairs who clearly runs the place?'

'No. I thought that if anyone should do that, it ought to be someone of the rank of Superintendent. I was terrified of her and she kept coming down, asking when we would be finished. Smart lass, though.'

A PC spoke up.

'We did a thorough house to house. Nothing emerged as they are quite used to seeing vans with darkened windows going in and out on what they preferred not to think about. However, from one house almost immediately opposite, by the tennis court, a lady was convinced that at about 7-00, and she remembers the time because The Archers was about to begin, she saw a van leave and possible a woman get into it.'

'Did she see the driver?'

'No. It was almost dark.'

'I suspect that if it was nearly dark it won't hold up in court. Did you get a description?

'She said that from the way she got into van she must be fit.'

'Ok. So we're almost there guys. All we need is fit female who doesn't mind missing the everyday story of country folk!'

They laughed.

'Let me tell you what DI Middlewood and I have discovered about our dead bishop.'

He went on tell in detail everything they had learned at Lambeth Palace, leaving out the obstructive behaviour they had encountered. Secrecy in an institution they knew all about, working for the Met.

'At the moment it looks like an especially unpleasant sexual-orientated murder, although what is odd is that the victim is 82. You can all go home tonight but I want everyone in by 7 in the morning. Inspector Middlewood and I will need to go to visit the complainant if only to rule out any involvement. One of you will have to go to Church House, Westminster, to talk to an old friend, Sally Makin, who when she left us took on the job of the head of Church of England Safeguarding. Sally will give you bugger all in the way of information but you might just shock her with the news of the murder and tempt out of her an indiscretion. By the way, whoever goes had better know that the former Detective Inspector Makin will only respond to flirting and innuendo from a lady. Two of you will go to the vicarage where our man lived and be prepared to take it apart and if you think you need SOCOS, get them. Check the neighbours and find out when he last seen. That's going to be key. I want you, Bob, to pay a visit to the Bishop of Southwark. Tell him the news and then get from him everything you can, asking why he let a man with such a past roam freely in his patch, or diocese. Take Karen with you. The rest of you need to be finding known associates and who he might have been engaging in homosexual acts with at his age. There will be a press statement from the Yard at 3:00 tomorrow. Until then, make full use of the element of surprise. Now off you go. 7:00 am is not a gentle request. If I'm now a Super, I have to give you all cause to hate me.'

The police officers left amidst much ribaldry at the last remark, and even more when one of the officers said loudly: 'Don't worry, guv, we've hated you for a long time already.'

Martin grinned.

Charnley was nowhere to be found, and Martin realised that now he was a Super, he couldn't leave until every report from all the various teams had been seen and responded to. Before leaving for home he telephoned Devon.

'Is that the Revd Alan Isherwood?'

'Yes.'

'Good evening sir. This is Detective Superintendent Martin Peabody from the Metropolitan Police. As a matter of considerable urgency a colleague and I would like to call and see you at home tomorrow.'

'Can I assume it's in connection with my official complaint about a certain paedophile bishop?'

'I shall be able to give you all the details when we see you. Can we say 3:00pm and if we are delayed, I will let you know.'

'Of course.'

At long last Martin was able to make his way home having ordered a take-away curry before he left, which he collected en route.

Martin had often wondered why the most senior officers in the force spent so little time on the front line of policing but was now rapidly discovering why.

The biggest problem faced by Ellie and Martin as they drove Southwest was the A303 at Stonehenge, a notorious site of serious traffic hold-ups. Martin hoped that in October it might not be too bad and although there was still a delay, it being school half-term, they were soon away on the other side. They were in Martin's own vehicle which was equipped with concealed blue lights and siren, but he had not been tempted to use them.

'Where are we making for, Martin?'

'A tiny place called Yarcombe. When I put it into the satnav, she said "You cannot be serious".'

Ellie laughed.

'Couldn't we get there and back in a day?'

'Orders from the Super.'

'But you're the Super.'

'So I am. That's what I call good planning.'

'You're an idiot.'

'That's the nicest thing you've ever said!'

'How do you want to play this?' asked Ellie.

'Sympathetically. He's not a criminal as far as we know, and unless we come to know otherwise, we must take him at his word. He was, after all, a vicar, and in my experience, though there are some bad apples even in the Church, among them Peter Sherriff, most are not bad people and try to do things for the best.'

They stopped for lunch in a small café behind a garage and had a sandwich and non-alcoholic drink. It was empty apart from them and the owner looked relieved to have some custom. The sandwiches were freshly made and brought to them by woman who might have been the owner's wife, with whom they chatted about the area for a while, somewhere, she said, she had always lived. The couple were pleasant and as they were early it was possible for the four of them to sit together, though the eyes of both husband and wife widened considerably when Ellie disclosed that they were both police officers.

'Look,' said the man, 'charging people £100 for a sandwich and drink isn't against the law, is it?'

They laughed.

'Are you on holiday?' said the woman.

'Alas, no, though I wouldn't choose this time of the year if I was. No, it's work and it will almost certainly mean being back in London tomorrow. I imagine we'll find somewhere in Honiton to stay tonight.'

Ellie excused herself.

'Your colleague is extraordinarily beautiful, if I may say so, though a lot of black women are,' said the woman.

'I suppose she is, but she has the job she has because she's even more extraordinarily clever. Far sharper than me and that's not false modesty.'

The house was a small bungalow, but the setting in the picturesque village could not be bettered. The garden was well-attended and as they parked a head appeared above the garden wall. He was a nice-looking man and came and opened the gate for them.

'Hello,' he said. 'I'm Alan Isherwood and you must be Mr Peadbody and Ms Middlewood. I won't shake hands because I've been tidying up a bed and I need to wash. Do come in, and welcome to Yarcombe.'

The bungalow was small but well cared for and, once seated, a woman came in and introduced herself as Alice, Alan's wife and took orders for tea or coffee. The place had a nice feel.

Alan joined them.

'You're very welcome,' he said, but I can only assume that something serious must have prompted your visit. A Superintendent and Inspector suggests more than just a response to my complaint.'

'You're quite right, sir,' said Martin.

'Oh, please, Alan.'

'Of course. It's a sign of how things have changed in less than a generation. Years ago every vicar I might have known used their title, and every police officer likewise. I believe bishops were always called "My Lord" whereas now they're Bishop Fred or whatever. So, I'm Martin and this is Ellie though she likes to be called ma'am!'

'You lying toad, Superintendent.'

They all laughed.

Alice came in with cups of tea and a fruit cake.

'Ooh that looks good,' said Ellie.

'That's because it wasn't made by me but bought at the Church sale.'

Once settled, Martin decided that the time had come to begin.

'About now, at Scotland Yard, there will be taking place a press conference at which an announcement will be made that

Bishop Peter Sherriff was found dead yesterday morning in a South London hospital and that the circumstances point to foul play.'

'Ah, now I see why you're here. You are wondering if I had anything to do with what your "foul play" is: a euphemism for murder. That makes sense now, and I would think it a not inappropriate inference, though possibly Sherriff might have had more reason to want murder me. I'm sure you wouldn't expect me to say that I'm sad to hear the news, and it would be hypocritical of me to do so, but his death may well open up a can of worms which will not be good for the Church of England. I have had no contact with him for many years, when I accidentally bumped into him in London, but knowing a little of how he was, I cannot evade the feeling that he will have been associating with people who are not necessarily very nice.'

'Are you suggesting that gay people are potentially violent?' asked Ellie.

'Only in the sense that white, brown, black, yellow skinned people contain within their number some who are potentially and some actually violent. I have a lesbian niece who scares the living daylights out of me.'

Ellie nodded.

'The Kray twins were believed to be gay if I remember rightly and though of course I am biased because of what Sherriff did to me, it's possible, and I cannot say more, that he sometimes mixed in the wrong company.'

'Even at 82.'

'Some people, and not just men, continue to be driven by powerful sexual urges right up to their death. Perhaps he was one of them. On the other hand you haven't yet revealed your complete hand and informed me of the manner of his death.'

Martin and Ellie looked at one another, both with raised eyebrows.

'Sherriff's body was found inside one of the fridges in the mortuary of The Hospice in Forest Hill, by the night staff doing their normal security round. When the body was removed for examination by the pathologist, his testicles had been cut off and placed on his body and he was then shot through his forehead. Although death would have been instantaneous, the pathologist believes his testicles were removed while he was still alive, resulting in agony.'

'Oh my God. No one at all would deserve that. It's terrible though as I'm sure you must have heard people say that any paedophile should have their testicles cut off, even if I think it unlikely anyone, however motivated, would do it. I simply wanted him named as what he was. I didn't even want him carted off to prison like Rolf Harris or Stuart Hall. But what do you make of it?'

'It's only yesterday morning that his body was found,' said Ellie, 'so our investigations are at a very early stage.'

'I hope you can rule me out. We haven't been anywhere other than Honiton in the last week. But tell me, if this had not happened, would you or anyone else from the police be here responding to the complaint I made to Lambeth Palace?'

'No,' said Martin. 'I saw your complaint in the file of the bishop and I know that it had also been considered by the Church of England Safeguarding officer. The impression I gained was that not having provided the names of other victims could only lead to a case of "did–did not" which would never see the light of day in a courtroom. That this had not been communicated back to you is appalling, but I don't understand how the Church of England works other than by extending a considerable veil of secrecy over all it does.'

'It's all irrelevant now but you're quite right about the secrecy. Perhaps it's all an attempt to divert people away from the Great Secret, that there is no God.'

Martin's phone demanded his attention.

'Yes? Ok, are SOCOS at work with you? Good. Do a house to house and see if anyone saw the van. Also check the CCTV on that road and all the way to The Hospice. Keep me informed and I'll be back in the morning. Oh, and well done!'

He put his phone back into his pocket.

'In our job it's as well never to get too excited about what at first looks like being a step forward, for too often we discover it's not what it at first appears.'

'You are clearly very diligent though why have two senior officers come to see me?'

'I felt I needed to see if you had any part in the murder of Sherriff, and I am convinced that you did not but it struck me that we can talk as senior officers about wholly confidential matters relating to those who work for us, as well as important planning matters that come with seniority in our drive down.'

' Have you booked a place to stay?'

'Yes. Well thank you for your plain speaking and thank your wife for her tea and cake. Something may occur to one or other of us later, so are you likely to be in early tomorrow morning if we need clarification?'

'Yes, we're both early risers.'

Ellie took the wheel, enabling Martin to make some calls. As he had expected, Sally Makin revealed nothing, meaning that he would have to lean on her himself. The Bishop of Southwark had almost died of apoplexy when informed about Sherriff's death and behaviour but provided a list of recent engagements the retired bishop had fulfilled, and then, apparently, talked a great deal of baloney about not judging others and that although paedophiles did bad and unacceptable things, what they needed was to be set on a better course.

'I very much hope you set his lordship on a better course with a powerful kick in the balls,' said Martin.

He received other items of information which he passed on to Ellie, as they entered Honiton and made for the hotel. Martin let Ellie do the registration, and she used their real names. Somehow it seemed less like a sordid occasion if she did so.

'I'm sorry to have to ask,' said the woman, 'but have you any ID?'

They both produced their police ID cards.

'Good heavens,' said the woman, 'I've only ever seen those on tv before.'

Martin took their key card and made his way towards their room.

'Gosh, are there many husbands and wives or partners working together in the police?'

'It's always been a feature of police life, a bit like doctors and nurses. But to be honest we rarely see one another when we're working. Lewisham Police Station is extremely busy and usually as senior officers we're heading up different investigations. This one's special.'

'Well, I hope you enjoy your stay and don't spend too much time discussing crime and criminals.'

'Do you know,' said Ellie, 'even in this short time I bet that Martin will already be fast asleep on the bed snoring.'

The woman laughed as Ellie walked towards the room, where she discovered that she would have lost her bet as Martin was on his phone being debriefed by the team back home though nothing significant had come in. SOCOS could find no trace of the murder having taken place in the Vicarage, either in the form of gunshot residue or human flesh and blood. There was no sign of a struggle and the fingerprints they found were those of Sherriff. House to house had revealed nothing further other than one person seeing Sherriff's car pulling out at about 10:00 am and receiving a wave from the driver – much as usual.

'Ok, make finding that car a priority. Is Charnley there?'

'He's gone home, guv.'

'Thank you, dirty Dave.'

He put his phone down and looked up at Ellie who was grinning at him.

'Promotion's never what you think it will be.'

'Oh, I don't know, it's got you here with me. Come and join me and tell me what you made of our ex-vicar this afternoon. And then perhaps we both need a shower before dinner.'

'Well, he was an unusual character to have been a vicar, or at least I would imagine most other vicars believe in God. We already knew about his own history of disastrous relationships and failed marriages, but he chose not to mention them, which always means that someone with as suspicious a mind as I have, makes me wonder what else he didn't tell us.

'He is up together and sharp and seemed to anticipate our

questions and made clear, but was it too clear, that he wouldn't and couldn't have been involved in any way with the murder, but I nevertheless got the impression that he has the sort of logical mind that could set up and even control almost anything he set his mind to. There was no emotion of any kind, which concerned me, and he didn't relate the incident of sexual abuse from all those years back, which is after all the basis of his complaint against Sherriff.

'And then the wife was excluded and I wondered why? So, I thought he was trying to exclude himself from any involvement, but also that this was his intention from the first. The Vicar "doth protest too much, methinks" but it was very subtle, a deliberate understatement I would not have expected. His track record in terms of relationships might suggest it would be otherwise. Yes, he was pleasant, well-spoken, up together and articulate, but he was clever enough to need to get a glimpse of us when we arrived and then to excuse himself to wash hands and comb his hair, and I could see that that piece of garden had already been attended to and there was nothing he would have been working on there. What about you?'

I've always found working with you difficult because you leave nothing for me to add. I agree with all you've said, but you've said things I wouldn't have noticed in the way you did, and I need a little time to think about them further. But you're not ruling out some involvement?'

'I very much doubt he was responsible for the castration or the shooting, but I am far from convinced that he didn't have some part in it.'

'H'm,   I   agree.

Boston

As he felt it often did, it was pissing down in Boston as he locked up the station door behind him, but the advantage was that it was unlikely that criminals would want to venture out into it, or at least he hoped not, as he was on call for the night. He headed up the A52 towards his home in the village of Wrangle, almost ten miles away. It was he thought, a good name for a detective inspector to live in, though Marjorie was always going on at home about moving much further away from the busy road taking day trippers and holiday makers up to Skegness, which used to be heralded as "bracing" but which she thought was now better called "disgusting".

Connor was reflecting on this as he drove home. At this time of the year the local roads were full of tractors and trailers carrying potatoes and onions, and soon it would be the sugar beet and that meant weeks of mud on the road about which there would be no shortage of complaints made at work though that was part of the price that had to be paid if the nation wanted good quality and relatively cheap vegetables.

As he pulled into the drive, he imagined the smell that would greet him when he opened the door. It was Tuesday and Marjorie had promised him Leek Pudding and Roast Potatoes, and he was not disappointed. Perhaps there was something to be said for living in the Fens after all, in which friendly farmers kept their garage well stocked with the finest veg, at no cost, other than perhaps as an inexpensive insurance premium against the police concerning themselves overmuch with life on their farms.

'What sort of day have you had?' asked Marjorie.

'We're still getting burglaries in Wyberton and Frampton, so we'll need to double the patrols.'

'But if they see a car coming, all they have to do is lie down until it's gone by.'

'I know, but I'm more concerned with pleasing the customers than catching the little shites who are doing it. If the pressure rises, we have one or two likely candidates to pull in.

'Shouldn't you do that anyway?'

'It's a thought.'

The leeks were followed by apple pie and ice cream.

'Nothing else today?'

'Marney Edmonds has been reported missing but it's not the first time and as likely as not he'll be away somewhere in a caravan with one of the Slovenian girls.'

'Slaves, more like.'

'Marney's a gang master, perhaps the biggest in Lincolnshire, and somehow or other, against all the odds he's managed to get a full contingent of East European workers over here, unlike most others. They're not here because he treats them likes slaves. I know he can be a bit tough on the idle but they're here to work and if they want their money that's what he makes sure they do.'

'And are Slovenian girls a perk of his job?'

'I can only investigate complaints and so far, there have been none.'

'Poor Mary.'

'Poor Mary my foot. You know as well as me she's as hard as nails and enjoys spending the money he makes and we've both seen her on a Saturday night knocking it back at the Admiral Nelson and disappearing outside for twenty minutes or so for a fag, when we all know she doesn't smoke.'

'So, you think he'll turn up by morning?'

'I'm certain of it.'

The night passed without incident as far as CID were concerned though as he drove in the still driving rain towards Boston a car passed coming from the town with blue lights flashing. He took no notice and was in his office by 7:30. His DS, Graham

Hollioake, brought him in a cup of coffee.

'I was giving thought last night to bringing in those two little toe rags from Skirbeck we suspected of breaking into the Spar shop on London Rd.'

'We couldn't prove anything.'

'That doesn't matter. All we need is to bring them in for questioning about the burglaries and let it be known that suspects are helping us with our enquiries. That will please the punters and give us a bit of breathing space. When it stops raining, take a couple of uniforms and bring them in.'

'If you say so, guv.'

The phone on his desk rang.

'DI Hannah. Ah, that explains the blue lights that passed as I came in. Any clues to identity. Ok, well keep me informed.'

'Looks like a farming suicide in the river at Midville. Tied himself to a fence so he could be easily found before he threw himself in the dyke. Not the first and won't be the last.'

'Do you want me to go?'

'No, I'll go and show willing. You mind the shop and look through all those burglary reports and see if we've missed anything.'

'Ok, guv.'

Connor wrapped well before going to his car only to find that it had stopped raining. He was also carrying his wellington boots because the bank of the river was sure to be muddy. He passed the Pilgrim Hospital where, he imagined, the body would be brought for a postmortem carried out by the resident pathologist Dr Andrea Morgan. It took him little more than 10 minutes before turning off at Stickney, where in summer he often called in for an ice cream and a chat at the Post Office. Ahead he could see blue lights, a police car, an ambulance, and a fire engine. As he emerged from his car, he could see a group of men pulling on the rope and then came the appearance of a body which was pulled up onto the bank. Connor knew that bodies that had spent time in water were far from pretty, with engorged features, so as he wandered over, he thought he knew what he would find.

'Not a pretty sight, sir,' said one of the young constables.

'So my wife tells me but there's not a lot I can do about it. Anyone know who it might be?'

'We might to have to wait for the pathologist and for the swelling to go down,' said a sergeant Connor knew well. 'But what's a bit odd, or at least I've never seen it before, is that his eyeballs are almost completely out of their sockets.'

'Let's have a look,' said Connor, and the paramedics pulled their sheet back from the face. 'I see what you mean and I agree with what you say about waiting for the facial swelling to go down, but I'm pretty sure that this Marney Edmonds.'

'The gang master?'

'Yes. Ok, let's get him to the Pilgrim and the tender care of Dr Morgan. Until she confirms the identity, no one at all is to give expression to my guess, no one at all. Is that clear, everyone?'

Mutters of assent could just be heard.

Connor waited until the ambulance had received its cargo and set off for Boston. He then went and thanked the fire fighters for their work which they clearly appreciated. 'He's the only bugger who ever says thanks,' he heard someone inside say. That he thought was a pity because saying thank you went a long way. Finally, he spoke to the men from his own station.

'Was that your first?' he asked the young constable.

'Yes, sir.'

'Well, your sergeant's a good man to be with. I've long suspected him of deliberately laying on suicides for new officers to experience but have never been able to get the proof. Anyway, well done the pair of you.'

Connor had not said so at the scene but had known it was Marney at once by a mark on his neck which had been inflicted by the knife of a Pole working cauliflowers up near Wainfleet. It had been a close-run thing as the young Polish worker slashed out at Marney but almost certainly wished he had not done so afterwards, requiring hospitalisation for what was explained as an injury caused by a machine, but the scar on Marney's neck remained.

Back in his office DS Hollioake was going through the burglary files and looked up when Connor walked in.

'Anyone we know?'

'Marney Edmonds.'

'You're kidding!'

'Not that it looked like him after lying in the water but do you recall the fight with the Pole and the scar on his neck?'

Hollioake nodded.

'I saw it at once, though until we get official identification that must remain between you and me. They've taken him to the Pilgrim.'

'I'm sorry, but I could never think of Marney committing suicide and didn't we think yesterday that he was probably away somewhere with one of his female workers? Are you going out to tell Mary?'

'All I can do is to warn her that it might be Marney and that later she may be called on to make an official identification. Telling her it's him and then finding it's not, would be a licence for her to print money in the hands of a lawyer. In the meantime, Marney is officially a missing person, but don't set anything in motion for that until I get chance to get to the hospital later and we see what he looks like once the water swelling has subsided. What I need now, and so do you, is coffee and breakfast.'

The crossed the River Witham, and like all residents gazed up at the Stump on their left before turning right and heading for the Dales Tea Rooms which if it was not yet open would soon be once they hammered on the door. This morning it was, and they were greeted by the owner, Brian.

'Two full English?' he asked and was met by broad smiles.

'Anything on the burglaries?'

'One thing stands out and that is that in no instance did the culprits reveal any sophistication. They missed all sorts of valuable things and only went for cash, of which of course in this day and age there was precious little, plus a few knick-knacks such as the sort of medals perhaps they saw on Antiques Roadshow which are worth a great deal, though most are not. And of course, they like to make a mess, pissing on everything.'

'That could be worse, I suppose. Can you find out whether they're in school today? Thomas Middlecott Academy in Kirton, if I remember aright. They try to do a fantastic job there but they're always up against it. I really admire their teachers.'

The full English breakfast arrived, and they tucked in silently, both clearing their plates and washing it down with strong coffee. A couple of other customers had come in and were also in search of equally wonderfully tasty food, just wholly shorn of nutritional value.

'Brian', said Connor, that was brilliant as always.'

'Thank you, Inspector.'

'If I remember rightly, it's my sergeant's turn to pay.'

'It's always my turn to pay.'

'I'm glad to hear you admit it, but don't worry, Graham, you'll be an Inspector one day and begin to recoup your money.'

The three of them laughed, but all the same, despite his bluster, it was in fact Connor who paid – on expenses, of course.

Back in the office, Connor said the breakfast had fortified him enough to face Mary Edmonds and Graham said he would contact the school and if they weren't there he would call in on their homes.

'Yes, don't turn them in into heroes and remove them from their mates. Wait until later, in front of their parents.'

After all the rain of the previous 24 hours Connor's car was filthy so he reckoned that driving out to Marney's place out on the fen would make little difference. He took with him a female PC, Linda Andrews, a willing if not especially bright local girl. It was nearly ten o'clock by the time they arrived and as he stopped the car the front door was opened by one of the girls here to pick vegetables but in fact working as a servant in the house. Perhaps she preferred it, and it certainly saved her from the vagaries of the autumnal weather. She smiled a greeting and didn't look as if she were operating under duress.

'Police,' said Connor, showing her his ID, 'I've come to see Mary.'

'Please come in and take a seat. She is on the telephone, perhaps to Marney.'

Connor smiled.

'And you are?'

'Ljubica, and I am from Slovenia, and all my paperwork is correct.'

'It's alright, I'm not here to arrest anyone. Do you prefer working in the house?'

'Oh yes, Mary and Marney have always been so kind to me, and this is my second year here helping them in the house. All my friends out in the field get very wet, and I am dry.'

'Do you go back to join them at night?'

'No. I stay here. They have no children and I feel they treat me like a member of their own family.'

Mary came into the room.

'Have you any news about the old rogue?'

'Perhaps it would be best if we spoke alone.'

'No. Ljubica can stay, and your colleague.'

'Ok. Marney is registered as an official missing person, but this morning I was called to an incident in Midville where a body was found in the river. It isn't easy to identify a body after it has been in water for a length of time but I happened to notice that this body had a significant scar on the left side of his neck. I cannot tell you that it was Marney, but I think you ought to know that it might be, and if we come to think it is, we shall have to ask someone to make an official identification. The circumstances suggest suicide.'

'Marney would never commit suicide,' said Mary. 'You know him well enough to know that.'

'I do, and that was my own first thought, but if it wasn't suicide, then someone has set it up exactly like a fenland farmer's suicide with a rope tied to the fence so that he could easily be found.'

Neither of the two women showed any outward emotion and he was about to comment on this when his phone rang. It was Dr Morgan from the Pilgrim.

'Connor. I need you here as soon as possible and when I say as soon as possible I mean yesterday if you can.'

'Ok.'

He pocketed his phone.

'I have to go, but I'll keep you completely abreast of any

developments and if Marney should turn up, please let me know at once.'

Connor and PC Andrews made their way slowly across the mud, and then dropping the constable off in town, drove on towards the Pilgrim. For some obscure reason the Pathology Department and mortuary lay at the heart of the building and Connor had to drive round and find somewhere to park which wasn't easy. He approached Andrea's office, knocked, and was called in. Andrea and a colleague were talking over a mid-morning coffee.

'Connor, this my good friend and appropriately named, Dr Arthur Goodfellow. He's my opposite number in Lincoln and I asked him to come and join us.'

The two men smiled and shook hands.

'I should warn you that neither of us have seen anything like this, and almost certainly never wish to do so again. I would prefer it if you came alongside us rather than stand in the viewing area and you'll see why. So, shall we go in.'

There were two mortuary assistants already in there waiting for them, one with a camera and the other operating an overhead tape mechanism. The place was typically spotless and the stainless steel shiny. There were two plinths in the middle of the room, one empty and the other occupied, the body covered with a green sheet. Connor was well-used to post-mortems and could even cope with the smell of formaldehyde.

'As you can see we've already done some front and top work, and the guys here have removed the vital organs and the brain. It was when we turned him over that we all stood back amazed.'

The assistants turned the body.

'And that is what we found.'

'Good God,' said Connor, as he looked down upon the number 11 that had been branded on his back.

'And then we looked further down and discovered the likely cause of death. Arthur and I both think a single barrel shot gun was inserted into his anus and fired. We both agree too that the branding was done before death which would have been pain of an extreme kind and perhaps the shock of that killed him, but if not, the gun certainly would have done so. This would have happened whilst he was secured by hands and feet using rope and the marks are clear to see. We shall need to get a toxicology report to know whether he had been drugged and it may well be that he was, as he's a big, strong man and I can't see how else this was done, but in all my years, and Arthur's too, I've never seen anything as brutal as this.'

'I almost think I want to go back and check that the Krays are dead. Why would someone wish to do this?' said Arthur.

'You said "someone"; surely you're not thinking this could be done by one person alone?'

'Sorry, it was a careless figure of speech. You're right. This was done by at least two and maybe more.'

'And where would they get a branding iron and know how to use it, and why 11?'

'Well, I'm sorry Connor, we've done our bit, now it's over to you and that will involve finding out who he is first. He does have a recognisable scar on his neck and the swelling has begun to go down.'

'That bit is easy. I knew who he was when they pulled him from the river, and yes, it was the scar that I recognised. He's Marney Edmonds, born in Southern Rhodesia, now Zimbabwe, but living here for a long time now, and is the leading gang master in the county. Clearly someone didn't like him.'

'Has he got a widow?'

'Yes. When will you be ready for her to identify?'

'About 4. I've got someone else due in at any minute. Should be straightforward but you never know.'

Connor took off his green kit and left the building to sit in his car. He took out his phone and called the Superintendent, his boss in Lincoln.

'Teddy, it's Connor. We've got a big one, a horrific murder more brutal than I or the two docs have ever seen. I shall need help as soon as possible.'

'It will be on its way in no time. Do I need to come?'

'I think you will think so.'

'Ok'.

Why 11?

Connor alerted everyone at the station to both the murder and an imminent influx of colleagues from Lincoln. The station would have to serve as murder HQ which meant it would get very crowded and more local matters would have to be dropped. Brian would oversee logistics and a whole host of computers would be coming and needing to be put online. There was a procedure for all this worked out in advance and now was the time when it is was to be put to the test. Connor announced his intention to brief everyone as soon as the Super from Lincoln had joined them. Now he had to go back out to the fen and he took with him Jo Enright, a young officer who, if she played her cards right, might go very far indeed. On the way there he told her the full story.

'That's incredible. Who the hell is so barbaric that they could do something like that? I've seen Marney in action in the pub sometimes and I grant you he's not the nicest bloke around but to use a branding iron whilst he was still awake is the most disgusting thing I've heard of since I came into the force.'

'I'll not disagree. The most obvious suspects, but I may be being racist, and I know you will tell me if I am, which is one of the reasons you are so trustworthy, are among the huge numbers of those he controls as their gang master.'

'Obvious maybe, guv, but I have my doubts about that. They know Marney and handle him remarkably well from what I've seen. Of course, he treats them as shit, and there have always been rumours about him and some of the young women, but whether the rumours are true, well perhaps in the investigation we'll find out. There are also rumours about Mary Edmonds and men, local ones in the main.'

'Yes, I know that, and I've also seen her disappearing for twenty minutes at a time from the pub. What about her? Might she have done it?'

'No chance. From what you have described, there is no way she could persuade Marney to lie down whilst she branded his back. That took force I would image and if were to hazard a guess, guv, in the presence of your deaf ear, I think it much more likely that this was the work of local men, perhaps rivals, paying him back for something or wanting rid of him in a great deal of pain, and of course someone who knew the area well enough to know the river at Midville.'

'Jo, the boss is on his way from Lincoln. If you're in agreement I shall propose your immediate transfer to CID. We need a DC urgently, and you are by far and away the best candidate. What do you say?'

'You know me, guv, I always do as I'm told.'

Connor laughed.

'That's not what I've heard. I'm told you're always using your initiative and doing your own thing and getting results. That's what I need in CID. It's plain clothes for you from now on.'

'Thanks, guv, that is brilliant.'

They were almost at the house.

'And how on earth are we going to deal with this?'

'Leave it to me, guv.'

Connor gave her an amazed look and he could see that she meant it.

As before Ljubica met them at the door and led them into the kitchen where Mary sat, nursing a mug of tea.

'Well?'

'I'm Detective Constable Jo Enright and you already know the Inspector. I'm sorry to have to tell you that we have found a body in the river at Midville which has been identified by the Inspector as that of your husband, Marney, though we shall need you to make a formal identification later today if you will at the Pilgrim Hospital. We are having to treat his death as unlawful in the light of various injuries inflicted upon it. We are, even as I speak, bringing in a lot of extra police officers so that we can discover who might have done this terrible thing to your husband, and it goes without saying how very sorry we are for your dreadful loss.'

Mary was silent for a moment or two and then looked at Connor.

'Have you any leads?'

'None at all, at this stage, but as you can probably imagine we shall need to speak to every member of Marney's workforce.'

'It's also your workforce, Mrs Edmonds,' said Jo, 'and for us to do this we shall need all the help you feel you can give us, or at least guidance as to how we might arrange this.'

'Yes, everyone will be working right now and won't be back until tonight. There's a lot of them, you know.'

'Might you be able to give some thought to this between now and your visit to the Pilgrim, and if you feel up to it, you can discuss this with Jo afterwards,' added Connor.

'Jo will be taking me, then?'

'Yes, I will,' said the new detective.

'I'm glad about that. You mentioned injuries. What sort of injuries?'

'The doctor will explain those far better than I can,' said Jo.

Connor was wondering why he had come and sensing this, Ljubica offered them both a cup of tea and a seat. Connor leapt at it before the constable spoiled his opportunity for a drink.

'Good idea. Mary, we need some details about Marney, boring but unfortunately necessary. Date of birth and things like that. Are you up to it?'

'I've known you a long time, Connor, and you me. Since when did you begin to see me as some sort of emotional weakling?'

Connor smiled. She was quite right.

Details collected, the two detectives returned to the station though Jo would soon be back across the fen to collect Mary.

'I knew Marney quite well, and often had a drink with him, but I never knew he was called Emmanuel Edmonds.'

'"God with us",' said Jo.

'I hope so as we're going to need all the help we can get.'

'No, the name Emmanuel, it's the Hebrew for God with us.'

'I'm sure you'll find being able to speak Hebrew will come in handy on the Fens,' said Connor with a grin.'

'I'll bear that in mind, guv, though in this case I recall it from nativity plays at school.'

'Where was that?'

'Downham Market, in Norfolk.'

'That's really bad luck. You've come up market.'

'What are you going to do when we get back?'

'Meet with the Chief and plan how we're going to interview all these workers for which we shall need some interpreters, and I can't imagine Slovenian speakers are two-a-penny in the land of the Yellow Bellies.'

'What?'

'Haven't you heard that before? It refers to those living on the Lincolnshire coast between here and Grimsby, though some use it for everyone in the county.'

'It's not very flattering.'

'Nor is Brummies or Scousers.'

They arrived at the Police Station.

'There's no need for you to come in, Jo. Just turn round and collect Mary, and if she wants her to come with her, bring Ljubica too. That'll make four women. Marney's dreams come true.'

'Do I need to be in with them, guv.'

'Have you done a mortuary visit before? '

'You've sent me often enough.'

'I imagine Andrea will have finished by now. I really need you to see the body and what's been done to it.'

'I will do exactly what you ask, boss.'

'And when you get back here, Jo, I want you to write those words down on a piece of paper and pin them to the CID wall.'

By the time they got to the Pilgrim, the postmortem had been completed and Andrea told Jo she had sent the results through to Connor, though there was little to add to the initial impression. Andrea then led the three women to a metal table where a sheet lay over the body. She raised the top from the head.

'Mrs Edmonds, can you identify this body as that of your husband Emmanuel Edmonds?'

'Yes,' she said quietly. 'That is Marney. Are you able to tell me how he died?

'Only the coroner can give an official cause of death, but unofficially it is my medical opinion that he died as the result of a violent asaault which, either there at the site or after moving him he was thrown into the river attached by rope to a fence post so he could be easily found.'

Mary's hand was at her mouth.

'Finding out who did it and why is for DC Enright and her colleagues to discover.'

When Jo returned to the station after taking the two women back to their house on the fen, she found the station remarkably empty.

'Has everyone gone home?' she asked the desk sergeant.

'I'm not talking to you,' he replied with an apparent lack of mirth. Joining the enemy in plainclothes.'

'Aren't we meant to be on the same side?'

'Now, whoever told you that? Of course, we're not and now I lose the opportunity to work with one of the smartest police officers in the station. Mind you, you look impressive in plain clothes so that might make up for it.'

'Be careful, sarge, or I might have to report you for sexual harassment.'

'But really Jo, I'm delighted for you. Upwards and onwards from here on. And how was the visit to the late Marney Edmonds.'

'Not as shocking for me as it was for him.'

'So I believe. And what about Mary? How was she?'

'She was shocked at first, I thought, when the doctor explained how he had died, but afterwards seemed more thoughtful than anything else.'

'Doing the sums I imagine. Anyway, to answer your first question, they're all out on the fen questioning workers as they return for the evening. The chances must be that it was one of them whom he had rubbed up the wrong way, so it'll be a process of elimination. You're on CID duty now and you'll find the big Chief is still here waiting for you.'

'Thanks, sarge. You never know, if I say the wrong thing I might be back in uniform in half an hour.'

Out on the fen a rather clever system of waiting in line had been designed and implemented by DS Graham Hollioake, the outer extremes protected by two uniformed officers making sure everyone was corralled before being directed to officers brought in from Lincoln. Those completely without English came to Connor who was being assisted by a teacher from Lincoln University. No one could eat or wash until they had been interviewed and it was taking a very long time. From time to time Connor went to each detective to see if anything had seemed useful, but there was nothing and the only anxiety the workers had was whether this would result in the work ending and an unexpected early return home to Slovenia. As yet the workers had not been told why they were being questioned though it didn't take them long to work out that this was something to do with the Boss who hadn't now been seen for almost two days. Many of them joked when being questioned, that almost certainly he had chosen for himself a girl and was away with her somewhere, but gradually it began to dawn on them that it might be something much more serious given the presence of such a large contingent of police officers. It was only when several workers listened to the English news on their radios that this much more serious matter was Marney's death.

At about 9:00 there was a meeting of all officers who had been interviewing back at the station in Boston, but to the frustration of Connor and the Chief who had remained, there was nothing to go on other than that he had been last seen driving away from one of the fields of workers doing cauliflowers at 3:30 two days earlier in the direction of the A52. After that nothing, and no hint from him in the form of the leer he sometimes adopted that some poor unlucky girl was in for a night she would endeavour to forget for the rest of her life.

The Lincoln lot departed, leaving Connor, Graham and Jo almost literally scratching their heads and wondering where they would begin in the morning.

'Home time,' said Connor. 'The PM report said that the toxicology check indicated traces of a restricted anaesthetic drug in his liver called Propofol which might have been given to shut him up, but otherwise tells us nothing we didn't know. This was as brutal a killing as there can have been. She thinks death might have taken place two nights ago but that the river makes greater certainty difficult. She's also clear that it was a branding iron which was used on his back and that he was alive when it was done, and that must have caused him to scream in agony before the shock led to him passing out. The shotgun was fired whilst he was conscious however which reveals a determination to inflict the maximum amount of pain and misery upon him.

'Fucking hell,' said Graham. 'He must have rubbed someone up the wrong way on a huge scale.'

'Yeah, and that's where we shall to start tomorrow. But for now, go home and get some sleep. We'll all think more clearly in the morning – or I hope we will. 7:30?'

All three were in the office before 7:00 having been unable to sleep especially well. Connor and Jo had both seen the body and the thought of it returned throughout the night; Graham's mind was just working overtime. Connor had brought in some croissants which they heated with some coffee and ate in silence. Once they had finished eating and drinking they looked at one another.

'What does the number 11 mean? I can't help feeling that answering that is most likely to lead us forward, said Connor. 'I spent half the night pursuing that on the internet but got nowhere at all, so I think we've got to go through Marney's books and papers today with a fine tooth-comb to see if the answer is there. Is there someone he's cheated or to whom he owes money – that's the most likely direction we should be looking in, so I've asked the chief for a couple of lads from Serious Fraud to come over the day and to go through the lot. I'd like you, Jo to go with them to make sure Mary holds nothing back. Insist on every safe being opened and every cupboard, and have a go again at her about 11. She must know something.'

'Yes, guv.'

'You and me, Graham, are going for a drive round the country roads, not together though, and I mean every country road. The vehicle Marney was seen driving away was a long-based landrover, not easy to hide and it must be somewhere. We'll divide the area up and get going.'

'Ok, boss.'

'We're looking for a Land Rover Series II long wheel base for which you both have the registration number. Once you've finished with Mary, Jo you do the roads out by the prison and on the east side of the A52.'

'Hang on, guv. Tell me again what you just described as the model of the vehicle?'

'Series II long wheel base.'

'Exactly. What if the number on his back isn't eleven but two, in Roman Numerals as used by Land Rover. And just suppose there's been a number 1 we don't know about?'

Connor and Graham looked at one another.'

'Ok, run with that until the Fraud guys arrive and see what you can find on the Holmes 3 National Police Computer. If you do, let me know. You'll need to register to get on. You'll find the registration passwords in my desk and I hereby give you permission to pretend you're me.'

'It's the bottom drawer on the left,' added Graham helpfully, as the two of them set off.

It took Jo half an hour to register herself and find her way round the programme though it insisted it was intuitive and user-friendly, though once in it took her hardly any time to find a similar brutal murder in South London in which a retired bishop had been castrated and then shot though the forehead. What was interesting was the presence of a single playing card, the Ace of Spades, which had been nailed into the spine of the bishop. There seemed no obvious common element in the victims, and she decided that having let her boss know what she had discovered, there ought to be contact made with the Met based in Lewisham.

The call to Connor would have to wait as the men from the Fraud Squad had arrived expecting to check out the significance of the number eleven and being told they had also to look out for the number II in Roman numerals.

Mary Edmonds

'Oh, they've sent you again,' said Mary catching sight of Jo with two men as she returned from an outhouse. Is it a case of the "gentle touch"?

'No, not at all. These gentlemen are officers from the Fraud Squad and they will need to go through all your papers, and I mean all, including any in safes you might have.'

'I can assure you there's no fraud here. Accusing Marney of fraud would be a wicked thing to do now he's dead.'

'I totally agree and that's not why they're here,' added Jo.

'Our sole concern,' said one of the men. 'is to find if there's any link with known criminals and your work on the farms. It could be any sort of link and we shall be looking out for them however well they are disguised,' .

'My husband was no fool and we have an accountant who has served us well.'

'Yes, and we shall have the chance to spend some time with him later in the day.'

'The thing is, Mrs Edmonds,' said Jo, 'the majority of murders such as that of Marney have an underlying concern with money, and whilst I know how much you and Marney shared, it is not beyond the realms of possibility that if there was a problem of some sort, he might not have wanted to worry you with it.'

'That's highly unlikely,' Mary replied, 'as most of the time finance was my responsibility.'

'That's good,' the first man said, 'it means we shan't need to be long about it.'

With reluctance she let the men in once they had collected

their equipment from Jo's car.

Once they were in the house, Jo remained in the yard and called Connor on her radio and told him all she had discovered on Holmes 3.

'Can you ask them to send us everything they've got?'

'I have done.'

'Ok, abandon the landrover search for now, and get back to the station and look through their material. Let me know if anything looks like a serial killing?'

'Ok, guv.'

Connor diverted a car onto the eastern section near the prison, and now had a number of cars scouring the area within and around Boston. It then occurred to him that the best place to conceal a vehicle would be in a vehicle park. He called one of the cars on the south side of town.

'Gerry, go down to Duckworth's at Kirton and take a look around, just checking if it has been parked apparently innocently and not spotted.'

'Yes, sir.'

Almost immediately after issuing that instruction, Graham called.

'Vehicle located, Boss. Up the drive and well concealed by bushes, trees and undergrowth, in the churchyard of Wainfleet St Mary.'

'Well done, Graham. Get on to SOCOS at once. Can you see anything through the windows?'

'It's so dark under the trees that I can't see anything even with my torch.'

'In which case just tape it off and I'll get uniform to come and relieve you.'

Connor turned his car and made his way back to Boston. At last they were getting somewhere though even as he drove he began to feel that the possibility of a link with the London murder was highly unlikely. This had all the hallmarks of a local job. Who else but a local would know that churchyard and its proximity to Midville? What he wanted now was a thorough search of the area and every building where the murder might have been committed. For this he would need many more officers to come from wherever it could be arranged as soon as possible. As he drove he told all this to the Chief on his hands-free, who said he would make it happen.

Arriving back in the office, he found Jo still at work on the computer.

'Anything more?'

'I've been doing a lot of searching. This is a fantastic programme. I've discovered all sorts of things.'

'Almost all of which you must make every effort to forget.'

'That goes without saying, guv, but it's a great education for a new DC.'

'As I said, have you found anything more?'

'No, though what I found about the murdered bishop is a great deal and I'm sure there are links.'

'But could someone in South London know the details of a churchyard in Wainfleet and a river in Midville? I very much doubt it could be anyone who isn't local.'

'Which is exactly what the South London team have said about their murder, that the detail of where his the body was found indicated extensive local knowledge, almost to an extreme degree.'

'And are they any further on?'

'No. In fact they said that my phone call represented the nearest thing to a breakthrough they've had. A Super and a DI are coming to pay us a visit.'

'Ok, you look after them when they get here and fill them in with everything they need to know. I need to get maps made for all those about to join us. Can you do that on the computer and then photocopy them for me?'

'Yes, guv.'

She smiled as she turned away, assuming that Connor didn't know how to make the map he would require at an adequate scale and get the photocopier to copy them directly. Connor was suddenly very thirsty and made a cup of tea for himself and Jo. He sat in the office with his new DC and watched her work.

'You're quite good with that thing.'

58

She laughed.

'That's because you went to school too early to learn how to use a computer.'

'I've been on courses.'

'How much did you learn?'

'I learned that the old way of detection cannot be bettered, but I admit that computers can speed some things up.'

'I agree totally. You've passed the test and I will continue to work with you.'

'Thank you, detective constable.'

'Don't mention it, sir, and I've done 40 maps for you.'

'Show off.'

'There's a large bus just arrived which I imagine contains the hired help. They'll be impressed with the speed of your computing skills, but to thank you for the cup of tea, I'll not tell.'

The next hour was extremely demanding of everyone. Jo reported on what had been found in Midville which they could see on the map, and the nature of the injuries on the body. Connor took over and pointed out the location of the concealed landrover, and then divided the area up into twenty, each with 2 officers working together. There would also be dogs available on call. Everyone was to keep their radios on at all times and to mark the maps when they had searched the land. Co-ordinating everything would be DC Enright. They were all told to stay in touch and suddenly they were up and away, all wearing wellington boots and carrying long sticks. Outside it was raining again.

Just before noon, when Jo was due to give the order to stop and eat and drink, the fraud team at the farm called in. Far from Marney being the good, almost innocent dealer in financial matters relating to his work as the leading gang master in the East of England, it turned out he had a scam bringing in a great deal of money into a private bank account in Nottingham, of which, it was clear, his wife knew nothing, some of the money from which was being paid into the account of someone with a female Slovenian name.

'How much of this have you told Mary?' asked Connor.

'Very little. We thought we'd leave that to you.'

'I'll come now as I shall need you to guide me through the finances.'

'Ok, guv.'

Jo looked round.

'Something come up?'

'Yes. The Fraud boys have apparently made a big discovery of a financial scam set up by Marney – big time, and not least benefitting a Slovenian girl. I need you to come now with me out to the farm in your own car to gather information before you set out and find this lady, if you can. Before you leave I want you to put all calls from those searching the area through to my phone. Can you do that?'

'Yes and no. Yes, I can do that easily enough, but no, you can't do both things at the same time, sir.'

'Don't tell me what I can and can't do.'

'Yes, she can,' said a voice behind him.

It was the chief.

'Don't be a stupid twat, Connor. You know she's right. Get out to the farm, you two, and be nice to each other. Before you go, call Graham and get him to cover here. It's not good for him to be out on the fen by himself for such a long time – it will drive him mad, as it would any sane individual. In the meantime I'll man the phones. You're doing well, by the way, so kiss and make up and be gone.'

Connor and Jo looked at each other for a moment and then Jo walked over to him and literally kissed his cheek. Connor smiled.

'Thank you for that. Now let's go and see bloody Mary.'

'Of course, guv.'

Connor led the way out of the room.

'DC Enright,' said the Chief.'

She stopped and turned.'

'Sir?'

'You did well.'

'Thank you, sir.'

The rain had stopped and a watery sun was trying to break through as Connor and Jo arrived at the farm, where the two

60

fraud officers were outside, smoking and waiting for them. As succinctly as possible one of the men explained to Connor what they had found. When they named the sum of £520,000 as the content of the account in Nottingham, they also said that a further sum of £125,000 had been withdrawn and paid for the purchase of a house in Heckington, on the way to Grantham. They had traced the purchase and had the address. Connor looked at Jo and she nodded, and returned to her car. It would take her about 40 minutes at most to get to the house, and she decided that she would need uniform backup and called through to Grantham.

'So, Mary,' began Connor, 'these gentlemen have been going through all your papers and computers. You said there was nothing illegal to be found on them and overall they wouldn't disagree. The government keep a close watch on the finances of those working with immigrants though always acknowledge that they can't see everything. We shall, however, need to be talking to your accountant for it appears that without having broken the law in any way, on instruction from Marney he has been siphoning more than £½m to an account in Nottingham, and that this account has been used to purchase a house in Heckington.'

'What on earth are you talking about? That's ridiculous. Marney and I had no secrets from each other. How do you know any of this?'

'It's all there in the financial records, Mary.'

'Is the account in his name or has he done it in both our names?'

'The account is in the name of Katarina Horvat. Does that name mean anything to you?'

'Not at all. What about you, Ljubica? Do you know the name?'

'No, though there are many Katerinas here for the work among the girls. But I now have very little contact so I wouldn't know the names of more than just a few.'

'She was listed as working here three years ago,' said one of the fraud officers, 'but not listed since.'

'And do you think that Marney's death may have something to

do with her?' asked Mary. 'Was she after getting the money for herself?'

'The money is hers already,' said Connor. 'The account is in her name. And to answer your underlying question, Mary, we have no idea whether she has any part in Marney's death, but believe me, if she has, we shall find out, and I have a team on their way to her now.'

The "team" on their way was a novice detective constable and two constables in uniform from Grantham, who had arrived before Jo and were sitting in a marked car outside the house and generating interest from neighbours. Jo glared at them as they left their car and made her way to the front door.

'Clear the crowd,' she said, and one of them turned back and asked everyone to return to their homes, though not everyone did as he asked. Jo returned to the garden gate.

'In fifteen seconds these officers will officially inform you that you are obstructing the police in the performance of their duties and you will be arrested, and when a vehicle arrives from Grantham you will be taken to the police station, fingerprinted and officially questioned about all aspects of your life. So I recommend you go now.'

Jo and her colleague heard words such as "bitch" and "cow" as the remaining neighbours left, but they all did so, and the two looked at one another and smiled.

'Sticks and stones,' said Jo shrugging her shoulders.

'Could we actually do what you said?'

'No idea, but they thought so.'

Jo approached the door and knocked vigorously, and then went and looked through the window, but there was no sign of life. Again she knocked on the door.

'A taxi picked her up yesterday afternoon,' said a disembodied voice which emerged from a head eventually appearing at the next door's upstairs window.

'Did you recognise the taxi firm?' asked Jo.

'Silver Cabs from Grantham.'

'Thank you very much,' said Jo. 'Can one of you guys chase

that up straight away and find out where she was taken. The other can witness me breaking and entering.'

She withdrew from her jacket pocket a small case containing a number of short metal rods each with a hook on one end, and a slightly larger device.

'It's a Yale,' she said. 'Why do people have them? Any idiot can get in.'

She inserted two of the rods into the keyhole and they both heard the click as it opened.

'You look downstairs, and I'll go up.'

There was little to be seen on either floor. Many of the drawers were empty suggesting that her departure intended to be permanent, but Jo did unearth some male clothes, possibly belonging to Marney but not necessarily so. Toiletries and other signs of daily life were also gone.

The other officer returned from the car.

'The Railway Station. Predictable I suppose. Said to the driver that her mother was suddenly unwell and she was going home.'

'Thank you,' said Jo.

'No, she's not,' said the other, holding up a passport. 'She won't get far without this.'

'When does it expire?'

'2026.'

'Ok, guys. Go and do a bit of door knocking and see what people know and what it was that drew them in such numbers when we arrived. What unusual cars and visitors has she had. You know the form. I'll try and discover if she had a second passport and find out from the bank if she's moved any money.'

The section-by-section search around Wainfleet St Mary yielded nothing at all and the force from Lincoln were thanked and allowed to go home although according to her report it might be that Jo was on to something with the disappearance of Katarina Horvat, but by the time she returned to Boston that hope was somewhat dissipated.

'She doesn't have a second passport and I've checked every airport and no attempt has been made by anyone trying to board a flight to Ljubljana without a passport, nor anyone with her name. Then it occurred to me that we had been assuming she would be travelling South towards London, but what if she were going North? And guess what, I discovered that she has a sister in a place called Bishop Auckland in County Durham.'

'How the hell did you manage to do that?' asked Graham.

'The ultimate in hi-tech. I found an envelope in a bin with her sister's address on the back and that's where she is now and possibly in something of a state because her lover is dead. If she had been involved in his death, I think she'd have gone as soon as it took place, but she only learned about it on the news. I found her sister's number and called her and asked her to check in at the local nick and I'll give them a call.'

'Anything else?'

'Not really. Smashing furnishings and she often had deliveries of stuff. No accounts of visits other than from the one we know about in his landrover, but they did say that on a couple of evenings every week she went out on foot, they know not where, but always looking smart and they have no idea when she got back. Extremely nosey neighbours who wouldn't miss a trick. But they assumed she must be being picked up by someone on the main road, which suggests that Marney may have had competition. We ought to try and follow that up or at least ask Grantham to do so, though there's next to nothing to go on.'

'Ok, give Grantham a call in the morning,' said Connor without enthusiasm.

There was a noise in the corridor and the desk sergeant opened the door and admitted a tall white man and an immediately striking black woman.

'Detective Superintendent Martin Peabody and Detective Inspector Ellie Middlewood.'

The all rose to greet them and shook hands.

'Welcome to Boston where nothing ever happens,' said Connor.

Martin and Ellie smiled.

'I gather you would like to have the chance to see the body.'

'Just to compare one gruesome act with another. There may be no link between them but ever since DC Enright made the possible link on Holmes we've been wondering.'

'Ok. Jo will take you. She's seen it already and knows what to expect. Dr Andrea Gordon is waiting for you, so I think it best you go straightaway. Jo can also fill you in with some of the details en route.'

The way Jo dealt with both the background to the murder and her ability to speak about the body as, with the pathologist, she showed Martin and Ellie the extent of the injuries and then spoke about the effect of being immersed in water, impressed both Martin and Ellie, and even Dr Gordon who had hardly needed to speak. And on the way back she even ventured a thought she had not previously uttered:

'As you know, cattle are branded to help prevent theft but these days almost always by a means called freeze branding which is regarded as considerably less cruel than the older form of heat branding with iron. Marney was heat branded and the pain must have been intense and probably caused him to pass out though wouldn't have killed him. On humans however, the use of heat branding goes back to slaves. So, what if this is the murder of the largest gang master, and in effect indicative of their beliefs that what he does is little better than slavery?'

'Look, Jo. Our hotel is close by your station. You may have family to get back to, but could you spare us half an hour to talk things through over a drink in the hotel bar?'

'Shouldn't that be with my Inspector?'

'No. He asked you to fill us in and though I'm sure he's a good man in every way, it's you I want to hear further from.'

'Ok, sir.'

'Do you agree, Ellie?'

'One hundred percent.'

'Good, that's settled. Oh, and by the way, we're Martin and Ellie. Ok?

'Does that mean I'm buying the drinks?'

'You're a quick learner.'

Inside, Martin went to the bar, leaving Jo and Ellie to chat.

'How long have you been a DC?'

'Ooh it's so long I can hardly remember. Four days maybe.'

'You're kidding.'

Jo shook her head.

'That's not good enough. You should be a DS at least by now and you've undoubtedly got the nouse. It's not about timeserving but about ability, that willingness and capacity for thinking out of the box. You have that. Your colleagues are, as Martin said earlier, no doubt good and reliable, and perhaps that's ok in Boston, but you're not just reliable – you're much better than that.'

Martin arrived with the drinks, and had persuaded Jo to try Campari and soda, which she found quite wonderful.

'Should I be drinking this on duty?'

'You're not on duty. I called your boss and told him that we'd finished for the night and instructed you to finish. We'll speak to him in the morning.'

'Our victim,' began Ellie,' was a paedophile and a bishop of the Church of England who had got away with things for many years. And then his body turned up in a mortuary fridge at a Hospice in South London. He had been castrated, almost certainly when he was alive and a playing card nailed into his spine, before he was shot through the forehead.'

'You don't think it was the Spanish Inquisition, do you?'

'I hadn't thought of that,' said Ellie, allowing space to Martin and his line:

'"Nobody expects the Spanish Inquisition".'

The three dissolved in laughter.

'So,' said Martin, 'put what Ellie's just told you alongside your case here and tell us what you come up with.'

'First and foremost, both imply considerable knowledge of the immediate vicinity – the mortuary and its routines in yours and the back roads, churchyards and rivers here. That's why Connor, my Inspector, is convinced it's a local job, but I'm unconvinced. Then we have the overwhelming supposedly moral element, as if someone has to be punished for doing bad things – sex with young boys and keeping slaves – as the perpetrators see it. Their aim is first to humiliate and cause a great deal of pain and then to kill. Your man got away lightly with a bullet through the forehead. Marney had a shotgun fired up his arse but perhaps they're perfecting their technique. But if it is the same killers, then we have to acknowledge that they've done their research and have planned everything in considerable detail, suggesting that if there is to be a III, it won't be just yet as they will need to prepare, but the whole point of numbers suggests a continuity, that there will be more to come, but we have no idea who and where. It's being done with ruthless efficiency.'

The three sat silently for a for a couple of minutes.

'Have you got a family here in Boston?' asked Ellie.

'No. My parents live in Downham Market in Norfolk. My dad was professional huntsman for the local pack of foxhounds until it was banned. I grew up seeing animals shot and skinned and all sorts of gory detail every day and thought nothing of it, so I don't struggle too much in a mortuary. I live alone at present and perfectly happily so as it means I can watch what I want on the tv and keep the anti-social hours demanded by my job without anyone complaining.'

'And hopes for the future?'

'I think I've been denied promotion and the opportunity to move to CID for a long time and I suspect Connor only moved me to make it look better in the eyes of the Chief who's quite hot on equal rights for officers.'

'I don't know about you, Ellie, but I've heard enough to convince me that Jo's bang on in the links she has made between the two murders and the likelihood, if not certainty, of a third and maybe more. I think behind this is an organised body of fanatics, and extremely dangerous fanatics too, who are seeking potential victims and spending time checking them out. How and if they are related to the statue down-pullers I have no idea, though I think on the whole they are not. We are dealing with people who remain hidden and want to inflict the maximum amount of pain on someone before they are killed. And if this is so, Jo, you and your team will waste all the energy they have pursuing nothing at all, because they've gone and who knows where they will surface again.'

'I agree' said Ellie, 'but there remains one overarching question. What are we going to do with Jo.'

'Hello,' said Jo. 'I'm still here, even though I've acquired a definite addiction to campari and soda. What do you mean by "do with Jo"?'

Martin and Ellie both smiled at her.

'I shall be pressing for the establishment of a national team to deal with this. It must remain hidden and quite secret, with its headquarters in some wholly unlikely place such as Newark or Redditch. It's frankly pointless you remaining here, Jo. You're much too valuable to the police service and eventually you'll get utterly fed up and leave. If I get this team up and running, I shall want you in it. In the meantime, I think you should seek a transfer to the Met as soon as possible and get familiar with the policing we take for granted and which you're not going to get here.'

Jo's face had paled, and she looked at Ellie.

'We're serious, Jo. You have what it takes, but if you stay here, you'll end up not becoming what you have it in you to become, so you need to be serious too.'

Chickens

The Oxford Farming Conference takes place each year in the first week of January and a lot of ale gets drunk. Livestock farmers mostly can't attend unless they have staff on their farms but for the cereal boys, nothing is happening in January ("bloody six-monthers" they were often called by those getting out of bed each morning at an unearthly hour to do the milking every day of the year). Keynote speakers usually include the Secretary of State for the Department of Environment, Food and Rural Affairs who, this time, unusually was also a farmer and unlike all his predecessors knew, to a degree, what he was talking about, the President of the NFU and a host of others including some representing firms selling foodstuff and chemicals who were sponsoring most of the event, as a result of which there was now also a "Real" Farming Conference taking place each year, a time for what those at the OFC regarded as cranks.

There were always some lively debates and at extraordinary cost a so-called celebrity from the BBC would come and host a session, even though not one of them showed signs that they knew anything about the subject other than what was contained on the briefing papers they had been sent in advance, but all possessed an astonishing ability in the art of bluffing.

In addition to the official speakers there was no shortage of opportunities for others to speak and these often were welcomed by participants more than the more staid propaganda in the set-piece events. In most years Tony Hendry made every effort to speak, and his words were always looked forward to with a measure of relish as he was very much a rabble-rouser and unquestionably wouldn't be being called on by the organisers of the Real Farming Conference, the members of which regarded him either with contempt or out and out hatred.

Tony was a chicken farmer, or he might even be called THE chicken farmer in the chicken county of Powys, with five sheds each containing 31,500 chickens slaughtered at 39 days. He always spoke of them as "cheap and cheerful" chickens, the sort that most people bought of the one billion sold each year in the UK. His chickens always bore the "Red Tractor" motif on their wrapping in the supermarkets, there to indicate the minimum standards of welfare used as they were raised. Each year at the conference, and on any other occasion he was cheerleader for those who felt no shame about their work, and always turned his animosity towards the "animal loonies" who broke into farms disturbing and distressing animals to make films of dubious authenticity. He was always cheered and hardly ever had to buy his own drinks in the bar that night.

He farmed just outside Builth Wells close by the River Wye which caused his opponents to claim he polluted the river with ammonia, which he vehemently denied. His farm was protected by somewhat frightening electric wire (to keep out the foxes he maintained, though all his birds were indoors) which deterred any one trying to break in to take photographs. His wife, Danny and their two grown-up children, worked with him on the farm, together with three others, and all were used to him disappearing for a day or two speak or appear on television.

He had phoned that morning, whilst Danny, Poppy and Gordon were having their coffee break together, to say he would be leaving after the evening session and would be back about midnight.

'Don't drink, then,' said Danny. 'You know what the roads are like at the moment, all covered with mud.'

'I know. Ok, see you later.

'Of course.'

It would take the best part of three hours to get home and Tony was feeling good. His speech had gone down well and he had received a number of invitations to repeat it to various audiences across the country. Tony knew that the majority of the people of this country (and by that he meant 97%) were not interested in whether a chicken was organic or free-range but within the means of their pockets and that was what he was providing. He felt truly proud of the chicken farmers of Powys. As he slowed down to go through Clyro (home of the 18th century Revd Francis Kilvert) he saw someone ahead clearly looking for some form of assistance, and as he slowed down he saw a vehicle with what looked at first sight as it if had a flat tyre. He stopped the car and got out.

It was not until the following morning that a police vehicle spotted the car and stopped. A request to look out for it had been issued at 2:00 in the morning when Tony had not returned home. The police noticed that the door was unlocked though it didn't have the keys in the ignition and, having reported in, began knocking at doors and ascertained that it had been there from at least first light when it had been noticed. In the meantime, there was no sign of the owner and they checked out the places Hendry might have stopped to stay if for example, he had been unwell, but there were no reports.

Sergeant Ronald Bowie knew both Danny and Tony well and was a regular visitor at the farm, not least when Tony was away.

'When did you last speak to him?' he asked Danny.

'Yesterday morning. He was cock-a-hoop about the reception received for his speech and instead of waiting for the conference to end officially this morning, said he would leave after the final session last night.'

'The car shows no signs of having been in an accident and is neatly parked by all accounts. Do you know anyone who lives in Clyro?'

'Clyro? Why Clyro?'

'That's where his car was found, on the main road through the village. We've checked the hospitals and there is no sign of him nor has there been a report of an ambulance. He just seems to have disappeared.'

'Where on earth can he be, Ronnie?'

'Are Poppy and Gordon here today?'

'Yes, Poppy's always here but Gordon makes sure he's here when Tony's away?'

'Will they be in huts 4 and 5?'

'Yes. Make sure you put the proper boots on before you enter and wash your hands thoroughly.'

'Of course. I've done it often enough with Tony.'

Danny had a bad feeling. Tony had never done anything like this before and she knew just how many people Tony had turned into enemies though his plain-speaking. He received hate mail on a massive scale and was often offensively barracked when he spoke. At times he had needed the police to ensure his safety, and she was certain the electric fence surrounding the place kept out those who would want to come in and make mischief. She, Poppy and Gordon had also regularly received threats.

These people, they knew, cared a great deal more about chickens than they did for humans. Tony's disappearance was first mentioned on the local news and then picked up by national television and the subject of much speculation and generating greater interest in Francis Kilvert of Clyro. Two days went by, and the police were no nearer solving the mystery or discovering the whereabouts of Tony.

On the third morning a working party was preparing Brilley Village Hall, across the border, for the annual Christmas Fair, setting out tables for the sale of homemade gifts and decorations for the trees. It was something the four ladies did every year and they brought coffee and a cake so they could have a break and a gossip. As they concluded their business, Marjorie opened the back door so she and Shelagh could put into the bins what was left over from their efforts. They were still chatting when they reached the bins and stopped.

'What on earth's that?' asked Marjorie, pointing ahead.

'It's a cage,' said Shelagh, 'but there's something in it.'

'Oh, my God,' screamed Marjorie, 'it's a body.'

The other two ladies appeared at the door only to be met by Marjorie and Shelagh yelling for the police to be called.

The first police vehicle to arrive brought a female officer who as she approached the caged body was immediately sick. She radioed for urgent assistance which in the furthest reaches of rural Herefordshire was slow in arriving. It was a full hour before an ambulance and a full cohort of police and a pathologist were in place.

Photographs were taken at every stage of the opening of the cage which was supervised by the doctor. The knees of the body had been bent to fit it into the cage. Everyone was horrified to discover that the mouth of the corpse had been stuffed full of chicken heads and then it became clear that the body which appeared to be male had been killed by having his throat slashed from below one ear to the other. Even the experienced attendants from the mortuary stood back a moment and took deep breaths. This was carnage.

The senior police officer there was Detective Inspector Cate Greene from Hereford.

'I think this is the missing person from Builth Wells, the controversial farmer, who disappeared leaving his car in Clyro. We shall need a proper identification of course, but I'll alert Powys police. In the meantime, what we have seen here must remain known to us only. If it makes the tv or papers I will hunt down whoever has let it out and that person will be out too.'

Those present knew her of old and could from experience confirm that she meant every word.

The search for Tony was being monitored from the police station at Hay-On-Wye, but with the body having been found in England there would have been close integration of resources across the border.

'Hay-On-Wye,' said a voice answering her call.

'Hay-On-Wye what?' she asked with considerable firmness.

'Police station,' came the reply.

'In future, make sure you say so. This is Detective Inspector Greene of West Mercia Police. Who's in charge of the search for Tony Hendry?'

'DI Ianto Howell, ma'am.'

'I need to speak with him urgently.'

'If you would like to leave a message, ma'am, I will make sure he gets it.'

'Constable, you don't even know how to answer a telephone properly let alone pass on a message. Get him for me and get him now.'

'He's out in the field but I'll give you his mobile number.'

'Thank you.'

Armed with the number, Cate rang his straight away. As he answered she could hear he was less in the field and more in a pub.

'DI Howell.'

'You're not going to find what you're looking for in a hostelry. You're meant to be out searching for a missing person.'

'Who's this?' said Howell.

'DI Cate Greene of West Mercia Police, and whilst you have been engaged in drinking and laughing, we have found your missing person and I warn you in advance, it's not a pretty sight. We shall require formal ID but not until after you and I have attended the PM which will be at 2-00 pm in the mortuary at Hereford County. Until after then I recommend you only say to your troops that there has been a significant find across the border and that for now they can all stand down. Agreed?'

'Of course. Ok, Cate I'll see you there and then.'

He'd heard of Cate Greene and knew she had a reputation of putting the fear of God in all those with whom she dealt, including her superiors, showing neither fear nor favour to anyone however exalted, but he also knew she was rigorous in her seeking out crime and criminals and that was good enough for him.

He passed on Kate's words and went to his car and set off.

Why III ?

As the day wore on it turned very cold and there was the possibility of snow coming from the Northwest which wasn't present now but very well might be on his way back, which Ianto was not looking forward to. Even between 1:00 and 2:00 it was getting darker and he needed his headlights on. He didn't enjoy mortuaries and as often as not sent a junior to attend the autopsy, but he was under orders from Cate Greene and who was he to disobey?'

She was waiting for him at the door but offered neither hand nor smile and like someone out of a Scandi Noir film on television, just nodded her head in response to him giving his name, and opened the door. They had to wear gowns and masks and then joined the team in the PM room. The pathologist was Dr Godfrey Summers, someone Cate knew well, and she introduced Ianto to him.

Ianto stood nearer to the body than he might have wished to but was stunned to see that at the top of the table were at least a dozen chicken heads.

'Yes, odd isn't it. I have perforce removed all sorts of items from the orifices of the deceased and quite a few from the living when I worked in A & E, but this is the first time I have ever removed the heads of chickens, fifteen in total, forced down the gullet, and in case you wondered, they are all real. The evidence suggests that this was done whilst he was still alive which will have been quite a ghastly experience. His life was ended not by choking as you might imagine but by the cutting of his throat from ear to ear. I would suggest it was done slowly enough to cause considerable pain before he became unconscious. However, before this happened (please turn the body over, guys) this was done to his back. The number 111 was written into his back with an extremely sharp knife which went deep into the flesh, again causing what I imagine would have been excruciating pain.'

'Ye Gods,' uttered Ianto. 'Who could so such a thing and why?'

'Before we can do much else, we need a positive identification of the body,' said Cate. 'We cannot begin investigating the murder of Tony Hendry until we know Tony Hendry is dead and that this is Tony Hendry.'

'I have spent a number of days looking at his photograph and as far as I'm concerned this is Tony Hendry.'

'And I think there are solid grounds for thinking it is so, the chicken heads, the means of slaughter and the fact that we found him tightly packed in a metal cage all point in the same direction but until we have a positive ID we must wait patiently for the starting gun.'

'He has a wife, Danny, and a son and daughter. I'll be in touch with the family liaison officer and see if one of them will come. When?'

'Today.'

'But it looks like snow.'

'If it does snow we may lose all possible ground evidence so we have to get on quickly.'

Ianto decided not to argue on the grounds that he knew he would lose. The FLO answered the phone quickly.

'Cherry, it's DI Howell here, and it's not going to be good news you will be delivering.'

'Ok, sir.'

'A body has been found over the border in a place called Brilley. There is every reason to believe that it may be that of Tony Hendry but we urgently need someone from the family to come and see if they can identify the body, not least to rule out the possibility that it is someone else, though I can tell you now that it's not. You know the form and I'll arrange for a car to collect you and whoever, to take you to Hereford Hospital. In advance I must warn you that what you will see when you get there is not a pretty sight. Ok?'

'Of course, sir, thank you.'

Danny looked at Cherry.

'Well?'

'A body has been found answering the description of Tony in the village of Brilley across the border, and has been taken to the mortuary in Hereford. Before investigations can proceed there has to be a positive identification by someone who knew him well, and preferably a member of the family. My inspector believes it is Tony but only one of you can say so for certain.'

Danny had her eyes closed and was shaking.

'I'll go, mum,' said Poppy. 'You should stay here, besides which it looks like snow, and you don't want to be driving in that.'

'It's alright,' said Cherry. 'A police driver will be taking us, and I'll call Sergeant Bowie. Knowing you all as well as he does, he'll come straight away.'

They were on their way, with Cherry holding Poppy's hand, sitting together in the rear of a marked police car.

'What are you expected to do, being with us I mean, at this time?' asked Poppy.

'I'm a trained Family Liaison Office and a police officer at one and the same time. As well as caring for you all to the best of my ability and helping you understand what's happening, I try to make a map of family and friend relationships which can help investigating officers do their job when family members may be involved in some way. I am not there to judge anyone whatsoever, no matter how unusual their relationships and I don't think I ever have.'

'And what of our family's map?'

"It's like a jigsaw puzzle with a major piece missing but, yes, as I know you are wanting to know, of course I have included on the map the close relationship between your mum and a certain person outside the immediate family whose name it is best we do not mention here and now.'

'Do you think they love each other?'

'That's not an easy question to answer.'

'Will your detectives learn about it?'

'It will be investigated, I'm sure.'

'In his position should he be doing such a thing?'

'I'm sorry, Poppy, you've used a word I don't understand.'

'What do you mean?'

'You used the word "should"; it's not a word I understand.'

Poppy laughed again, and squeezed Cherry's hand tighter.

'Would you condemn a butterfly for landing on a particular flower, this rather than that?'

'No.'

'Well, who knows where the heart leads?'

'But isn't that a recipe for chaos in society and the destruction of relationships?'

Cherry didn't reply, thinking briefly of someone in Colwyn Bay she loved and almost certainly shouldn't.

'The snow's coming,' said the driver. 'We'll get there ok but it might be a bit slower on the way back.'

'Cherry, what will happen when we get there?'

'When you are ready, and not before, I will lead you into a room with a large, curtained window. The curtain will be pulled back and a body with a sheet over it will be there and the doctor will pull back the sheet and you will be asked if this is your father, and you be asked to give his name. Then we go to the doctor's office and you will be asked to sign the record of identification, and that will be it. You won't be asked any other questions.'

'I'm not looking forward to it.'

'I know, but I won't leave your side and you can hold my hand throughout, if you choose.'

It was all over in next to no time and soon they were on their way back through the snow which was falling even heavier than before.

'I knew it was going to be him,' said Poppy as they left the city lights, 'but with you there with me I experienced considerably less pain that I might have imagined.'

'Were you close?' asked Cherry.

'You never knew him. I always felt I was being completely ignored by him and even found myself working in the lowest hut, number 5. He was full of words and hot air. Reactionaries in the farming world liked him because he voiced some of the dreadful things they thought, social things and not just about farming. He was racist even where we live, homophobic and completely misogynistic. His language was crude and offensive at home, but I know that at some gatherings he said things that were disgusting and his disciples cheered his every word. In my experience most farmers are neo-fascists with little interest in animal welfare unless forced into it.'

'So why do you stay?'

'He didn't let me go to university as he said that educating women was a total waste of time and money and though my A-levels were good, where could I go? I hardly know the world outside Powys and most of the time I smell of chicken shit and trust me, no end of showers and baths seems to get rid of it.'

'Boyfriends?'

'Can you really imagine a boyfriend taking to the smell? Anyway, in my experience most men are total arseholes. And though the one we mentioned earlier is close to mum, he does have a wife and 2 kids at home he's meant to be there for. What about you?'

'Do you mean have I got a wife and 2 kids at home?'

'Idiot!'

'I live alone in a flat in Welshpool. Police officers have a reputation for not being able to sustain good relationships. In part that's because the anti-social hours we have to keep and some of things we have to see in the course of our work which unsettle us inside. I suppose that mindful of these things I have been reluctant to go out looking for someone to love and be loved by.'

It wasn't quite a blizzard, but it was snowing heavily and the driver had to use all his skills to keep the car securely on the road. The two women huddled closely together.

'How long will you be staying with us, Cherry?'

'Until I'm told to leave.'

'Do we get a say in that?'

'Oh yes. You will soon be subject to extensive questioning from senior detectives and it's vital that I'm there with you throughout.'

'Will it be difficult?'

'Rigorous rather than difficult.'

The snow was turning to rain as they dropped down into Builth Wells and then turned off towards the farm when Cherry noticed Ronnie's car was parked discretely away from the house. There was no sign of Gordon, who would be at home. Cherry wondered whether she should call him and inform him of the identification but waited a while to see if either Danny or Poppy would do so.

'There's no doubt, mum. It's definitely him.'

'No, well, I thought as much. Your dad made an enormous number of enemies and it was perhaps inevitable that sooner or later they would catch up with him. I tried to tell him over and over, but he wouldn't listen. What happens now, Ronnie?'

'Detectives will come tomorrow. They always start at the victim's home. I'm afraid they'll want to poke their noses everywhere. When something like this happens, people tend to lose their privacy and they won't mind washing dirty linen in public. Your Liaison Officer will support you through it.'

They looked at Cherry.

'She's been brilliant this evening,' said Poppy.

'As no one knows where the death occurred, the coroner will be English, and all he will do is open and then after hearing that the police are investigating a murder, he will adjourn the inquest for at least 28 days.'

The West Mercia Assistant Chief Constable to whom Cate had made her report was astounded by what she was told.

'Jeez, Cate. What the hell are the press going to make of this? Where are you going to make your base?'

'Does that mean you're making me Senior Investigating Officer?'

'It's your territory, Cate.'

'Ok. Well, the obvious place is where the body was found, in Brilley Village Hall. The locals won't like it and they'll need to be in there first thing to clear out the Christmas crap. I'll try and get it set up by tomorrow night, and in the meantime put together a joint team with Powys..'

'I'm probably wasting my breath but, Cate, please be tactful.'

'That goes without saying, ma'am.'

'Oh God, why do I always get full of dread when you call me that? Anyway, I'm sending someone from the Press Office to you in the morning. Ok?'

'Ok.'

Because of the snow Cate decided she wouldn't begin interviewing the family tonight but get her team together and inform the ladies of Brilley that the Hall needed to be cleared by 9-00am in the morning, and to make all the arrangements for moving in computers and phone lines by first thing. Talking to BT was never easy at the best of times but by emphasising that they were talking about a murder investigation brought the full attention of the area manager who said the overnight team would make it a priority.

At long last she got home shortly after 11-00 pm. There was a message on her answering machine from Godfrey Summers, the pathologist, to say that toxicology had found small traces in the victim's liver of a drug, Propofol, which anaesthetists used to induce unconsciousness, but the question most playing on her mind as she lay in bed concerned the meaning of the number 111. She had looked it up on Google earlier but found nothing that made any sense. She was sure it would provide the key to solving the mystery.

Questions

Overnight the snow had turned to rain just about everywhere and Cate was in her office shortly after 6:00. Far from tiring as an investigation proceeded, she found herself increasingly energised, something largely unappreciated by those working for her. Although the base for the investigation was to be the Village Hall in Brilley (chosen not just because it was the place where the body was found but for its proximity to the border and the knowledge she would be required to work with Dyfed-Powys police. She even found herself wondering whether those who had committed the murder had deliberately chosen the border area to confuse detection. Not that confusion would necessarily make it more difficult than it already was, something not at all helped by the snow of the previous evening. The base at Brilley would take at least 24 hours to set up, and she knew she would send her lieutenant, Sgt Tommy Enders, there to make sure it was ready for her arrival on the following morning. Her plan this morning was to set up a press conference to be led by her boss, Superintendent Adam Douthwaite whom she needed to brief when whoever from the Press Office arrived.

In the meantime, she telephoned several farming friends to enquire about the significance of the number 111 in the circles in which Hendry had operated. They had not come across it but she noticed that not one of them expressed even the slightest regret when she told them of Hendry's death though each recognised how many enemies he had made, and not just among the animal lobbies. There are many chicken farmers in Powys, she was told by one friend, and they constantly wished he would keep his mouth shut.

'Enough to kill him?' she asked.

'Let's say there might have been a queue.'

The Press Conference was called for 9:30. The Police Station in Bath St was not exactly equipped for a large gathering and Hereford was far enough away from most other places in the world not to attract many journalists quite so early. Cate sat at the back of the room and watched how her boss got on. She had told him as little as she needed him to know without reference to the state of the body'

'So, to sum up,' said Superintendent Douthwaite, 'we are concerned to contact anyone who might have been driving through Clyro on the night I have mentioned, and also anyone in the vicinity of Brilley in the 24 hours following. Any activity that might have struck you as odd should be reported to us at the Incident Room which is being set up in Brilley as I speak.

'We are anxious make contact with and will be most grateful to anyone in the farming community who can supply us with information relating to the number 111.

'Finally, we extend to the family and friends of Tony Hendry our sincerest condolences. We shall do all we can, working with our colleagues in Dyfed-Powys to bring the perpetrators of this dreadful crime to justice.'

The tail end of the Press Conference had appeared briefly on Breakfast TV where it was seen in her flat on a day off by the newly promoted Detective Sergeant Jo Enright in South East London. She smiled when the Senior Police Officer mentioned something he named as the number 111. She knew at once what it was and in seconds had picked up her phone and called her DI, Ellie Middlewood.

'Ellie, it's number 3. Up near Hereford. They're still talking about the number 111 but you and I both know what it signifies.'

'Jo, is there any chance you can go and tell them. It will be no use unless you're there in person, and once you are there you can find out if the death is like the others. I know it's a long way but you'll need a car because it's in the middle of nowhere. Clear it with the locals on your way but use blue lights throughout.'

'Where's Martin today?'

'In court again. The case is taking longer than we thought. But if this really is number 3, then I can't see the National Unit any longer being put on hold. Keep me in touch, and of course it goes without saying how well you've done spotting this.'

'Ellie, I was about to turn it off, so it was an accident.'

'No such thing, Jo. You are blessed with the gift of serendipity. Wrap up well and come back safely.'

Jo knew what Ellie meant: the ability to be in exactly the right place at the right time without any planning or forethought. That had enabled her escape from Boston and the bleak fens to a new life she was enjoying in London, though it had also been hard work. She had passed her sergeant's exams in Boston but knew she had no chance of promotion there and to get it here she also had to train as a qualified firearms officer, a qualified police driver and to acquire the skills and authorisation as an operator on any piece of police technology. Martin's boss, "Dirty" Dave Charnley, couldn't at first understand why Martin was pushing Jo into all these things.

'Are you knocking her off, Martin? I thought Ellie was your preferred piece of action.'

'I'll think you'll see, Dave, that DS Enright is the best you'll ever get entering your station. Besides which I am going to want her for my national squad when it gets going.'

'There's not a lot of enthusiasm for that at present.'

'There will be when number 3 happens.'

'And what about you and Ellie?'

'I think she's having yet another go at mending her marriage so we haven't been seeing quite as much of each other as we were.'

'And DS Enright?'

'Dave, please, credit me with some sense. Besides, I think she may not exactly be the right sort, if you take my meaning. I have no evidence, so I may be completely wrong.'

On her way along the M4 as far as Swindon then across to Gloucester, Jo rarely went under 90 mph but kept each local force aware that she was doing so. It was the first time she had been out of London since her arrival there shortly after the murder of Marney Edmonds. She was now encountering the sort of policing in Lewisham she was excited by and experiencing the realities of urban life and for the very first time in her life, relatively late in time, at 26, she was in love.

Cate had been told just before leaving for Builth Wells that someone was coming from the Met about which she was far from pleased, as she feared that the case might be taken over. It was bad enough having now to relate to a DCI from Welshpool who had been allocated to the case and to whom she was subordinate when in Wales. In England the case was hers and no Detective Sergeant from Scotland Yard would be allowed to muscle in on her.

She had arranged to meet DCI Gwilym Jones at Builth Wells Police Station in Garth St. He seemed relaxed and assured her that they would work together. She smiled at what he took as an agreement and they set off together to pay a first visit to the Hendry Farm. The demands of biosecurity meant it was not a straightforward task but eventually they made it to the door where they were by Sergeant Ronnie Bowie.

'Good morning, sir, ma'am, I'm Sergeant Bowie based in Builth Wells. I'm sorry not to have been at the Station to welcome you.'

'Ronnie, isn't it,' asked Gwilym.

'Yes, sir.'

'Have you picked up anything which we might find useful?'

'No. They know Tony had made a lot of enemies and they are always suspicious of animal activists, with whom, as I'm sure you know, we've had more than a few encounters in the county with so very much intensive farming going on.'

'So, they think that's what this is?'

'Don't you?'

'Ok, take us in.'

'Before that, what are you doing here sergeant?' said Cate. 'I understood there's a FLO on site.'

'Yes ma'am, but they're a family I know well and I'm just here offering support.'

'Don't you think four of us here will be rather over-egging the pudding. I'm sure you have other matters you should be attending to.'

'Of course, ma'am. I'll just tell them I'm leaving.'

Ronnie walked ahead and Gwilym turned to Cate.

'It is a small community and the community police officer knows people well. It's not unrealistic that he's here.'

'Ok,' said Cate, singularly unimpressed, 'your call.'

Entering the room where everyone had gathered, Gwilym gave the nod to Ronnie that he could remain. He therefore decided to become Master of Ceremonies, introducing the detectives and all those present to one another.

'Thank you very much for coming,' said Gordon, who, unlike anyone else in the room knew, from a visit to the family solicitor first thing, that the farm and everything associated with it now belonged to him, which meant he could and would dispose of it as soon as possible. 'Although none of us have the first idea who could have done such a terrible thing, we will try to give you all the help we can.'

'Thank you,' said Gwilym. 'At the moment I think it is fair to say that we have very little to go on but one or two things are clear. The first is that the death of Tony Hendry had everything to do with his very public championing of chicken farming in the style he had adopted, producing what he called "cheap and cheerful" chickens for the supermarkets. He was very good at this but didn't help his cause by not just boasting about it but deliberately going out of his way to offend those who see things differently. I take it you would all agree.'

People nodded or muttered their agreement.

'The second thing is that from the way in which this was planned and carried out suggests considerable local knowledge – the back roads round Clyro and Brilley, for example, which must have been used without leaving a trace, certainly might well lead us to think we are looking for some locals.'

Cate thought she might explode. What sort of cretin was he?

Coming out with this when perhaps, unknown at present, someone in the room might be involved and not least the son Gordon, whom she had herself already discovered by a phone call to the same local solicitor, was the inheritor of the whole farm and all its buildings including the house they were in at present, or perhaps the widow Danny who kept looking at the Sergeant in what she thought might be a suggestive way?'

'However,' she said firmly, 'we know very little at this moment and therefore it is customary for us to begin with those closest to the deceased and to ask where each of you were at the time Tony's car was left in Clyro and on the following day. I think we should begin with you, Gordon, as you are now the owner of the farm and land.'

'What?' said Danny and Poppy, almost in unison.

'Gordon?'

'Well, er yes, I called to see the solicitor this morning and the will is clear. I inherit everything – farm, land, buildings and this house.'

'That is typical of the bastard,' said Poppy. 'If I had known that I would quite happily have killed him myself. I'm glad he's dead and I hope he suffered.'

'It is terrible,' said Danny. 'I've supported him through thick and thin and he repays me by leaving me homeless and without a penny.'

'Perhaps he thought you were making arrangements of your own, mother,' said Gordon.

'What do you mean by that?'

'Do you really want me to spell it out in the presence of strangers? '

'I'm sorry Mr Hendry but we shall need to have an explanation of that remark, now or at some other time, probably at the Police Station,' said the DCI.

'It's the elephant in the room or should that be the elephant in the bed and has been for some time? My dad saw it, I have and I imagine Poppy has too – the relationship between my mother and Sergeant Bowie there.'

'Ok,' interrupted Gwilym, 'I think in the circumstances,

Sergeant, it might be best if you were to be about your business.'

'Yes, sir.'

'We'll speak later.'

Gwilym continued, 'Our concern is only with the death of Tony Hendry. Whatever elephants there may be concealed in a family are not of any interest to us unless they directly relate to the central question. We are not policing your morality. Now back to the question of your location on the night Tony disappeared and on the following day.'

Satisfied with their replies, Gwilym and Cate departed for a pub where they could get a late sandwich and share thoughts. They would have welcomed the chance to hear from the FLO but that would have to wait.

'Once you scratch the surface of a family it's amazing what comes to light.'

'And nothing scratches quite like money.'

'How did you know about Gordon inheriting the lot?'

'The town solicitor used to practice in Hereford and I knew him well, besides which I had sort of guessed that might be the case. Will you see your Sergeant?'

'Yes indeed. As well as opening himself to possible blackmail with a family at home, I just wonder whether he is more involved than we realise. Was he screwing Danny in the hope of an inheritance?'

'Right, I've got to meet a DS up from the Yard, believe it or not, with important information about this case. Are you coming or are you attending to the Sergeant?'

'He'll keep. Your DS sounds more important.'

'Well, I imagine she probably thinks so.'

Jo had stopped for lunch in Hereford and made an unscheduled visit to the Hospital and its mortuary. Somehow or other she managed to persuade Dr Godfrey Summers to allow her to see Tony Hendry's back which she obviously already knew about. He then let her see the full report.

'It fits,' she said to him, 'completely.'

'Really?'

'Oh yes, and that's the news I've come from London to bring to Detective Inspector Cate Greene.'

'Oh my God. I can only wish you the best of luck with that. I might find some form of shelter whilst you're doing so. She's a brilliant detective, highly intelligent and has the shortest fuse in West Mercia.'

'She sounds like fun.'

By the time the three of them arrived at the Village Hall, those preparing the place had made it warm and installed computer equipment. Locals would have been amazed and perhaps appalled that BT had managed to install the fastest internet possible in the shortest time possible ready for the following day when work would begin in earnest. Cate and Gwilym were impressed.

'Tommy, we're waiting for a DS Enright from London.'

'She's already here, boss. She's somewhere around. I think she wanted to get a sense of the area where he was found.'

The front door of the hall opened and in came Jo.

'Hi there, 'she said cheerfully. 'I'm Jo Enright and I think we need to talk as a matter of urgency.'

Cate and Gwilym looked at one another and at once sat down.

Jo began to recount the murders of Bishop Peter Sherriff and Marney Edmonds, both of which remained unsolved and characterised by three features in common, the first being the horrendous torture and disfiguring of the bodies, the clear indication that each must be the work of locals, and then the number on the back, nailed to the spine of the Bishop and hot branded on Marney. The first was the Ace of Spades, the second the Roman numeral II, and now, the Roman numeral III or 3.

'Shit,' said Cate. 'However could I have missed that?'

'By being busy today and not having your computers to hand, I'm sure you would have found it as soon as you went on Holmes 3, and that's why I'm here. It's not for to me to tell you to cease your enquiries, though I would have to say that from previous experience they may need to be set in a much wider context. All three of the victims were singularly unpleasant people but my Super thinks the time has come for our betters to realise that the only way in which this can be responded to is by the setting up of a National Unit. At the present time we are each in our own area getting nowhere and what is going to be necessary, as I say, is a dedicated team. Your man fits the template exactly with the chicken heads, the cage and the slit throat which is how chickens are slaughtered. These people exact appalling injuries as they kill. His back looked to me as if it was done when he was alive. The pain must have been excruciating, as of course it was in the Fens, when it was done a hot branding iron and in all three incidents there was the presence in the blood of the anaesthetic drug Propofol. That suggests more than a coincidence.'

'How long has there been between each incident?' asked Cate

'About three months.'

'Enough time to find a new target and prepare in depth in such a way as to suggest a local job and lead us round the mulberry bush.'

'What happens now?' asked Gwilym.

'I leave you to get back to London with some stuff to look at on-line, and then my Super is going to arrange a meeting with the powers that be to see if the task force can be appointed and get going.'

'Isn't it a job for the Security Services?' continued Gwilym.

'No,' said Cate in the sort of way Gwilym was beginning to recognise as determinative of the shape of the rest of the conversation. 'This is for us to do. Jo, it's ridiculous trying to drive back tonight, so you can come and stay with me in my spare room. I want to hear the thoughts of your team in London and see if we can't get our ACC to throw her weight behind it.'

'Is that an order, ma'am?' said Jo with a smile.

'It certainly is.'

'Then I'll do as I'm told, though my boss would tell you that there's a first time for everything!'

Martin returned from his meeting with the Association of Chief Police Officers in Birmingham knowing how much he owed to DS Jo Enright. She, Ellie and Martin himself were sitting in a Pizza Express in Lewisham High St.

'You know how to spoil us, Martin,' said Jo as she tucked into her garlic bread.

Ellie laughed.

'Yes, it's not like you to splash out.'

'That's because we're having food and drink in honour of Jo.'

'Really?'

'Yes. ACPO is exactly as you might imagine: a bunch of the self-important mostly discussing matters far removed from what we do day by day. I only got the chance to speak when they were over-running and in danger of missing lunch, because the chief of West Mercia insisted that what I had to report had to be heard, and that is all down to Jo. Isn't that right?'

'Possibly.'

'Possibly be buggered. You have made the new Unit possible. He reported on the murder of Tony Hendry in graphic detail as reported to him by his ACC whom you met on the morning after you went there and DI Greene called for her to come. I followed up with the first two and said that a fourth was almost certainly inevitable. I then made the case we've drawn up and the hungrier they were feeling, the more amenable they were to getting us going and financing us for a year with my choice of team.'

'Brilliant, Martin,' said Ellie.

'Yes, well done,' said Jo, 'though a year's not a long time.'

'I know, and the team will be small, but first we need to find a base.'

'Any thoughts?' asked Ellie.

'I'm told Jersey is pretty warm most of the year,' said Jo.

'That's exactly the sort of creative thinking we're going to need,' said Ellie.

'Unfortunately, ACPO have suggested we set up in Royal Leamington Spa. There a is facility there which they think ready-made, meaning it will cost them nothing, but is central with good access to motorways and railways.'

'And the Royal Shakespeare Theatre in Stratford,' added Jo.

'I think we'll be dealing with quite enough drama in our work

not to have to witness more murders on stage in the evening.'
They   laughed.

Comrie

At almost the same moment, but a long way north, Jocelyn Hoosen was in full flow at a gathering in Glasgow. Although the Scottish government liked to keep an eye on her when she was speaking publicly, because she strongly favoured independence, they decided to tolerate her views on other matters. The other matters were what some would call extremist views on matters of race. Hoosen was a white South African who had lived in what she called "involuntary exile" in Scotland for almost twenty years and if being away from her homeland had lessened the force of her utterances, you would never know it.

Tonight, as on most nights, she spoke about the dreadful long-term effects of so-called racial integration in Britain, though in Scotland particularly. She was a great devotee of Enoch Powell, the "Ulster MP" as she called him quite correctly but oddly, as it would be if she called him the Australian Professor of Greek, which he also had been. She denied that neither he nor her were racists, simply those who could see the terrible long-term effects of black and whites living together, marrying and producing children who were neither one thing nor another. When reports reached her of the many black on black stabbings in London, she echoed Powell's words about "rivers of blood". And she made full use of the experience of Southern Rhodesia as she still called Zimbabwe under Mugabe and the horrendous years under Black rule in South Africa where the natives murdered one another on a terrible scale, on average 57 a day.

'So much for Black rule, and it will be always like that where Blacks rule. Just look at Africa as a whole and you will see the effects of such rule in terms of utterly corrupt regimes where, if you ever get in the way, you are killed.'

Her audiences lapped it up. Mostly she remained in Scotland despite frequent invitations to come south and speak to gatherings of those would relish were words in England. She did sometimes appear on television and would be asked questions such as "If you were taken very ill, would you object to being treated by a black doctor?" to which her reply invariably was "Is that the best you can come up with?"

She lived in a small village called Comrie, situated in the South Highlands, but was increasingly finding journeys in the evening to Edinburgh and Glasgow very tiring and now relied increasingly on a local man, Scott Miller, to drive her to events. Local people had no interest in her reputation and just liked her for her friendliness and willingness to join in all local events.

Scott dropped her off at her home on South Crieff Rd at about 11:15.'

'Will ye be needing the car tomorrow, Jocelyn?' asked Scott.

'No. Use it as you see fit. It's Perth next.'

'I'll give it a clean then. Good night.'

'Good night, Scott, and as always, thank you.'

Generations of boys (and, later, girls) know Comrie best for Cultybraggan Camp, a little south of the village where, though once the domain of the real army has for many years been used as the summer camp for school CCFs. If you like dreadful food, the cold, and days of following of silly army rules and regulations, it's the place for you, but at least in time off you can wander over to the nearby Auchingarrich Wildlife Centre. For many staying at Comrie the worst time of all is the over-night exercise, most of which is spent lost on the nearby moors, the only respite coming with the early rising of the sun in the Scottish summer. Wise were those who anticipated the night and had spent wisely at the NAAFI on the day before and now chomped their way through chocolate bars.

Andy and Nigel from a school in Cumbria were more used to moors and fells than some of their peers and spent a lot of the night sitting smoking, eating and drinking. They had no intention of completing the task asked of them and thought that others would be like them or well and truly lost. They were near something known as the Milntuim Hermitage but put their rucksacks down to allow themselves to replenish their water supply in the burn that ran nearby.

In the half-light of dawn, Andy almost slipped into the burn which he definitely didn't want to do as wet boots were not a lot of fun. As he steadied himself, he noticed something peculiar a few yards away, and approached it.

'Oh Jesus fucking Christ,' he yelled to his friend.

"What is it?'

'It looks like a dead body but without a head. O God, I'm going to puke.'

Andy vomited into the burn as Nigel took a closer look.'

'Shit. It's horrible. Come on we need to get to someone to tell them.'

'It's alright, I sneaked my phone down my underpants which they were checking us. I'll call the police. An ambulance is going to be no fucking use.'

There was no signal. We need to get back to the camp as soon as possible and they can say what they fucking like, I'm going home as soon as I can get out of this ridiculous uniform, and I'm not taking no for an answer.'

'Me too,' said Nigel. 'If I can get to speak to him, my dad will come at once.'

They made their way across the relatively short distance to the camp where, just before they got there, Andy had a signal on his phone and used it to call the police. When the boys arrived at the camp and tried to tell their story, the masters pretending to be officers seemed much more concerned that they had not completed the task. It was too much for Andy.

'Just shut up, will you, and listen. Over there, near the so-called Hermitage is a dead body with its head cut off and lying nearby wrapped in something. Fuck your night task. This is not a game.'

'Watch your mouth boy or you'll be on report. I'll call the

police but if this is a joke you are both in for the high jump. Now get to your quarters and wait there.'

'Too late. I've already called the police and we'll remain nowhere. We're leaving as soon as possible and will arrange for Nigel's dad to come and get us.'

'How have you called the police? You were expressly forbidden to take mobiles.'

'Oh, piss off you stupid wanker,' joined in Nigel.

The boys moved off leaving a teacher with not the first idea how to respond. He needed his fellow teachers with him.

A vehicle was approaching and he could see it was a police landrover and he went out towards it. He pointed before he spoke.

'Two of our cadets claim to have found a body over there, near the Hermitage and by the little river.

'We call it a burn. Where are they?'

'Gone to their hut.'

'Get them.'

The teacher ran towards the hut and found the two boys already changed.'

'The policeman wants you, probably to show him where.'

They looked at one other.

'I'm not going back to it,' said Andy.

'Nor me,' said Nigel

'Just come and tell him where to go and then go and get yourself something to eat. If what you say is true we'll all have to pull out today.'

'It *is* true,' said Nigel.

The boys followed the teacher to where the policeman was waiting.'

'Tell me again what you think you saw.'

'We didn't think, we saw it. We saw it,' said Andy, now thinking all adults were totally committed to thinking all teenagers were liars.

'Aye but the light wasn't good and you'd been up all night.'

'In which case, sod you, tosser,' said Andy. 'Go and find it yourself. We're off.'

They turned and left.

The policeman didn't speak again but set off for the Hermitage.

It wasn't far and then he drew nearer to the burn and looked across to the other side. There could be no doubt what he now saw and had a terrible sense that he knew whose body it was. Immediately he called for backup which would have to come from Perth as Crieff wouldn't have the resources to deal with what he realised was a beastly murder.

By the time he arrived back at the camp, groups of boys were arriving in from the exercise, cold, wet and wondering why the police landrover was there. The teacher saw the policeman coming and went out to meet him.

'When the boss gets here, he will want the camp cleared completely and everyone sent off home though he will want a quick word with the two lads who found her.'

'Her? You know who she is then?'

'Aye. Now make sure everyone has returned safely. Get some food and warm drink into them and then make ready to leave. This area is completely out of bounds and I shall tape it off.'

Almost a further hour passed before those in the camp heard sirens approaching. Word had got round as to what it was that Andy and Nigel had found and it generated a great deal of excitement in those who had made their way up to the exclusion tape in large numbers.

Detective Inspector Robbie Douglas merged from the front car and unceremoniously said to the officer who had been there from the beginning: 'Get rid of them, Ali, and extend the tape back so no one from there can see the road. I also want them away from the camp as soon as possible, other than the two who found her.'

'Ok.'

If they were wise, no one argued with Robbie Douglas. A former second-row rugby player he towered over everyone from his 6' 6" height.' With a couple of other officers Douglas made his way along the route marked out by Ali. No one spoke. They reached the former Hermitage and then jumped the burn and came upon the terrible sight before them.

'Good God,' said Inspector Douglas, as he moved close to the corpse and what they assumed was her head, three feet away and wrapped in the flag of South Africa. Even more bizarre was that he could see she had been stripped of her clothing and then painted black. He went to the head and slowly tried to pull the material to see her face. He stopped and withdrew.

'No question. It's Jocelyn Hoosen. There's nothing we can do now other than just take a look around the immediate area. There's blood near the neck but where was this done? We have to wait for the pathologist. Any word how long he might be?'

'Another fifteen minutes the driver reckons.'

'Good.'

'It's like some of the murders I've read about in England, sir, the ones on the police computer. I guess we won't know more until the doc turns the body over and we see what's on her back.'

'M'm. But say nothing about that to anyone. The thing done to the back in terms of Roman numerals has not been released to the Press and it has to stay that way. If she hasn't got them, it may just be a repulsive copycat killing, but if she has, that will be another ball game altogether.'

'Don't you think it shows all the signs of being local, sir,' ventured on the young constables. Who else would know the back roads here but someone from the area?'

'There are such things as maps, constable.'

'Of course sir, but this is in such an out of the way place.'

'We'll get back to the cars and wait for the doctor and I'll have a word with the two lads who found her, though it's only for form's sake. They'll have nothing for us, I'm sure.'

By the time the pathologist arrived, Inspector Douglas had praised the lads on their courage when faced with something so terrible and wished them a safe journey home.

'Oh shit,' said Inspector Douglas when he saw that the pathologist was Dr Alexandra Jenkins from Dundee, and not the miserable old git from Perth, whom he knew so well.

'Good morning, Inspector.'

'I should wait until you've seen what we've got for you before you say that. And where's miserable Angus today?'

'He's in hospital in Edinburgh with pneumonia.'

'Oh, poor thing. Will he live?'

'With antibiotics I should think so. Shame, but there we are.'

The officers standing round all laughed.

'So I'm covering Perth and Dundee, and here I am brought at a quite frightening speed by one of your men. So, tell me, what am I going to see?'

'The corpse of the South African racist rabble-rouser Jocelyn Hoosen, as far as I can make out, but I've never seen anything like it, so prepare yourself.'

The doctor clambered into her blue jump suit and Inspector Douglas and a couple of others into their grey equivalents, one of the constables leading the way, the doctor carrying her bag. Jumping over the burn was no problem and then she approached the site.

'Have you given the immediate area the once-over, Robbie?'

'Yes, nothing we could see.'

'And how long since it was discovered?'

'Two hours. Two boy cadets from the army camp on a night exercise. Nice lads with a fine turn in the less delightful aspects of the English language according to their teacher, but I thought they were good lads.'

It's not surprising if they came across this. Photographs please.'

Her technician came forward.

'Did they or you open the flag?'

'I did, to see who it was.'

'With gloves on.'

'Dr Jenkins, I didn't get to my present position as a result of my good looks.'

'Oh, I don't know. In the half light of dawn you're more than passable!'

'Thank you.'

The doctor now had a tape recorder in her hand and was recording impressions in situ. At first, she concentrated on the torso and then turned her attention to the head which she handled with an ease the Inspector could never have managed.

'Are you intending to turn the body over, doctor,' said her

technician.

'No, that wouldn't be fair on the police officers present. When we get her to Perth we can do that? Is the van here?'

'I imagine it will be by now.'

'Go and tell them what we've got. They will know the form about handling the head. Robbie, I can't at this moment tell you anything you probably don't know already, other than that she has been here about 24 hours and judging from her eyes was alive when her head was chopped off. I think it's a fair surmise to reckon that she suffered a very great deal. The paintwork could have been done before or after and I can only let you know that after I have had time to spend more time on the head.'

'Thanks Alex. How do you do it, how do you deal with this without flinching, without throwing up?'

'My uncle was a funeral director and from a very early age I spent loads of time with him in his workshop. I got used to death and it's never troubled me. Pathology is such a fascinating discipline. Ah, here are my guys. Will 2:00 o'clock suit you, Robbie?'

'Of course, if I can stand it.'

The rest of the morning was spent in a house to house in Comrie together with a final check on those leaving the camp that they had not seen or heard anything unusual, but his question was greeted with silence and soon some coaches arrived to take them to Perth and to the trains heading south.

One name did keep cropping up as the police chatted with her neighbours and that was her driver Scott Miller who used her car for his own needs when not transporting her hither and thither. Inspector Douglas and one of his detective constables together called to see him, but he was out in the car getting it cleaned in Crieff.

'Who's in Crieff this morning?'

'No one, everyone's here.'

'Shit. Ok, drive quickly with siren and blue lights. We've got to stop him cleaning the car.'

The officer did as he was told.

'There's a Suzuki garage on the main road that may have a car washing facility behind it. Go there first.'

At the speeds he was driving the constable entered the small town in no time at all and pulled into Gordon Motors. Douglas was quickly out of the car and in the show room whilst inside everyone inside staring from the plate glass windows at the police car with flashing lights.

'Who's in charge? This is urgent.'

A man raised his hand.

'Have you got car washing facilities here?'

'Round the back but not for the public. It's where we prepare cars for delivery.'

'And what exceptions do you make?'

'You mean for yours?'

'No. Answer the question. This is important.'

Sometimes for particular people.'

'Is Scott Miller a particular person.'

'Well, occasionally.'

'And what about this morning?'

'Yes, he rang about an hour ago and asked whether there would be a space for him to do Ms Hoosen's car?'

'And has he done it?'

'Not yet, no. I said to him it would have been at noon when the lads go for their lunch break.'

'Thank you.'

'I need to see him, but if he should ring before then and cancel, please ask him to come anyway.'

Why IV ?

The two police officers wandered around the car showroom, marvelling at the prices, whilst keeping a sharp eye open for the arrival of Scott Miller. It is was the constable who noticed his arrival first as the car drove over the forecourt towards the back.

'Leave him to me, unless I need your help. A uniform might frighten him.'

'Yes, sir,' replied the constable, thinking to himself if Douglas thought that a plain clothes officer of about 6' 6" wouldn't!

Inspector Douglas went out the back door and saw Scott as he approached the same door,

'Mr Miller?'

'Scott, please.'

'That's a nice motor car you've got there.'

"I know and it's my good fortune to get to drive it.'

'Oh, so it's not yours?'

'Sadly not. It belongs to a well-known local lady to whom I'm chauffeur and who allows me to drive it when she doesn't need it.'

'So regular cleaning is part of the job, I imagine.'

'Yes, the other night she had to go to Glasgow and she always likes it to look good for the next journey, so I have a deal with this garage that I bring it when the the lads are having their lunch and give it the once over. Are you one of the directors? If so, I pay for what I do and don't delay their normal work.'

'I'm sure, but no I'm not one of the directors, but Detective Inspector Robbie Douglas and I'm sorry to have to let you know that the lady for whom you work, whom I take it is Jocelyn

Hoosen has been unlawfully killed. I'm still waiting for the results of the post-mortem but I gather that the manner of her death was not pleasant.'

If Scott had known about this beforehand, Robbie felt his face didn't show it. Instead, it registered shock in such a way as he thought not contrived.

'Oh my God, that's terrible. A lot of people thought her a monster because of her speeches but in our village she was much loved and generous in every way.'

'Did you feel that way about her?'

'Certainly I did, Inspector, but you'll be wanting to take the car for examination, I imagine. Please ask your people to be careful with it.'

'Of course. What about you? Can we take you back to Comrie?'

'Are you going back there yourself?'

'Yes, though I should warn you that my constable believes that Formula 1 drivers go far too slow. But first I have to get him to tape this whole area off and then let the garage know the car wash area is closed until your car can be collected.'

'Of course. I can hardly believe this.'

On their way back to Comrie, it was possible to question Scott in a more relaxed context.

'So what was she like?'

'As I've said, those of us in the village liked her very much and could hardly believe how many others spoke of her as akin to the devil, just as those in her audiences would never believe that we knew her as a nice lady in every way.'

'And how many black people live in Comrie?

'None.'

'I have to say I don't take a great deal of notice of fringe political activity, so is it just blacks in the sense of West Indians or Africans she is opposed to?

'No. She wasn't especially politically correct, so Asians, East Europeans, Chinese, in fact just about everyone she lumped together as blacks.'

Robbie smiled wryly.

'But wasn't she an immigrant from South Africa?'

'She said that was different, being white and of European heritage. She wasn't troubled by the obvious inconsistency.'

'You saw her last when exactly?'

'Two nights ago, after I dropped her outside her house at about 11-30. We had been to Glasgow and I think it had gone well.'

'Did you go in with her when you arrived home?'

'Good heavens, no. She would not have welcomed being treated in that way, though I always waited until I saw the lights go on.'

'And that happened?'

'Yes.'

'And there was nothing you saw to suggest that anything was different?'

'No.'

'Would you have expected communication from her yesterday?'

'No, and there was none.'

'She provided me with a list of commitments for which she needed me every couple of weeks and we worked from that. We've been working like this for some time. Nothing was different.'

'Did you ever go into her house?'

'Of course, mainly to talk through upcoming journeys.'

'I'd like you to come with me to the house now, before we take you home, so you can take a look round and see if there's anything you notice that's different?'

'Please just wait in the car for a few moments as I need first to speak to one of my men.' said Robbie.

A uniformed constable stood by the front door.

'Is Sergeant Marsh still here?'

'Yes, sir, with SOCOS, inside.

'Ok. Can you please go in and call him?'

'Yes, sir.'

Marsh was chunky (in his own words), fat in the eyes of

others, and he came out of the door.

'Hello, boss. How did you get on with Miller?'

'Seems genuine enough. I've got him in the car and thought he might look round and see if anything's unusual but with SOCOS here, I'll send him home and rely on you getting him here later.'

'No problem.'

'And is there anything to see?'

'Not in the house or garden. There are no signs of a struggle and there is no blood anywhere. I don't know where she died, but it doesn't seem to have been here.'

'And have any of the neighbours heard or seen anything?'

'Nothing.'

'Ok, I have to get to Perth for the PM which I'm not looking forward to one bit.'

'Even with Dr Jenkins standing in for old misery guts?'

'Do you know, when she reached the body this morning she didn't bat an eyelid.'

'I suppose they get used to it.'

When Alex had arrived in the mortuary her first task was to completely unwrap the South African flag from the dead and bag it. There were no clothes which had presumably been removed to allow the black paint to be applied to her body, not exactly a subtle protest against her views but she took a little of the paint for testing though it looked ordinary enough. She asked her colleagues to lift the torso on to its side so she could see the back. There was no doubt about it and at a nod they laid it down again. She then covered the torso and head with a green cover.

'Time for some food, I think,' she said, and was greeted with smiles. 'We'll make a start at 12:30, ready for the police coming at 2:00. You make a start, Charlie,' she said to her senior technician and I'll join you.'

By the time that Robbie Douglas arrived and changed into his mortuary kit, most of the physical dismantling had been done for which he was hugely grateful. It never did him any good to hear a saw and the removal of the brain, nor the opening of the abdomen and the removal of the organs.

The first thing Alex wanted to show Robbie was IV deeply cut into the back.

'An extremely sharp knife did that, and I believe she was conscious when it was done. You should have been able to hear the screams for miles around. Decapitation was done with a large axe and like Mary, Queen of Scots, was done with two blows. I cannot say whether she was alive when the first blow was struck. Nor yet can I tell you if there was anything in her blood that might account for being able to move her without her objecting. I've asked for a rapid toxicology report but it has to go Edinburgh and they'll call me, but it could be late.'

'That's fine, Alex. Just let me know. I have a feeling this will be passed to another team altogether as almost certainly it has been done by the same lot who carried out the preceding three in the series, all brutal murders of the politically incorrect. The word is that a special Unit is being set up and hopefully they can find those responsible before number V takes place.'

'How long is there between them, Robbie?'

'Usually a few months and, other than the Roman numeral, details of which have not been made public, they all give the appearance of being local because of the apparent knowledge they display. This one fits perfectly and I shall need to communicate all this to the Superintendent at the Met who's coordinating everything. But I suspect he'll be stunned by this one – an actual decapitation.'

'And one à la mode of Mary, Queen of Scots, with the double blow to the neck – no French expert with a single swing of the sword, as with Anne Boleyn.'

Deliberate, you mean?'

'It looks like that to me. I would have imagined that a strong enough blow could have done it in one, but as this is my first decapitation . . .'

'Alex, you haven't lived! In Glasgow there's at least two every Saturday night,'

'Robbie, get out!'

Robbie had been back in Comrie for less than an hour when his phone rang.

'Robbie, it's Alex. Edinburgh have already done the toxicology testing and there is unusual evidence of Propofol, sometimes called Diprivan, in her liver.'

'Tell me more.'

'It's the basic drug used by anaesthetists (and probably also vets) to put someone to sleep instantly before an operation. I've checked again and there's a possible entry point on the back of her left hand but I couldn't guarantee that it is so. What's unusual is that the body does not normally retain it, but this might suggest at least a double dose.'

'It hasn't been mentioned in relation to the other murders but it's the sort of detail that may be being deliberately withheld. I'll be in touch with them before long so they may be able to confirm if it is so. Thank you, Alex.'

Robbie returned home to complete his report which he was immediately able to send by encrypted email and he followed it up thirty minutes later (as he was instructed by Holmes 3) with a call to a dedicated phone line.

'Good evening, Inspector,' said the female voice. 'Please make a note of the following reference. When you call again, tap it into your phone when you are asked to, so we know who you are: 852045. Have you got it?'

'Yes'.

'Good. And let me say at once how superb your report is. Thank you for that. We have no doubts, which you clearly share, that we are dealing with the same people, though we were all taken aback by the decapitation which is even more barbaric than anything we have seen before now.'

'It's not a pretty sight.'

'I can imagine, though none of them have been and so far I'm the only one who has seen all the other corpses, and I'm determined to do all we can to prevent number V, even though the victims are not necessarily the nicest people.'

'What now?'

'It's vital you continue acting as if this is a local crime, not something you suspect isn't. If they begin to think we're setting up a national team, we suspect they will take cover and become even more inaccessible. But one of the team, though membership is not yet finalised, will want to meet with you tomorrow, and with the pathologist, if possible, at the mortuary in Perth Hospital at noon, and then come with you to Comrie. Ok?'

'Yes, of course. I'll call Alex, that's the pathologist, straight away.'

'Ok, once again thank you for that superb report, Inspector.'

The phone call had ended.

Jo turned on her chair to the others, knowing full well she was the only one present.

'Ok,' she said, to the absentees, 'if no one is willing to do it. I guess I will have to.'

Turning back to her desk she quickly booked a flight to Edinburgh. Martin and Ellie would have expected no less of her, and all three had built up considerable trust among them. Martin was in Hereford seeking to recruit Cate Greene to the team, although he had already decided with her ACC that she would say "yes".'

Ellie had left an hour earlier and had gone home to cook "something special" whatever that might be.

Robbie was left puzzled by the phone call. Whoever spoke to him gave no name but seemed already to have grasped the essence of his report which was impressive in itself, and no one could fault the speed with which they were responding and they extent to which they were taking his report seriously. He picked up his phone and called Alex.

Martin was already chatting with Cate Greene in the restaurant in Hereford when the call from Jo came. He listened intently and without interruption for five minutes before he spoke.

'Would you prefer Ellie to go? ... Oh, I forgot the visit to Warwick. Well, have a nice time. The last execution by guillotine in France was 1977 ... Ok, thanks Jo.'

Cate looked across to him.

'Is that the Jo I met?'

'Yes.'

'She's a class act. Why is she only a sergeant.

'Don't worry, it won't last long, and that call was to report number IV in Scotland, complete with decapitation. There's no doubt. The Roman numeral on her back, which we've never released, but use of the other concealed information – clear traces of Propofol in her blood.'

Cate nodded her head gently.

'And here – anything?'

'As you would expect, nothing whatsoever. A station sergeant was knocking off the wife of the victim, but absolutely nothing to link the two. The daughter of the victim developed a crush on the FLO, which she denies was mutual and frankly I don't care either way. The son of the victim inherits everything and already he's selling up, the chicken farm, land and house, which has made him very unpopular with his mother and sister, who are going to be without a roof over their heads. As for the many other chicken farmers in Powys, and I mean many, they are delighted the main competitor is finished.'

'Lift up any rock and it's amazing what crawls out. Thanks too for suggesting we eat here. This is very good food.'

'So, when is the Police Handbook to Good Eating due out, Superintendent?'

Martin put his knife and fork down and looked at Cate, before smiling.

'You might well have been impressed with Jo when she came but it's as nothing with how impressed she was with you. She's our recruiting sergeant and has superb judgement and as a result of what she told me I spoke to your ACC who understands better than anyone what is at stake in these murders. I told her I wanted someone from West Mercia in my team, someone familiar with that happened here, and who could exercise imagination and acute intelligence in a team dedicated to sorting this lot out. I then told her that I wanted you and she replied that you were exactly the sort of brilliant pain in the neck I could make most use of. I said I would come and sound you out, but she said, "No. She will do it.'

Martin began eating again and this time it was Cate who put

down her cutlery.

'Did she mean I was brilliant but a pain in the neck, or a brilliant pain in the neck?'

'Good question, Inspector. Welcome to the team. Now let's concentrate on the food.'

As Jo made her way home, she found herself wondering whether being in love allowed you to be late in getting back to the flat, and then decided she didn't care because she knew she was loved utterly and completely. It had taken her years of emptiness and a great deal of loneliness, but she had arrived.

Meetings

For both Ellie and Jo, it was an early start. Ellie's train left Euston at 7:40 and Jo had to be at London City Airport by 8:00. Ellie was arranging with the Warwickshire Police Force the authorisation she, Martin and Cate (Martin had texted her to let her know Cate was on board) required to allow the members of the team who were designated as Specialist Firearms Officers, which would be all apart from one, to bear arms when appropriate.

She was met by the Deputy Chief Constable, Derrick Blowes, whom she had known when he was at the Met, and sometimes saw at meetings of the Black Police Association.

'Hello Ellie, you're looking well.'

'And you, Derrick, promotion obviously suits you but I thought that at the very least you'd greet me in your uniform. Just fancy – DCC Derrick Blowes.'

'It sound very grand but I regret to say there's very little actual policing involved in the job. Budgets and planning are the mainstay of my day-to-day life, and meetings until they come out of my ears, and I do feel there's quite a bit of racial tokenism involved – the chief often wheels me out for tv and the press, but I'm not complaining. At least no one has yet attempted to shoot me.'

'Racist hate mail?'

'That, I'm afraid, is par for the course. You?'

'No. I'm much too unimportant and mostly invisible, though in court I sometimes get it, but no worse, I suppose, than the abuse white colleagues receive simply for being police officers doing their job.'

'From what I have been told, you are now onto something very big indeed. Three horror show murders.'

'Keep this to yourself, but it's now four and the most horrific has just taken place in Scotland. We're holding on to it at the moment but I very much doubt we shall be able to do so much longer. It involved a beheading.'

'O blessed Jesus!'

Derrick stopped in his tracks and momentarily closed his eyes. Ellie knew he was a devout man.

'We have some paperwork to complete here in Warwick and then we'll pop to Leamington and see your new base. Actually I'm really pleased you're coming here. We are a small force and need a treat.'

'I'm not sure it will be that, but it's got you, Derrick. I know you and for heaven's sake, don't let the job crush out of you all you have to offer. You are an outstanding police officer and you need to be able to show it.'

'Thanks Ellie. That you're doing what you are is more than adequate testimony to the regard with which you are held.'

'If you could, would you join a team like ours?'

'Of course I would, but you don't get DCCs doing that sort of things. We're much too important.'

'Oh sorry, I was forgetting.'

They laughed as the car pulled into the force headquarters.

The paperwork was straightforward and then Ellie surprised Derrick by asking for a word with the Chief Constable by herself.

'Good morning, sir,' she began as he motioned her to sit.'

Good morning, Inspector and welcome to Shakespeare's county where you are to be based. I'm not quite sure whether this means you come under us in some way or whether other means of authority are to be applied.'

'I'm pretty sure you won't want to lose sleep over what we might be doing, sir, and as you say these things are still being sorted in links with both the Met but also the Security Service. However, I want to ask an odd favour of you, sir. We have no wish at all to be without a proper link to the local police service and, please forgive my cheek in asking but if you don't ask, you don't get. I think we would find it extremely beneficial doing our job with proper guidance from a much senior officer, not active day by day with the team of detectives but so we know that level of support is there. So, though I have said nothing about this to him and he might not want to do it, I wondered whether you might lend DCC Blowes to us, say for two half days a week. Detectives don't always observe the boundaries and I think he could help us a great deal.'

'Do you know Derrick?'

'I knew him when he was at the Met and I was greatly impressed by him. I was not all surprised that he was promoted.'

'And you maintain that he knows nothing about what you have suggested?'

'No, sir. He has great integrity, as I'm sure you know, and would have stopped me saying this if he had known. He knows nothing of what I have asked you, and for my part there is simply no way I would have undercut your authority by mentioning it to him before I discussed it with you.'

'I appreciate that very much, Inspector. It would require some planning of course and more responsibility for the ACC, but I would welcome some involvement in what you are doing, even if not in terms of direct action. You have three terrible murders to deal with according to what Superintendent Peabody said at the meeting of ACPO.'

'I regret to say, sir, that as of yesterday it is now four, and the most recent, the most barbaric of them all.'

'Ye gods. Look, Chief Inspector, I gather Derrick is going to show you Leamington Spa and your new base. Please inform him on the way what you have said to me and see what he thinks about the idea. By the time you return after lunch I will be able to speak to you both together. Ok?'

'Thank you, sir.'

Ellie stood and shook his hand and left the room and found Derrick in his own office.'

'Ok, sir, let's go to Leamington Spa.'

'Royal!'

Jo had booked a car she thought fitting and arrived at the hospital early, making her way to the mortuary and immediately bumping into Alex.

'Hello,' she said, 'I'm DS Jo Enright from London.'

'Have you come this morning?'

'Odd world isn't it?'

'You'll certainly think so when you see what I've got for you.'

'So I gather.'

'Do you want to wait for Robbie?'

'I imagine he's already seen her, so I'm happy to get on with it.'

'Do you want her brought right out of the fridge?'

'I'm sorry but yes, as more than anything I want to see her back.'

'Of course.'

Alex went for a fork lift vehicle and wound it up the required level and then withdrew the tray with its burden on to the lift and then pulled the lift away whilst Jo closed the fridge door. They went into the PM room and again raised the life allowing the body to be moved onto the metal plinth.

'Don't you have technicians to do this for you,' asked Jo.

'They've gone out to bring a sudden death in for me. I'm also trying to cover two hospitals because the guy who works here is in hospital. Normally I'm based in Dundee, so it isn't easy to get a colleague's technicians to work in my way.'

She had by now unwound the cloths.

'I've never seen a decapitated human head before.'

'Does it disturb you?'

'It's not exactly pleasant but my dad ran a kennel of foxhounds and from an early age I was used to seeing lots of dead animal bodies including some with heads separated. You can get used to anything as I imagine you say to people who can't understand why you do this job.'

Alex smiled.

'Oh yes! But I like the job. It's fascinating though I've never seen anything like this before. It must have been a horrible death. Whoever did it, did so with two goes.'

'Like Mary, Queen of Scots.'

'I'll lift her from your side. She's not heavy.'

Jo looked at the back. It had clearly been done with a knife and the wounds were deep.

'Thank you. The pain must have been intense. Please can you explain to me how the anaesthetic forensic tests discovered in the liver, is normally administered in an operation?'

'A cannula is inserted into the back of the hand allowing the drug to come straight into the vein and it produces sleep within a very short time, usually in less than ten seconds but in anaesthesia it is used only for induction, to give the anaesthetist time to do the rest which is required for the operation. So, what I'm saying is that it would have knocked her out quickly if administered correctly but the effect would not have been for long and if it was the intent of moving her, they would have to do it at once.'

'Are there signs that a cannula was used?'

'All I can say is "possibly". She was left in the open and whilst I can show you the back of her hand where an anaesthetist would administer it, I can't honestly swear that is the mark left by a cannula.'

'How else would it have been possible to get it into her system?'

'By no means easily. It has to be intravenous to get to the brain not a muscular injection which would do nothing.'

'My next question is purely speculative so I shan't mind a speculative answer. Who would know how to insert a cannula knowing it to be the only way Propofol would do its work?'

'A nurse, a phlebotomist or an anaesthetist.'

'A pathologist?'

'Thanks for the vote of confidence. I haven't put one in for a long time.'

'It's ok, I don't see you as a murderer, but could I do so?'

'The real question is not technique, which can be learned, but the knowledge involved in using the drug. How did they get hold of it? And if it's been used in all four killings that suggests a ready supply, and believe you me, your local chemist shop won't sell it and won't even stock it.'

They heard voices.

'That will be Robbie arriving with my men and my next customer. I'll ask them to put Ms Hoosen away and perhaps we can go and get some lunch. The food here is better than in Dundee.'

She began wrapping the corpse and preparing her for the return journey to the fridge.

'Hello there,' said a very tall nice-looking man coming towards her with arm outstretched, 'I'm Robbie Douglas. I'm sorry I'm a bit late.'

'Hello Robbie, I'm Jo Enright, we spoke on the phone last night. It's great to meet you and what a job you have been faced with. Alex has suggested some lunch here. Would that be ok with you or do you want to get on with the task of getting rid of me as soon as possible?

'Not at all. To be honest I'm especially glad you're here. It's been proving a wee bit isolated having to deal with this by myself.'

In the main over lunch, they talked about wider issues, not least those espoused by the late Ms Hoosen. Once done Alex had to return to the PM room and Robbie offered to drive Jo to Comrie with the promise of returning her to Perth to pick up her car later.

'This reminds me a little of John Buchan country.'

'Do you read him?'

'I certainly do. Oh I know his views on things are remarkably like Jocelyn Hooson's, but he is such a good writer that after all this time we can forgive him for living when he did and reflecting the views of his time and not ours.'

'I love John Buchan too and have most of his works.'

'Are you married?'

'I was. The policemen's disease is divorce. We're never there and then we discover that someone else has been. It was my own fault so I can't complain. Sad though.'

'Have you children?'

'Aye, a son who's an engineer in Bahrain, and a daughter who's still living with her mother, but who I hardly ever see.'

'And the future?'

'Like the past.'

Robbie showed her the Hoosen house and drove up the side of the camp opposite to where she was found.

Jo got out and walked over to the Hermitage and Robbie showed her where across the burn the body was found by the two cadets. Jo leapt across the water and studied the ground.'

How far around did you search?'

Twenty yards radius and found nothing.'

'Do you think she was dead when they brought her here?' asked Jo.

'I think there would have been much more blood if not.'

'Yes, but where on earth could it have been done – in the open air, do you think, but that would have been very dangerous. In the dark it would have required strong torches at least, and like the other three killings, it shows all the hallmarks of local knowledge.'

'It's bewildering.'

'It is if we continue to treat it as a local crime, but I've seen the other three and I know it's not a local crime, and the more we treat is as such the more it won't be solved.'

'That would take a lot of explaining to my Chief Constable: "three days in sir, and I've given up".'

Jo grinned and again thought to herself what a good looking man he was, though found herself wondering how, unless she was up there with him, his wife could hardly have ever kissed him – no wonder she went off and found someone shorter! She was herself daily discovering for the first time the joy of being kissed and kissing. She quickly pulled her thoughts together,

'There may be a way round that, Robbie.'

'Oh, what's that, and it had better be good.'

'Let's head back to the car,' and she once jumped across the burn.

'I need to be at the airport by 5:00.'

'That won't be a problem,' he replied as they set off, 'but what about this other problem?'

'As you know, a team is being put together to work nationally on what is a national problem, based in the unlikely setting of Royal Leamington Spa in Warwickshire and headed by my boss, Superintendent Martin Peacock. Martin maintains that to remain credible with the ACPO we need a detective in the team from each of the crime areas, preferably the person who has led the enquiry. Having someone from Scottish Police in the team would undoubtedly be a politically wise move but if we could get you transferred, and some lucky DS will temporarily be made up to replace you here, we would have the benefit of you in the team. We've been given a year's funding but hope to take less than that of course, but we're under no illusions about how tough this is going to be.

'Your chief has been informed about the nature of the killings and the extent of their sheer brutality. He has given his support to the task before us and Martin will be in touch formally requesting your loan if I give him the word, and trust me, Martin is very convincing when he is in his persuasive mode. I assume you are an authorised firearms officer.'

'Yes, though it would do me no harm to visit the range.'

'Are you saying that you wish this to go ahead and be considered by your CC.'

'Yes, though I'm still somewhat amazed to receive such an offer from someone so young and junior.'

'And beautiful?'

'Goes without saying.'

They both laughed

'I'll get Martin to confirm.'

Whilst waiting at the airport Jo called both Martin and Ellie and reported on the day and especially her conversation with Alex and the issue of how the Propofol was administered. She spoke too of her time with Robbie Douglas and said there really was no alternative possible though he clearly wasn't in the Premier League of detectives such as Cate Greene.

'It's great that that you've been up there, Jo,' said Martin. 'As far as I'm concerned, you're in the Champions League.'

'Hey, please don't push the football metaphor, Martin. Remember I'm in Scotland and I gather they only have two teams!'

'Don't let anyone hear you say that or you may wake up in the mortuary.'

'Hopefully   with   my   head   still   in   place.

Leamington Spa

'It's *Royal* Leamington Spa,' said the man in the paper shop as he handed The Guardian over to Ellie, even to darkies.'

'And does that "even to darkies" extend to those who are senior plain clothes police officers?'

She reached into her pocket and produced her badge.

'Oh God, I have a feeling it's not going to be my lucky day.'

Ellie couldn't resist a laugh.

'I think it might be after all. One of my darkie colleagues is the Deputy Chief Constable of the County, and if you'd said to him what you said to me, you'd be wearing handcuffs by now, and I'm not exaggerating. And the next time I hear you use those words I shall do likewise.'

Walking back along to the flat she knew she had been wasting her time but it gave a few moments of emotional satisfaction. It was hate speech but more born of ignorance than anything really malicious. She had known it before and would do so again, and probably experience it in a far worse form.

It was their second morning in "Royal" Leamington Spa and were expecting to work seriously today. Yesterday had been all to do with meeting new colleagues and familiarising themselves with equipment and the desks at which they would be working. There were also housekeeping matters related to their hotel just 400 metres away from the office. All but two were in single rooms and most people seemed happy with their lot.

Shortly after 8:00 am Martin summoned everyone to his desk at the end of the main room – no one was hidden away in an office.

'Well, welcome everyone, here we go and what a task we have ahead of us. Over here to my right is the only one of us not a police officer, though he did used to work at Scotland Yard for a while as a computer genius. Not only can he help overcome any of your technical problems, but he is our technological wizard. Please do not attempt something you're unsure about, that might betray you or us to others, but come to see Eamonn first. In the end he could be the most important member of the team.

'The first rule we live by is that as we come through the door we lay down our ranks, and that includes me. I'm Martin, and I'll always welcome hearing from you as the day goes by. If I'm absent, then Cate Greene can help you out, not least because she heard only last Friday that West Mercia are so delighted to be losing her that she has been promoted to DCI, so well done, Cate.'

Everyone applauded and she looked totally embarrassed.

'From Scotland I'm pleased to welcome Robbie Douglas who had the misfortune to be faced with the most gruesome of the killings. Ellie Middlewood and I have worked together for some time in London, and that is also now the case with Jo Enright who worked on the Lincolnshire murder before joining Ellie and I in London. Most of you know Jo and I'm sure you're all glad to do so. By the way, and I speak from personal experience, do not accept an invitation to play poker with her. This gentleman is Derrick Blowes who will be with us a couple of days a week at least and will also coordinate what we are doing with both Warwickshire Constabulary and ACPO. It is also possible that from time we shall have visitors, possibly from the Security Services, but more especially and more importantly from the sandwich bar along the road. We may also co-opt into the team when appropriate. Our aim must be to press on and make sure there is no number V.

'I've had conversations with officers of the Security Services. They are inevitably concerned with some of the groups currently making a massive nuisance of themselves protesting, most notably XR – Extinction Rebellion. As we already know, it's clear that groups such as this are being infiltrated by those of an even more explicit political nature, and who are parasitic on them. We here in this room will have our own social and political views even to the extent of supporting various causes, but we are concerned only with those who have murdered our four victims. If it should happen that the Security Services and we overlap, they have their work and we have ours.

'I said earlier that Eamonn could be the most important member of the team but in fact I want to say that about each of you. Remember we will consider anything no matter how unlikely in our task of getting these people (and I think we must assume it's in the plural). Brainstorm when you need to. You're all very experienced so you know the form: however unlikely it might just be so. Remember and continue to recall the words of Mr Holmes: "How often have I said to you that when you have eliminated the impossible, whatever remains, however improbable, must be the truth?" Now, you've all had details of each crime and you each know one better than anyone, but they're not your possession and make sure you welcome the insights of others, perhaps offering something you might have missed. Equally don't hesitate to offer your own ideas to others.'

'As I read through the various reports,' said Cate, 'what stood out for me and upon which we might all focus for a while was the first. Yes, castration fits in with what followed with others, but he was killed with a single shot to the head and on his back was a playing card nailed to his spine, not a Roman numeral. He was then wrapped in a sheet as he would have been in any hospital by what is universally known as the "last office". But no traces of Propofol were found in his blood as they were in the others. Was this a case of different people from the other three and a decision made by some to take that initial killing further. In other words, are we dealing not with 4, but 1+3?'

'I think there's a lot to work on. I know you will have done a check made on former nurses who worked there and were they cross-checked with, say, the files of the Security services? Knowing in detail the Hospice and how it functions is still, I would suggest, that is still the most likely way this could have been done.'

'The cross-check produced nothing,' said Martin, 'though the fact of what you call the "last office" suggests that a nurse might have been involved and the absence of Propofol only means it wasn't found, not necessarily absent. A further check with MI5 might we worth doing as we have Eamonn with us. What do you think. Eamonn?'

'That would be straightforward,' he replied.

'I think we've always assumed,' added Jo, 'that after murder one something in their modus operandi changed. Kate's quite right. The Roman numerals were introduced and the level of violence against the victim was greatly increased, though the bishop might not have agreed. Also, the victims were much more politically selected. I'd also like to know a little bit more about bishops and homosexuality by talking to them face to face.'

'Ok. Cate, you liaise with Eamonn and do that cross checking with MI5. Jo, can you and Robbie, look into seeing bishops as soon as possible and see what literature has been produced by them. So, go to.'

They all moved swiftly back to their desks, other than Ellie.

'Tell me, O Great One, am I on tea making duty?'

'I want us to go out for a coffee now,' said Martin.

'Ok.'

Martin wandered over to where Cate talking to Eamonn about some technological matter.

'Cate, Ellie and I will be out for a while. Mind the shop and see if you can fix up a flight for late morning.'

'Of course,' she replied with a warm smile.

Martin and Ellie passed their hotels and continued up the road, passing the newspaper shop Ellie had used earlier.

'The guy in there called me a darkie this morning. I said that the next time I would bring a man called Derrick Blowes with me and suggest he call Derrick a darkie to his face.'

'Would you like me on the way back to call in and scare the shit out of him?'

Ellie smiled.

'I'll think about, it but you do know, Martin, don't you, that I don't need a man any more to protect me, or even a man anymore for anything?'

'I had noticed,' he replied, matching her smile.

They entered the coffee shop and Ellie, knowing his taste, bought the drinks for Martin and herself.

'When did the place acquire the prefix "Royal"? asked Martin.

'1838. One of the young Queen Victoria's first acts. Apparently the Spa water is good for constipation.'

'And our rather grand looking hotel. Is that comfortable enough for you both?'

'Martin! You're in territory where angels fear to tread.'

'I know, I know. Sorry. It's just that I still hurt.'

'What hurts most? Is it your pride?'

'Don't be horrible.'

She smiled and squeezed his hand, and he laughed.

'I'm not surprised in a way, however. We are talking about someone who is very special in many ways, and I still can't get over the way the cretins in Lincolnshire treated her.'

'Oh, it's like the guy in the paper shop this morning. Dickheads the lot of them. Anyway, I would have thought you were already casting your line towards another, much bigger, fish in the sea.'

'Cate, do you mean? Don't you think she's an Ice Queen?'

'Yes, but you're pretty affective at thawing.'

'Tell me what you make of Robbie Douglas?'

'When Jo returned from her visit to Scotland, she told me of this huge good-looking police inspector and when I met him she was absolutely right. You know the way some men turn to continue looking at a woman, so women do the same with Robbie. Jo did say however, that she thought he wasn't necessarily the sharpest knife in the drawer, and that may be right, but he has other talents, not least that of putting others at their ease and yet still obtaining information. When the time comes, as I hope it will, that Edinburgh accent will be of great use when we are interrogating suspects. I think it was clever of you putting him and Jo together in the task of speaking to bishops as they will make formidable interviewers.'

'And Eamonn?'

'We both know how highly he was regarded at the Yard, and I

can only assume that if he has gone on from there to work for the security services, he must be very good indeed.'

'He tells me that he has a boss who is even better than he is, arguably one of the very best in the world, but that unfortunately she is taking maternity leave, so we have to put up with him, but personally I'm very pleased about that.'

'How long have we got him?'

'I can't say and neither can they. It very much depends on what emerges in the course of their own work. You go back to the hotel and get your passport. Cate will have all the details and have arranged a taxi to take you to East Midlands Airport.'

Ellie did as she was told and arrived back at the office. Cate came towards her holding a slim file.

'These are the makers of Propofol and I've arrived arranged with the Garda that you'll be met at the airport in Dublin and they'll accompany you. I've already checked you in and your E-ticket is in there too. I wish I was coming with you. I'll get Jo to come and meet you tonight. Ok?'

'When was this arranged?'

'I've no idea. The instruction was on my desk when I came in and Martin said he would let you know about it.'

'Well, let that be a lesson to you too, Cate. I've got used to him but he sometimes behaves in wholly unexpected ways.'

Ellie received a text.

'My taxi awaits!'

'See you in the morning and by the way, where is Martin?'

'He wanted to pop into a shop on the way back.'

There were two people in the queue ahead of him but he pushed to the front and waved his police badge in front of the newsagent who went pale as he did so.

'Good morning, I'm Detective Superintendent Martin Peabody. This morning you used racist language against one of my senior officers, who I might add, has more brains in her little toe than you have in your head. If it is ever repeated against anyone of whatever colour and a complaint is made, you will be arrested and this shop closed down. I hope I have been able to make myself clear.'

Martin turned to those whom he had overtaken in the queue.

'I do apologise,' and left the shop.

The newsagent tried to regain his composure.

'I wish they would do their job and catch real criminals rather than threatening the likes of me.'

'I think those who are offensive to people of colour *are* real criminals,' said a customer, who walked out, which shut him up completely.

'Oh, look at this, Robbie.' said Jo, showing him something on the screen.

'I might leave that to you to mention.'

'Oh gladly. Do you want to let Cate know where we're going?'

'Of course.'

Jo meanwhile wandered over to where Ellie was sitting.

'Has anyone ever told you how stunningly beautiful you are,' she said quietly to her, as she rested her hand on her shoulder and leant forward as if looking at her screen.

'I only want one person to say that to me and that's you.'

They smiled and Jo left and joined Robbie as they left the office and went to their car. With the sat nav they found the Bishop's House in Davenport Rd easily enough and had already agreed on the way they would conduct the interview. A young woman opened the imposing front door.

'Good morning,' said Robbie holding up his badge, 'I'm Detective Inspector Robbie Douglas and this is Detective Sergeant Jo Enright, to see the Bishop of Coventry.'

'Of course, please come in. The bishop is on the phone just now, but if you would like to take a seat, he will come and collect you when he has finished.'

'And you are?' asked Jo brusquely.

'Francine Hart, his PA.'

'Well, Francine Hart, I've been in this business long enough to recognise the ploy of keeping people waiting as a means of intimidating them, so please tell the bishop to end his call now. We are engaged in trying to solve four gruesome murders.

Whatever you claim he might be doing is considerably less important and needs to stop now.'

She said nothing but walked towards what was clearly the bishop's office or study. Moments later the man in a purple shirt and wearing a cross on his chest appeared.

'Do come in. Can I get you a drink?'

Jo smiled.

'Do you mean you would make it, or would that be the task of the PA?'

The bishop laughed but did not reply.

In the room there was what appeared to be a full-sized grand piano and a great number of books, a large cross on the wall and photographs of what Jo assumed were family members. Once they had sat down, it was Robbie who began things.

'Of the four utterly brutal murders we are trying to solve as a team, one is that of one of your fellow bishops, Peter Sherriff, sometime Bishop of Kennington. Did you know him?'

'He had retired before I became a bishop.'

'But had your paths crossed before that?'

'I knew his name of course, but I don't think I ever met him. We came from quite different traditions in the Church. I am an evangelical and he was an anglo-catholic.'

'You must have known he was homosexual,' said Jo.

'It's no longer a crime, sergeant.'

'Is it a sin?' she continued.

'That's a complex theological question.'

'I have no idea what that means so I'll ask it in in a different way. Is it a sin to engage in homosexual activity.'

'The Bible implies that it is.'

'And what does the Bishop of Coventry imply?'

'As I say, it's a complex theological question.'

'Which I take it means you can sit on the fence and not reply. So let me ask if it is sinful for a clergyman to solicit trade in a public convenience as a court found one of your own clergy guilty of, whom you continue to employ, and how would this differ, say, from the activities of a clergyman inserting his erect penis into the anus of ten year old boys, especially when he becomes a bishop sometime later? Or are these complex theological questions too?'

'As you are not investigating matters related to those who live in my diocese, I think it would be a good idea if we ended our conversation now.'

The bishop stood but Robbie and Jo remained seated. The bishop resumed his seat.

'You see, bishop,' said Robbie gently. 'It's more than possible that Peter Sherriff was killed because of the complex theological views of others, Christians, who found his homosexuality objectionable, and then on discovering that it had led to certain major indiscretions in the past, decided that their religious faith should put an end to the man. We both know that religious believers are not all Anglicans pondering complexity in their studies.'

'That is why we have come to you for help,' said Jo, herself for once as gentle as Robbie. 'Neither of us would profess or call ourselves Christian, even if there are possibly one or two we respect, and it is hard to understand the dynamic that light lead some Christians to do this, and the fact that the bishop's testicles were cut off, whilst he was conscious, suggests that it was indeed objection to his homosexuality that underlay what happened to him.'

'O my God! I didn't know that.'

'Sometimes we have to hold back information,' said Robbie.

'Yes, I can see that. Well, my own position as a sort of middle of the road evangelical is not easy to hold and yes, perhaps I am sitting on the fence. I accept homosexual orientation as a given, something for whatever complex reasons some men and women are either born with or somehow develop. Some Christians cannot even accept that much. Sexual desire and energy belong to most people, heterosexual and homosexual alike, and I have knowingly ordained gay men and women because they are going to be good priests. The rules say they should remain celibate but I'm not as stupid as I may look, and I have developed a fine capacity for selective blindness when the gay clergy, women and men, just get on with everything and make no fuss. It is more difficult if a priest gets into difficulties as you obviously know one of mine did. This happened in London and I thought he should be given a second chance. He was lonely and unhappy and I didn't think he should be punished further, so as it did not make the local news or television, I encouraged him to continue. Hypocrisy? I plead guilty, if it is so, but I don't regret it.'

'But if a bishop behaved as this bishop did, what then?' asked Jo.

'That is where you come in as enforcers of the law, I suppose, and he would have to answer for his actions in a courtroom, but capital punishment in the way you have described it is unacceptable.'

'Though I believe that's what the Bible recommends,' said Jo'

The bishop said nothing.

Well, Bishop, you have helped me sort out one conundrum,' said Jo. 'I now know that a complex theological question is essentially trying to find a way of having your cake and eating it. It reminds me of a story told when the first six women were due to be ordained in America in 1976, before I was born, but told to me when I was on holiday in the US. One of the bishops couldn't make his mind up whether to take part in the service. The woman due to be ordained said to him, "Bishop, either shit or get off the john".'

She stood and Robbie followed suit.

'Thank you for your time, Bishop. We'll see ourselves out,' said Robbie.

Once in the car, Robbie said, 'We do an effective "good cop-bad cop" routine. But what did you think of him?'

'Not a great deal, to be honest, because he daren't be honest. Most of those who come to see him in his grand study approach him as some sort of spiritual superior and will be intimidated by that. But we didn't show the deference to which he imagines he is due and shorn of that his weaknesses of thought and action became abundantly clear. In his fancy dress in the Cathedral, he is no doubt impressive. But he's not, and the priest caught in the London toilets would not have got away with it had it made the local press.'

Arriving back at the office it was clear a lot of work had been taking place. Martin was eating his sandwiches with the others, but Jo noticed the absence of Ellie. Sandwiches had been saved for them.

Martin smiled at Jo.

'You won't perhaps be surprised to learn that shortly after you left him, we had a call from the Bishop of Coventry complaining about the "heavy-handedness" of the police.'

'Not surprised at all. Actually, Robbie and I thought we let him off rather lightly. I don't think there was anything we learned from him about the official position on homosexuality in the clergy we couldn't have got from you. But I found the blatant dishonesty about his position plus the smugness inherent in his official position as he sat there surrounded by privilege, not something that impressed me.'

'Hey, I'm not even remotely reprimanding you, just reporting his call, indicative I think, of the anxiety someone in his position has about anything they say being reported in the papers.'

'That's not going to happen,' said Robbie. 'I think there is no one in this room likely to leak. I notice Ellie is missing, so would anyone like to share her pack of sandwiches with me?'

'I will if no one else wants it,' said Martin.

'Where is she?' asked Jo.

'Probably approaching Dublin Airport right now,' said Cate. She's gone to visit the manufacturers of Propofol, to learn about the security measures they have in place when it is exported to the UK, but also to find out if there have been any security lapses in the Republic or here that they know of. And I'm hoping you won't mind collecting her from East Midlands Airport at 7:15 this evening.'

'No problem.'

XR et al

That afternoon Eamonn forwarded to everyone the latest product of the Security Services assessment of the various groups hiding under the umbrella of Extinction Rebellion. Some were hard left-wing groups who had realised that with the disappearance of Corbyn after the 2019 election there was nothing there for them anymore. Some advocate violent revolution whilst simultaneously continuing to enjoy the fruits of the very capitalist system they claimed to despise and making use of its technology, most of which was financed by commercial advertising. The results of undercover conversations, undertaken at great risk, revealed increased impatience and a determination to find the best ways to engage in what they called "direct action". None of the undercover agents however, had picked up anything suggestive of one of the groups having already done so.

At Dublin Airport she saw a sign with her name on as she emerged from Arrivals.

'Hi', she said, 'I'm Ellie.'

'Good to have you here, Ellie. I'm Phil Tom.'

'Unusual names for a woman, if I may say so.'

'I know, but I've got used to having two male names and I'm not trans in case you were wondering.'

'You don't look like a former man.'

'Thank you. Phil is what I called myself when I started in school, instead of the Philomena my mother chose for me.

'Hasn't the film helped that?'

'My mother's a devout catholic still in spite of everything we now know about the nuns, the priests and the Church, and says she wishes she'd never called me by the same name as that woman, so even she calls me Phil now. Anyway, let's get to the manufacturers of Propofol. It's not far so would you welcome some lunch here before we set off, and you can tell me about your interest in anaesthetics.'

'Ok.'

As they ate their lunch, Ellie explained that they were exploring the possibility that some sort of anaesthetic had been used in a series of murders. Propofol was the most obvious to check out first as it was often used first in inducing unconsciousness, so she was beginning here to check from manufacturers the security measures in place when transporting it to hospitals. Tomorrow it would be the turn of Amsterdam, and then Germany, seeing which drugs might have been used and leave no trace.'

'It's all quite speculative, then?'

'We are trying out as many possibilities as we can think of in the hope that we might get lucky, though between you and me, I'm not sure we aren't barking up the wrong tree completely. I asked my own GP about this and he said he thought I'd get nowhere, as he thought nothing would be left in the bloodstream, and if there was nothing found that was most likely for the simple reason that it hadn't been used. Well, maybe, but at least I'll build up my air miles.'

'How does your family cope with so much travelling?'

'My husband thinks I'm safer doing this than being around nasty killers, so he doesn't mind, besides which Derrick is often away himself. What about you?'

'I have a boyfriend who works as a clerk in the prison system but well away from inmates, I'm pleased to say.'

Once they arrived, Phil said she would wait for Ellie in the car, where she could sit and read and be paid for it. Ellie went in and was warmly greeted by a man with a badge on which read "Anthony Cummins, General Manager"'

'I'm not only pleased to meet you Mr Cummins but thank you for letting my visit be arranged at such short notice.'

'I only hope I can be of help, Inspector. Shall we go to my office?'

The office walls showed posters of some of the products they produced.

'I gather you have an interest in Propofol.'

'Yes. I'm a member of a team investigating a series of murders in which the only explanation we can produce for moving someone was that they had been drugged. Our thinking has been strengthened by a toxicology report in one instance that revealed traces of Propofol in the bloodstream of the victim.'

'That would suggest to me, Inspector, that death must have taken place soon after the administration of the drug or it would not have been found, and indeed in postmortems on both sides of the Atlantic following death on the operating table, it has never been recorded as present. It disappears quite quickly once it has done its initial job. To continue to be in the blood stream and therefore in the brain when other anaesthetics are being applied would be dangerous.'

'Thank you. That's helpful. My other question you may now think irrelevant, but assuming this one application of the drug to our victim, would it be easy to obtain the drug?'

'Not at all. You certainly can't obtain it from your local pharmacist, and neither could your local pharmacist obtain it either. Under measures of the strictest security, it is delivered to hospitals and to the best of my knowledge, is secured on arrival under lock and key, the realm only of an anaesthetist. I cannot account for what happens to it after that, of course, but there is no record of our security being infringed. Unless your murderer is an anaesthetist, I'm not sure I can add anything further.'

'And is a cannula the only way it can be administered?'

'No, but it would still have to be intravenous. It won't work just injected into a muscle. That happens only in films. But I would like to give you some papers to back up what I've said about our record and security procedures, and then, if I may, I would like to give you the grand tour of the place. If further questions occur then I'll try to answer them as we go round.'

'I would like that very much, Mr Cummins.'

'Tony.'
'Ellie.'

The flight was on time and Jo was delighted to see Ellie coming through the Arrivals automated doors matching her own broad smile.

After the closest of greetings, Jo muttered, 'Welcome to the United Kingdom.'

'Thank you, my darling, I'm so pleased it is you here. I thought it might be clever-clogs Cate.'

'She asked me to come.'

They were walking towards Jo's car which she had parked illegally but with her police parking warrant in the windscreen window. That hadn't stopped a young police constable beginning to write out a parking fine notice.

'Excuse me, constable,' said Jo, 'what are you doing?'

'Is this motor vehicle yours, madam?'

'You will need to begin the sentence again and this time say something like "Is this motor vehicle with a police parking warrant on the windscreen yours, sergeant, or is it yours, ma'am?" which is how you address a Detective Inspector who just alighted from an aeroplane in pursuit of those who have committed a serious crime.'

'Have you had any success, ma'am?'

'I will need to share it with the team in the morning but maybe. Here's my badge.'

'I believe you both and good luck.'

'Thank you, said Jo.

In seconds they were on their way.

'One thing I must thank our killers for is bringing you to Boston. Had it not been for that I would still be trailing round the streets checking cars.'

'And had you not come to Lewisham, then I would still be as dead as our bishop.'

On the way Ellie ordered a takeaway to be delivered shortly after they arrived at the hotel.

'It's been an odd day. I was met by a woman officer called Phil

Tom which was pretty strange, and I spent all my time deceiving her about why I was there. I had to do so because we just don't know where, if anywhere, information on Propofol might be coming from, and I had to dot a repeat performance when I was shown round the factory where it's made and exported to the UK. The manager who showed me round was a nice man and I found the whole thing fascinating though I had to dress up like a nun to maintain biosecurity!

'But the most important part of the journey was the flight back on a half-full plane, when something that might be very important struck me but which I will need Eamonn to check out in the morning. It may, but no more than that, suggest a way forward with the London killing.'

'That's fantastic, Ellie. You're no less clever than Cate and very much prettier!'

'Thank you, but tell me how you got on with the bishop.'

'Well enough for him to have complained straight after Robbie and I departed.'

'I'm impressed, but then again, I always am with you.'

'Mutual admiration aside, I could murder a curry let alone a bishop.'

They looked at one another and burst out laughing.'

Jo knew as did Ellie that no matter how great the reality of their love, they were also police officers and the reality of their different ranks had to be always taken seriously. Jo never doubted that if Ellie wanted to share with her something to do with work she would, but she did not feel troubled in any way when, as now, they both knew that the correct way forward was for Ellie to speak first to Cate and Martin on the following morning.

There was each morning a whole team meeting at 8:00 to share and allocate, but this morning Martin said he wanted everyone to stay where they were because Ellie had some things to report from her visit to Dublin, and then something from her flight back which has to be pursued today. So, over to you Ellie.'

She gave them a rapid account of the life and times of Propofol and the security that ought to be in place in the anaesthetist's room.'

'So, in II, III and IV, death would have had to have been rapid after becoming unconscious?' said Robbie. That throws aside much of how we have been thinking of anaesthetic used to move victims, followed by torture and then death, unless the torture happened astonishingly quickly which is more or less impossible. I think we should get a second opinion from those who are using the drug day by day in operating theatres.'

'Ok, we'll return to that, Robbie, or more likely, you will!' replied Martin to all-round laughter. 'Now, back to Ellie.'

'It was the air hostess really; she gave me the thought. I asked her if she always did this route and she said that sometimes she did the City of London Airport route. She meant London City of course, but it triggered a series of thoughts. When we began work, we did a check on Peter Sherriff with every force in the country which produced no results. Most of our attention was focussed inevitably on London. We checked and cross-checked doctors and nurses who had worked at the Hospice but nothing emerged. Martin and I even went to Somerset to interview the complainant who had not been listened to by the Church, and everywhere we drew a blank. The second killing, in the Fens, began to change our thinking into seeing both as serial murders.

'But back to the City of London. All of us are aware of villains who constantly manage to evade arrest, the wealthy who can buy their way out of anything and the clever who are able to wriggle and lay the blame on others. Their names we know, but they're not on our records. But what if there are those who are profoundly homophobic, to the degree of absolute hatred and disgust, who learn things about someone who is totally abusing their position to get young boys who can't protect themselves, and yet proof and evidence are almost impossible to gather for all the reasons we know in terms of blackmail and shame?'

'Are you suggesting we might have to consider a probation officer?' asked Robbie.

'No,' interrupted Cate, answering Robbie, 'Ellie is talking about a police officer.'

'I regret to say that Cate has put into words the possibility that came to me on the aeroplane last night. In case you wondered, I said nothing about this to Jo, and only spoke to Martin on our way here this morning,'

'It's true,' said Jo, 'and we both know that's the way it is. Yes, we're a couple and we love each other, but I am a DS and she's my boss and we honour that boundary to the letter. In fact, some mornings when I say "good morning" to her and she doesn't reply, then I assume it's a secret I'm not allowed to know.'

Everyone laughed and it achieved the break in tension Jo had hoped for. Ellie and Martin knew instinctively what Jo had accomplished and smiled at one another.

'Eamonn, you and Ellie need to get to work on this. Cate, you need some fresh air, so you and Robbie should make some contact with anaesthetists. Check on how long they assume the various drugs of anaesthesia remain in the blood. Jo, you and I are going out to see the Bishop of Warwick, who for some reason lives in Leamington Spa and not Warwick.'

'It will be for a complex theological reason.'

Robbie struggled to suppress a laugh.

Jo and Martin were able to walk to the house of the bishop, but it provided Martin with an excellent chance to talk to Jo.

'You know that Ellie and I had a fling.'

'Of course, and I know that even though that may be over she still thinks the world of you, as I do, though in a different sort of way.'

'I discovered how professional she was in our time together in that her notion of confidentiality is absolute, as you are no doubt discovering.'

'Yes, and I'm very happy about it. I value the fact that information I receive has been filtered to enable me to respond accordingly and not to get above my station.'

'Yeah, well Jo, you'll be up there soon enough. I'm therefore pretty sure she hasn't told you the full extent of what she told me before we had our meeting this morning, but I'm telling you now because I'm going to need you to act on it.

'Ellie mentioned and you could confirm all the checking and

cross-checking we did following the discovery of Sherriff's body in the morgue at the Hospice. Every member and former member of staff was examined, and I think you went over it all again when you joined us.'

'I did and we found nothing either time.'

'That was where the air hostess came in last night when she mentioned the City of London airport and it occurred to Ellie that one group we hadn't considered was the City of London force. We did the Met as a matter of course but overlooked City. They're small with just 4 police stations and mostly deal with a very small range of activities. But it was a serious error on my part. So, as we walk along this road to see the bishop, Ellie and Eamonn are busy seeing if there are any links that might help us. I think Cate is correct, that this first murder may be unlike the others, and that the other three are copycats designed to make us think there have been four, when perhaps there has been just one, plus three.'

'And where do I come in?'

'The staff at the Hospice are no doubt sick and tired of the faces of Ellie and me. If what we are thinking is so, then I shall want Cate and you to go down and pursue enquiries.'

'As her bagman?'

'I very much doubt that,' he said with a laugh. 'Here we are.'

It was a much more ordinary house than the one she had visited on the previous day and the bishop himself answered the door.

'Hello, welcome. I'm Terry Hill. The kettle's just boiled so come and join me in the kitchen and decide what you want to drink.'

They moved with drinks into his study which was once again full of books and photographs but without a grand piano. Pride of place among the photos seemed not to go to his wife, but to one of himself with Sir Alex Ferguson sitting chatting together.

'I gather you gave the boss a tough time yesterday. Well done. Often people in our positions get away with murder because people think they can't say what they want to. Or is that an unfortunate metaphor?'

'Because neither of us are accustomed to church life, it would help if you could explain why one bishop is the boss of another. You're the Bishop of Warwick, so is your diocese the diocese of Warwick.'

'Confusing, isn't it? Yesterday you or your colleagues visited the Bishop of Coventry, and his area extends well beyond the city of Coventry. Among those working with him is the Bishop of Warwick, a sort of assistant, what the church calls a suffragan bishop. It's a bit like when a Superintendant calls but brings with him a sergeant though perhaps a inspector would be a better analogy.'

'Trust me she will be that soon,' said Martin.

The suffragan detective decided to ask a question.

'What did you know about Peter Sherriff?'

'I knew he was gay, of course. Most of us did, and to be honest most of us took very little notice of the fact. There are others, even among the bishops, and no end of gay clergy, male and female. My own attitude is less trapped in theology than that of the Bishop of Coventry. Those I know to be gay don't get any trouble from me provided they can keep out of trouble with you people. But that's no different from everyone else surely, no matter what occupation you have.'

'Are there any particular circumstances pertaining to clergy whereby they are more likely to have difficulties that might get out into the open?'

'Certainly, because people in the parishes hold them to a higher standard than others. Am I right in thinking that a police officer's skills are not thought the less of because she or he changes sexual partners, or those of a scientist because she has an affair? I can appreciate that a priest knocking off one of his parishioners may well be manifesting some underlying unhappiness, but does that really affect the substance of his preaching, providing he or she doesn't stray into the area of hypocrisy.'

'Why do you do it?' said Jo.

'Do what?'

'Keep up the pretence. Your boss, as you describe him, must be a contortionist in his brain to deal with homosexuality and left me feeling he was in fact being utterly hypocritical. You on the other hand adopt a thoroughly laissez faire attitude with the powerful proviso: don't get caught. If you will excuse me for saying so, it's just a slightly different variation of hypocrisy.'

'Well, I can't deny what you say, but I'm in an institution made up in the main of people who claim to love God. With that comes many different other thoughts and feelings, some of which I sympathise with and some I don't, but they are all the people I have to relate to and care for. Some of those thoughts and feelings are strong and emerge from minds that are highly opinionated, so very often it's like walking on eggshells. I do it because I too claim to love God.'

'And Peter Sherriff?' said Martin.

'I can only assume the urges were just too powerful, and which of us doesn't know that force when we're having sex? He obviously had it at other times too. Perhaps he was also guilt ridden and as an anglo-catholic went to confession as some in that tradition do but we shall never know.'

'So those in the Church, bishops and priests alike who knew that he was gay, assumed he was celibate, or was it is a case of everyone turning a blind eye to those clergy you have said you do?'

'I never worked for him or was in his diocese, so I cannot say and he was in any case a different generation from me, so I wasn't aware of him to much of a degree. He had retired before I became a bishop.'

'Thank you, Bishop,' said Martin, for being so candid in your answers. Nothing that you have said will be repeated or reported, because what we were wanting was background and nothing pertinent to our investigation.'

'Thank you for that, Superintendent. You clearly have an extraordinarily complex and difficult task before you and I wish you well. Unlikely though it is, if you were to require further help, please don't hesitate to ask.'

They all stood and shook hands.

'One further point,' said Jo. 'Do you describe homosexuality as a complex theological issue?'

'No. It's a complex issue for some church people, but not for others.'

'But in practice there's a lot of nodding and winking?'

'For now, but I hope it will change.'

At first neither of them spoke as they made their way back to the office. Finally Jo spoke.

'He was considerably less pompous than his boss was yesterday and I wasn't totally unsympathetic to the difficulty of his position and his rationale. But it's all founded on dishonesty towards those who differ from him, with regard to the gay clergy whose heads be bids keep down, to the outer world where he has to profess one thing buts believes another, and of course to his religion itself. I'm left wondering whether any God he might claim to believe in bears even the slightest resemblance to the many Gods the people who go to church believe in.'

Martin laughed.

'Thanks, Jo. You've said it all and I've nothing to add, other than to say we won't be attending All Saints Church here on Sunday morning. But don't overlook the fact that the force of your feelings are no doubt also being shaped by the discovery that you are gay. This isn't some sort of disinterested investigation for you, is it?'

'Are you implying, Martin, that I've let my personal circumstances interfere with my work and duty as a police officer? That would be a serious matter.'

'No. I don't think that, but all police officers have always to keep a close eye on their functioning when the subject is close to their own heart.

'H'm. Changing the subject, I'm glad to say or at least I hope I shall be glad to say, I wonder how Ellie and Eamonn have got on? I'm feeling bad that we missed City of London out when we cross-checked and part of me is hoping she's found nothing to make me feel worse.'

'Her too, remember, and, albeit to a lesser extent, me as well.'

They walked through the front doors and into the office and found Ellie looking very cross and addressing a man Martin at once judged to be a journalist.

'Can I help you? I'm Superintendent Peabody. Who are you and what are you doing in here? This office is out of bounds to everyone other than those who work here, so leave at once.'

'Hello Superintendent. I'm Kevin Docherty and I work for the Leamington Courier. Someone reported intimidation from a senior police officer in his shop and that person was seen entering this building in which I notice there is a lot of high technological equipment. I just wondered if anyone might like to comment.'

Before anyone could reply, Jo noticed a bulge in the jacket pocket of the man and put her hand into it and pulled out a tape machine that was recording every word.

'Would you like me to arrest him, sir, and take him to the police station to be charged?'

'I think so. Did you not notice the sign as you entered about not entering at all without permission and not bringing in equipment such as this?'

'I don't take any notice of such signs. We have a free press and I was acting on behalf of the people of the town.'

'Who is it you work for? The Times of London, the Washington Post? Oh, I remember, the Leamington Courier. Well Mr Docherty, always check your sources and ask the complainant about the abusive terms he used to one of my officers which led me to warn him as to his further behaviour. On this occasion, as then, I shall let you go with a warning about your further behaviour. If you come here again or follow one or more of my officers in their lawful activity, or if there is even a word about this office and what might go on here in your newspaper, I will report what you have done here this morning to the local police and request that they charge you. So, please leave.'

He reached out to Jo.

'My machine, please.'

'I'm sorry,' she said, 'but it may be required as evidence. If not, it will be returned in due course if you leave me your address.'

He handed her a card and left, muttering something about

"fascists" under his breath.

Audit

Cate and Robbie were sitting at the far end of the room with Eamonn and describing something of their two hospital visits and encounters with anaesthetists. The others walked over and listened.

'It was a new experience to me,' said Cate. 'The doctor said that instead of telling, he would show, and invited us to don gowns, gloves and masks, and to stand behind the patient, to whom he introduced us and from whom he secured permission. He chatted with her and then explained he would be putting a cannula into the back of her hand so they could easily administer whatever medication might be necessary during the operation. He warned her about a sharp scratch but he got into the vein first time. He then said she might feel a cold sensation going up her arm and he then injected the cannula with what he told us was Diprivan, another name for Propofol apparently, and continued to ask questions of the patient but in less than five seconds she was unconscious.

'At that point, one of his colleagues took over, as she was the anaesthetist for the operation, so he and we left and went with him for coffee once we'd shed our gowns. We were then able to ask questions. He said it was almost universally used not just in getting someone unconscious for an operation, but in helping keep someone sedated in intensive care on a ventilator. It is quick acting but its effects would only last about 5-6 minutes unless a second dose was given. Other drugs were used together with anaesthetic gases to keep someone unconscious for an operation. It has a half life of between 2 and 24 hours and therefore in theory could leave traces but maintained that the normal initial dose would leave no trace behind either in the liver or the blood.

'I have to report that Robbie and I enjoyed every moment. We never got to the second hospital because there was an emergency operation and our anaesthetist there had to attend but hearing what he told us and showed us and checking it against everything I've looked at on the internet, I'm confident what we heard was the truth.'

'Robbie?' asked Martin.

'It was great to watch and see these doctors handle people who need to be unconscious and then restored, but I totally agree with Cate about it being clear that what he said is the case, not least because the other anaesthetist was in the room before taking over and she didn't object to anything he said.'

'Well, that's going to help us with timings and after lunch I think we should make a start with working them out in the case of numbers II-IV. And now, Ellie and Eamonn, what if anything have you got for us?'

'In terms of serving officers in the City and current staff at the Hospice, there is nothing, but when we came to former staff, both in City and the Hospice, we have two married couples, both of whom seem to know each other well and worked together. Michael (Mick) Ellam was a DS and his wife, Elizabeth (Liz) Ellam, a state enrolled nurse. The others are Neville (Nev) Sturgess (also a former DS) and his wife Gloria Sturgess, also an SEN. None of them have form, but I interviewed both women at the time. Gloria Sturgess is an attractive second-generation West Indian woman whom I liked and found helpful. Liz Ellam was very defensive, almost verging on the aggressive, and tarted up to the nines. They both now work for the local authority as nurses visiting people at home. The men I never met, and it took a while for Eamonn to find out what they're doing now, but typically for ex-coppers, they're doing security work in a warehouse in Dartford.'

'You four have certainly had a more profitable morning than Jo and I, trying to engage with the Bishop of Warwick, Terry by name. He was nice but so compromised it must tear him in two. I don't think we learned anything new about Peter Sherriff though. He may be an absolute pervert who got what he deserved or he may be a man who struggled and failed to cope with his own rampant sexuality, but those things are not for us to decide. He was brutally and unlawfully killed and that is our sole concern.'

Ellie could see, as they ate their sandwiches for lunch, that Martin was thinking hard. He was saying nothing and often looking up at the ceiling and she knew better than to disturb him when he was like that. Robbie asked him a question but received no reply and Ellie shook her head towards him.

As sandwiches were finished and tea drunk, Martin suddenly said, 'I want you all to have the afternoon off, to relax and see what Royal Leamington Spa has to offer or catch up on your sleep. All that is, apart from Cate and Jo.'

When the others had departed with smiles on their faces, Martin asked, 'Cate have you ever done an unsolved case audit?'

'I've assisted in two, but you have to be at at least a DCI to do them.'

'Well, you are a DCI now and I want you to do one, assisted by DS Enright from the local force which is another requirement. I want you both to meet the Ellams and Mick and Liz Sturgess. The force records of both men mention warnings for racist and homophobic language. Familiarise yourselves with those and also Ellie's accounts of her interviews with the two women at the time. In an audit, as you know, you can repeat questions asked at the original interview, and compare the answers.

'We shall need a number for them to call to verify.'

'Leave that to me. I'll make sure Detective Chief Superintendent Dirty Dave Charnley will be there.'

Cate and Jo went down the road to the Jephson Gardens by the river and sat quietly together reading the papers drawn up by Eamonn and Ellie. Jo, representing the home team did the telephoning, booking times when she and the auditor could call. She also gave the number for verification at Lewisham Police Station. Martin had done his work. Both could see them tomorrow though it would mean an extremely early start.

After the traffic of Leamington Spa, London as always came as a shock, especially to Cate who was more used to Hereford. Fortunately for her, Jo was driving and they went through the Blackwall Tunnel on to Woolwich where Nev and Gloria Sturgess lived. They were in an unmarked car and waited ten minutes to be on time. Cate rang the bell and clutched a folder containing just about nothing.

An attractive black teenage girl opened the door.

'Hi,' said Cate, 'we've called to see Neville and Gloria.'

'Oh, you're from the police, aren't you,' she said with a smile. 'It would help me a great deal if you could arrest them and lock them up so I could go to a party I'm invited to on Saturday night.'

'OK. I'll try, but I can't promise.'

They were allowed in when a man and a woman warmly received them with handshakes and smiles.

'The thing is I don't approve of 14-year-old girls going to parties such as the one she's invited to just because she could pass for 18,' said the woman.

'14!' said Jo. 'Perhaps I should put the word out to keep an eye on that party.'

'I wish you would,' said the man. 'Anyway, please sit down and I'll bring in some drinks.'

There was further party talk before the drinks came.

'Ok', said Cate, ' first may I call you Nev and Gloria? I'm Detective Chief Inspector Cate Greene of West Mercia Police and this is Detective Sergeant Jo Enright of the Met, based in Lewisham (though I guess somebody has to be).'

They laughed, and Jo was impressed as it was first time she had heard Cate say anything funny.

'You, Nev, will know only too well what I'm doing here. An audit on an unsolved case is automatic in the instance of a homicide. All I want to do is to go through with you, Gloria, the questions you answered about the murder of Peter Sherriff, whose body was found in the mortuary of the Hospice where you were working at the time. Nev, if you have any observations as

Gloria and I chat, please make them.'

Directing the question to Gloria, Cate asked, 'Did you know Peter Sherriff?' and was quietly overjoyed when it was Nev who replied.

'The City of London force knew of him even though he didn't live or function in our area in any sort of official capacity, and we were never able to catch him in the act, but there was evidence of his presence among young boys who found themselves with more money than we might have expected. We believed he was procuring and rewarding for homosexual favours quite a few boys.'

'But he was a bishop in the church,' said Jo. 'However could he get away with that sort of behaviour? He was a public figure.'

'But not the first, I'm sorry to say. We had a bishop in our area who in terms of being queer was as bent as a nine-bob note. The Chief Constable went to see the Bishop of London and said that unless he was moved, we would have no choice but to go public. A month later he took up a new appointment in Africa. He's dead now.'

'Have there been others?' asked Cate with a pained look on her face.

'I don't know about bishops and anyway some are women now, but there is no shortage of bent vicars in London. It's appalling and yet the Church doesn't seem to want to do anything about it.'

'Well, someone did in the case of Sherriff,' said Jo.

'And what about you, Gloria. How much of this did you know?'

'Not much as Nev couldn't talk about his work, but from time to time he arrived home fuming about the whole thing and it shocked me deeply.'

'And did you talk about it with anyone else?'

'The only person I ever mentioned it to already knew it from her husband, and that was Liz Ellam, who heard it from Mick who worked with Nev.'

Cate turned to Jo.

'I think they're on our list for later today.'

Jo produced a sheet of paper from her handbag and nodded.

'When you were interviewed about your knowledge of the functioning of the mortuary at the Hospice, did you feel the questions were adequate or did you rush home and say to Nev that you'd been interviewed by a cretin who'd failed to ask something important?

'No. She was thorough and so kind and thoughtful. I really liked her.'

(Jo wanted to say, "And I was making love to her in our bed about 12 hours ago", but then decided against it).

'You obviously enjoyed working at the Hospice? Why did you leave?'

I suppose I'd had enough of death and dying. Liz and I decided it would be a good idea to change.'

'I can understand that. Did you have to do things like "Last Offices"?'

'I must have done hundreds.'

'I can't envy you that.'

'At the time you do them as the best last thing you can do for a patient, but I don't miss them.'

Cate asked some further inane questions that would feature in a real audit and then announced that everything was fine, and unless they had questions, she and Jo would move on to their next location.

Jo drove for a couple of miles until they saw a pub, which they entered and ordered some food and non-alcoholic drinks. Whilst Jo was ordering, Cate called Eamonn.

'Hi, it's Cate. Have you anything for me?'

'Both called in for verification and about ten minutes ago a call was made from the Sturgess number to the Ellams.'

'That would be straight after we left and its useful to know that. We're due at the Ellams at 2:00 and it will be interesting to know if they reciprocate.'

'I've warned you before about using those big words, Cate.

He heard her laugh.

'Message received. Speak later.'

Jo looked at Cate.

'So, Chief Inspector, what did you make of that?'

'I think about these things more slowly than you, Jo, so the real question is what did you think? After all, you said little and I imagine that means you were listening hard.'

'If it was an audit, he would have known it was entirely inappropriate for to me say anything unless asked. He jumped in to answer your first question to Gloria, almost as if he was determined to direct the conversation, yet you had made clear that it was an audit of Ellie's conversation with Gloria at which he wasn't present and you were asking her if she knew Sherriff. He was answering questions you hadn't asked, as politicians do, something we both know from our experiences of interrogation suggests a measure of unease.'

'Yes, that's true. We had better get on our way. Is it far?'

'No. I will show you as we pass the place where Stephen Lawrence was murdered and the Ellams live on the other side of Eltham.'

'You seem to know round here quite well – you haven't been using the sat nav.'

'My flat is in a place called Lee, a little further in than here and very handy for work, but I know round here quite well. I certainly know North Park where the Ellams live and quite posh it is too.

As they drove down Well Hall Road, as she promised, Jo pointed out the Stephen Lawrence plaque which had fresh flowers nearby, impressive after 25 years.

Jo pulled up outside the house.

'Posh indeed. Not bad on the salaries of a DS and SEN,' said Cate. 'Right, let's get on with it.'

Having introduced themselves, Cate began with the same question as earlier and as before, though asked to Liz, it was answered by Mick.

'Sherriff was a nasty piece of work and he was also very devious, making sure he didn't leave his metaphorical prints behind. We were pretty sure he was paying out large sums for the bums of boys.'

'Mick!' burst in Liz, 'don't be crude.'

'They'll have heard far worse. I went to see the Bishop of Stepney about it but he was just mealy-mouthed and said that in any case the places I was mentioning were outside his area and belonged instead to the Bishop of Chelmsford even though they were within our area. He also said that we would have to prove my accusations by the production of proof in the form of boys I claimed were assaulted by Sherriff. Clearly I was getting nowhere at all but I knew what he was doing. So, one day I stopped Sherriff in his car in the Commercial Road as he was heading out to his normal pick-up places. I hadn't seen him before and was shocked that he was much older than I had realised. He denied what I put to him as his intention for being where he was and said he was visiting a priest friend but wouldn't give me his name. I had to let him go.'

'You would have liked to have stopped him though.'

'I would hope any police officer would do so. He wasn't just gay, as we say now, though I prefer less polite terms, he was a corrupter of the young and he should have been given hemlock to drink.'

'Well, someone did in a manner of speaking. And what of you, Liz. How much of this did you know?'

'Mick never pretended what Sherriff was like to me. He was after all a Bishop in the church and it was a scandal that the church officials did nothing about it. They must have known and did bugger all to stop him, and bugger all was what he was clearly intent on doing.'

'But do you think my colleagues in the Met satisfactorily investigated why it might have possibly been that whoever did it should have chosen the mortuary at the Hospice to leave his body?'

'Is that why you're here? To check up on them? To find faults?'

'I'm sure Mick can tell you what an audit on an unsolved crime is. It's for a senior officer from another force to come, accompanied by an officer from the home force not to find fault but to see if anything now stands out that wasn't obvious before.'

'Well, yes, they did all that I would have thought was expected of them. I don't think anyone was missed and we found the whole business as perplexing as them. It was like a joke – a body in the mortuary.'

'And yet there had to be an element of inside knowledge – wouldn't you agree?'

'I suppose so. Whoever did this had to know the site and how best to get a body in by pretending to get a body out and at the most sensible time of day.'

'Were you a regular visitor to the basement?'

'When someone died, two of the nurses on duty wheeled the body on the bed to the end of the corridor, stopped people coming up or down the stairs so they didn't see, and then called the lift. We had a key which prevented anyone stopping the life on its way down and once there we placed the body onto a tray and into the fridge. I did so no more but no less than others.'

'How many would have known that at that time of day, the staffing in Reception would be at its lowest and take for granted the arrival of a van from a funeral director.'

'I have no idea, but not nurses. For that was the busy time on the ward, clearing up supper, doing the 6 o'clock drug round, straightening beds and preparing for the arrival of the night staff.'

'Can I ask a question, ma'am?' said Jo.

'You're not supposed to, sergeant, but go on.'

'It's harmless, but I'm just interested to know what it was like working at the Hospice. I've never been there but I gather that a lot of people die there each year, and I just wondered how as a senior nurse you coped with that almost every day. Wasn't it a bit depressing?'

'You should go and pay a visit. You'd be very welcome. I loved it. To care for people at the end of their lives and provide proper pain control was a real privilege, and I worked with some really good people who have become lasting friends.'

'Do you really think it would be alright to visit?'

'Definitely.'

Cate was by this time glaring at Jo, who looked down to the floor.

'Why did you decide to leave?' said Cate.

'I'd been there a long time and my body was no longer quite so able to work with heavy people. I did my back in and decided that the time had come to leave.'

'And are you working now?'

'A bit of home visiting of old ladies and gentlemen. Some need injections and others require help with their medications.'

'And what about you, Mick?'

'Warehouse security. Easier than being spat at and called names in the Force.'

'Doing an audit is a very artificial task but it has to be done. Sometimes it highlights things that might have been missed but I can well understand why in this instance the local force were baffled. Some crimes never get sorted.'

'Were you in on the original investigation?' Mick asked Jo.

'No.'

'You should know better than that, Mick.' said Cate with a laugh, 'It's not allowed in an audit.'

She stood and signalled to Jo to do likewise, something noticed by Mick and Liz and caused them to look at one another with raised eyebrows, as if to say, "no DCI would have done that to me".

They shook hands. Cate led the way down the garden path, and Mick whispered to Jo, 'Don't let the bitch get away with treating you like muck. You're a DS after all.'

She smiled her thanks.

In the car as she drove away she reported his words.

'I thought you were brilliant, Jo,' said Cate laughing. 'But how did you rate their performance?'

'I thought that for certain the Force is better off without the likes of him. And I wondered what an early morning visit would unearth. I noticed on the shelf behind the tv a violent snuff porn DVD that I know is banned in the UK, but might it be that somewhere in the house there is also a gun firing .22 bullets he came across in the course of his work.'

'Eamonn will let us know whom he calls now we've left the house, and for someone with a bad back Liz moved easily.'

'Yes, I noticed that.'

It was as they emerged from the northern end of the Blackwall

Tunnel that Eamonn called Cate.

'Thinking of asking for a transfer to the Met, are you Cate?'

'Oh, I can't wait. All this traffic is wonderful. So, tell me.'

'He's made two calls since you left, but none as yet to Neville Sturgess. I have the numbers and I'll trace them and let you know.'

'Thanks, Eamonn.'

'Two different numbers called straight after we left, though not to Nev,' said Cate to Jo. 'Both men despised Sherriff and had the motive. They also knew how to get the body in there, and indeed, as Liz said, it might have struck them as a joke. Because neither man was involved in the original investigation and therefore beyond the scope of the audit, I couldn't bring up the matter of Mick Ellam's force record and the warnings he had received for hate language towards Pakistanis and homosexuals. He escaped punishment for an alleged assault on a homosexual man in a public toilet because his Federation rep persuaded Professional Standards that the other man hit him first whilst looking to make his escape. The comment in the file is that judging from the injuries sustained, the man would not want to make the same mistake again! Objection was raised about this comment by the Federation but it was not allowed.'

'He said he left to avoid being spat on and receiving abuse, but those are mostly the lot of uniformed officers and he had been in plain clothes for a long time,' said Jo.

'The file says he took early retirement voluntarily but I would love to know more.'

Kate's phone rang. It was Eamonn.

'The phones called after your visit were made to the phones of two men: Andrew Robinson and Warren Roland, both of whom have done time for violent crimes. I've also received further information about the Ace of Spades. Generally, it isn't thought of in relation to the number one but is sometimes used to designate the sexual longing by a white woman for a black man.'

'H'm, I'm not sure where that fits in but we shouldn't overlook it, that's for certain. Ok, thanks Eamonn. See you in the morning.'

'No you won't. Martin has given me a couple of days off to go home and see the family, but unless you've got everything solved by then, I'll be back.'

Jo was first into bed that night, and Ellie spent some time talking to her about her day as she set out her clothes for the following day and then began to undress, talking all the while. As she approached the bed she realised that Jo was already fast asleep and without a doubt had not heard a word she had said. She leant across and gently kissed her. She slept on.

Team Building

Martin was determined that all the team, and not just Eamonn needed time off, so arranged for the morning briefing to take place not in the office but in the lounge of their hotel. Although Robbie had had no connection with the first crime, Martin still thought he should hear all that Cate and Jo had to report. Later he was hoping to visit Stratford in the hope of a ticket for Coriolanus in the evening.

Jo was impressed by the depth and quality of Kate's report. She missed nothing out and even included the reflections of the two of them as they came back up the M40.

'None of us would lightly even consider the possibility that a fellow officer or former fellow officer might be involved in any crime, let alone one as serious as this,' said Martin, once Cate had completed her report. 'If it is so then it might suggest we should discount it completely from our enquiries and pass it back to the local force to pursue and regard it much as Cate suggested earlier about the essential differences between it and the others, and then allow ourselves to focus on the three with Roman numerals.'

'That may sound right,' said Robbie, 'but doesn't allow for the possibility of development in the minds of the killers. When you do something for the first time and come to do it again, you learn from your first efforts and make changes.'

'That is true,' interrupted Ellie, 'but from Kate's report I had a profound sense that despite all the killings deliberately made to look local, the body in the mortuary really was local. It had to involve person or persons who knew the setup in some considerable detail. I still believe it has to have been an insider who gave that information.'

'And I tell you what has struck me,' said Jo, 'and I hadn't really considered it before, but that inside person didn't have to be on duty whilst it took place. All he or she would have to know was that the routine was still the same and he or she could be at home watching the television.'

'But that would depend on certainty that the routine was in place which couldn't really be guaranteed. For example, if another body was being brought down from the wards they might clash,' said Robbie.

'Ah, but that was the time when, according to Liz Ellam, the wards were at their busiest. My guess would be that if a patient died at that time, the last office would be held over for the night staff to do.'

'So what are we thinking?' said Martin. 'Do we keep hold of this, given that the castration and shooting link with what we know in the others, or do we hand it back to the Met with what we think may be extra information for them to work with?'

'It would be tempting to do that, Martin,' said Ellie, 'and all that Cate and Jo unearthed points in a new and different direction, but we're not handing them any evidence and at the moment this is our crime and I think we need to stay with it a little longer.'

'I agree with Ellie,' added Cate. 'We only have what I would call enhanced suspicion and I'm not sure others would thank us for that just now. We need more and we are just at the beginning, but we do have something to work on at least.'

'I'm just thinking how I would receive this new material,' said Robbie, 'if I was part of the team that had worked on it before. Having Eamonn with us has meant we have access to those Ellam made contact with, but for all we know they might have been discussing the latest football results. I think I would be unconvinced that I was receiving anything especially helpful and new.'

'I think the three of you are right,' said Jo, 'and I will go along with my betters, but I felt something was not right at the Ellams.

That posh house in Eltham for example, his record in the Force, his total contempt for, or perhaps fear of gay men, and phone calls to men with form, straight afterwards. Yes, we don't hand it back, but I think we've also got something to go on.'

'I am convinced by you all. Thank you. Take the day off now and let's gather for a curry together at the Paprika Club in Victoria Terrace. Shall we say 8:00?'

Being given a day off when it's cold and raining is not necessarily much of a kindness and even Robbie was having second thoughts about a trip to Stratford and a phone conversation with the Box Office decided him. There were no tickets available for the evening but "if he stood by the door there might be a return", was the best he could be offered and helped him decide to stay in and read, and at least share the curry with the others. He did however, discover there was a Leamington Spa Rugby Club which advertised a match against Warwick University 1st XV at 2:30 and he decided that he would get a taxi to take him. It was quite a way out of town up the Kenilworth Road, but he knew he would enjoy it when he got there and could get a couple of pints in the Clubhouse and forget murders for a couple of hours.

Cate booked herself into the hotel gym, Martin wanted to catch up on sleep, whilst Ellie and Jo decided to walk hand in hand around the shops and see how many people stared. Very few did, and it was hard for them to know whether they felt good or bad about this. Shortly after arriving in London Jo had mentioned to another woman officer that she was getting fed up with men staring at her breasts. She had replied, "As Oscar Wilde didn't say, there's only one thing worse than having men stare at your tits, and that's not having them stare at them". Since then, she had ceased to bother about it as long as Ellie looked at them!

'I have to confess that I do,' said Ellie with a big smile.

'That's quite alright. You can do anything you like with them.'

And there and then in the street in Royal Leamington Spa, the black woman kissed the white woman, but more alarmingly, the Detective Inspector kissed the Detective Sergeant. Was the world coming to an end?

'Did you play the game when you were younger?' asked Ellie.

'At school, for the University, for the Police. It's a game I have always loved and even though this afternoon's game was not of the highest standard, I enjoyed the way both teams threw themselves into it.'

'What position did you play?' asked Martin.

'Mostly second row and sometimes Number 8. I'm 6 foot 6 so those positions were obvious.'

'Where do you watch it now?' asked Martin again.

'Alas, mostly on television, but now I'm single I like to go abroad and follow Scotland and the British Lions. I went to the World Cup in Japan and I went to South Africa with the Lions in 2009 which was an extremely rough set of encounters. It's a great country and they know and love their rugby. They defeated England in the World Cup Final in Tokyo, I'm pleased to say, though like all Scots, I always love it when England lose.'

'What about Scottish independence? What's your point of view on that?'

'I have one of course, but I make a point of never discussing politics.'

'Wise man,' said Cate. 'I live on the Welsh border so I'm pretty close to English haters.'

'Have you been back to South Africa since you went out to support the British Lions?' asked Ellie.

'Yes. I allowed myself a three-week-long rugby holiday in 2014, on which I met and became friends with the great Chester Williams, the only black player when the Springboks won the World Cup in 1995 in front of Nelson Mandela. We stayed in touch by phone and then on 6 September 2019, I had a call from his wife Maria, to say that he'd died suddenly and could I come to cast an independent eye as a British Police Offer over the claims being made that he had died of myocardial infarction. So, I went and found no evidence of foul play but I lost a great friend and a good man

'South Africa had as its head for just a little while the great

Nelson Mandela, once pressure was put on the government like a scrum pushing relentlessly forwards. Chester and the other black players adored him, as I did. I love that country and one day perhaps will get the chance to move there but perhaps best of all was that moment in Japan in 2019 when Siya Kolisi, the South African captain, became the first Black South African to receive and lift the World Cup.'

Everyone was conscious of the rising tone of passion with which he spoke and were moved by it and the sight of tears rolling down his cheeks. There was a period of silence once he had finished, eventually broke by Cate.

'You may find it difficult to believe,' began Cate, 'but for two seasons I played international sport for England.'

Everyone turned, a little stunned.

'That makes sense,' said Jo. 'You're the only one of us who visited the hotel gym this afternoon.'

'How did you know that?'

'I was passing and I could hear someone and because I'm nosey I went and had a look at the list, but I only have to look at you to know how fit you are. You're taller than most and netball is obviously your sport. According to my laptop you played Goal Attack five times and Goal Shooter four times, for England.'

The others spontaneously clapped their hands, turning Kate's face quite red.

'Your applause is misdirected,' she said. 'It should be reserved for the genius detective sergeant in our midst.'

Before breakfast on the following morning, Cate received a call in her room from Martin.

'Good morning Cate. I'd like you and I to meet after breakfast, but here in the hotel rather than at the office, if that's ok with you, but I don't think it should be in a public room. Can I come to you after the others have gone up the road?'

'Of course, but won't they think it odd?'

'I don't expect them to think anything about it.'

At the breakfast table the only instruction issued by Martin was to ask Ellie if she could check on anything Eamonn might have been able to send when he was due to call in at work briefly on the Saturday evening, and to follow it up between the three of them. Ellie, who after all had been Martin's lover for some months until the appearance of Jo, both knew and respected him enough as a senior police officer not to enquire what he himself was intending to do.

'Come in,' said Cate, opening the door to Martin. 'I think I know what you have come to talk about. It's about the quality of the naan bread we were given at the Indian last night!'

'Oh God, Cate however did you get to be so sharp a detective? Brilliant, I'd call it. It must have been all that netball.'

'Perhaps not, but I really do think I know what you want to talk about and it's that powerful speech we received from Robbie last night, not so much about rugby but about his powerful emotional links to South Africa and the death of his close friend Chester Williams.'

'Anyone who shared such views in the rugby world would have a powerful motive to kill a white South African racist living nearby who blames her exile on the triumph of black South Africans.'

'It's also possible for killings III and IV, that a police officer had looked on Holmes 3 and seen details not known to the public. Tomorrow, I want to send Ellie and Jo up to Scotland and send you and Robbie to Boston to see if you can pour fresh light on the killing of Marney Edmonds.'

'I'm pleased about that Martin. We both know how often when a crime is unsolved for quite some time, perpetrators get over-confident and careless, but without doubting their abilities, shouldn't you be the one heading to Scotland?'

'Jo's been to Scotland before and already knows the pathologist and the crime scene and besides which they might accuse me of being homophobic by not letting them ever work together.'

'Jo is something special in terms of her acute brain and good looks, and if I didn't know that she bats for the other side, I might even fancy her myself.'

'Well, just in case you were wondering, I don't fancy her or any women, nor sadly, most of the men I've met, but I remain ever hopeful.'

At the office Ellie opened the emails from Eamonn's computer at MI5, one of which contained goodies:

"Andrew Robinson and Warren Roland are well known to the Security Services as well as to the Police. Both have served time as young men for drug importing, since when they appeared to use a gang to do the risky jobs whilst concentrating on organised crime in the East End of London behind the front of an export-import business in Shoreditch. There is no evidence but it was not beyond the realms of possibility that they have police assistance. Both are known to be aggressively anti-Semitic and have been photographed participating and perhaps even organising protest rallies in London to counter gay pride gatherings. This intel has been shared with senior officers of the City of London Police Force."

When Martin arrived and read it, made a noise which expressed a considerable measure of scorn.

'Why were we not given this information when both men lived in our area, and where it looks possible that we have a bent copper who might well be party to a murder? It almost makes you want to give up. But anyway, it's here now, and again we have to ask what *we* do.'

'Nothing has changed, Martin,' said Jo. 'These two may smell, even stink, but in terms of evidence we have none and it sounds to me as if they're accomplished at making sure there could be none. Nothing has changed from when we recognised this yesterday.'

Ellie and Robbie looked back at Martin who was reluctantly smiling.

'I wondered which of you would notice that first.'

They all laughed.

'Right, tomorrow we're heading out in pairs, so I need you to do some hard work today getting to grips with where you are going. Cate and Robbie, I want you to go to Boston. We've heard next to nothing from there in a while, so do your best to shake them up, to ruffle their feathers. See the pathologist too, if you can, and the widow. I imagine that by now most of the workers will have returned to Slovenia but do what you can.

'Ellie and Jo, you're off to Scotland. Meet the pathologist again, Jo, and then visit Comrie, the site where the body was found.

'That leaves me and it's becoming clear that we need another member of the team so I'm going looking for one. you'll be pleased to know it's not going to be the Bishop of Coventry. I have someone in mind but we'll have to wait and see.'

Robbie and Cate quickly left with their files and made their way up the road to the Tea Society tea rooms which Cate had discovered. At this time on a Sunday morning it was still quiet.

'How do you think the boss is doing?' asked Robbie once their drinks had arrived.

'He's had a full range of experience. He was in Special Branch for two years and then a section leader in the Armed Response Unit based at the Yard. His experience of marriages and relationships may not be quite so special, but as you know from your own experience, marriages and partnerships do not always thrive among us. But in terms of what we're doing, it's early days but I'm impressed. As earlier, when Jo spoke to him in a way I wouldn't have dared when I was a DS to my Super, he listens before he acts. What do you think?'

'I think he's doing a great job in terms of team building and management. What I don't know is whether we shall ever be able to solve these crimes. I also know we'll need a very early start to get there and have some daylight.'

Ellie and Jo were waiting for Martin to finish a call.

'It's a long way and that was your hotel for tonight. It's on the Dunkeld Road, heading out of Perth to the north but close to the hospital where I'd like you start first thing in the morning. You've met the pathologist, Jo, so call before you leave here and arrange to meet tomorrow.'

'Martin, I find myself wondering what's going on. Has this anything to do with what we heard in the curry house last night?'

What are the three things we look for in a suspect?'

'Motive, opportunity, means,' said Jo.

'The motive is obvious and could hardly be greater. Opportunity and means are what you are looking for. I have however arranged for you to collect a warrant from the Perth Sheriff Court House in Tay St. I do not like having to do this but I think I must. Please do not take the place apart and if you find nothing, leave it as you find it. If there's nothing, then I don't want Robbie to know anyone has been, and make sure you spend time with those officers still trying to make sense of the case.'

'You don't think you should be asking Robbie to pull out of the team?' asked Ellie.

'A man talking about his love for rugby, South Africa and Chester Williams would be an odd reason to ask him to leave. I am hoping that tomorrow night you'll return with nothing to go on. Now you two, be gone.'

'Quis custodiet ipsos custodes?' said Jo as they left the office.

'Do you think so?' replied Ellie. 'I thought it looked like rain myself.'

They looked at each other and laughed and took hold of the hand of the other.

About Turn

They stopped for lunch at the Woodhall Services on the M1 and largely wished they hadn't, and both wondered whether they should arrest the management and charge them with daylight robbery!

It was after they returned to their journey and via the M18 onto the A1(M), that they began to discuss the task ahead.

'I remember being struck almost as soon as Robbie began to speak last night that he was making a trap into which he might himself fall, and I could hardly believe the way he did so,' said Ellie.

'Yes, and I kept remembering the severed head wrapped in the South African flag. I want to ask the pathologist if SOCOS can tell us whether it was of South African origin or manufactured here.'

'And yet,' said Ellie, 'I don't want to find anything even remotely incriminating. I like Robbie; he's a gentle giant and I would find it hard to believe that he had beheaded anyone, however racist. Surely there must be someone else who thinks like him who might have done it. I desperately hope so.'

Ellie and Jo arrived in Perth and their first point of call was at the mortuary at the Infirmary with Dr Alex Jenkins the locum pathologist who mostly worked in Dundee.

'Hello Doctor Jenkins, it's good to see you again.'

'And you Sergeant Enright.'

They burst out laughing together.

'Alex, this is my boss, Ellie.

Hello, Alex.'

'Hi. Welcome to the morgue.'

'Are you still doing a locum here, as well as your own job in Dundee?'

'Jo, this is the NHS and they have now appointed me senior pathologist of both.'

'Senior? That implies a junior.'

'Trust a detective to notice that. Do let me know if you find him or her!'

'We'll try not to keep you long then.'

'I would love you to do so had I not to prepare for an inquest in Dundee this afternoon.'

Jo looked at Ellie.

'Do you want to see her?' she asked.

'I was hoping you wouldn't ask so instead I'll ask some questions of Alex. You reported traces of Propofol in her liver. Was it unusual that you should find that after a body had lain in the open air for at least 24 hours?'

'Not if more than the usual amount was inserted. As you may know, it's used primarily as the basic drug to bring about unconsciousness by an anaesthetist on top of which she or he will give others whilst intubation is taking place.'

'Might the anaesthetist give a double dose?'

'Definitely not. That really could never happen under any circumstances unless the anaesthetist were a total twit and knew nothing.'

'But what would happen if he or she did?'

'It would prolong the first stage of anaesthesia and not be good for the patient. In the wrong hands, such as mine or yours, it could be quite lethal.'

'Yours? But you're a doctor.'

'But I'm not an anaesthetist.'

'And would it be more likely to leave traces if it were a double dose?'

'Possibly. It has a short half-life and I don't usually find it even in the blood of someone who has died in theatre, close to the administration of the drug.'

'Your report indicated a possible entry point in the back of the left hand.'

'It was a mark but no more than that.'

'If you were a potential murderer and wanted to use Propofol to render your victim unconscious, however could you get them still enough to apply it?'

'Trichloromethane.'

'Chloroform,' said Jo.

'Yes.'

'But you did not mention that or anything else like it in your report,' said Ellie.

'But it doesn't mean it wasn't used, it's just that there were no traces and I wouldn't have expected there to be. It doesn't hang around which is why it was the drug of choice for rapists at one time.'

'And how would I get some?'

'You might make it yourself. There's instruction on the internet, I imagine.'

Ellie looked at Jo.

'When the flag was removed from the head, you will have bagged it and sent it to forensics.'

'Yes.'

'Did you examine it first?'

'Yes.'

'Did you notice a label of origin?'

'Yes. Unsurprisingly for the South African flag, it said "Made in South Africa".'

'But companies in this country make flags of all nations,' said Jo, 'so it's possibly a little surprising to find an actual South African manufactured South African flag here in Scotland. Given the victims view on the country she left, it is hardly likely that she had one in the house.'

'We're not here fault-finding with the previous investigation, by the way,' said Ellie. 'When an investigation gets stuck, the policy is to ask two pairs of fresh eyes to look at everything again. Almost certainly the fresh eyes will see one or two things that might have been different because they will ask different questions, but the task here will have been thorough and I can't see us making an early arrest.'

'In which case, I think you should be made familiar with the victim.'

'Ok, not least because if I don't, my Sergeant here will spend the whole day teasing me about it.'

'She was quite small and I imagine quite light even when her head was attached.'

As they were preparing to leave, Alex said, 'Do you know, I've been racking my brain as to where someone could get hold of Propofol. Security is tight in main hospitals but considerably less so in what we used to call Cottage Hospitals and there is one not so far away, the Blairgowrie Community Hospital. It has a 17 bed GP Unit and does not do surgery except in an emergency for something relatively minor, but I would be surprised if against that remote possibility they do not have a supply of Propofol. I may be wrong but it might be worth pursuing.'

'Thank you, Alex. We will do so.'

They were late for the Sheriff Court House though on arrival no one seemed to mind. They went in together, Ellie making the appropriate notes whilst Jo took the oath. They collected the warrant and then made for the Police Station where they were warmly welcomed by the team still working on the Comrie murder. Their questions to these officers were somewhat perfunctory given that they were pursuing a line at this time they couldn't share with them.

'It's not an ordinary Audit,' said Ellie to the detectives working on the case, 'and please don't feel under any sort of judgement from us, 'but I will say that the case is odd. Beheading a victim is not just unusual, it's unheard of outside of gang murders in London and the pages of crime writers. As with the other crimes we're investigating the appearance is of both something local and related to crimes committed in other parts of the county. We now have one at each point of the compass: North, South, East and West. So, if those of you still struggling to make sense of this have anything to offer, however unlikely or outlandish an idea, we need to hear from you.'

'Our real difficulty,' said the SIO, 'is in finding where the thing happened. It would have had to be far enough away from housing for screams not to be heard given what was done to her back and how on earth do you manage a decapitation?'

'One of those in Iraq with Saddam Hussain had his head come off as he was being hanged, but this certainly didn't happen like that as those who have seen the body and head will know. Someone took an axe or something akin and had two goes,' added a sergeant.

'Yes,' said Ellie with a trace of sarcasm in her voice, 'we paid our money and went to ogle. But what I can tell you is that in the light of the other three investigations we are carrying out, you are largely wasting your time. Whoever the perpetrators of these crimes are, they are revealing a determination to lead us all a merry dance. They are well planned to give every appearance of being local but cannot be if they are related by the numbers inscribed on the backs of the victims, information so far withheld from the public, though for how much longer as more people know I cannot say.'

'Are you suggesting we lay off it, ma'am?' said a sergeant.

'I cannot make that decision but I could make the case for it. I have no doubts that you, in common with the police forces in Wales, Lincolnshire and South London, are excellent in what you do as detectives, but you are all baffled in exactly the same way and I think that the force in the Midlands are best placed to tackle these cases as one, and that is where we think the answer lies.'

'That certainly makes sense, Inspector,' said the SIO, who was one rank above her. 'I shall need to discuss it with the powers that be of course, but it would seem not the best use of resources for us to duplicate what others are doing when the crime is related to others. Does anyone disagree?'

Those present shook their heads.

'Dare I ask if a cup of tea might be possible before we head off?' said Jo. 'Oh, I apologise for that regrettable pun. It wasn't intended.'

There were groans.

'I'll take the orders,' said a young Detective Constable. 'It's what DCs are for.'

As he got up to go to the kitchen, Jo left the room having asked the way to the loo, and once outside the room stopped the young officer.

'Tell me, then.'

'What do you mean?'

'What's your name?'

'Sandy.'

'Well, Sandy, whilst my boss was mentioning things unlikely or outlandish, I was aware of your face giving off signs of unease or concern. So, let's make the drinks together and you can tell me.'

'You will think me disloyal.'

'No. You're wrong. My boss meant it and I can promise you there will be no reporting to anyone of anything you say.'

'Ok, and it's probably nothing, but about two days before the murder I was with Inspector Douglas on our way to investigate a burglary at the Blairgowrie Cottage Hospital. He always liked to have the radio on, and it was time for the twelve o'clock news on which there was a report about a meeting in Dundee being addressed by Jocelyn Hoosen which had got wholly out of hand when anti-racists let off fireworks and played loud music to drown her out. She had complained that the police had failed to protect her right to free speech. That was when Inspector Douglas suddenly burst out and said "Free speech, my arse. She should be fucking killed – hanged, drawn and quartered, as far as I'm concerned". I was completely taken aback and said nothing. When we got to the surgery, he told me to wait in the car, which was most unusual, and I then saw him go into the Cottage Hospital but he was in there just a couple of minutes before he came back to the car. He told me it was more vandalism than a break-in and we came back here. And what was most odd was that he said he would do the report which, as I'm sure you know, is totally unknown.'

'When we've taken these drinks in, Sandy, is there any chance you could print off a copy of that report?'

'Sure.'

Shortly before they left, Sandy passed close to Jo and whispered, 'If I were you, I'd pay a visit to the ladies before you set off and I recommend the far cubicle.'

'Well, it's been great to be made so welcome and thanks for the tea.'

'My pleasure.'

'I'll just pop in here before we leave,' said Jo.

Ellie was more than used to her sergeant and lover doing the unexpected and took no notice, and moments later they had driven out and were on their way towards Blairgowrie.

'I assume you were making a surreptitious date with that young man,' said Ellie.

'Yes, it was a "meet me in the ladies loo" sort of date, or rather he left me something in the ladies loo, something I'd asked him to print out for me, a report on a sort of break-in at the Cottage Hospital, and a report written up by his inspector, someone called Robbie Douglas.'

'You mean an inspector wrote up a report on a break-in?'

'Strange that. But the best is yet to come. The report says that the Inspector had a look into a drugs cupboard in the hospital from where some bottles has been taken. No mention is made of which bottles. And all this happened after a news report in the car on Jocelyn Hoosen at which my young friend said Robbie blew a gasket and said she should be killed – hanged, drawn and quartered.'

'Saying dreadful things and wishing death on someone is not the same as doing it, but I would like to know if one of those bottles contained Propofol.'

Jo drove into the car park and together they went into the hospital, where Ellie introduced herself and Jo to the receptionist who gave them a puzzled look.

'Isn't it a little odd to have someone from the Metropolitan Police here in Scotland?'

'Without a doubt. Ring Perth CID if it will make you feel easier,' said Jo.

'You had a break-in attended by DI Douglas some weeks ago.'

'Yes. It was nothing much. After drugs I imagine, but they got nothing, mainly because we don't stock them.'

'But were there signs that they had entered the premises.'

'Oh yes and made a right mess they did too over the waiting area.'

'Thank you,' said Ellie. 'Judging from the empty waiting room there are no doctors here now.'

'No. Having their lunch, I imagine though Dr Reynolds might be somewhere about. She tends to have her lunch here when she has an early afternoon clinic.'

They went the past the receptionist's desk and saw a nurse talking to a woman who looked vaguely medical.

'Dr Reynolds?'

'Yes.'

'I'm Detective Inspector Ellie Middlewood and this is Detective Sergeant Jo Enright. Can we go somewhere private?'

The doctor led them into her own room.

'We are part of a team seeking to bring to justice four murders across the country which have aspects in common. We are based in the English Midlands but we have countrywide jurisdiction. The pathologist in Perth indicated that it was just possible that you might have here, locked away, a bottle of Propofol.'

'I've certainly never had need to use it myself,' said the doctor. 'It would be most unusual for us to do a procedure requiring that sort of anaesthesia. If there were, we would send it through to Perth immediately, but I suppose it's just about possible in an emergency.'

'If you did have it, where would it be kept?'

'It's a dangerous drug and it would be locked away with others in one of our treatment rooms.'

'Could you take us?'

'Of course.'

She led them down a corridor and into a larger room than they had anticipated.

'It's quite a large room for a treatment room,' said Jo.

'That's because sometimes we have to have the space necessary to respond to something bigger than a sprained wrist.

Look,' she said pointing to a cupboard, 'this is where we keep dangerous drugs.'

She touched the door and it swung open.

'Presumably it's normally kept locked.'

'Well, er, yes.'

She opened the door. There, tucked away, at the back was a bottle of white liquid bearing the title "Diprivan" and in smaller letters below "Propofol".

'Please don't touch it doctor.'

'No, but it's odd because as you can see it has been used but the date on it means it must have been used in my time here at the hospital, and we certainly have not made use of it in that time.'

'Are there bottles missing?'

'I would have to check on the list, but I can't see anything missing that I would expect to be there.'

'Please can you check your list now and do you have CCTV in the corridor?'

'Yes.'

'I have an awful feeling this is going from bad to worse,' said Jo.

'Jo, can you hunt out the CCTV tapes? You know the date. What do you think about fingerprints? Here or back home?'

'Back home without a doubt or else we shall alert Perth to something we don't yet know for certain.'

'You're right. I'll wait for the doctor and then place it in an evidence bag and she and I can both sign it.'

The CCTV tapes clearly showed Robbie in the corridor and that he entered a side room but were not clear enough to show which. However, the orderly who had shown her the equipment said that she had seen Inspector Douglas again a few days later. They looked for the tape and there he was, two days after the murder, back in the corridor and once again entering and then leaving the room. Jo took out an evidence bag from her pocket and put the tapes inside.

They said little as they drove down to Robbie's house in

Balhousie Avenue in the north of the town, close to where Perthshire Rugby Club had their ground on the edge of the golf course. It was a quite unremarkable semi-detached house and certainly not the place to transport and behead a body.

Getting in was a doddle to Jo and once in they stood and took in everything before them. As far as they knew it was not a crime scene but they had to treat it as if potentially so and were determined to disturb it as little as possible. There were photographs of those they assumed were Robbie's parents and siblings, and quite a few of him with Chester Williams and his family, including one of Robbie proudly wearing a South African Rugby Shirt. There was one of him with his arm around the shoulder of a black South African rugby player and underneath it said "With Siya Kolisi after the final in Tokyo". There was an older photograph of him lifted high in the air catching a ball at a line out. The sideboard drawers revealed nothing of note and so they passed through into the kitchen. Once again there nothing much to see to excite their interest other than an old PC on the kitchen table. Jo opened the back door and found a car covered with a tarpaulin which was not visible from the front of the house. They removed the tarpaulin between them and discovered a Dacia Duster Estate, not new but with four-wheel drive and plenty of space once the rear seats were put down.

'We need to see if we can find the keys,' said Ellie, and went back into the kitchen to root around possible places for hiding keys.

Jo stayed and looked through the rear windows but could see nothing. The exterior of the car was muddy. Ellie appeared holding the keys in the air before throwing them to Jo, who opened the door. The smell greeting her was horrid, and she understood more when she opened the door at the rear of the car. There was dried blood and some hairs congealed in it. She closed the door at once.

'The car has to be taken away, Ellie, and we have to come totally clean with our colleagues here in Perth. We're in the realm no longer of speculation but of evidence and unless I'm mistaken, it's going to be necessary for Cate to arrest Robbie in connection with the murder of Jocelyn Hoosen.'

'We must indeed inform the station here, but at a higher level than those we met earlier. The car will have to be collected for forensic examination but until that is completed, we still won't have the compelling evidence we need to get Cate to arrest him. Besides which it would be neither fair nor safe for her to have to do that and then drive him back to Leamington. Let him come back and have him arrested by officers from here who are the ones who can decide if he is to be charged or not.'

'Yes, I'm wrong, I'm sorry.'

'Hey, I've got a bit more experience than you with matters of procedure, that's all.'

'I foresee a problem though.'

'Go on. This is where you're cleverer than me.'

'We don't know if there is anyone here, a friend or a housekeeper, who won't try to inform him that his house and car are being taken apart. If he received that news on the way he might very well pose a real danger to Cate. I would suggest that here and now we speak to Eamonn and see if he can block Robbie's phone before the troops arrive here.'

'I said you were cleverer than me. Do it now and see if it's possible. Then I'll make the call to the station here.'

Jo explained to Eamonn the reason for her call, and he said that he had already done it as she was speaking. He would not be able to receive or make any calls. Eamonn also suggested a text to Cate, reading "Robbie to drive back".

'Eamonn, you're a genius.'

Jo nodded to Ellie.

They heard the sirens almost immediately and in a short while the road was blocked and tapes stretched across the paths in front of the house. In the meantime, and probably against regulations, Jo turned the computer on and finding nothing obvious at once called Eamonn and asked him how to find something that might have been erased. He had talked her through checking the hard disk and there it was: an internet description of to blend chemicals together at a very low temperature to make Chloroform. When the Detective Super arrived, Ellie gave him everything she knew and they had discovered, although when she was just reaching the end, Jo approached, apologised for interrupting and informed them that she had found the equipment and chemicals used in making chloroform in the garage: acetone and bleach, together with an erased file on Robbie's computer explains how it can be made, and hidden away at the back of a cupboard full or rubbish that looked as it had been piled on just to conceal it, an axe. The head was clean but she said she had left it in place for the forensic team to examine.

'I don't quite know what to say to you two. You'll go back home leaving me with the absolute nightmare of the possibility that one of my senior officers has not just murdered but beheaded a minor celebrity and tried to disguise it by copying something he read on Holmes 3, and then joining the team looking to solve it. You also leave me with a team who in their investigations seem not to have been able to see what's under their noses. You turn up and in one day you may have solved it completely.'

'Not quite completely, sir. There is a possibility that this is a set-up. DI Douglas is away and so the house has been empty and it's quite possible that someone has planted evidence. And even more, sir, you have no idea and we have no idea where the killing and decapitation was done. If Douglas is the man, then you will have to try to get it out of him, but he's not stupid, and he knows that if you don't find that, your case will be weaker and purely circumstantial.'

'Inspector, do you delight in bringing me bad news?'

'I think you will have enough, given what Sergeant Enright discovered in the boot.'

'Where is the bastard?'

'Somewhere in Lincolnshire, sir, probably driving back to Leamington Spa, which is our base,' said Jo.

'Lincolnshire? That's punishment enough for any man. So how do you want to play things from here?'

'We can perhaps persuade our boss to bring him tomorrow. Martin can mislead for England and find a reason for them both to come,' said Ellie.

'There's no chance of either or both of you coming here to

work full-time, I suppose.'

'It gets dark too early, sir. By the way, here's the warrant we obtained to enter the house.'

'Thank you, both of you. Have a safe journey back.'

Look East

'What an awful place to have to live,' said Robbie, as they crossed the fens towards Boston. 'It's completely flat and the fields are the full of cabbages. And what's that great big black thing sticking up ahead?'

'It's the Boston Stump, the huge tower of St Botolph's Church in the town, and a landmark when people are lost. It's also immediately across the river from where we are heading, the local police station. Boston ought to be a pleasant place, welcoming visitors, but in fact it had the highest vote for Brexit in the referendum and has a mass of racial tensions. Immigration has changed the character of the place considerably.'

'And this is where Jo was a lowly PC before the arrival of Martin and Ellie.'

'Yes, and I gather there have been other changes since the murder. The DS who was here has transferred elsewhere though the same DI is still in place.'

Robbie being extremely tall could not be missed as he entered the police station walking behind Cate who was herself quite tall and also gave off a sense of not to be messed about with.

'DCI Greene and DI Douglas to see DI Hannah,' said Cate to the desk sergeant.

'Yes, ma'am. If you go through the door on the left, you'll find CID at the end and I'll let him know you are here.'

Before they got to the office Connor was out in the corridor and welcoming them, and then introducing them to his new DS, Nigel Stancliffe, and his new DC, Christine Halton.

'I'm sure, Inspector, that you will have undergone an audit on

178

an unsolved case before, as most of us have. We're not here to find faults so much as to look over the investigation with fresh eyes. Most of the time we come to the same conclusion as did the original team but sometimes we can suggest a new line of enquiry.

'We have both read your extremely thorough report with which we are impressed. What we don't have are the two missing former members of the team. One of them we know well because she is now a member of our own team and that is DS Enright, and I have had, of course, the chance to speak to her. DS Hollioake has, I believe, been transferred to the Durham Constabulary. Was that his own wish?'

'Like many people who are not natives, Graham found the flatlands just too much to bear and decided to move to be nearer his family in Newcastle and is working with traffic, I believe,' replied Connor.

'Then he should hope not to be called to too many road traffic collisions. They can be grim experiences,' added Robbie.

'They can indeed,' said Cate. 'Ok, Connor, we're all ears. Take us through it.'

Neither Cate nor Robbie interrupted as Connor spoke during the following 25 minutes, recounting everything from when Marney went missing to the arrival of Superintendent Peabody and Inspector Middlewood.

'The most immediately obvious shortcoming of your account, Connor, is your lack of follow-up of Katarina Horvat, the alleged mistress of Marney Edmonds, to whom he supplied an enormous amount of money and bought her a house. She disappeared after the murder and was traced to Bishop Auckland by DS Enright and spoken to by telephone and checked by the local force, but not interviewed face-to-face by you or anyone else. Nor do you indicate in your report that any sort of attempt was made to trace whoever she might have been seen seeing on at least the nights of the week when Edmonds was not her caller.'

'We had nothing to go on and no idea in which direction she might be travelling if indeed she was. We did a house-to-house but no admitted to seeing her leave the estate which of course might even mean she stayed there and was having a relationship with someone on the estate who had no wish to tell us.'

'So I take it you drove up to Bishop Auckland to find out.'

'No, but DS Hollioake spoke to her and asked about it. She said she went out with a Slovenian friend who picked her up and they went out for a drink in various pubs around the place.'

'And did Hollioake ascertain the name of the alleged Slovenian woman?'

'Yes, of course but it did not correspond to any we know from Marney's gang. By the time we learned the name, Katarina said her friend would have returned home by now.'

'Did it not strike you as odd that a Slovenian woman should have a car?'

'Graham tried every means he knew of tracing the car and the woman, but to no avail. I think she was lying and that it was a local man. He went round all the local pubs but no one recognised her photograph,'

'Robbie, have you anything that you want to ask.'

'No thanks, ma'am.'

'In which case we need to visit the mortuary. Is it the same pathologist who performed the PM?'

'Yes, and she knows you'll be coming.'

'After that, DI Douglas will need to see the widow and I the place where the body was found, er, Midville, I believe.'

'I'll take you to the hospital, and DI Douglas out onto the fen to see Mary Edmonds. She knows me. Nigel can stay here and Christine will take you, ma'am, to Midville.'

'No. I'd like you to stay here, Connor, especially as you say, Mrs Edmonds knows you. This is an audit, remember. We're not here to solve a crime but to concern ourselves with the way in which your investigation was carried out. DS Stancliffe and DC Halton can both accompany us to the mortuary and then onwards.'

'You're in charge ma'am.'

Robbie accompanied the DS and Cate the DC to the hospital.

'It's an unusual arrangement having the mortuary in the main part of the hospital,' said Cate.'

'I know. In most places it's on the periphery.'

'Have you seen the body of Marney Edmonds?'

'No, ma'am.'

'Then it's up to you, but I have to.'

'I will come with you ma'am.'

'Good.'

They met the pathologist waiting by the door, who couldn't stop staring at Robbie, much to his acute embarrassment.

'Please don't die today, Inspector. We have nothing that you would fit into.'

'I'll try my best, doctor.'

'Do come into my lair. I have prepared what you need to see. Please ask anything you like.'

Even after all the time the body had been in the deep freeze (as no order permitting burial of a murder victim had yet been issued by a coroner), what they saw was still shocking to them all, especially the letters on his back put there by a branding iron before the shotgun wreaked fatal havoc with his insides.

'Your report, Dr Gordon, was outstanding. Thank you for that and it answers all the questions that occur to me now, bar one, and it invites a purely speculative response. Was this done by human rights fanatics concerned with what they saw as human slavery, or was it done to give that impression for another reason altogether?'

Dr Morgan thought for a while.

'I could say, and I know many if not most pathologists who would say. that such questions are not my business but that of the police, and of course they would be quite correct, but it is an enticing, almost irresistible question. The thing is, and I recall saying it to my colleague at Lincoln Hospital, that everything seemed wrong about this murder.'

'Wrong?'

'Yes. Marney may have had a bit on the side, but he really was not a slave owner and quite the opposite, provided work and good conditions for those he brought over from Slovenia or wherever. He was the most trusted gang master of them all and I have found no evidence from conversations I have had with some of his workers that they were exploited though they always joked that he paid close attention to some of the girls, but you know I think it was a joke. So, to use a branding iron was not only horrendously cruel, savage even, it was an error. And then to shoot him as they did which suggests revenge for a sexual misdemeanour is once again inappropriate. And then, why did they use a branding iron to put the Roman numeral II on him? Or did whoever did this, know there had been a numeral I somewhere else and a III to follow?'

Cate smiled.

'Thank you for that. Can you also repeat what you said in your report about finding traces of the drug Propofol in the liver of the deceased?'

'It's very quick acting as you will know if ever you had an anaesthetic and that is its purpose – to induce almost immediate unconsciousness and then other means are used to keep a patient wholly unaware of what is being done through what we call intubation – inserting a tube which delivers anaesthetic gases. It has a very short half-life and usually disappears from the blood stream quickly. That there was the tiniest amount in the liver is highly unusual, unless a second infusion has been given.'

'Ok. Robbie, Nigel, Christine, have you any questions for Dr Gordon?'

'Yes,' said Christine, 'if I may, ma'am. I had an operation two years ago here, for ... well, it doesn't matter what for, and I assume the drug you are talking about was used because I went to sleep almost immediately. The anaesthetist told me he had to put in what I think he called a cannula in the back of my hand, which was a convenient way of putting in anything else needed during the operation. He said it went straight into my vein. So, if this drug, Propofol, was used on Marney, would it have to be done using a cannula? Surely that would be extremely difficult for someone not a doctor or nurse to insert.'

'So?' said Dr Gordon, 'finish your question.'

'So, if not by that route, how was the drug administered?'

'Excellent question, Chris. Please all four of you, come and look at the hands of the deceased. There's a mark here over a vein but isn't the mark that would be left by a cannula. So, I can only assume that who whoever used the Propofol knew that it was for intravenous administration only and used it directly with a syringe. Intramuscularly it would have no effect.'

'You said in your report that this would have to have been done by at least two people because of his weight and size,' said Robbie.

'I suppose someone of your size might have been able to do it, Inspector, but even then, it wouldn't have been easy, so I think we can discount you, or at least you working alone.'

They all laughed.

'You have been most generous with your time doctor and so we should be on our way, but before we do so, none of us were involved with the investigation. This is an audit on the past not an attempt to investigate in the present, so as clearly as possible can you give me your opinion of the way in which the investigation was carried out in relation to your own work?'

'It was as I would have expected it to be – professional and wholly competent, though, perhaps a little less so once Constable Enright was stolen by the Metropolitan Police. My assistants all called her Sherlock.'

'I'll pass on the compliment when I see her next.'

Nigel took Robbie to see the widow.

As Chris drove away from the Pilgrim Hospital towards the turning for Midville, she said to Cate, 'Ma'am, may I ask you something.'

'Don't be daft, of course you can.'

'Well, you're the senior officer and yet you're not seeing the widow. I assumed you would.'

'That's because it's an audit rather than part of an investigation. Inspector Douglas will ask if she is satisfied with the conduct of the investigation so far. Because it is not yet resolved she will still be hoping that somehow or other it might be, and it does sometimes happen that an audit provides a breakthrough, otherwise we wouldn't do them.'

She indicated right.

'This is Stickney, where DI Hannah tells me he calls for an ice cream at the Post Office in Summer. Midville doesn't really exist as you will see, for we are here now. There's just a short riverbank and a narrow river. The body had been placed in the river and attached by a rope to the fence. Believe it or not that is something fen farmers do when they commit suicide to aid those searching for them.'

'So, whoever killed him knew that and I imagine it wouldn't be widely known outside the region. There's obviously nothing to see but is it very far for you to take me to Wainfleet St Mary churchyard where Marney's landrover was found by Sergeant Hollioake?

'It's not far, ma'am.'

'DS Enright who worked here before you felt she was not being taken seriously by her senior officers because she was a woman, and that this meant she felt she was being overlooked for promotion. Now, I know her to be an outstanding police officer so it vexes me that this was her experience in this day and age. I am neither writing anything down or recording it, and I want you to give me an accurate account of your experience as a DC here in Boston under DI Hannah.'

'There are not many good jobs around the area for someone like me, so the alternatives are not obvious, but I have wanted to be a police officer since I was about 12, so I am disappointed that as a career it's not working out as I had hoped. I work hard and whilst I'm obviously not another Jo Enright, I think I am a good police officer and a good detective, but if there is to be a future for me then, as with Jo, it will have lie elsewhere.'

'Do you think there are added difficulties because of your colour?

'In Boston, yes, because we have problems with immigration and I get abuse from locals because I'm perceived to be from Asia, when I actually come from York.'

'And do you get grief, however mild, from colleagues too?'

'No. They wouldn't dare and in either instance I am more than capable of taking care of myself. I am a black belt in Taekwondo, believe it or not, for which I have my dad to thank.

In fact, if you'll excuse my boasting, I'm the current British champion in my weight.'

'Have you a particular sort of policing you're especially interested in.'

'Yes. Working in CID. It stretches my mind in so many ways and is more fun than a crossword. Now, here we are ma'am. I'll park on the road which will enable you to see something interesting, or rather not see.'

They got out of the car.

'Excuse me asking, Chris, but where are the houses and the village?'

'They're about a mile away. Nobody lives here though it's a lovely churchyard.'

'And overgrown. Where was the landrover?'

'That the interesting thing, ma'am. From here it was completely concealed and only accessible from the long drive and the right turn towards the Church porch. That is where, so I am told, Sergeant Hollioake came across it.'

'Was he a religious man, do you know?'

'I've never heard that said of him.'

'You said., "so I am told" that Sergeant Hollioake found the landrover here. That tells me you are not convinced.'

'No, ma'am, I'm not convinced at all.'

'Have you raised this as a concern?'

'Inspector Hannah said there was nothing sinister or surprising about it as the Sergeant knew the area well and would have checked it as a matter of course.'

'And were you any more convinced?'

'No, ma'am.'

Cate approached the porch and tried the Church door which to her amazement was open. Both women entered and almost gasped in unison.

'It is so beautiful. I've rarely seen a country Church as beautiful as this anywhere and here in the middle of nowhere.

'"A serious house on serious earth it is

In whose blent air all our compulsions meet

Are recognisd and robed as destinies."

'Philip Larkin wrote it in 1955 and it's part of quite a long poem called Church Going and it could have been written for here. The odd thing is that he was an atheist and is probably better known for the first lines of one of his other poems: "They fuck you up your mum and dad / they may not mean to but they do".

Chris finished off the verse: "They fill you with the faults they had /And add some extra, just for you." I am a great Larkin fan, or perhaps the only one left. He was his own person and I admire that in anyone.'

As they walked back down the drive to the car, Cate stopped for a moment.

'Chris, I need a Detective Sergeant in Hereford and though Inspector Hannah will hate me for this, I would be very happy if you would consider accepting the post. You would have to pass your sergeant's exams first but for someone who can quote Larkin that will not be a problem.'

'Less of a problem than you might imagine, ma'am, as I've already passed them, more than a year ago. There was no poetry, but I scraped through anyway.'

'Ok, in which case I'll clear your promotion with my ACC. Because you will be appointed under me and I am away on attachment I shall specify that because of the situation you are having to put up with here, it would be best for you to join the team in Leamington Spa, and as soon as possible. It will also be good experience for you. But first we need to play a little game. Please say to me you wish to apply for the position of Detective Sergeant in West Mercia Police based in Hereford under you, ma'am.'

She did so exactly.

'In which case, I am pleased to inform you that your application has been successful.'

Chris was numb with amazement as they set off back for Boston and feared that at any moment she might drive off the road. For most of the way they talked about T S Eliot, and to Chris's relief it was Cate, not her, who pointed out that his name was an anagram for toilets!

When they arrived back at the Police Station, Cate received a strange text from Eamonn about making sure Robbie drove back which she didn't understand but would obey without question. Before she sat down with a welcome cup of tea and a conversation with Robbie and the team, she wrote a note for Chris asking her before she went home to send to her email a list of all those who were registered holders of shotguns in the past five years. Chris smiled and gave the tiniest of nods.

'Ok, good people,' she began, 'let's begin to draw things to a close. Robbie, what have you to report?'

'I'm big by most standards and I've played a great deal of rugby, but I still would not like to get on the wrong side of Mary Edmonds. She has a companion in the form of young Slovenian woman called Ljubica, who is also tough and very protective of her.

'I made the point several times that this was audit of an unsolved crime not a continuation of the investigation itself, but I'm not sure she took that in. When I asked about the investigation and how it had been carried out she had nothing detrimental to say and said that the Inspector here and his team had worked hard and done the right things, save in one regard, and that concerned the money that had been given to the woman Katarina Horvat whilst her husband was alive, her house in Heckington, near Grantham, and in his will, which she insisted had to be for the purposes of blackmail. She doesn't believe you have been into this anywhere near thoroughly enough.'

'That is not so,' said Connor, 'as you can read in my report.'

'I know,' said Cate. You could not have been more thorough in terms of working closely with the accountant, bank and solicitor. You and DS Hollioake did a very good job there, but we both know what happens where money is concerned. So very often it matters more than even the murder, though from what you say in your report Mrs Edmonds won't exactly be without.'

'She'll scrape by!'

'My report to the Chief Constable will stress that although the case remains unsolved, our audit has shown that every possible line has been explored by you and your team with one exception, and that is that no member of your team visited Bishop Auckland to interview Katarina Horvat in person, though I share your view that the likelihood of her having committed the crime is small – she was just the mistress of Marney Edmonds and took flight when she learned of his murder for fear, probably that she might be next, though that is pure speculation on my part. So, Inspector, have you anything you wish to say?'

'Perhaps, in retrospect, a visit to Bishop Auckland might have been desirable, but a small team such as ours has to balance that with the enormity of the murder investigation here, not helped by the officers of the Met encouraging Jo to an act of treachery and leaving us just two officers.'

'I undertake to make that point to the Chief Constable.'

'As for Mary Edmonds, I believe she measures life by the number of noughts she has in the bank, and no one will ever convince her that Marney had a young bit on the side, whom in fact he probably loved, long after he had stopped loving her. I now accept that this crime belongs with the others your team is trying to make sense of. It was made to look like work of locals but almost certainly was not. The three of us will, however, continue to keep our wits about us for anything that can be of assistance to you.'

'I'm sure you will, Inspector and thank you for that undertaking, though in fact it's not strictly true, the bit about the three of you, I mean. Probably unknown to you Detective Constable Halton applied for a position in the West Mercia Police Force and I have been able to deliver in person today the news that she has made a successful application, an appointment the ACC wishes her to take up as soon as possible to meet a shortfall.'

'Christine?' said Connor.

'It's an opportunity and a promotion I'm unlikely to get here, though I have learned ever so much from you, guv.'

'Oh, well there's nothing more to say.'

'Well, actually there is, Connor. Twice now you have failed to give women police officers the proper opportunity of promotion and greater responsibility which is why we in West Mercia have not asked you for a reference and account of her record, which would be the normal procedure. You have had two outstanding women officers working in your team and have failed to see what they could have offered the people of Boston simply because as women you regarded them as not essential to the task and therefore denied them the opportunities both have now received. In my audit report I shall be making this point strongly and urge your Chief Constable to ensure you have more, or at least, some diversity and leadership training. Do you even understand what I am saying, Inspector Hannah?'

'If you say so.'

'If you say so, ma'am.'

'Ma'am,' uttered Connor with clear contempt in his voice.

Making their farewells in the car park and commenting on the size of the Stump, Cate heard an email arrive on her phone, presumably the list of shotgun licence holders being sent by Chris.

'Will you drive, please, Robbie?'

'Of course. There seems to be something wrong with my mobile. The battery level is ok, but it's dead. Oh well, I don't suppose I shall need it on our way back to Leamington Spa.'

'No, but what I shall need is some food. I imagine we might get something in Grantham and if so, we shall pass Heckington en route where Katarina lived. What did you make of that?'

'I think a conversation with DS Hollioake might be in order.'

'Me too. Perhaps Hannah doesn't realise that Bishop Auckland where Katarina allegedly lives with her sister is in County Durham, where our DS now works "to be near his family".'

'Do tell me, Cate, what time was it when DC Christine Halton made her application to join West Mercia Police?'

'Oh, it was such a long time ago I cannot possibly be expected to remember.'

'Do you by any chance come from a family of sly old foxes?'

'Less of the old, inspector.'

'Yes, ma'am.'

'She's not a Jo, but then again, who is? But I think she will be very good indeed and deserves the chance to flourish in a way she will never get in Boston. Ah, look here's the sign for Heckington. Turn right and let's look.'

Cate had the address in her file.

'It's pretty ordinary but perhaps to a Slovenian it was the last word in luxury. Ok, let's get into Grantham and some food.'

They found Juliano's, a nice-looking Italian place, not yet busy and were quickly served their food.

'This is good,' said Cate.

'Yes, but tell me, is it a case of a condemned man's last meal?'

'What do you mean?'

'I'm happy for you to pretend for the time being, Cate, but I'll tell you exactly what I mean.'

Great Scot

'Suppose you were to commit a serious crime, Cate. Would you really want to be part of a team appointed to solve it? Yet, my team, the team I'm part of, and which therefore includes you, the one with arguably the clearest mind, has become convinced that this is what I have done, that I killed and tortured and beheaded someone whom I freely admit I detested for her views and utterances, because I spoke about my love for South Africa and for Chester Williams in particular, you all realised my motive for the murder, and then, I think you all stopped thinking. You've seen it happen before, Cate. It's an obvious and easy route through to the apparently intractable. So Eamonn sent Ellie and Jo up to Perth, and you and I to Boston. They have gone to investigate the horrendous possibility that a member of the team, our team, is a brutal murderer.

'I have seen today that as a senior police officer you are quite willing to break all the rules when it suits you in terms of not technically lying to DI Hannah about the appointment of DC Halton, but deliberately twisting reality to suit you. Isn't Eamonn doing exactly that by sending the lesbian twosome to investigate me without informing that he was doing so? I have not been placed under caution nor am I under investigation in the technical sense we now use of that term, and I seem to be now rendered out of communication with a lawyer or my federation rep, or anyone for that matter' who might be able to defend my interests when I am so far from home, because my phone has developed a mysterious fault.'

'Aren't you being paranoid, Robbie? You are respected and

already loved by every member of the team, not least for all you said about South Africa the other night which, speaking for myself, deeply moved me. You could hardly be expected to do an audit on yourself and your own team. Who else but Ellie and Jo could Eamonn send?'

'Oh for heaven's sake, Cate, get real. However much we pretended in Boston that we were doing audits, we were not, we were investigating, and that is what Ellie and Jo are there for – to investigate me. Knowing Jo's skills they won't need a warrant to enter my house, but perhaps Martin has arranged for them to collect one. If they do, they won't find anything though they will get something of a shock if they open the boot of my car. I didn't have time to clear it up properly but they will notice a deposit of blood and hair. In fact, it belongs to what remains of a fox I shot and carried in the car. No doubt they will get excited and call forensics. I wish I could be there to see their faces when they get the results.

'Otherwise, Cate, they will find nothing – of course not. I have been a police detective for a long time so do you think if I had done this terrible thing, I would leave them a blood stained axe and a signed confession on my dining table? I think not.

'And all I've got on my side, possibly, is the best detective in the force, whom, I hope, when she has wiped a piece of pasta off her bottom lip, will advise me as the best way to proceed, and I include the possibility that the said detective might want to arrest me.'

Cate sat silently for a while, watching Robbie finish his now cold spaghetti. Perhaps five minutes passed before she spoke.

'I have received nothing in the way of information or a report from anyone that would give me cause to detain you. If, for example, you were to ask me to drive you to the railway station here where you could catch a train to Edinburgh, where you might stay overnight before returning to Perth in the morning, then, as far as I'm concerned, you are wholly free to do that and, indeed, should do so. Being there to defend yourself is a fundamental right. However, Robbie, I can't do that until I have some tiramisu, so you'll just have to be patient.'

They smiled at one another.

It would be another 45 minutes before the next train to Edinburgh arrived but Cate decided to leave him at the station and continue her journey. Those who had worked with her throughout her career believed that at some stage in the past she must have done a three-month course in stubbornness with a mule-pack, and this was well known to barristers and even judges when she appeared in court. She always gave careful thought to any and every question, and on a famous occasion when a judge had said "Oh do get a move on, Inspector", she had turned towards him and with a look that could kill at thirty paces replied: "Are we here to serve justice or speed, judge? I will answer the question when I have given it the consideration it deserves". That judge always tried to avoid her subsequent appearances.

She had received no evidence of a crime having been committed by Robbie, but, unusually for her, she was also relying not just on that fact, but on her intuition. It wasn't just that she liked Robbie and knew how good he was at his work, she enjoyed his clarity of thinking.

She arrived back at the hotel at about 9:30 and before going to her room suspected that Martin and Eamonn would be in the bar and lounge. Eamonn went to get her a brandy and ginger.'

'I take it Robbie's gone straight to his room,' said Martin.

'Robbie? As far as I know he's not here.'

'His car's here.'

She nodded.

'Well, it will be. He was good today. I gave him the toughest tasks and he handled them ever so well, but so he should. I imagine he will be north of the border by now.'

'Cate, what have you done?'

'I did what every police officer should do: assume someone is innocent until they are proved guilty, but, sir, I would like you and Eamonn to listen to my account of a conversation we had in a restaurant in Grantham this evening, doing so remembering I have heard nothing whatsoever from Ellie and Jo today so I don't know what they have reported to you, nor had Robbie, not least because someone had stopped his Sim Card from working.'

She repeated all that Robbie had said in Grantham.

'So what is your evaluation of his account?'

'His intention is to return freely to Perth and defend himself against claims that he murdered Hoosen.'

'In which case I had better stop the convoy heading South and tell them to return, and that includes Ellie and Jo, as I want them there with him. Are we able to reach him?'

'I will have to go up to the office to undo the block on his Sim card. Do you want me to?'

'I'm sorry, Eamonn, but please do so. I'll call a halt to the cars. but it would be good for Ellie and Jo to liaise with Robbie, perhaps in Edinburgh and take him to Perth in the morning once he's convinced them as he's convinced you that he should be allowed the opportunity of self-defence.'

Martin took out his mobile and called Ellie and asked her to cancel the cars. She and Jo should head back towards Edinburgh and further instructions would be given in due course.

'Martin, you are a total tosser.'

'I think, Inspector, you mean "you are a total tosser, sir.'

She sniggered.

'So I do. Received.'

Cate rolled her eyes.

'Let's wait until morning before you let me know about Boston.'

'That's a good idea, especially when I tell you about the new member of the team I've appointed.'

Martin stared.

'Good night, Martin.'

Eamonn returned having restored and tested Robbie's phone and ascertained that he was about half an hour from Edinburgh Waverley.

Martin checked the Internet on his phone and quickly booked a single and a double room in the Travelodge, just north of Waverley station, in their own surnames only, no titles, and told them to meet up in the morning to talk before going back to

Perth, and he said he expected to see all three back in Leamington in the evening.

'You're putting a lot of faith in Cate, Martin,' said Eamonn.

'Yes, I know, but I happen to think she is very special so my faith is well-founded"

There was a pause.

'I hope.'

They looked at one another and burst out laughing.

Cate lay in bed, tired but wide awake, and wondering if somewhere north of the Border the person laughing there was called Robbie. It was as she had been undressing that she was struck for the first time since leaving the restaurant in Grantham that there could be no doubt that Robbie was the murderer of Jocelyn Hoosen.

She got out of her bed and turned on the kettle, making a cup of tea. In part she was disappointed with herself as she prided herself on never being duped by the lies of a criminal. She could only put it down to stupidly relying on what she had felt was her intuition instead of the straightforward logic of her mind's normal functioning. Well now she had to use that mind.

She picked up her phone and called Jo. It rang a couple of times.

'Cate, you do know what time it is in Edinburgh, don't you?'

'Please listen, Jo, and put in on speaker so Ellie can hear as well.'

'Ok.'

'But first tell me what you found.'

Jo recounted all that they had discovered at Robbie's house including the blood and hair in his car which forensics said belonged to a fox, plus an axe supposedly hidden but which could barely chop wood into sticks, containers used for making chloroform left in a prominent position, and elsewhere CCTV which showed him entering a room where Propofol was stored and easily accessible, plus a conversation with a DC who heard Robbie shout in a violent rant that Hoosen should be hanged, drawn and quartered.

'He is in Edinburgh tonight aiming to return to Perth in the morning, or should I say, later this morning, ostensibly to defend himself, but be prepared to face accusations that he is being framed, and possibly by you two who have set everything up.'

'And is this what, Cate, you have woken us up at this ungodly hour, to tell us?'

'Do you mean you had already worked it out?'

'Of course we hadn't, but we felt yesterday,' said Jo, 'the very real possibility that that we were being played in a game with a double bluff. In the morning we are planning to give every indication that we shall support him all the way but ensure he is handed over to the investigations of his superiors. We shall drive him up to Perth and chat normally, hearing about your day in beautiful Boston. Any further on, by the way?'

'This is not the time to talk about Boston. You need some sleep.'

'You're right, though I can't quite remember who it was who called and woke us up. Can you, Ellie? No? Thought not. Night night, Cate, dear.'

It was at about the same time that Martin woke up and was also wondering what he should do. It was an act of cruelty, he knew, but as her phone was engaged, he went and knocked on her door.

'Put your clothes on, Cate, and meet me downstairs in ten minutes.'

Cate was about to object to Martin, when she realised that it was her Superintendent, and he had given her an order, without the word "please". She thought she knew what was coming and when she reached the lobby he was already by the door, and soon in his car, and still without having said a word.

'Can you let Warwickshire and Leicestershire know we shall be travelling with blue lights and once on the motorway keep us ahead of the game with each force?'

'Of course.'

In a way it was a compliment that he didn't need to tell her what was happening because he assumed, quite rightly as it happened, that she knew and understood. Once on the M1 he did not travel at less than 100 mph and although she was very tired, she was enjoying this, though she did wonder what he would do when they reached Northumberland and the motorway ended.

'I want us there before Ellie and Jo arrive with him. I want to talk to their Super before the questioning and answering begins, so as we get a little nearer, I shall need you to get him for me, even if it involves getting Eamonn out of bed up to the office to get his home number.'

By 7:00 am they were already well into Scotland. Martin had turned off the motorway near Darlington onto the A68, which runs up through the heart of Durham and Northumberland, but had mostly not lessened his speed, and Cate had discovered that when you went on the radio and announced to a local force that an unmarked car with blue lights containing a Detective Superintendent and a DCI, they were happy to acknowledge and oblige!

By 8:00 they were on the A720 Edinburgh by-pass heading for the A90, across the Forth Bridge and then on to the M90 towards Perth. Martin asked Cate to call the Detective Superintendent in Perth and leave it on the hands-free.

'Good morning Superintendent, this is Superintendent Martin Peabody heading the inquiry into the four brutal murders of which you have one in Comrie. I have travelled up during the night from England to see you before two of my officers bring in Detective Inspector Robbie Douglas. You will have to take it from me as I travel up the M90 at high speed that it's vital we speak before the others arrive.'

'I'll be here but I'm a bit confused.'

I'll try to explain when I'm with you.'

'I was just thinking that we should perhaps have come in two cars,' said Cate to Eamonn,' one of us bringing Robbie's car which is parked outside the hotel.'

'What did you say?'

'Robbie's car – it's outside the hotel.'

'Yes, it is, and I bet that's where he wants it to be, far from Perth. Please can you get me Derrick Blowes at Warwickshire Police HQ?

'Good morning, Martin, how can I help you?'

'I can't go into details now, Derrick, as I'm in the middle of something that might lead us to killer number IV, but outside our hotel there is a large dark blue Mazda CX–5. It needs to be isolated at once and taken away for a forensic examination, especially of the boot and folding seats area. I can't stress how important this is, Derrick. Can anything found be phoned through to me? The whole team apart from Eamonn is up here with me and the car could well contain evidence which could convict a killer.'

'Received.'

'Surely he wouldn't have done that – leave the car he used under our noses?'

'He'll have cleaned it, I'm sure, but we both know that only very rarely does that get rid of all the traces of evidence. Ah, the turning for Perth and I reckon we'll be ahead of them.'

Ellie insisted that it was Cate who had brought reason to bear when she enabled Robbie to catch the train in Grantham.

'Even with seasoned police officers we can get things somewhat distorted. She was clear that we should meet you and take you up to Perth so you can deal with the claims that have been made, some of them, I regret to say, by us.'

'Aye, well that's the whole point when you are being framed. That's why they are so accomplished at doing the things that make you look bad,' he replied.

'I'm dying to know how you got on in my old stomping ground, said Jo. Did you solve the case?'

'No, but Cate has one or two ideas to do with the Slovenian woman who was the mistress of Marney Edmonds and expressed concern that she hadn't been interviewed face to face.'

'We spoke on the phone a number of times, if I remember rightly.'

'I also had to go out onto the fen to interview the widow, Mary Edmonds. What I wanted to say to her was that if she took a long look at herself, she might discover why her husband not just had a fancy woman but siphoned off so much to her. The money was all she seemed to regard as important, far more that the murder.'

'Then something happened that will ring bells for you. Whilst I was out on the fen, Cate went out to the scene of the discovery of the body.'

'In Midville, which doesn't actually exist.'

'And then on to where the landrover was found in a place called Wainfleet St Mary. Cate found this most odd and thinks we should be going to see DS Graham Hollioake as he has transferred to Durham. She thought his finding of the vehicle was suspicious. She has been driven everywhere by a woman DC whom, I suppose had been your replacement. She's called Christine Halton. When they arrived back Cate revealed that Christine had applied for a new job as a DS in West Mercia and was able to announce that she had been appointed. Because she is appointed to Cate, that means she will be joining our team until Cate leaves.'

'Well, well, well,' said Ellie, 'lightning obviously can strike twice in the same place.'

'Yeah, well if you ever worked for Connor Hannah, you'd understand why, the old misogynist. Now then Robbie, guide me to the police station.'

Offside at the Back of the Line

The three officers walked into the Police Station and a couple of constables waved a silent greeting to Robbie as he continued his way to his office, the door of which he discovered locked.

'And I haven't got my keys; they'll be at home. As I imagine you've both been there, could one of you please go and bring them to me? I expect you've seen them.'

Neither spoke. The voice that broke the silence was an unexpected one.

'Good morning, Inspector Douglas,' said Martin. 'Please can you come with me as your commanding officer?'

Martin led Robbie down a corridor with which we he was more than familiar and into an interview room where three men were awaiting his arrival. The first was the Detective Superintendent, Jock Reeman, under whom he had worked for many years; the second, Paul McFadden, a solicitor he knew well, but the third was unknown to him.

'This is Superintendent Adam MacCaig from Edinburgh where he is head of Professional Standards.'

They all sat and Reeman turned on the recording tapes with their familiar long drone.

'DI Douglas, at the moment you are neither under arrest nor have you been cautioned as we understand you have returned to Perth to claim that you have been deliberately set-up by others to give the appearance that you unlawfully killed Jocelyn Hoosen. You are therefore here in a voluntary capacity. Is our understanding correct?'

'Yes, sir.'

'Go on then.'

'What do you mean?'

'What matters DI Douglas, is what you mean. Give us the evidence for your claim.'

'I can't possibly be expected to do that if I am not given the evidence that is allegedly being given against me.'

'I think the time has come,' said Superintendent MacCaig, 'to place you under caution. As you know that is not the same as arrest.'

Jock Reeman issued the caution.

'Now you are under caution, DI Douglas,' said Reeman, 'Can you confirm for us and for the tape that not only have those responsible for the killing of Jocelyn Hoosen conspired to make it appear that you were the killer, but that this has been a conspiracy by police officers here in Perth and in Leamington Spa where you are currently attached. Are you able to account for the conspiracy by your fellow police officers?'

'No, sir, but it is nevertheless so.'

'How much had you told the team about your investigation into the death of Ms Hoosen. For example, had you told them, as you did a detective constable of this force that you thought she should be hanged, drawn and quartered?'

'That was a regrettable outburst following a radio report of a speech she had made.'

'Well, in point of fact,' said Jock, 'your fellow-officers went to Blairgowrie Cottage Hospital but do you know why?'

Douglas said nothing.

'Because the Senior Pathologist of the Dundee and Perth Hospitals suggested to them that there might be a bottle of Propofol in a cupboard which indeed there was the doctor they spoke to could not understand why the seal had been broken and some removed before being replaced. They were also given access to CCTV camera tapes which clearly showed you entering the treatment room where the Propofol was stored and returning there on the day after the murder.'

'Time and again, sir, we have been shown in court how unreliable evidence from CCTV can be.'

'You're quite right, Inspector, but even the best lawyers cannot evade the fact of someone 6 foot 6 inches tall. So can you account these two visits?'

'I made only one following a reported break-in I was investigating.'

'What remarkable police force we must be that we can send a Detective Inspector to investigate a suspected break-in, especially when you asked the detective constable accompanying you to remain in the car, and in whose presence you had just in a furious rage in response to a news item on the radio shouted that Hoosen should be hanged, drawn and quartered.'

'I do not deny that I hated the woman intensely, much as I hate the England rugby team intensely, but I have no plans to murder them either.'

'The pathologist told the detectives, your colleagues, remember, that one way of causing immediate loss of consciousness which might allow the administration of another drug, such as for example, Propofol, would be to use Trichloromethane – Chloroform to you and me. In your garage which they entered with a warrant, they found equipment for making chloroform which you would presumably maintain was placed there deliberately to incriminate you.'

'Yes, sir, I would.

'The method there tallies exactly with instructions on the internet.'

'And it is likely that I am the only person in Scotland with the internet so that it could only have been I who saw and used this?'

'Subsequent search of your hard drive found that this page on the web had been used by you before the date of Hoosen's death but are you wanting us to believe that this was deliberately placed on your hard drive to incriminate you in anticipation of the event?

'No comment.'

'Robbie,' said Martin, 'our whole team so admired you when you spoke to us about your passion for South Africa, for the late Chester Williams who became your close friend, and for South African rugby. We loved hearing you talk about your visit to

Japan and the World Cup Final. With such a love and passion for those for whom you care so much, and knowing that a woman who lived within a few miles of you epitomised everything you despised in the way she encouraged racism, can you understand how we might begin to wonder whether in another burst of feeling such as characterised your outburst in Blairgowrie you might have decided to end her appalling diatribes once and for all?'

'Yes, I can understand why you might erroneously think that, but thinking something is not evidence and so far, you have not produced any evidence for what you think.'

'My client should now have a break, gentlemen,' said the solicitor. Are you wishing to charge him with some offence? If not, he is here in a voluntary capacity and therefore should be allowed to assume his freedom.'

Superintendent MacCaig stood.

'Robert Henry Douglas, I am arresting you in connection with the handling of dangerous substances likely to cause death or harm, you do not have to say anything, but, it may harm your defence if you do not mention when questioned something which you later rely on in court. Anything you do say may be given in evidence. You will be given a break and lunch but you will be brought back for further questioning later.'

Martin wandered outside. He was dog-tired and beginning to wonder whether he should allow the team to remain in Scotland for a good night's sleep, returning home tomorrow. He and Cate must. Outside were Jo and Cate chatting cheerfully to one another. Martin moved towards them.

'How's it going?' asked Ellie.

'I think it could end quite quickly if Derrick came back to me with positive news. He's being held on handling dangerous substances, namely Propofol and the results of his prints was unequivocal. In terms of circumstantial evidence, we have a good deal, mainly gathered by you two but we need more.'

'Do you think he did it?'

'I have no doubts about that and to a certain extent I can even sympathise. You may recall when he joined us we weren't altogether convinced he was up to it, but we now know that Robbie is a very clever man and his capacity for bluff and double bluff is considerable. It takes something special to mislead Cate Greene, but he managed it. Look, dear ladies, I can't have you two just frolicking the day away. Unlike Cate and I you've been to bed last night. There's no reason for you to be here any further, so why not head off home and take Cate with you. If I'm finished, I'll stay here in Perth at the Holiday Inn and return tomorrow.'

'Good idea, said Ellie, 'though the lady on my left has an idea we might just check out before we leave.'

'Go on.'

'Just before lunch I was talking to the DC who told me about the trip to the Cottage Hospital at Blairgowrie, and he happened to mention that all this was very sad for Robbie. He'd lost his close South African friend Chester, then his aunt to whom he was also very close had died and now this. I assumed great sympathy and asked about the aunt and found she lived in a tiny village called Tibbermore, just four miles from here and who was caretaker of the local church which is now closed other than for the very occasional wedding and funeral. I wondered whether we might take the scenic route back to Leamington and visit her house and the Church.'

'Find Cate and go.'

As their car drove away, Martin's phone rang. It was Derrick.

'I'll give you the bad news first. The car had been recently valeted, but the good news is that it may well have been valeted by a bunch of cowboys and in the circumstances probably had to be well-paid cowboys who were encouraged thereby to forget him. Forensics have taken it apart this morning and have found hair and congealed blood in the joins of the boot and rear seats, blood that is of the same group of your victim – O+. Obviously further tests will have to be done including DNA and somehow that will have to be organised, presumably someone from here going to the Forensic labs in Scotland, but it's pretty damning, I would say.'

Derrick, you're a genius, and the next time we have a team

curry, you'll be guest of honour.'

'I expect that means I shall have to pay.'

'That's very kind of you, sir. I'll inform the team. Oh, by the way, we have a new member of the team on the way, from Lincolnshire via West Mercia, a DC working for a misogynist who the West Mercia ACC is promoting to DS as soon as she arrives. She passed her exams more than a year ago.'

'She'll be very welcome.'

Whilst he was on the phone, he saw Jock come out for a cigarette and went towards him.

'Not good for you, Jock.'

'Yeah, my doc says I should stop or else I might stop altogether, but having to deal with an issue like this makes me wonder if that wouldn't be preferable. He was such a good detective.'

'Am I to conclude that you think he's guilty?'

'Of course. I've known him a long time and I used to watch him play rugby before that. He was good second row even if given to the odd foul play he hoped to get away with and almost always did. Do you recall the famous Andy Haden in the match between the All Blacks and Wales when, worthy of an Oscar, he fell as if he had been pushed and they got a penalty which won them the match? Robbie must have taught him!'

'He's very clever. However, our boss, the Warwickshire DCC has just called to report that a forensic examination of Robbie's car in Leamington has found significant amounts of hair and blood which had not been moved when he had the car valeted. It's the same blood group as Hoosen's. And I'm now waiting to hear from three of my team who are pursuing a possible location for the killing and beheading, one not considered before, when Robbie was running the case, but to which he had access.'

'Did you mean what said earlier, about having sympathy for him if he had done it?'

'Yes, I did. I've seen her on YouTube and I found her repulsive and disgusting but unfortunately we can't destroy people with whom we disagree no matter how awful they are. After all, if perhaps he had met with her and tried to convince her just how wrong she was, it might not have been necessary to cut her head off.'

'I doubt it, but you may be right. Come on then, let's get it done.'

Robbie was brought into the interview room with his solicitor and opposite him the same team as before.

'Well, gentlemen, I very much hope you have had sufficient time to realise that you have no evidence against me other than that I foolishly moved a bottle of anaesthetic and replaced it, which as far as I know is not the sort of offence you can realistically hold me for.'

'You left behind in Leamington Spa the motor car you came down in, a long-term hire car, I believe,' said Martin. 'Behind your house here in Perth, I am informed you have another car which you own, a rather swish car covered in a tarpaulin and apparently smelling of dead fox. Why did you not come in your own car?'

'What does it matter which car I came in?'

'Is your own car experiencing difficulties?'

'No.'

'Yet the records in the garage here in Perth show that you took out a long-term hire some time ago, before you came to Leamington, before Jocelyn Hoosen was murdered. I'm interested to know why.'

'Why not. That is what I chose to do. I have no other calls upon my income as a single man and I can do with it as I choose.'

'Some time recently you had the car valeted. Yes?'

'Yes.'

'This morning in Warwick, that car was taken apart by the forensic team, and in the area between boot and rear seats, they discovered that those you paid for the valeting should return your money. They discovered hair and a considerable amount of congealed blood of the same group as Jocelyn Hooson. Can you account for that, Detective Inspector?'

'I don't know how it got there.'

'We are now talking about material evidence,' said MacCaig, ' I would judge that you're in serious trouble which you might make a little easier for yourself by telling us the full story.'

Martin's phone rang and he could see that it was Cate calling.

'Yes, DCI Greene.'

'It's DS Enright, she's got to go, sir. She's far too clever and shows the rest of us up.'

'Tell me.'

'In the house we found nothing other than the key of the Church, which is more or less redundant. Inside we found a lot of dried blood and what seems to be pieces of bone and hair and minute pieces of clothing, and a pot of black paint and a brush. There can be little or no doubt that the murder took place here and when we returned to the house and rummaged about, we found in the coal bunker what we feel may be the axe that was used. I could see nothing on it but I imagine forensics will look closer than me.'

'I know you will be keen to get back to Leamington, Cate, but please will you wait for the arrival of the forensic team? Once you have signed off with them, please tell Miss Smarty Pants to drive the three of you home.'

'Received.'

'Jock, as a matter of considerable urgency will you please arrange for a forensic team to proceed to the village of Tibbermore, and there to liaise with DCI Greene and two other members of my team and ask them to focus upon the house of the former caretaker of the Church (now probably owned by Robert Henry Douglas, the nephew of the late lady), but more especially on the village Church where the team has found all the evidence of a serious crime having been committed.'

Jock stood, stared at Douglas.

'Robert Henry Douglas, you will now be remanded in custody and I shall make application to the Procurator Fiscal to charge you with the murder of Jocelyn Hoosen of Comrie in Perthshire.'

'Robbie, this is so stupid,' said Martin. 'I really do want to cry. You are a far better man than this and I shall do my best to enable Mrs Williams to come from South Africa to speak on your behalf,' said Martin.

Jock left the room and returned with two uniformed officers, one of whom handcuffed Robbie as he stood. Before leaving the room, Robbie turned to Martin.

'Thank you for what you just said to me, sir, they are probably the words I shall need to hang on to most in the following months.'

He was taken from the room.

'There are no winners in a case like this,' said Jock.

'You're quite right,' echoed MacCaig, 'in fact I'm not sure why I do my job, except it's a great feeling when we're able to find someone wholly innocent.'

'Well, all I want to do,' said Martin, 'is sleep, which I haven't done for a long time having driven up through the night. There's a Holiday Inn somewhere here and although in my experience they're not the sort of holiday I would choose, I'll go there and have a very early night.'

'No you won't,' said MacCaig. 'Have you got it in you to drive down the M9 just as far as the outskirts of Edinburgh? If you have I insist you come and stay with Megan and me. I have a good single malt which after one of Megan's meals will send you off to Slumberland and you can make a good start in the morning.'

'I've had one of Megan's meals, Martin. Don't even consider refusing, said Jock.'

'I'm not, I can assure you. Lead on MacCaig.'

Martin was underway by 9:30 on the following morning. He had greatly enjoyed the company of Megan and Adam and, despite the day that they had just endured, they laughed a great deal, not least at a recording of Michael McIntyre at his dentist. Now he found himself thinking that there might be one down, but there were still three to go, and the terrible realisation that Robbie had cut the IV into the back of his victims because he had seen all about numbers I to III on the Police Holmes 3 computer. He desperately hoped that the others were not the same and all perpetrated by police officers.

He called through on his hands-free phone to Cate and

discovered they were still together at the breakfast table.

'Ah, well please inform them that you can all take off the next few days, until Monday. Could you please call Derrick and let him know that we have solved number IV. I must also give thought to bringing someone else into the team, a man preferably to take Robbie's place.'

'No, Martin, you need to find the best person for the job, regardless of their gender.'

'You listen to me, Detective Chief Inspector Greene, I am already outnumbered and for the sake of operations and my sanity, we need a man, I need a man.'

'Don't we all, sir. Oh, I've already spoken to Derrick and he offers his congratulations. Drive safely and we'll probably all see you on Sunday evening.'

Ahead of him lay not only miles and miles of tarmac, but the writing of a long report which would not be easy (however would he explain away the fact that he selected as a team member the person who had committed one of the murders they were meant to be investigating?). It did occur to him that when ACPO learned of this they would want him replaced. He would understand if they did and could think of no one better to lead the team than Cate Greene though it ought to be Jo Enright! He smiled to himself.

A Matter of Licence

The team gathered on the Sunday evening in Bill's, the restaurant nearest to the hotel and each was eager to hear what the others had been up to in the recovery period after the events in Scotland. Jo had gone by train from Nottingham to Norwich to visit her parents where she had been joined a day later by Ellie which occasioned astonishment and great amusement in the Enright household, but which gave way to a joyous time together and Mrs Enright telling Ellie she was always welcome, and not just when Jo was here! Jo said she was extremely proud of her mum and dad, not least when her dad had said to his daughter about her black lesbian partner "I have to admit I did rather fancy her myself". The others were convulsed with laughter.

Cate had returned to Hereford and enjoyed the longest sleep she had ever known, from 9:00 pm to 3:00 pm on the following day.

'I might still be asleep now had it not been for a phone call from my good friend the ACC to say she had received a complaint from the CC of the Lincolnshire Force that I had attempted to poach one of his officers. She was laughing as she said this and fortunately, I had already emailed her with the info on Christine, pointing out that she had applied for the job (which, believe you me, she had done, not least because I told her to apply in person when I was with her) and properly appointed by me to work under me as my bagman. The ACC, who is in no small part responsible for the existence of our team, reported this to the CC, and then said that I was intending to make a formal complaint about the level of misogyny in Boston Police Station, and that as a result of the audit there were a number of important matters that needed to be addressed in the way in the investigation had been carried out. She said that all this had come as news to the man, who there and then gave his consent to the transfer of Chris Halton.'

'Oh, please promise me, Cate,' said Jo, 'that if ever I get into trouble you'll be on my side.'

'You're the last person in the world who would need my help, Jo.'

'But the most important thing she said was that you, Martin, had done an outstanding job leading the team to solving the Scottish murder, especially given that the perpetrator had managed to get himself incorporated into the team. She and Derrick have kept in close touch. So that has been my holiday though I also saw some friends and once got very drunk with a couple I was seeing for an evening and had to stay over. It did me the world of good.'

The others were all laughing.

'Anyway, my bagman arrives in two days' time.'

'That's great, Cate (apologies for the unforeseen rhyme)', said Martin.

'So boss, what have you been up to?' asked Ellie, with great affection in her voice.

'Well, after I returned from a pleasant night with the head of Scottish Professional Standards and his delightful wife, I came back here to work on the report, and half-way through received a call from Jock, the Super, to say that Robbie had requested an interview, in the course of which he made a full confession and indicated that he intended to plead not-guilty to murder but guilty of manslaughter on the grounds of diminished responsibility, and though you may not agree, I very much hope he is successful in that. I know what he did was terrible in the extreme, and that to cover it up he applied his considerable intelligence to the art of lying and deceit, but I liked him.'

There was a murmur of agreement.

'His full confession made writing the report a little easier. Since then, my holiday consisted of some days with MI5 in

London, staying with Eamonn and Marie and their children. I wanted some lowdown on XR and Animal Rights extremists just in case that's what we are dealing with in Kate's territory, although I suspect I mean Wales.'

'I would agree with you, Martin,' said Cate.

'But I did at least get to The Globe and saw Richard II. They were doing Titus Andronicus on the following night but I decided I'd had enough gore for one week.'

'A wise decision, if I may say so.'

'Eamonn will be back by lunchtime tomorrow and Christine by Wednesday. For operational reasons we also need another male member of the team and Derrick has suggested we take a look at DS Bobi Jones, who though he works here is a Welshman by birth and a Welsh speaker.'

'And presumably named by poetic parents after the great Welsh academic and cultural historian, added Cate.

'I was just about to say that.'

'Liar!' they said in unison.

'The truth, Martin, is that you're not cut out for a life of crime and deceit,' said Ellie.'

'Or poetic licence,' said Cate.

'What is he doing at the present?' asked Jo.

'He's been working for Professional Standards.'

'That may come in useful when we pay a visit to Durham,' said Cate.'

'Durham? Why Durham?' said Ellie.'

'I think I can guess,' said Jo.

'Be quiet, sergeant and let the rest of us play,' said her lover who leant over and kissed her.'

'Ok, ma'am, I will wait until Cate is ready to tell us tomorrow morning.'

'Notwithstanding the guessing game, Bobi will be joining us in the morning.'

In Boston, Connor Hannah was not a happy man. Not only was he losing a member of his team which would leave him having to cover more of the drudge work the junior CID officer had to deal with, but he had received a call from the Chief Constable on Friday who in turn had received a call from the ACC of West Mercia, who had the reputation of one not to be messed with. The CC pointed out that the DC had applied for the job in a proper way, not least because she was no longer wishing to accept the misogynist ethos of the Boston station. He was also aware that the audit was drawing attention to serious shortcomings in the investigations into the murder of Emmanuel Edmonds in which an important lead had not been followed. He told Connor that he would be required to attend a diversity course and that thought was being given to bringing in a new DCI as his mentor. He was not a happy bunny and he knew whose fault it was and she would feel his wrath on Monday morning, which the CC had told him was to be her last day.

All these thoughts were going through his mind as he drove through the drizzle to the station. He had always believed women were not equipped to be detectives. It was all very well being a smarty-pants like Enright but detection was a slow and steady gathering of evidence, not making mighty leaps of imagination as she had done and attracted the attention of the Met who had then claimed her. It must be grim for good men at the Met having to work with a Commissioner who was nothing more than a lesbian dwarf and whose judgement had been found seriously lacking in the past causing a tragic and wholly unnecessary loss of life on a underground train. The only masculine thing about her was her name: Dick.

He parked the car and went in barely muttering a greeting to the desk sergeant who was quite used to the old misery.

He entered his office and glared at the two waiting for him by his desk.

'Haven't you two got better things to do?'

'We were simply wondering if you've heard back from the audit,' said DS Stancliffe.

'Why don't you just ask Chief Superintendent Halton? I imagine the Chief Constable informed her first.'

She neither replied nor even blinked at the sarcasm, catching Connor off-guard.

'Er, well, on the whole it was positive, as DCI Greene indicated before she left with the exception of our not following up in person rather than on the phone, the matter of Katarina Horvat. Do they think we have an unlimited budget, and there is simply no way that on-the-make hussy could have had any involvement in Marney's murder, so I'm intending to let sleeping dogs lie and let the wonder squad sort it, and did you read about it, how one of the murders has been solved because it was done by one of their own team? What kind of tossers are they, trying to tell us how to run an investigation, when they clearly couldn't organise a piss up in a brewery? So much for having Miss Mastermind Enright in the team.'

'You really don't like women, do you,' said Chris, 'and especially if they have skin the colour of mine.'

'That's ridiculous. Get out and do some work. I want you to call and see the Vicar of St Nicholas, Skirbeck who's reported a theft of something trivial from his church.'

'Gladly,'

She stood, smiled at Nigel Stancliffe and left.

'Traitorous scheming bitch,' muttered Connor.

The door opened again.

'Traitorous and scheming are more or less tautologous,' said Chris. 'One word would do.'

She went out, collected everything that was hers from her office, carrying them out to her car. She came back into the building and went round some colleagues and made her farewells. The desk sergeant, whom she liked very much was more than sympathetic.

'Good luck in the west, Chris. All but one of us will miss you. We've enjoyed working with you and know you have a very bright future.'

'Thanks Sarge. That means a great deal. I'm sick of him and so I'm going sick on my final day.'

'In which case I give my consent.'

She kissed him, which made his day.

At his meeting on Monday morning, Martin was surrounded

by women, and only breathed (a totally false) sign of relief when the office door opened and in came Derrick Blowes – in uniform. Instinctively, the whole team stood.

'As you were,' said Derrick, and behind him was a man with very curly black hair, wearing a grey suit and looking almost shy.

The team sat down and Derrick proceeded to introduce them to their new colleague.

'This is Detective Sergeant Bobi Jones, not the American golfer, but until Friday last was a member of the Professional Standards Team. If you wish to be rude about him, don't say it in Welsh, as I gather he is fluent in his native tongue.'

Bobi came and shook hands with them all.

'You are extremely welcome to the team,' said Martin. 'Your arrival is timely in that today we have to decide which target we are going to throw ourselves towards next. Later, we shall be re-joined by Eamonn, our computer expert from the Security Service and on Wednesday by another new team member, Detective Sergeant Christine Halton who will, technically, be working to DCI Greene who recruited her last week, as her bagman, but in practice will just be another member of the team.

'We don't distinguish between ranks and we use our own names to speak of and to one another. Isn't that correct, Derrick?

'From the standpoint of an observer I think it works very well but I wouldn't recommend it if the Chief Constable decides to drop in.'

'Do try to deter him,' said Ellie, to general amusement.

'It's hard guys, to decide whether what happened in Scotland, was a good thing or a bad thing. We solved the fourth murder and brought someone to justice, but that someone was not just a fellow police officer, but a fellow member of this team.'

'It was a regrettable occurrence, Martin,' said Derrick, 'but the important thing is that you dealt with it in double quick time. I'm sorry and sad for Robbie as well. I guess all of us can imagine how even within each one of us passion can lead to anger and a regrettable chain of circumstance. If I had the friendships and contacts with South Africans that Robbie had and had to listen to that woman disseminating hatred as she did, who knows how I might have reacted too.'

'I have spoken to the widow of Chester Williams,' said Martin, 'that great South African wing and Robbie's closest friend, and she has said she will come to Edinburgh for his trial and speak on his behalf to the court, which is wonderful. She is such a nice and dignified lady.

'Ok, let's get down to business. We exist for one purpose and that is to do ourselves out of a job by solving the remaining three brutal murders – in London, in Boston, and in Herefordshire. So which is it to be? Last night, Cate, you uttered a name we haven't given any thought to, so now's your chance to tell us all about the city of Durham.'

'It's the county of Durham rather than the city we need to be thinking about. When Marney Edmonds was murdered, it was soon discovered that he had been paying large sums of money, and I mean large, for three years to a Slovenian woman in a village called Heckington, near Grantham. He bought her a house and provided a healthy income for her. He visited her a number of evenings a week and managed to keep it a secret as far as we can tell. The neighbours were very useful for telling Jo how often he was parked outside.'

'Indeed they were,' added Jo. 'It was as if all the Lincolnshire gossips had been gathered into one place and I genuinely believe that if even one of them had known where Katarina went on those evenings out by herself, they would all have known and told. Of course, I left soon after and wasn't able to see it through and Graham Hollioake took it over.'

'Katarina left Heckington once she learned the news of Marney's death and claimed to be in Bishop Auckland with her sister. Marney's will served her well and of course the house in her name was sold, and she received the proceeds,' continued Cate. 'She is now a wealthy woman which she could hardly have expected to be had she stayed in Slovenia.'

'Was Katarina a suspect? She certainly had the motive,' said Bobi.

'Oh yes, but it didn't make sense. She was already on to a good thing and there seemed no way that a woman could have done to Marney what happened to him and manipulated his much larger frame, nor could we understand how she might possibly have known Midville, which doesn't actually exist except in name, have known how well concealed his landrover would be in the Churchyard of Wainfleet St Mary, nor that fen farmers committing suicide tie themselves to a fencepost before throwing themselves in a river.'

'I can see the logic of that,' said Martin.

'Nor was it conceivable that she would be able to hire a killer to do it for her, and in any case, he would have had to be a local person too.'

'So, tell us why Durham,' said Martin.

'It's quite simple really,' said Jo. 'After I moved to the Met, Graham Hollioake also decided he wanted a transfer or early retirement. His reason was that he had come to hate living in the flat Fens and wished to move nearer to his family in the Northeast. He said Newcastle on his official application, but in point of fact he is living in County Durham.'

'Oh sweet Jesus,' uttered Martin, 'please not let less this be another murder by a police officer.'

'I persuaded the officer joining the team on Wednesday to print off for me a list of licensed shot-gun holders for the last five years', said Cate, 'and I regret very much having to report the presence on the list of one Graham Hollioake, occupation: police officer.'

'Is the woman Katarina living with Hollioake?' asked Bobi.

'I don't know.'

'In which case I would have thought we need to find that out, but in any case, arrange to visit and interview them face-to-face,' continued Bobi.

'Yes,' added Ellie, and I would therefore like to suggest that is where we start again now our holiday is over.'

I didn't get a holiday,' said Bobi with a huge grin, 'I came straight from writing a report yesterday morning to here.'

'I think you'll find that life in our team is one long holiday,' continued Ellie.

The others almost passed out in their paroxysms of laughter.

'Ok, maybe not,' Ellie concluded.

'Eamonn will be back after lunch, especially so if you Jo, can go and pick him up at the railway station. I know it's not far but you're best placed to brief him on this, so that when he gets here, he lands running.'

'Received.'

'Bobi, I want you to immerse yourself in Kate's murder in Herefordshire. Read her superb reports, talk with her, and discover all you can about those who will have most benefitted from Tony Hendry's death in terms of his competitors. I've been talking to MI5 about the animal people, but we mustn't overlook the possibility that the manner of his death was deliberately staged to look like their work. At the moment I can't see much point in your being involved with Durham and Boston, but if you think it would help to go to Builth Wells to pursue matters, then wait until Wednesday and go with Chris when she arrives, and perhaps, Cate, you can find out when we can expect her.'

'I'll call her later when she's finished her final day with Inspector Hannah. She'll be here early enough for Bobi and her to get going in good time.'

'The rest of us must focus on Durham. Let's have a look at Hollioake's record and find out anything we can about Katarina Arvot. I was about to say that I find it hard to believe a police officer could kill anyone in the way that Marney Holden was killed until I remembered Robbie.'

'"If you can keep your head when all about you
   Are losing theirs and blaming it on you ..."' recited Cate.

'An unfortunate quote, I think, Cate, and it's on that subject that you and I need a conversation and I need a coffee up the road to accompany it, so let's go.'

The disappearance of team members at various times was so common that it was always a matter of indifference to the others. People had a task, and any given to others was not of concern of them. That was the discipline the police shared with the armed forces and groups such the Security Services and the ethos was knocked into them at a very early stage of their initial training:

"Do what you are asked to do and leave others to do likewise".

It was a bitterly cold day with a wind coming straight from the Urals (not the urinals as Cate had once heard someone say) and both were properly dressed for the elements. They entered the shop and gave their order.

'You have a fantastic taste in clothes, Cate. Not just that coat which I admire greatly, but all you wear. How do you do it living in Hereford?'

'Brum's not so far away, but more and more I do it online. It's always a bit of a risk but most companies are more than happy to exchange and provide ready-paid labels. And of course, I'm single, well-paid and have no children, so I can be as selfish as I wish.'

The coffees arrived.

'Ok. I'll cut to the chase. Would you be willing to take over the leadership of the team?'

'What? I thought you said you're enjoying the support of those above you.'

'I'm sure there have been times when you've known a copper do something foolish, perhaps something quite serious, and when you've spoken to them and offered them a second chance, you nevertheless felt inside that you might be making a mistake.'

'Yes.'

'Well, I feel that's what's happened to me. I brought Robbie into the team, no one else did, and I made a monumental error of judgement. Derrick has been very gracious as you would expect and as a sincere Christian is more than ready to forgive a repentant sinner. But your ACC, Dani Thomas, is much more of a pragmatist. In the upper reaches of ACPO it is well know that she lay behind the setting up of our team, and what has happened inevitably reflects badly on her judgement in appointing me to lead it. Derrick is here and a good man, but in effect, just as you do, I recognise her as my boss.'

'I can see that, but she's good and fair and supports her people.'

'I have no doubts about that. Nevertheless she called me at 7:00 this morning telling me that she had received an offer from Greater Manchester Police for me to head up Vice. It wasn't an offer, you understand.'

'Oh, Martin, I'm so sorry. That's really bad. We need you much more than they do. And who will she put in your place. It could change the whole ethos of the team and we have done amazingly well in exposing Robbie. That was a first-class piece of work.'

'I know that, and so does Dani. Indeed, she used the same expression, but you know as well as I do, that as in so many other areas of life, policing at that level is a matter of politics, which is why when she asked me the best way forward for the team, I had to say that only one person able and qualified to take over the team and that is Detective Sergeant Enright!'

'Well, you got that right,' said Cate with a smile.

'No Cate, it must be you. This is not flattery, but you are an outstanding police officer and first-class detective. Dani knows that and believes you are best placed to continue and complete the work of the team, and when you say that you will, as you will and that's an order, I am to tell you that your acceptance includes promotion to the rank of acting Detective Superintendent.'

'This is a very odd conversation in a coffee shop in Royal Leamington Spa.'

'All I need to hear you say are the words brides and bridegrooms say on their wedding day: "I will".

'Don't they say "I do"?'

'No. Except in films and on tv. I know that because I've said them a couple of times when perhaps I should have said "Maybe".

Cate smiled.

'To lose you, Martin, is to lose a great deal and it is going to be a huge shock to the others, but now you're asking me: "I will".'

A passing waitress had caught the end of this conversation and stopped at their table.

'Ooh,' she said, 'that's so romantic, but shouldn't you be on one knee, sir.'

'I knew there was something wrong,' said Martin, 'but the important thing is that she said yes. And now we shall go back to the office and celebrate with our friends.'

'Aah, how lovely!.'

In The Realm Of The Dead

The Shock

Superintendent Greene and Superintendent Peabody walked back up the road, but not hand in hand as a watching waitress might have hoped, but in silence, until Cate said she thought it would be best for Martin to tell the team in her absence of his departure. She had a phone call to make and would come in afterwards. Martin continued on his way.

There was a bench on which Cate sat.

'Assistant Chief Constable Thomas, please.'

'Who shall I say is calling?'

'Cate Greene.'

'Good morning, Superintendent,' said a familiar voice, 'I thought I might hear from you this morning.'

'You're making a big mistake getting rid of Martin, ma'am.'

'I know that, of course I do, but there's no way he can stay, and he knows that. The result was good and the result was also a catastrophe, and if you are to continue, he knows and I know, and you know, that his departure was inevitable. He recommended you at once and I didn't need telling twice but he also mentioned a DS of unusual quality. Is he right?'

'Oh yes, she is outstanding. Jo Enright she's called and came with Martin from the Met and she's the best detective I've ever known.'

'I think you need to go and gather your group together and massage the bruised, then get on with it. Your new team member arrives on Wednesday and I think you could also use an extra man to which I'll give some thought and have some conversations. So, Detective Superintendent Greene, set to.'

'"Acting", surely ma'am.'

'Never use that term, Cate. Years ago some people who failed their degrees at Oxford had cards printed with the words "B.A. Oxon (Failed), on the grounds that it was better to have been to Oxford and failed, than never to have been to Oxford at all. Ranks and titles are best used with discrimination. You are Super.'

The phone went dead.

Cate rose and made her way to the office, and when she entered everyone stood.

'As you were,' said Cate, 'and do that again and I'll boot your arses into touch, as our much-missed former colleague DI Douglas might say.'

It was a sentence that won them over completely.

As they returned to their work, Cate asked Ellie to come and join her.

'How are you feeling, Ellie?'

'Sad, of course. Martin and I have worked together a long time and we also had a brief fling, and I have great respect and love for him, but knowing the force as I do, I knew this was going to happen.'

'There is likely to be another new male member of the team, possibly a DCI. How do you feel about that?'

'As long as whoever it is integrates quickly it will be ok, but we both know that not every man can do that. Will we have the right of refusal?'

'On behalf of the team, I will, and I won't go against you. In the meantime, you have to be acting DCI, and in that new capacity tell me what you think we should do about Durham, Arvot and Hollioake.'

'Jo's left for the station in Warwick to pick Eamonn up and to get him fully onside before he gets here. Once we know where they are living, and especially if they are living together, I think we should be looking to call on them tomorrow. Martin wanted us to work closely together and I still thinks that's right, but I believe that it's you and Jo who need to do the business with them, as you two know the situation best.'

'Not really, it's Jo who must take the lead. She knows them both and worked with Hollioake as a DC under Hannah with him. Once Eamonn can give us the intel, we should think of making an early start tomorrow.'

'Hey, boss, I've only just caught up on my sleep.'

'I won't ask why!'

They smiled at one another.

The sandwiches arrived and then Eamonn and Jo arrived, the computer expert insisting that he'd come back for a rest after some days of MI5 and two small children, the latter of which had utterly exhausted him. There followed anecdotes about nephews and nieces, and horror stories about other people's children, though Bobi insisted that his were perfect in every way, especially when he was away from them!

Lunch over, Cate informed everyone that the hope was for a very early start tomorrow, with Ellie driving, Jo, who would be lead, and herself, with Bobi and Eamonn going over everything to do with Wales. Another team member, Chris, would be joining on the following day and her ACC hoping to recruit a further member soon. In the meantime, she announced congratulations to Ellie, now DCI, and Jo, now acting DI, which would be needed in the event of a formal interview with Hollioake, being one rank superior to his own.

'As I say, she is lead tomorrow. Sad to say, when I told her this, the first thing she wanted was to change our starting time to 9 o'clock, and I had to overrule her.'

'Ooh, you fibber,' said Jo.

Everyone laughed.

For a technology expert working primarily for MI5, the immediate task of discovering the whereabouts of Arvot and Hollioake was not difficult, nor discovering that his shift on traffic did not begin until 2 o'clock on the following afternoon. As both Jo and Cate had suspected, they lived at the same address in a village called Bowburn, just off the A1(M), south of the city itself. Cate said she was hoping that they might live in the small town of Crook, but no such luck!

The journey was a long one, just shy of 200 miles but mostly on the motorway and once again the facility of blue lights was used once the various forces had been properly informed. They set off just before 5 o'clock and both Cate and Jo slept a good deal of the way. Ellie was regarded as the best driver in the team and kept up a good 90 mph all the way. They had a short break at the Woodhall Services for the loo and a very quick breakfast and then continued on the A1(M). In an attempt to fool everyone into using the next interchange, and succeeding in fooling no one, the road authorities did not sign Junction 61 "Durham" but "Spennymoor". It was however the "Bowburn Interchange" and Bowburn itself was just a mile or so on the A177 towards Durham.

As with so many communities in the county, it was a former pit village and some of the housing still reflected this and on a dark winter's morning looked bleak and dispiriting. Ellie turned right off the main road towards newer housing, a 60s Wimpy estate and in its own way equally dispiriting. Behind that there was, however a small group of detached houses which immediately gave off the appearance of being the domain of the (relatively) wealthy of Bowburn. It was in one of these that Katarina and Graham lived. It was a quarter to eight, and Ellie felt so tired from the early morning driving that she was tempted to ask the pair if she could use their bed upstairs whilst they answered questions downstairs.

The first discovery was that Eamonn had failed them in one significant regard – a baby had not been anticipated. Jo and Cate left the car and immediately heard a baby's cries and looked at one another with surprise. Jo rang the doorbell which was opened by a pretty young woman holding the baby.

'Hello Katarina,' began Jo, 'I am Detective Inspector Enright and this is Detective Superintendent Greene. We would like to ask you and Graham some questions.'

'I don't understand what you are doing here. Graham works for Durham Police and surely you can speak to him at work.'

'Is he at home?'

'Yes, he's getting dressed.'

'Please call him and allow us to come in.'

'Of course.'

The baby was very interested in their appearance, and obviously less so was Graham when he came into the lounge.

'Jo! What on earth are you doing here and please introduce your partner.'

'This is my boss, Detective Superintendent Cate Greene, and I now, alas, Graham, am Detective Inspector.'

'I'm not at all surprised at that, Jo. Well done though, you were streets ahead of Connor and me. But what are you doing here and at this time in the morning. With a relatively new baby sleep is at a premium I'm pleased to say.'

'How old?' asked Cate.

'Almost three months.'

'Congratulations to all three of you then,' said Jo. 'Sex?'

'Not a lot,' said Graham with a wry grin

They all laughed.

'A girl – Anja, with a j, but pronounced Anna.'

'Slovenian?'

'After Katarina's mother.'

Jo needed to shift the mood.

'Katarina and Graham, we are part of a team investigating a series of brutal murders in different parts of the country which we believe may be linked, one of which was that of Marney Edmonds. The only conversation about it that I had with you, Katarina, was on the telephone while you were you in Bishop Auckland.'

'I was at my sister's home.'

'And a serious mistake was made when no one came to see you.'

'That was Connor's insistence. You left soon after the killing and he was always anxious about our finances.'

'Yes, I remember that, but much more important is the matter of whether or not he knew about your relationship with Katarina.'

Graham and Katarina looked at one another.

'Yes, he did.'

Jo wanted to explode but managed a smile instead.

'So, he knew all along that when Katarina made her mysterious trips out on foot at least twice a week, you were the person picking her up and presumably that when you claimed to have gone round all the pubs with Katarina's photograph, he knew that you hadn't.'

'Yes.'

Jo looked at Cate, who raised her eyebrows.

'For how long had you been in a relationship?'

'I prefer to say we had been in love – for 2 years before Marney's death, shortly after he had bought the house for Katarina. She came into the police station when she was working on the farm to say she was uneasy about how she thought she was being used by him, almost as his own personal prostitute and that by giving her so much money, he felt he could do whatever he wished. I took her out to a nearby tea and coffee lounge we knew and wanted to spare her anyone at the station knowing about this. That was the beginning and I have no regrets about it.'

'Nor me,' said Katarina. 'Graham was wonderful and we began to meet.'

'But Marney continued to come to Heckington.'

'Yes and I didn't know how to stop his visits. It may sound dramatic but in some way I felt I was his property.'

'What a relief you must have felt when you heard he had been murdered.'

'I was terrified and Graham told me to get to my sister's as soon as possible.'

'Was that wise, Graham?'

'No, but in the circumstances it worked out well. Connor knew Katarina couldn't have killed Marney and so was happy to allow her go.'

'So he knew that before he sent me on what he already knew was going to be a total waste of time?'

'Yes.'

'Did it, do you think, occur to Connor, that the murder of Marney had been done by you? After all, that would explain your fortuitous but unlikely find of his landrover in the churchyard of

Wainfleet St Mary, and that you possessed a shotgun licence plus access to Homes 3 which might have given you the idea of the numeral II on his back. And that's not to mention your potential as jealous lover, being forced to share what you most valued with a rough and probably unpleasant gang master.'

'If it did occur to him, he never gave the slightest indication to me. To you?'

'No. But it does occur to me that you had every reason to wish Marney dead and possessed the means and the local knowledge with which to do it. So did you?'

'Am I under caution?'

'Not at the moment. Do you wish to be?'

'I can see that you may be here with the intent of accusing me of murder, and I can also see, because I too have been a detective, why you might have come to that conclusion and that had it been others in my place I might have come to the same conclusion as you, but I deny it completely.'

'I think, sergeant,' interposed Cate, 'and you will fully understand why I think it, that we need to conduct the interview on a more formal basis so that you have representation from your federation and also a solicitor. There are questions still to be answered about your involvement, but more importantly, matters relating to the behaviour of Detective Inspector Hannah which are serious and need to be formally addressed before being attended to.'

'Are you arresting me?'

'Good heavens, no, and presumably you're happy to travel to the Professional Standards HQ at Neville's Cross freely with us.'

Graham looked at Katarina.

'You know I did not kill Marney, so my beloved wife and daughter you can rest assured that I will return safely home.'

Katarina came towards him and they kissed, and Graham also kissed Anja.

'Because this was a possibility, Graham, we arranged in advance for a solicitor to be on hand and a fed rep. They know nothing about any of this nor do they as yet know your identity. If you are not happy about this, the alternative will be to take you under arrest to Lincoln. You will be allowed plenty of time this morning to meet with the solicitor and federation rep before we begin formal questioning which will largely take the form of the questions you have already answered. I might add, that unless you did murder Marney Edmonds, there is nothing whatsoever that we would fault you with.'

'I understand, Jo. I suppose that I always knew that these things would have to come out into the open one day, so now it's happened I feel great relief and I just want to get it over with.'

As the three of them got into the car they had to wake up Ellie.

'Our driver today, when she surfaces, is none other that Detective Chief Inspector Ellie Middlewood.'

Good morning, ma'am. We've met before when you came to Boston after the murder and stole Jo from us.'

'Can you blame me?'

'Not at all.'

Neville's Cross was on the western side of the city, away from the headquarters of the County Police Force. It was an old building with "character" as an Estate Agent might have claimed. Graham was met by his solicitor and Federation Rep, and the three officers by most welcome cups of coffee. An officer in the uniform of a DCI came over to them and introduced himself, welcoming them and realising from their own introductions that they were senior officers, one of them senior to himself.

'Can I just be clear, ma'am. This interview is taking place here for the sake of your convenience and not dealing with any matter of Professional Standards.'

'That's right and thank you for the facility. We could take him back to Leamington Spa where we are based or even to Lincoln where the matter we are seeking information on took place, but as he lives here, it just seemed sensible to make use of what you have on offer.'

The interview room was standard. A long table with the tape machine at one end three chairs on either side. Cate, as senior officer would take over from Jo as lead but would still leave most of the questioning to her. Graham and his supporters came in and sat down.

'This is most unusual,' said the fed rep.

'I know, said Cate, ' but for all sorts of practical reasons I am designating this place a police station. Are you happy with that, Graham?'

'Of course.'

'And shouldn't you address him by his rank?' said the fed rep.

'As in the sentence "And shouldn't you address him by his rank, *ma'am*?'

They all laughed, including even the rep himself.

'We want to keep this as an informal interview as possible, but it has to be formal because there are certain matters relating to another officer, not here present, which are serious. So, Detective Inspector Enright, will you please caution Graham and then turn on the tapes and we will begin.'

They went over the same ground as earlier and each question and answer sounded as it had come from a script.

'Graham, you have just told us as you did earlier that you knew about the Ace of Spades playing card that had been nailed to the back of Peter Sherriff. How?'

'Like many officers I looked through the pages of Holmes 3 regularly which is what I believe is meant to happen, to keep the forces in touch, going back to the fiasco of the Ripper murders. I saw it there.'

'Have you ever had an operation in hospital?'

'Odd question. No.'

'How familiar are you with the drug Propofol?'

'Again I know of it only from reading accounts of the crimes you are investigating.'

'But before that?'

'Not at all.'

'Were you aware that fenland farmers determined on suicide tie themselves to a fencepost before drowning themselves.'

Graham smiled.

'Not in Lincolnshire they don't. The rivers round Boston are very shallow, apart from the River Witham. This is perhaps a little more common in the Cambridgeshire fens where their rivers, usually called Drains, were drained in the 17th century and are wide and deep, but even there it happens rarely and hasn't now for almost ten years. Farmers shoot themselves these days. Messy for everyone else but quick.'

'You admit you had the motive?'

'Oh yes, without a shadow of doubt. I detested the man with every ounce of my being, but I wasn't alone in that. Although she denied it, Mary Edmonds had as much motive. She knew about the money being siphoned from the business to Katarina, and she knew that she existed but didn't know where, or else it might have been Katarina who died. And she had a Slovenian woman who lived with her, Ljubica. Ostensibly she was functioning as a maid, but her role in the household was more complex than that. Between them, she and Mary tyrannised the Slovenian workers. That emerged on day one when all the workers were being questioned. I also know that Marney tried it on with Ljubica and received what she told me would have been an extremely painful twist of his testicles, something, she said, she had learned back home. I made a mental note never even to flirt in fun with her. Shortly before I left to come here, I managed to do a trace on her. She had spent time in the Slovenian army yet when later, I reopened the file, that had been removed, presumably by Connor, and when I questioned him he said it was utterly irrelevant.'

'Go on.'

'I think there must have been someone else involved, a man of necessity, perhaps a boyfriend, perhaps a Detective Inspector.'

'Hey, that's quite a leap, Graham.'

'You asked me to go on.'

'I was not in CID at the time. But can you recall what happened after the report that Marney was missing came in?' asked Jo.

'Nothing. Connor said he would turn up after a night of screwing a pretty Slovenian girl from the farm.'

'Nothing at all?

'No, and what was also odd is that when word came in that a corpse had been found in Midville on the following morning, he attended but then came back and insisted he and I went out for a full English breakfast in a café in town. I couldn't have done that if I'd seen what he had just seen. Only then did he go out to the farm and took with him a junior woman PC.'

'Who?'

'Linda Andrews.'

'A local girl,' said Jo to her colleagues by way of explanation, 'but not the sharpest knife in the drawer.'

'I think ma'am,' said the Federation Rep, 'we should stop now and call it a day. Graham has been more than co-operative and I can't see how you can take it any further.'

'Yes, a break is a good idea, so thank you for suggesting it, but we have to conclude our business in Durham today,' said Cate, or face meeting again tomorrow morning either in Lincoln or Leamington Spa, neither of which, I imagine, will appeal to you.'

'I'll see if I can hunt out some coffee,' said Ellie rising up.'

'No, it should be me, ma'am,' said Jo. 'You have a long drive ahead of you.'

She left the room and Cate invited Graham, his fed rep and his obviously deaf, dumb and blind solicitor to withdraw to a nearby annexe. She and Ellie followed Jo into a kitchen. Coffees and teas sorted, they then moved into a small sitting room.

'Any thoughts anyone?' asked Cate when they had sat down.

'As a neutral can I say something?' asked Ellie.

'Please do.'

'It's abundantly clear that Connor Hannah could be picked up in the morning and charged with perverting the course of justice, and on a number of grounds. What we have been hearing points to his further involvement in a conspiracy to murder, something he shares with Mary and Ljubica, who may or may not have been in the Slovenian army, which is something I should ask Eamonn to check for us. Graham also hints at the presence of a further man and perhaps he was or even still is the boyfriend of Ljubica.

'But, and this is my main point, this is to place all the weight on the words of Graham Hollioake, and to overlook his own clear motive for killing Marney. We have two factions, you might say, the Mary faction made up of Connor, Ljubica, and possibly A N Other. We also have the Graham faction which seems to consist of Graham by himself. The Graham faction has love as its chief motive; Mary wanted not love but to punish. We already know that she spread her sexual favours around. Ljubica may hold the key.'

'Jo, can you please ring Eamonn now and ask him to see if he can find if she really was in the Slovenian army and what she might have been doing there and gently point out that we need the answer an hour ago?' asked Cate.

'Of course.'

She went out at once and chose to go out into the street outside to call so as not to be overheard.

'Ellie, I'm finding myself on unfamiliar ground, so I have to talk you as a DCI for a moment.'

'Go ahead.'

'You sat in on the interview. How do you think DI Enright handled it and Graham.'

'As her superior officer I thought that she was good in ascertaining information but not as direct in challenging him as I would have been. I would have given him a much harder time.'

'Me too, but the last thing I want to do is knock her confidence.'

'You must tell her, Cate, straight and direct. She is one of those people who prefers to know how things are rather than be given platitudes meant to disguise critical words. I adore that woman, but I'm perfectly happy with her knowing these things and so will she be. Perhaps you should now take over and show her how to go in for the kill.'

The door opened and in came Jo.

Moving On

'That man's an absolute gem,' she said. 'He had it in no time at all. Ljubica Kovač was in the Slovenian army for a year doing National Service which is compulsory, but then moved to their form of Special Forces. She left when pregnant but according to the file had a miscarriage and did not return to the army.'

Her words were greeted with knowing looks among three of them.

'Jo, you were a DC at the time. Did Graham mention this to you. He says he put it in the file and claims Connor removed it?'

'No. I never really understood why neither woman was more closely examined. Connor was insistent that no woman could have done the murder.'

'And certainly not a mere housemaid from Slovenia. I think we need another session with Graham which I will lead. Perhaps because you know him having worked with him, we neither of us thought that you were quite as willing to put the boot in as we might have done, notwithstanding that you elicited information so very well.'

'In which case I have to plead guilty. Martin told me that he hardly spoke during Robbie's interview for much the same reason. I think it's what I would call an important learning point. Thank you both of you. Ellie might tell you that I say to her that when we are working, she in my superior officer and I want to learn and therefore she has to treat me appropriately.'

'Ok, let's get them in and start again.'

As junior officer, Jo went and called them back.

'Earlier, Graham, you said that you learned from the internet,

234

somehow or other, that Ljubica Kovač had been in the army for a year. How did you obtain that information?' said Cate.

'On Facebook. That is what she had written.'

'Did she write anything else?'

'She said she had been climbing with the army in the Dolomites. And then she said she had been ill and left the army.'

'It's quite convenient for you for that to be the case. After all, if she had served in the army she might be more capable of taking part in a killing. That let's you off the hook.'

'Superintendent, I've never been on the hook. I didn't kill Marney and for one reason only, though I freely admit I would have liked to do so when I thought about the way he used the woman I was falling more and more in love with, and that reason is simplicity itself. If I had done it I had no doubts that you, or someone like you and almost certainly Detective Inspector Enright sitting next to you would have worked out that I had done so because I'm simply not clever enough, and so I would lose Katarina and spend many years in prison. I love and adore her, and there is no way I would risk that. What I was planning was a moonlight flit for us both. I didn't care about losing my job; all we wanted was to be together. Begging you to believe it won't help me, I know, but it is true.'

'Graham, you hinted at the possibility that Ljubica Kovač might have had a boyfriend. What do you know about him? This may be very important.'

I realise that, ma'am, and I realise why, and I wish I could give you a name but I can't.'

'Excuse me a moment. DI Enright, please can you come with me.'

They left the room. And she gave Jo her mobile. Ring Christine Halton immediately – you'll find her number in my Contacts. She might still not have left Boston for Leamington. Ask her the same question about a boyfriend?'

Once again Jo went outside to make the call.

'Hello, ma'am,' said the voice.

'Christine,' said Jo, 'I'm on her phone but its Jo Enright calling from Durham where we are interviewing a suspect in the Marney

Edmonds murder case. At the moment the boss is doing the questioning. So ... First of all where are you at this precise moment?'

'I'm almost ready to set off for Leamington, but still in my flat in Boston.'

'Ok. Second question. Do you know the identity of the boyfriend of the housemaid of Mary Edmonds who is called ... '

'Ljubica Kovač?'

'That's her.'

'Indeed I do and I'm rather surprised you don't. He's called Barry Kisbee and he lives in Camelot Gardens, just round the corner from The Spar shop on Priory Rd, which is where I first made his acquaintance. He had been accused of shoplifting and then wrestled to the ground, somewhat ironically, by two men from the prison on day release. I wouldn't have tackled him myself because he's a big bugger. Anyway Connor said to let him off with a caution or else he might lose his job as a Porter at the Pilgrim Hospital. Subsequently I've seen them together a couple of times in town in various stages of intimate embrace.'

'And you're sure it was her?'

'There's no question about that and believe you me, when she dresses for a night out with Barry, she clearly doesn't spare the cost though, trust me, she doesn't use a great deal of material.'

'To save my time here and now which would involve calling Eamonn whom you will meet tomorrow, did you check whether he has form?'

'Six months for ABH from magistrates, of which he served just three, plus some juvenile offences. And I hope the lady is turned on by tattoos.'

'Chris, that's brilliant. Thank you. I can't wait to see you tonight if and when we ever get back. Drive safely and welcome to the team.'

By the way, are we all very formal with titles and ranks in the squad?'

'We don't use them except in emergency for the cause of irony.'

'In which case, thank you, Jo. I've heard so much about you

and I can't wait to work with you.'

Jo knocked on the door of the Interview Room and Cate reappeared. Jo handed back the phone and quickly filled her in with the info from Chris.

'What's you're gut feeling, Jo?'

'I think we have no grounds for the arrest of Graham and should release him. I think we shall need to move as a team to Boston and do some hard questioning of Mary Edmonds, Ljubica Kovač, Barry Kisbee and, sadly, Connor Hannah, whom we should speak to as a suspect in a murder case, not in the context of dereliction of duty which would necessitate our taking it to Professional Standards. You will, however, have to inform the CC in Lincoln and whoever he insists joins us when Connor is interviewed.'

Cate smiled.

'I like working with you. It means I don't have to waste time thinking. You worked with him, you go and tell him the good news.'

Jo entered the room and remained standing.

'Graham, this interview is now over. Thank you so much for your time this morning, and you two gentlemen as well. You are free to go and as we have to go back your way, may we offer you a lift home, not least so we can see Anja once again, get to know the elusive and very beautiful Katarina, but most important of all, so we can call in at your local Fish and Chips shop which we passed and come and eat them with you.'

Graham turned to Ellie.

'I have to say, ma'am, that things have changed since I was interrogating. We never used to let anyone go with an invitation join us in a meal!'

'Come off it, Graham, you've worked with Jo before. Anything is possible.'

Even the dour solicitor, who had not spoken once all morning, laughed at that.

The relief on the face of Katarina was palpable once she saw everyone coming carrying fish and chips, not least for her. Anja was fascinated by Ellie, and discussing it later, the women decided that in Bowburn black faces, now the pits has closed, were little in evidence.

Ellie said she was happy to drive once again as she had done none of the talking, but did ask what the other two had concluded.

'We have to go to Boston again, 'said Cate, 'which is a burden it itself, and there we have to interview the four principals: Mary, Ljubica, Barry Kisbee and Connor. It's not going to be easy. I imagine that for Connor someone will have to come and sit in, perhaps a Super from Lincoln.'

'If it's the one I know,' said Jo, 'he's rough but fair, blusters a lot and I suspect he's based himself on Superintendent Dalziel in the tele programmes. Deep down, I think's he's a good and decent copper.'

Once again Cate and Jo drifted off to sleep, so Ellie turned on the radio for company.

When Cate woke up, not that far from Leamington, she said to Ellie: 'Tell me how you think we should do things when we get to Boston.'

'I've been giving it some thought as I've been driving, and have come to the definite conclusion that the best thing we can do is to get the Detective Superintendent, the officer in charge of our squad, to decide.'

'She often says how much she values you as a colleague – I can't think why!'

They giggled together like silly schoolgirls. Jo, the perpetual sleeper, never heard a word or giggle. You could say anything and she would sleep on oblivious.

They arrived in Leamington and went straight to the hotel, where they found Bobi, Eamonn and Chris chatting together in the bar. In seconds they too had ordered drinks and joined them.

'I know going out for a curry together has proved dangerous in the past as that was when we began to have our suspicions about Robbie,' said Cate, 'but I need to do a briefing this evening and that seems a good place to meet for it. Is everyone happy with that?'

There were nods and smiles.

'Welcome to Chris, joining us now, fresh from Boston, and thank you for that most useful information you were able to provide Jo with. Chris is in the room Martin had. Thank you, Eamonn, for your information too. I won't ask how you managed to get into Slovenian army files, but I can't tell you useful that was. Now this G&T is going to do a disappearing act and I shall have a shower and change, and shall we meet here at 8:30? I'll phone and book a table.'

Ellie and Jo went up to their room, took of all their clothes and had a shower together which they adored. They then lay on the bed fast asleep in each other's arms, and it was only the alarm on Ellie's watch which she had fortuitously set that woke her up. She smiled when she realised that Jo who had slept for most of the journey from Durham, had also slept through the alarm!

Chris was taller than Jo and had long blonde hair.

'I can't tell you how pleased I am to get away from Boston,' she said.' Working for that man was ghastly.'

'I know and I felt a similar amount of relief when I left to go to the Met with Martin and Ellie. Even South London villains seemed an improvement on Lincolnshire though the traffic is awful and I guess that when we've finished here, though that won't be just yet, I shall be returning there. But you may not quite have finished with Boston yet. We still have the murder of Marney Edmonds to sort out.'

'Of course.'

'And then one in your new neck of the woods which is all to do with chickens.'

'Oh. I guess I'd probably have lamb curry tonight then.'

Jo smiled and knew that Chris would fit in.

'What's happened to the men? We only have Bobi and most quads consist of men and a token woman, not the other way round.'

'Apparently your new ACC is trying to do something about that, but we've lost two senior men in the past week. Martin and Robbie moved on, you might say, so yes, here we are and let's hope we don't all get PMT at the same time. I'm told it used to happen in convents and all the nuns got ratty together. Men are lucky, at least in that respect.'

Once in the restaurant and having ordered, Cate said, 'I'm pleased to say that relatively speaking tomorrow's going to be a rest day, though only relatively speaking. I had a call after I had just got into the shower from Dani Thomas, my ACC, to say that she wants to pop in and see us tomorrow morning, and not least to meet one of her new officers, Detective Sergeant Halton. I am hoping and perhaps we're all hoping she'll be bringing with her another member of the team which we urgently need for what we shall be doing on the following day. I have no idea whether she will be in uniform, but we will not and we shall continue to use names rather than ranks. So we can enjoy our curries this evening with little immediate thought about what comes next. After Dani has gone we can have a full briefing.'

As they walked back up the street in pairs, with Jo and Chris sharing Boston horror stories and bursts of laughter, Eamonn and Bobi talking computers, Ellie said to Cate, 'Hey I was only joking earlier, Cate. I know how much forethought we have to give to going over to Boston, so I wondered if you and I might get up very early and have breakfast without the others and plan.'

'That's a good idea, though we can't really manage without Jo. She knows the ground and the people. I think we need her too.'

'I thought you might say that. She'll love you for yet another early morning. She's not at her best first thing. At least it won't be quite as early as this morning, but it was worth it. I know I'm a sentimental old thing but I really liked Graham, Katarina and Anja, and from the moment we arrived hoped you'd find nothing.'

'I know what you mean. That gorgeous baby. But he's not totally out of the woods yet, even though I personally doubt any participation in the killing and, like you, hope we don't have to return.'

'Did your boss give any indication that she might have someone with her?'

'She can be very enigmatic. I'm pretty sure that when she took her marriage vows and was asked the question by the vicar, she will have stopped for at least a minute, as if she had never considered it before, and replied something like: "I don't think any of us should assume a simple answer will really suffice because marriage is very complicated indeed and we need to be clear about all the ramifications of my answer, but given those considerations, ok, I will."

The pair laughed and laughed.

'Just you wait and you'll see what I mean,' said Cate.

Cate, Ellie and Jo met for breakfast at 6:30 with Jo protesting that she was only a Detective Inspector (Acting) and this was a time for the big girls, not her, but the others were unimpressed.

'So, the question is multi-faceted. First, we have to decide if we should travel this afternoon and stay overnight somewhere convenient for an early start. My thought is to let Dani and Derrick know this morning what we are planning and elicit their help in getting assistance first thing for bringing in the four for interviews. Of necessity that is going to reveal our hand somewhat in that we will have indicated the possibility that DI Connor may have perverted the course of justice and needs to have present a senior member of the Lincoln constabulary as well as myself.

'The other three must be picked up and separated immediately, but how we can do that, Jo, depends on your local knowledge.'

'The main problem is Connor and what might be possible depends very much on how persuasive Dani and Derrick can be with the Chief Constable and insist that this is a murder investigation at the moment and not one of discipline. They might want him to come to Lincoln otherwise and be interviewed by Professional Standards, but that will be to miss the point completely. One possibility would be to take him to Skegness Station for our interview. It's not too far and he wouldn't be known to everyone there.

'Mary will curse and swear and be very unpleasant. Ljubica will insist she cannot speak English. We did use an interpreter from a local college when all the workers were interviewed, but

Ljubica speaks English perfectly well. And then there is Barry Kisbee whom I do not know. He might well put up a fight when he is picked up.

'There are a couple of holding cells at Boston plus an interview room. The County Court has no cells, and we might have to consider the use of Sleaford. There are only a dozen or so stations in the county, which is common in rural areas.'

'Yes, I know that only too well,' added Cate. 'Herefordshire is just the same.'

'So, in a way, much will depend on the high-ups and what they want to do with Connor and our limited resources for interviewing as only the three of us know the situation well enough and that suggests we may have to divide and use Bobi and Chris alongside as silent participants providing moral support.'

'And hopefully,' added Ellie, 'anyone accompanying Dani this morning.'

Cate's phone rang at the precise moment.

'Speak of the devil! ... Good morning ma'am ... No, we're really looking forward to seeing you ... Parking is no problem, ma'am ... Oh, that's good news ... He sounds ideal ... What time are you hoping to get here? ... Good, because we urgently need your input and that of DCC Blowes who's coming to meet you. The things is we have made important steps forward with regard to the Boston murder and we want to bring in four people we suspect of being involved as soon as possible, hopefully tomorrow and for that we need you and Derrick to pull strings ... Of course we will, and in detail, but I ought to warn you that there is a police officer involved ... A not inappropriate word, ma'am, if I may say so, indeed I may even have used it myself ... Ok, Dani see you soon.'

'Dani?' said Ellie and Jo in unison.

'Don't worry, she'd had her full quota of "ma'ams" and was happy. She'll be here by "9:30 at the latest" which means earlier, and is bringing a DI called Sammy Burton whose been leading an armed response unitand is apparently bored but likes crosswords.'

'He'll be at home here then,' said Ellie. 'Puzzles r'us!'

'I have just had an outrageous thought,' said Jo, about where we might be able to the interviewing and keep people apart. Can you leave it with me, please?'

'Why not? In the meantime, can you go and wake everyone and make sure they are in the office by 8:00, Jo? Ellie, will you please ring your mate Derrick and tell him what's what in Boston and what time Dani is arriving? I'm going to stay here and have another coffee and distract myself with the paper and settle my nerves.'

Everyone was there on time and the first happening of the day was Eamonn's report to Cate that he had received info from his "home team" about a group that had infiltrated Extinction Rebellion, calling themselves Burning Pink (Beyond Politics), who were maintaining that they were only interested in direct action and had already done so on a number of occasions.

'If they get any word, however tentative, of an involvement in the murder of Tony Hendry, please make sure, Eamonn, that we get to hear that word.'

'I'm off there later today for the rest of the week so I'll do more about this when I get there, but it may just be the first link in the chain. It's odd how often these groups can't resist exhibiting themselves and adopting fancy names. In the end it's often the route to their downfall – a longing for some sort of publicity. I think they should read a history of the French Resistance where they would learn a very different way of functioning and up against an enemy who would have no hesitation in killing them if discovered.'

'Well, thanks for that Eamonn, and if you don't mind I might mention it to my ACC when she gets here. I think she's concerned that we haven't turned our attention to the murder of Tony Hendry yet.'

Dani arrived wearing jeans and a very smart jumper and was early as usual. Everyone stood and awaited the "As you were" command, but she just said, 'For heaven's sake, sit down. You're a specialist squad and we have to take liberties, hence I've come in my best dress uniform, so let's begin by introducing you to the man beside me, not just here to carry my briefcase which he appears to have left in the car!'

He looked suddenly shocked.

'It's alright, Sammy, just my little joke. It's a rare thing – a no briefcase morning. So, yes, this is the new member of the team, DI Sammy Burton, fresh from an armed response unit and wanting to get back to his first love which is detecting. Having cruelly, you may think, robbed you of a good man, here is another. Sammy is a qualified firearms instructor, so if you have quiet days I hope it might be possible to get you, Christine (and I'm assuming that is who you are), up to speed with that.'

'Thank you, ma'am.'

'I hope to get to speak with each of your informally, but I also know there are very important matters to discuss about an op tomorrow for which we need to wait for Derrick, so is it possible please, to begin with coffee?'

'She's very good,' said Ellie quietly to Jo. 'What a waste having her in an office most of the time.'

'You're not kidding,' she replied. 'But just look at Chris, she can't take her eyes off Sammy.'

'Well, even I know that he is gorgeous – for a man.'

'I'm glad that you managed to get in the last bit.'

'Something women sometimes have to say that to men.'

They both tried desperately to suppress their laughter.

When he arrived (on time), Derrick was wearing his uniform and he and Dani withdrew to the end of the room for an initial chat, though both knew the other well. Eventually, as the senior officer present, it was Derrick who called everyone to order and to gather together. That done, he immediately handed over to Cate, and she spoke for the next forty minutes outlining everything the others and their superiors needed to know.

Dani couldn't resist getting her oar in first once Cate had finished.

'I see what you mean, Cate, about needing Derrick and myself to secure all the help you will need from Lincolnshire Constabulary. But, I don't know about you, Derrick, I can also see the need for a measure of urgency. It's not possible to know what your visit to Durham might have stirred up in terms of a brief mention in a phone call to the friend of a friend in Boston, albeit unwittingly.'

'In effect,' said Derrick, 'you are wanting: first, a team to collect your suspects before dawn from their homes; second, somewhere to take them for holding; third, their thoughts about the best place to interview DI Hannah, making it clear that he will be interviewed by you Cate; finally, i where should everyone be held?'

'Sir, ma'am, may I just add something about the first of those points'. It was Sammy speaking. 'From what I have heard from Superintendent Greene, and in the light of my own experience, I would recommend that we ask for an armed response unit. Two of the targets are potentially dangerous, and if a firearm was used in the original killing it just might be immediately accessible again. That means the same unit for all four, including the police officer.'

'Thanks Sammy,' said Cate. 'You're quite right though to be fair Jo also mentioned it to me and Ellie over breakfast. And ... Sammy, the house rule is no titles used, except to the biggies.'

Everyone laughed though Sammy also blushed, and by now Chris was totally smitten.

'Derrick, can we go to your HQ to make our calls?' said Dani, 'for verification purposes?'

'Yes.'

'If you get the green light, Cate, when will you move?'

'Mid-afternoon. We'll head over and find somewhere to stay, ready for an early start in the morning.'

'Ok, then if I may, I'll come back here after Derrick and I are done and have some lunch with you and finish off my meeting with everyone. Eamonn has already given some positive news about a possible lead on the killing on the Welsh Border.'

They rose and left. Sammy was shown where and told to make the coffee and tea! They all agreed that his success in doing this boded well for the team as a whole.

It was 11:30 when Dani, without Derrick, reappeared. The

whole team gathered to listen.

'It's go for tomorrow. The ARU will collect from three locations at 5:30am and the targets will be taken to the North Sea Camp Prison, where there is space to hold and interview, and that seems to me to be an ideal solution, not least because it apparently came from someone here. Anyone wishing to own up to it? Jo, for example? Thank you, Jo. It was good idea even if a bit left-field. The CC insisted that a senior officer from Lincoln must be present for the interview with DI Connor who will join you there. So, I wish you good luck.'

HMP North Sea Camp

Synchronised by radio, the three squads entered the houses at 5:30. Mary gave no trouble at the farm other than a torrent of curses. Connor too was outraged and also full of abuse. At the flat of Barry, they also found Ljubica. He was not all all pleased and made the great mistake of trying to get his shotgun which gave it's hiding place away. He was handcuffed after he had dressed. At first Ljubica gave the impression that she thought they had only come for him and was not all pleased when a woman officer forced her out of bed and remained whilst she dressed. And just as Jo had forecast, she began saying she did not understand anything as she did not speak much English but her eyes suggested more than this on arrival at the prison when she, and the others too, were informed that they were being held for questioning in connection with a conspiracy to murder Emmanuel Edmonds. Solicitors would be coming to see them soon and would be with them throughout their questioning,

For Connor, this is was the most ignominious moment of his life – to be taken here, to a prison of all places, and he was devastated when locked in a cell and told breakfast would be brought. All were informed that they should prepare to be here for quite some time. The informer was Bobi, the other members of the team already inside and eating their own breakfasts away from the latest arrivals and the inmates, who had been aware of considerable disturbance and wondered what was going on.

Shortly before 9:00, Mary Edmonds was brought to an Interview Room with a solicitor, and joined there by Ellie and Bobi. Mary starcd hard at Ellie.

'I want to be questioned by an English person not by a foreigner'.

'I think you will find, Mrs Edmonds, that Detective Inspector Middlewood is as English as you, and the only foreigner in the room is me,' said Bobi

His Welsh accent made its point.

Ellie began the process with a statement of who was in the room and the tape recorder was turned on.

Mary immediately complained that the solicitor was not her own solicitor (whom she named) who she would want present before she would say anything more.

'That is of course your entitlement. The solicitor you named regrets he is unable to attend either today or tomorrow. If you wish to wait for him, with the weekend coming up, you will be held here or in a cell in Boston Police Station until then.'

She turned to the solicitor who merely shrugged.

'You have maintained in the past that you kept control of the farm and gang finances. One might overlook ten pounds missing here and there, but the Fraud Squad discovered that £¼m was missing. So how long before Marney's death had you become aware of this, for unless you were unbelievably incompetent, which I don't believe for one minute, you must have known?'

'Money had been going out for at least a year and maybe more. Some of the amounts were considerable – one even for £125,000 to an account I couldn't trace, but which paid for the house for that bitch he had starting seeing.'

'Was your accountant aware of this?'

'That bag of shite! Of course he was. I think he put together a scheme for Marney to take advantage of.'

'When did you become aware of the existence of Katarina Arvot as the person who was receiving all this money?'

'Ljubica followed his landrover one evening and found her name by chatting to a neighbour.'

Why did you not challenge your husband with either his adultery or his financial abuses?'

'I don't know, really.'

'Of course you weren't exactly the best example of moral

rectitude yourself, were you, Mary?'

'I don't know what you mean.'

'Twenty minutes here and twenty minutes there, outside the back of the pub.'

She said nothing.

'Let's get to the nub. Which of you decided that the only way forward was by means of Marney meeting a terrible end because he was a slave-owner at the hands of fanatics?'

'That's ridiculous.'

'Tell me how much you knew about Ljubica's past, in the time before she came to be with you.'

'She said she had been in the army for a year's National Service, mostly working as a nurse in their medical corps. She was bright and intelligent and she and I got on very well.'

'And she knew what Marney was doing financially, as well as with his girlfriend in Heckington?'

'She was the only person I could tell.'

'Apart from Connor.'

'Well ...'

Ellie smiled at her and hoped Mary would not recognise the crocodile teeth.

'Tell me about the way your conversations with Ljubica about Marley went in the months and weeks before he disappeared.'

'That's my business.'

'You see Mary, we know that your husband was brutally murdered by what we think was a conspiracy and we are confident that we know who was part of it. You had the powerful motives for the killing and of course you knew the area well.'

'Yes, but so did Connor.'

Ellie let her words sink in, and sat back in her chair.

'You're in serious trouble, Mary, and you wouldn't be here this morning if we didn't have our reasons. Helping us in our task is the best way in which you can help yourself.'

After the formal naming of those present, Ljubica sat facing Detective Inspector Jo Enright and Detective Inspector Sammy Burton, whom Ljubica could hardly stop looking at.

'Just so you know, we have managed to secure the assistance of an interpreter to help you answer my questions, but as you and I, both know, your English is very good indeed,' began Jo. 'Two years ago you had a moment of fame when you made an appearance on the tv programme *Countryfile* which was looking at the work of gang masters. May I congratulate you on how well you did, but also point out the quality and quantity of your spoken English, which I have experienced myself before now at the time when Marney was killed. So please spare us your pretence that you can neither understand nor speak much English. You know and I know that you can.

'Your Facebook entry says you spent a year doing National Service in the army and that for some of the time you worked as a kind of auxiliary nurse. For the purposes of the tape can you please confirm your Facebook entry.'

'Yes.'

'Is National Service compulsory in Slovenia?'

'Yes.'

'There is then a gap of two years before you decided to come to this country. What did you do in that two year period?'

The solicitor intervened.

'I don't see how this relates to the issue of why Miss Kovač is being questioned here this morning. It is not an immigration issue.'

Jo ignored him.

'Please answer my question.'

'I returned home and spent my time helping out.'

'In fact, according to your military record, you were a member of Slovenian Special Forces for those two years. Yes?'

Ljubica shrugged.

'Were there many women?'

'No.'

'It was then decided to send you here to look after the interests and well-being of your many fellow nationals. Do you try to keep fit?'

'I run each day up to 10 kilometres and three times a week I go to the gym.'

'Which gym?'

'The truGym in Boston.'

'If I remember aright, it's pretty close to McDonalds. That must be a real temptation after a hard workout?'

Ljubica smiled.

'Sometimes.'

'It would be to me. I'm guessing, was it as truGym that you first met Barry Kisbee?'

'Yes.'

'And how long did it take before you became more than just acquaintances?'

'Not long.'

'What did he tell you of himself?'

'He told me had spent three months in prison for being in a fight, if that's what you mean.'

'You didn't think this was a good reason to keep well away from him or when he was cautioned for shop lifting and affray – and this was after you had met and were together.'

'That is not true. He would have told me.'

'And if he had told you, what would you have done?'

'It cannot have been very serious as he was not arrested.'

'You told him about Marney and Katarina and all the money, I presume.'

Her solicitor leaned over to her.

'No comment.'

'What do you think of the Stump, St Botolph's Church?'

'It is very beautiful and very old, I think.'

'There are many fine old church buildings in England but most are locked all the time to protect them. Were you surprised to discover that St Mary's Church in Wainfleet, was open all the time.'

'Yes ... but I was never there.'

'I believe you have been there, and in the company of your boy-friend Barry Kisbee, and it may even be that the suggestion was made to you by someone that it was worth seeing.'

'I don't understand what you are saying.'

'Nobody comes casually across the Church at Wainfleet St

Mary. It is a mile from the village and enclosed within a small wood. So who suggested you go and pay a visit?

'I remember now. It was Inspector Hannah, when he had called in at the farm.'

'And you visited it.'

'Yes, that's it. On his recommendation Barry and I drove there one day, and I put on my running kit and ran back.'

'Why kill Marney and not Katarina?'

'She is Slovenian ...'

There was silence.

'I assume it was whilst you were nursing that you saw what Propofol can do?'

She lifted her hands from the table in a sort of resigned gesture.

Ellie and Chris entered the room and Barry barely looked up at them as Ellie named those present. Cate knew that with the suspected racist views held by Barry it was provocative move designed to produce a response of some sort.

Barry continued to feign boredom and unconcern.

'Have you ever read *The Art of the Deal* by Donald Trump, Barry?'

Taken aback by the question, he looked up but didn't speak.

'You should, and that is what we are now engaging in – the art of the deal, the deal which with encouragement from us when the case comes to court will enable the judge to pass sentence leniently.

'The thing is, we now have sufficient evidence in the form of your single-barrel shot gun (for which you do not possess a licence) with which you were hoping to resist arrest, together with our discovery of an electric cattle branding tool found, poorly concealed, by the Scene of Crime Officers who are still dismantling your flat. That branding tool will be examined in minute detail and I'm told that it if there are even the tiniest traces of human flesh, they will be found. So, you can perhaps see that attending to a deal might be a good idea after all. Why on earth did you have an electric cattle branding kit in your possession?'

'When I came to live here, I thought I might make some money doing jobs like that for farmers, only I discovered that there are no cows round here as it's all vegetables, and that anyway most farmers these days use what's called cold-branding.'

'But you did find a use for it. Who told you about the card nailed to the back of a murder victim in London?'

'It was a brainless thug I met inside and kept in touch with mainly because he was reliable supplier of stuff he sent, using a delivery firm.'

'His name?'

'You won't believe it when I tell you but it's Horace, but he shortened it and liked to call himself Ace, Ace Lumb, and said he used it as a sort of calling card, which he thought was really funny.'

'Who made the decision to burn the figure II rather than the number 2 into Marney's back?'

'I'd never used it and I found it difficult to operate except for straight lines. Ljubica said II was 2 and it struck me that it would mislead the police in two ways. In the first place they'd be looking for something involving "eleven" and then, they would assume a link with London.'

'I assume you were supplying drugs to the many Slovenians here to work, which is risky when there are so many and someone might let something out and the supplier is then identified.'

'I'm not that stupid. Others did it for me.'

'And Ljubica oversaw it all?'

'No, she didn't.'

'Oh, come off it.'

'No, she didn't. She never used herself, didn't even smoke. She was a fitness fanatic and still close to the army at home. I knew that and she wouldn't have approved if she'd known what I was doing. She said she was there to look after their interests and well-being.'

'But it was Ljubica, I assume. who asked you to try and get hold of a bottle of a white liquid called Propofol from an anaesthetist's room at the Pilgrim?'

'No, it was a bottle of Diprivan. She said doctors used it in the anaesthetist's room to help relax patients and that she needed it herself as she was experiencing a lot of tension being with Marney and Mary who were always fighting and rowing. It was easy. As a porter I was able to go into the room without causing suspicion of any kind. The bottle was on the side having not yet been put back in the cupboard whilst the anaesthetist was in the operating theatre. I regularly got syringes and needles anyway.'

'For your own use?'

'Some'.

'And the shotgun? Why that?'

'He liked shoving his dick up girls from Slovenia front and back, and Ljubica thought it an appropriate way to kill him and see how he liked it. She pulled the trigger and what was odd was that she hardly reacted to the recoil which made me wonder whether she had used guns before.'

'Who chose the river at Midville to dump him in?'

'Ljubica, and she said that if we tied him to a fence with rope, it would make the police assume it was a local crime, as that was what farmers did when they committed suicide so that they could easily be found.'

'Where is Horace Lumb now?'

'I don't know.'

It was the lunch break and the team sat together in the strange confines of a prison lounge, served hot drinks by inmates.

The morning's questioning was shared and it was a common feeling that it had proved much easier than they had anticipated.

'I'm satisfied,' began Cate, when they were alone, 'we have enough evidence already to go to the CPS and ask to charge Barry and Ljubica with murder, and Mary with conspiracy to murder. Putting bits and pieces together, I believe Ljubica gave a message to Marney from an unspecified girl asking him to meet her in the churchyard of Wainfleet St Mary where they could be together. He couldn't resist and went flying off, drove his vehicle up the drive where it couldn't be seen and waited. It was not her but Ljubica who turned up and tempted him into the Church which was of course open. Already there was Barry and between them he was secured long enough for Ljubica to administer the Propofol which Barry claimed she had said was a relaxant. They used an electric plug in the Church for the branding, dragged him outside, either unconscious or already dead and she shot him up the backside as a revenge for all his sexual abuse of other girls! We also have a very definite new lead with the London killing.'

'But why has Barry decided to come clean about all this?' asked Jo, 'and do we take seriously his claim that it was all done by Ljubica? He may be thinking that conspiracy with a word to the judge about his help, might lessen what he knows is coming, but is it the truth?'

'Yes, well, we have to keep those questions before us,' replied Ellie, suddenly feeling a little cross with Jo.

'What about DI Hannah?' asked Detective Superintendent Mann from Lincoln.

'That's what we will find out this afternoon,' said Cate.

Cate, Mann and Sammy sat opposite Connor and all were named for the tape. His lawyer immediately objected to the way Connor had been dragged from his bed and placed in a cell in a prison, and now had to undergo questioning on his conduct into the murder of Emmanuel Edmonds. This, he insisted, belonged only to Professional Standards, and he would only answer questions to them.

'This interview is not being undertaken by Professional Standards,' said Cate. 'There are matters which we are referring to them, serious matters, but it is not what we are here for. We are investigating a murder and a conspiracy to murder. As far as I am aware DI Hannah, you have not investigated the possibility of a conspiracy to murder. Is that right?'

'I always believed that there must be two people involved, given that the body was moved and manipulated into the river, but I found no evidence of a conspiracy beyond that.'

'When I did an audit recently, you indicated that you thought this was a crime from outside, part of a much larger national conspiracy.'

'Yes, and another member of your team turned out to be the murderer in Scotland which doesn't exactly show your team and superiors in the best of all possible lights.'

'You had therefore given up looking here for the killers.'

'We never give up, or at least some of us don't.'

'It was clear to me that you had. I asked about new possible directions and you said there were none and that you were waiting for our team to investigate a national connection.'

'Isn't that what you're there for?'

'Yes and look where it has brought us: Boston. In Boston, therefore, how long before the murder did Mary Edmonds inform you of what Marney was doing financially and paying for a house and providing large sums of money for a young woman?'

'I didn't know.'

'Really? That is not how others remember it. So perhaps you might try again.'

'I can't remember exactly.'

'Days, weeks, months?'

'She wasn't telling me in an official capacity, but as a friend.'

'So, if someone told you of a bank robbery in progress but as a friend and not in an official capacity, you would do nothing about it?

'Of course not.'

'But in this instance, you didn't try to find out whether what he was doing was legal or illegal, and therefore a crime.'

'After the murder I brought in two officers from the Fraud Squad who found nothing illegal.'

'Yes, locking the stable door after the horse had bolted. Why did you show no interest in Katarina Arvot, Marney's alleged mistress and recipient of considerable generosity on his part, who disappeared after the murder?'

'DC Enright spoke to her at the house of her sister in Durham and we excluded her from our investigations.'

'Even though you knew there was another man involved with her who might well have every reason to want to kill Marney?'

'I knew there was another man, or suspected it was so, even

though he didn't visit her at home. DS Hollioake followed this up and took her photograph to every possible hotel, restaurant or pub they might have visited without recognition .'

'Though you didn't check on this, did you, and that was because you already were fully aware of the identity of the man? Am I right?'

'No comment.'

'Then allow me to do so. DS Hollioake had already let you know that he was in love with Katarina, so you encouraged him after she had left for Durham to pretend he didn't know her and was visiting hotels and pubs when you knew he was not.'

'I cannot speak for DS Hollioake.'

'On the morning you had been to see Marney's body at Midville, before you did anything else, you insisted that you and DS Hollioake went into Boston for a cooked breakfast. After what you had just witnessed many would have felt unable to do that.'

'I know, ma'am, from our previous conversation at the time of your audit, that we have both seen unpleasant sights in the course of our work and we get used to them. I knew I was going to face a busy day and a cooked breakfast was what I needed.'

'It's not quite the same though, is it, when the body belonged to someone we have known? Marney's body had been subject to the most terrible abuse imaginable.'

'Perhaps women officers are less suited to this than men.'

'Well, I suppose DI Hannah, that might account for your obvious misogyny in refusing promotion to even extremely talented female officers, but we'll let that sleeping dog lie and pass on. Isn't it a priority in such circumstances to inform the family first? I mean before tucking into a hearty breakfast. Or was it for the same reason that on the previous day, when Marney was reported missing, you made the decision to do nothing about it in terms of alerting other officers, because you knew they would not come across him however hard they looked? And that was because you had learned of his fate from Mary and Ljubica. And for much the same reason you removed from the case file the information that Ljubica had been in the army in Slovenia where she had learned some nursing skills.'

'It didn't seem relevant.'

'It didn't seem relevant? Marney had a drug injected into a vein by someone who knew how to do it and who knew the effect of that drug on someone, rendering them unconscious in seconds? And tell me, DI Hannah, might it have been more relevant had you learned as we have, simply because we checked it, that Ljubica Kovač went straight from the army into two further years with Slovenian Special Forces?

He did not reply.

'DS Hollioake told you about her entry on Facebook doing National Service and you accepted that even though what someone writes on Facebook can be a pack of lies. You did not think to check.'

'I don't use social media.'

'I can't believe what you have just told me. A detective who doesn't realise how much crime is controlled using social media and you sit there and say you don't use it. Some, and I mean just about every detective I know would regard that as a serious neglect of duty.

'You said to DS Hollioake that no woman could have committed the murder. What about one who worked out in the gym three days a week and ran at least 10 kilometres every day, and knew how to render someone unconscious and was also quite used to firing guns?'

'It's alright for you with your big team and resources. I had one DCs whom you took away from me, leaving me with just two officers.'

'Please answer my question. Do you see things differently now knowing about Ljubica's background?'

'I have no idea what it means for her to have been in Special Forces.'

'On the morning of the shooting you took with you to the farm, ostensibly to deliver bad news, Constable Linda Andrews, and not DC Enright. DC Enright can run rings round you and smell out obfuscation, as you and I can smell newly baked apple pies when we walk through the front door. You weren't prepared to take the risk.

'On arrival, with Linda Andrews as witness, you informed them of what they already knew and had known for at least 24 hours, and the evidence suggests that you yourself were also in possession of that knowledge at least a day earlier too, which is why there was no urgency when he was officially reported missing for you to do anything, because you knew by then that he was dead. That encounter on the farm was a charade. You did not want DC Enright with you because you feared she would be able to tell that it was.'

'No comment.'

'May I ask where this is leading,' intervened the solicitor. 'Almost everything you've said is speculation. If you are going to charge my client, then do so or release him.'

Cate ignored the solicitor.

'Are you able to recall what time it was when Mary Edmonds, on the day before you notified her of his death, informed you that Marney was dead?'

'No comment.'

'How long have you been having a sexual relationship with Mary Edmonds?'

'That has nothing to do with the matter of the death of Marney. I didn't kill him.'

'So, who did?'

'You know who did.'

'And so do you, and the point is that you've known for quite some time and done nothing about it. They have not been questioned about this crime until today and must be rejoicing that they thought they'd got away with it, thereby allowing Graham Hollioake and Katarina Arvot to be together in a new life in which they already have a baby, allowing you and Mary to be together when you can until you leave your wife and allowing Barry and Ljubica to live off the fruits of his drug industry.'

'A baby? Graham has a baby? That's wonderful. It makes it all worthwhile.'

Connor was smiling.

'It makes all what worthwhile.'

'The murder of that horrible devious bastard.'

'Were you present as a participant?'

'No, I was not.'

'But you knew that it had happened?'

'Of course.'

'How would you describe your part in the whole thing?'

'Accomplice to murder, perverting the course of justice but above all the man who made it possible for Graham Hollioake to fall in love and for them to have a baby, and I am therefore really proud of what I have done, including ridding the world of a very nasty human being.'

'There may be a heavy price to pay, Connor.'

'No there won't because I'm not going to be around a great deal longer. I've been diagnosed with Advanced Congestive Heart Failure and my doctors here at the Pilgrim and in Lincoln will confirm that I have less than a year to live and probably considerably less. Therefore, I am determined to continue to eat cooked breakfasts and leek puddings and have have as much sex with Mary as I could manage, and preferably depart this life whilst doing so, though I bet you won't be letting that happen now. What's the baby's name?'

'Anja.'

'Ok, Cate, do with me what I know you have to. It doesn't matter any more.'

Cate could see that Sammy was about to caution Connor, but she shook her head. She nodded at Connor and the three police officers left the room. Moments later, Cate returned.

'You're free to go, Connor. We'll call you a taxi and you should go home. Superintendent Mann will not be recommending that you see Professional Standards but asks that you take sick leave with immediate effect.'

'Thank you.'

His solicitor looked utterly flummoxed.

Cate and Ellie spent some time on the following morning in contact with the CPS while the others had a lazy morning and a long breakfast. With instruction from the CPS, Jo and Sammy returned to Boston and charged Ljubica with murder, Barry with murder and many other things besides, and Mary with conspiracy to murder. The decision was made that they should appear before magistrates in Sleaford in the afternoon when they were remanded in custody. Bail was not sought and the magistrates announced that they would appear in Lincoln Crown Court on Monday. Barry was moved to Lincoln Prison, the two women to HMP Peterborough, the nearest institution for women on remand.

It was dark by the time they got away from Boston and none of them fancied ever coming back to the place, and it was just a week later that they heard via Graham Hollioake that Connor had tracked him down and spoken to them over the phone about his joy in the birth of Anja. Two days after that they heard from Lincoln Constabulary that Detective Inspector Connor Hannah had died from acute heart failure and that having died in office, his wife would receive a full widow's pension.

Jo had never been his greatest fan, but on hearing the news at they sat in the office, said, 'Connor Hannah was a misogynist, a liar, an adulterer, an accessory to murder and perverted the course of justice, but, ironically, I feel rather sad.'

'I thought you were going to say,' said Eamonn. 'that with those qualities he might have become Prime Minister!'

Washing Up

On the way back to Leamington Spa Ellie had noticed that Jo was unusually quiet and once back said she was very tired and wouldn't be joining the others for a celebratory meal. Ellie was concerned but thought it best to give her space. As she emerged from the shower to get dressed to join the rest of the squad, Ellie could see Jo already asleep in bed and assumed that perhaps she was sickening for a cold. Although everyone was tired, they also shared a genuine sense of achievement absent when Robbie had been arrested and charged.

When Ellie returned to their room she was at once aware that Jo was awake and her face showing all the signs of tears. She threw her coat onto a chair and sat down on the bed taking hold of her lover's hand.

'What is it, my darling? Tell me.'

The tears appeared once again, and Ellie put out her left arm to enfold Jo's head as she cried.

Ellie knew she would need to allow her time and space and had no idea what it was about except that she had never known her like this. Jo was strong and perhaps the ablest person she had known. To see her vulnerable was therefore profoundly unsettling. Inevitably she feared that it was something she herself had said or done, though she couldn't begin to think what it might have been. Or perhaps it was a comment by one of the team. She herself had known the experience more than once of living with a careless or deliberately wounding word made by a colleague or superior. Often it was trivial but it went deep. But again, she knew that everyone in the team thought so very highly of Jo.

She continued to hold her close and allowed Jo to fold into her.

'Come on, my love, tell me. Is it me? Have I done or said something stupid to upset you?'

Jo raised her what Ellie thought her exquisite beautiful blue eyes to look at her.

'My beloved, you wouldn't know how to hurt me. Your love is constant and true and you are the meaning of my life, and I adore you. No, it's me and it's all my abject failures, which have made me realise that I should resign from the force and go back to mum and dad in Norwich.'

Ellie placed her other arm around her and held her even tighter than before, the effect of which was to occasion even more tears to fall. Ellie did not yet feel it was right to speak.

Ellie had once been married and had had several other subsequent relationships including one with Martin, but it was not until she first cast her eyes on Jo on that first visit to Boston, that she had begun to realise what it meant to love someone and not just be drawn to them out of loneliness or sexual longing – not that there wasn't plenty of that in their life together. The prospect of losing her was just too enormous to consider.

Ellie had always loved the way Jo dressed so simply. Her clothes were obviously well chosen but never showy but she had often seen people turn and look at her, men for the obvious reasons that she was immediately attractive and women for the clothes she was wearing, even if there might also be some who fancied her. Ellie could not deny the incredible physical attraction of her partner, but even more than that she was stimulated and excited by the quality of her mind, the speed with which she thought things through, her remarkable powers of observation and discernment. Lots of women in this world were attractive, but she had met very few with these qualities in one person. Meeting her parents had been a source of sheer enjoyment and fascination, seeing that their daughter manifested so many of the gifts and talents they possessed. They were obviously proud of her, but possibly and wholly unconsciously because they saw in her something of themselves.

The tears came to an end and Jo began to speak, slowly and tentatively as if what she had to say was as much a source of fear to herself as it would be to Ellie.

'What we have had to face, not just in these last days in Boston but before it in Scotland is too much for me. We have been brought face-to-face with the terrible reality of human beings killing another for revenge or to satisfy their own longings. I grant that the woman in Scotland was a disseminator of hatred, and I accept that Marney in Boston was a despicable human being in so very many ways, but to have to face those who deliberately chose not just to kill but to do so with a brutally bordering on evil, has hit me deep inside. What a terrible world has come into being. And my failures have been so terrible.'

'Jo, my darling, you are the one who has surpassed us all.'

'But I was there when it all began, I was there before Marney was killed, when a conspiracy was growing. I failed to see it and failed to stop it.'

'You're right. And you also failed to stop the war in Iraq, not to mention the Brexit vote, for which the intelligent people of this country hold you personally responsible. You were around for both and, all things considered, you are a total failure, though apart from that, I adore you.'

Jo looked up.

'You're making fun of me.'

'Well, only to an extent. What I said was perfectly true, you didn't stop those things, nor did I, but you were not in a position to do anything other than just be there and recognise that some things are outside our control. There isn't a single member of our team who doesn't know that in terms of the functioning of your brain in the work of detection you are superior to us all. And we depend upon that. We rely on your insights and the leaps you make which take us forward. When you were in Boston, in the days before you and I had met – the dark ages – you were only a PC and your knowledge of the community was greatly limited by that. You only became a DC when Connor felt that following the murder, he had to have a woman in CID to please his superiors. It was nothing to do with you as such, galling though that is.

Therefore, you were not in any kind of position to know what was going on until after it had happened, and then some black woman from London came and stole you away.

'As for the rest, the regular encounter with evil, is a feature of human existence from earliest times. Read again the Greek tragedies. Much more than the sheer nonsense of the Bible, they take us into the depths of the human heart and reveal what is to be found there, and it's quite scary because it points to a constant tension, if not battle, between good and evil, in which we are all of us inculpated, but requires inadequate people such as you and me to protect the rest of us from the very worst consequences of our nature. So, before we get into the next piece of action which I think will be in London, I want us to have a day and night away, to go into the countryside. But as for resigning – sorry, Detective Inspector, no chance!'

Jo raised her face and they kissed.

'Do you know, my beloved, I need some special medication which only you can provide, so I would like to undress you completely and make love.'

'I'm unlikely to object.'

As they gathered in the office, Cate opened proceedings with a reminder that their task was only half accomplished.

'We were set up to solve four murders which when we began assumed were all connected and perhaps even done by the same people. We now know this isn't so. But two of those murders remain unsolved and will require our undivided attention. The first task is to discover the whereabouts of the man who likes to call himself Ace: Horace Lumb, who may be the person who carried out the first crime at the behest of others, at least one of whom may be a former police officer with the City of London force. Today I shall contact Eamonn at MI5 and with colleagues at the Met and see what they can offer in the way of help. It's quite possible that he is using a number of aliases.

'The second task is begin work on the murder of Tony Hendry, but here and now, today, we need to do a full debrief on how things were handled in Boston and what we might have done better. Tomorrow you can all stay in bed as long as you wish, all day if necessary.'

Cate made them work hard right through until the sandwiches arrived and gave them a break. Each person was invited to offer their comments on how the investigation and interrogation had gone. From the beginning Cate made it clear that no one, including herself, was to be excluded from appropriate critical observation. She emphasised that a supportive team enabled that, without it being felt as a personal attack on anyone. She did however surprise them with the news that after lunch they would be being joined by their former leader, Martin Peabody, who was intending to complete their work in Scotland by letting them know all that Robbie Douglas had confessed to. For Chris and Sammy this was all outside their experience, and Cate indicated that neither should feel they had to stay, though both made it clear that they wanted to be there with the other members of their team.

As they were eating their sandwiches and therefore expecting to switch off, Cate began to go into detail about what was to come next.

'Given the fact that we need to go to London to pursue Horace Lumb, I am going to ask Ellie to take the lead in this and she will be accompanied by Sammy and Chris. Because I am most familiar with the Herefordshire killing, it seems appropriate that I take the lead there accompanied by Jo and Bobi. Once the London lot have made their rapid and spectacular arrest, they will come and join us as we tackle the delights of the countryside of Wales. Once Martin has finished this afternoon, the two groups can meet and give thought to how they might begin their tasks. Are there any questions?'

'Will at least one of us have to go back to Lincolnshire for the eventual trial?' asked Chris.

'Almost certainly, but that is going to be some considerable time off and we'll give thought to it as we draw nearer to the trial date.'

Martin admitted that as yet he had not begun his new job in

Manchester and used the phrase "excited by it" to mean the exact opposite, and that he had therefore been on holiday since he had last seen them. He began by congratulating them on their success in Lincolnshire and that it was abundantly clear that without him they were much more effective as a unit, at which they raised an inevitable protest.

'The most painful part of my holiday, most of which was spent on the West Coast of Scotland, was the visit I had to pay to see Robbie on remand in prison. In Scotland no less than elsewhere, police officers do not have an easy time inside, and even though Robbie is 6'6", a few attempts at doing him physical harm have been made. He spent many an afternoon in the scrum, but as he said, there he had seven other people alongside him. In prison he is on his own.

'We know just how much rugby, Scottish rugby and South African rugby means to Robbie and I'm delighted to say that he has already received a great deal of support not just from the Williams family but many other supporters of South African rugby who know the part played by Robbie in its support. I didn't know, but he has given a lot of money to enable young black men to play the game who otherwise would have been prevented from doing so in the absence of funds to buy kit. To many people there, Robbie is a hero, and I have to say that from my own telephone conversations with Maria Williams and members of her family, it is clear that he is even more of a hero for what he has done in ridding the world of a foul and unpleasant white South African racist. Anyone of you who doesn't understand how a murderer could be a hero should look on YouTube at one of her meetings and just listen to the hatred she disseminated.

'But we were not there as moral policeman, we were there to solve a murder and I very much hope that no one will repeat this outside, but I very much wish we had not done so and could have persuaded Robbie to get on an aeroplane.'

There were quiet moments of agreement.

'He asks me to thank you for everything and sends special greeting to the one member of the team he knows made the difference, the one who in effect caught him: and that is you, Jo.

He said that soon after meeting you, he knew you were the threat, that you were the one most likely to discover the truth but he hopes that one day, you and Ellie might go and visit him.'

'It was a team effort, not the work of an individual.' pleaded Jo.

'He said you would say that.'

'But what a paradox: the person who murdered and decapitated his victim is also one of the loveliest people we who knew him, have come across. I hope South African Special Forces, or even those from Slovenia, can come and enable a daring escape and that he can spend the rest of his life in the country he loves. For me, he will ever be Richard Hannay, arguably John Buchan's greatest hero, and to think, something that scares me, I helped put him jail.'

'It isn't often, at least not in my experience,' said Ellie, sitting close by Jo, 'that police officers either wish or even have the time to engage in the sort of discussion we're having now and I think we should cherish these moments.'

Ellie had arranged a luxury hotel for an overnight stay in the Cotswolds to which she and Jo set out on as soon as the afternoon meetings were done. They had a lovely four-poster bed.

'Thank you, my darling,' said Jo as they lay on the bed before going downstairs to dinner. 'I shall miss you in the next few days whilst we are apart, but I think we are always together.'

London Life

Sammy and Chris moved into Ellie's flat with her but used Lewisham police station as their base. "Dirty Dave" Charnley was delighted to see Ellie again and expressed the hope that she was back for good but had to be disillusioned.

'Does the name Horace Lumb ring any bells for you, sir?'

'I can't say it does. Why? What's he done?'

'It's highly likely that he is the person responsible for the murder of Peter Sherriff. He, quite understandably, chooses not to use his first name, but has instead shortened it to the last three letters: Ace, and if you recall it was the Ace of Spades that was nailed into the back of the victim.'

'It isn't much used nowadays, but there was a time, say back in the 70s, when black men chose for themselves or were given the name "spade", presumably because of the colour of the playing card symbol. I'm not saying that this is what is going on here, but it might give you a way forward to reflect on that. It could be that we are talking about a black guy. I know that there's lots of them in south London but at least it's a beginning, if you want it to be. Oh, and that reminds me, until about 10 minutes ago you were an acting DI and that clever-clogs girlfriend of yours was a DS. So how has it come about that you are now a chief inspector and she's an inspector? Must be something wrong there!'

'Well guv, you can't keep good girls down forever.'

'Ah, the story of my life, Ellie: I only get to meet the good girls!

He smiled and gently nodded before leaving.

'Why do you call him "Dirty" Dave?' asked Chris.

Ellie laughed.

'It's a sort of affectionate tag that tends to follow those who have worked in Vice. He was head of Vice at the Yard for a number of years but in fact he is anything but dirty and everyone who has ever worked for him has such great respect for his wisdom and understanding. not least of the criminal mind. You might say he's the copper's copper.

'One of the great advantages of having you two with me, is that you are not known in south London, not known within the criminal fraternity, and although that will not last long, because word spreads like wildfire, it's important we make the most of it. You, Sammy, will know of the implicit dangers of this and you will probably hazard a guess that some of the villains round here are not necessarily very nice people. Chris, you will be on a steep learning curve but I have every confidence in you. Never doubt the authority with which you operate, and whatever you do always keep in touch with Sammy or me, and no heroics please!'

'It's most odd that you should say that, because I'd already more or less decided that anyway.'

'There's one other, rather boring thing to mention. Whilst we are in the nick here with any other officers, I am "ma'am"; when we are just us together I'm Ellie. Okay?'

'That's really not a problem to me, ma'am,' said Sammy.

'Nor me,' echoed Chris.

'Okay. I want you to spend some time with the computers this morning trawling through the criminal records of black guys old enough to have been using the word spade from the 1970s to describe themselves. Put it in as the search item and see what comes up. I'm black and I've certainly never used it nor even heard it so I think Superintendent Charnley may be accurate when he says the 70s and possibly the late 60s, so you'd be looking at someone in their 50s+. Experiment and play around. The equipment is good and the programs excellent. Talk to each other so you're not doing the same thing at the same time. I'm going to visit an old contact whose computer is in his head and see if I can find anything out. We'll meet back here at 12:30 for lunch.'

Ellie drove to Charlton where there was a club with a gym much used by men of the black community. One of the leaders there she knew well and trusted him within the boundaries that they both took for granted. When she entered she knew at once that there would be many eyes on her, some of whom would be fancying their chances, though others would laugh at them because they knew she had turned. She was looking for a man called Boomer, so described because of his quite astonishing capacity to raise the level of his voice when necessary. However, he saw her first and waved to her, inviting her into his office in which reggae constantly poured out of his speakers. He loved the music but he also knew that it prevented unwanted ears hearing what he had to say.

'Ellie my darling, I've missed you. Where have you been?'

'Sorry, Boomer. As for where I've been, I am presently working for a special murder squad in the Midlands, but I'm back here because of the one I'm sure you know all about – the bent Bishop.'

'Is it true that they cut his balls off? '

She nodded,

'It must have hurt.'

'Some people would say it was no less than he deserved.'

'But would you say that, Ellie?'

'I choose to work within the law because I believe in it. Much though I can understand why some people want to chop off the balls of rapists and child molesters, I still believe prison is the best place for them, but that's in part why I've come to see you this morning. We wanting to contact someone who uses the name of Ace, which is short for Horace.'

'Oh my God. How could a mother be so unkind, even a West Indian mother, to give her son such a name?'

'It's the name of a great Roman poet from the first century BC.'

'Perhaps it is but that's where it best belongs.'

'Is it a name you know?'

'No, and it's not the sort of name I would easily forget, is it?'

'And what about the Ace of Spades?'

'A spade was once the sobriquet black guys used of themselves to impress white girls and in their turn, impressionable white girls liked to use of the black men they had sex with claiming their 'aces' were bigger than those of their white boyfriends and husbands. Whether they were right or not I just don't know as I've never wanted to measure them. Perhaps you won't agree, Ellie, but the effect was to encourage some black guys to think too highly of themselves, to give themselves airs and graces, and the white chicks looked at their groins with longing, mostly, I guess, so that they could boast about it to their friends. It was a very silly time.'

'Are you implying that it was widely used?'

'Like every description it can only be used for a little while before it becomes so common it's meaningless.'

'And when did it stop being used?'

'I don't think I've heard it since the late '70s.

'What about one of the older brothers, someone called Lumb? He would be older than most of those who come here, and is perhaps in the pay of certain members of my profession.'

'I am deeply shocked, Ellie, as I thought you were all above reproach.'

'Boomer, you and I have known each other a long time and I don't think we should have any secrets from each other, certainly not on that subject. You and I both know there are bent coppers and I sincerely hope you know that I am not one of them.'

'Although if what I hear is true, you're not exactly straight either.'

He laughed and she laughed, knowing there was no animosity in what he said. Over the years in fact, she had often confided in him and told him he ought to train as a counsellor.

'Actually Boomer, I'd love you to meet her but I mean it when I say she's gorgeous and restraining some of your boys out there, might not be easy.'

Boomer smiled at Ellie and took hold of her hand.

'I'm so glad of that, my darling. I could have told you, come to think of it I did tell you, getting married to that man was a mistake, and then you took up with that cretin of a detective, Martin Peabrain. Now I feel a sense of relief and satisfaction that you have found the right person.'

'Boomer, you old flatterer, tell me about the Ace in the pack.'

'Lumb – If he's the man you're talking about, I've never heard that he is into killing anyone. He works in the import-export business across the river and quite where he imports from I don't know, but I'm told on good authority, that he has a thriving business exporting throughout the country. I'm not going to deny that I enjoy the occasional ganja, as these days it seems to me that just about everybody does, but I've never touched anything stronger and never would, but in the main I gather, that is his source of income. The rumour is he is well protected, not least by officers of the City of London force. If you are going to have business with him, please my darling, be wary. Whatever their colour he doesn't like people getting in the way, if you take my meaning.'

Ellie decided that she had taken her old friend about as far as he could go and didn't want any risk to come upon him either, so she changed the subject to his mother and his family, and he showed her the latest photographs on his mobile. One of the boys came in with some tea. She knew she could trust Boomer but also knew she could only trust him short of that place where he would be putting others, members of the community, at risk. They hugged and kissed and she left, once again running the gauntlet of the boys outside, ready to tease her – which she adored. These, after all, were her people, her family, and she loved them – well, most of them, oh, alright (she thought), some of them!

She returned to Lewisham and found Sammy and Chris still hard at work.

'I think you ought to call a halt and we can go and get a drink and a sandwich at the Joiners Arms across the High St. If we are stationed here in Lewisham we're not allowed into the local pubs in our working hours, but as we are based in Leamington Spa, that's nothing to do with us and there won't be any coppers there but us.'

Topped up with drinks of various kinds, Ellie began her account of the morning's visit to Boomer and bringing back information that would need to be followed up and would of necessity involve the City of London force, though, as she pointed out, that was not the first time they had been mentioned, and she told them about the visits made by Cate and Jo on the so-called audit, which was of course, no such thing.

'That's a great step forward it seems to me,' said Sammy, 'though quite where we start isn't at all immediately obvious but we also have turned up one or things.'

'I couldn't find any reference to anyone called Ace,' said Chris, 'but I then had the idea to turn them into initials. At first the computer wasn't all that helpful, so I gave a quick call to Eamonn on his mobile and he made a suggestion which, unsurprisingly, worked straight away. So it was that I found "A C E Import and Export" and it provided me with an address in the East End of London, so what in fact has happened is that we have come up with the same information from two different sources.'

'Needless to say,' added Sammy, 'the website did not specify which drugs are the speciality of the house, though I imagine there must be some other goods which serve as a cover. I then discovered that they have another base for their work in Southend, and I think it's only fair, Ellie, to point out that when I was moved to this team, I did specify with the ACC that this would never, under any circumstances, involve anything remotely approaching a visit to Southend. You may not think it but I do have some standards.'

The other two smiled at him.

'If we do to engage with them there, I can assure you we would only do it with full armed backup.'

'That's a relief – there's nothing like it in West Mercia.'

'There is one thing worrying me,' said Ellie. 'We are rather a close-knit body in the police service and mentioning names or entering them on computers when some of those names may be familiar, is not necessarily the wisest of actions. I'm not accusing anybody and despite our experience with Robbie Douglas, I still think almost all officers stay within the law, but there are a couple I'm less sure about and as they are local we need to double our efforts to be like Trappist monks and say nothing where their identities are concerned. Are you with me?'

They both nodded their heads.

'What you have in mind, Ellie?'

'Using my flat as our base we should speak to Eamonn as to how best to communicate with him on matters relating to computers and phones and take away Indian meals.'

Chris and Sammy grinned, and they all returned to the major task of eating and drinking!

'I know this sounds highly unlikely,' said Ellie as they later sat drinking coffee in her flat after she had made a call, 'but I've just had a word with Eamonn and he wants us to go to meet with him this afternoon in the coffee shop near to where he works in the MI5 building close to Parliament. He has something he wants to share with us which he cannot trust to a telephone. After that, Sammy, I think it would be a good idea if you were to take Chris to the Range at the Yard. Maybe I'm being overcautious but I can't help thinking that when we are dealing with the sort of unpleasant and dangerous men we may soon encounter, we ought all of us to be properly equipped, if the need should arise.'

'I don't see that as a problem,' replied Sammy. 'From our first attempt the other day it was clear, Chris, that you have a good eye and so what we need to concentrate on is handling various weapons so that you don't shoot yourself in the foot, and more, especially me, somewhere else! I think we can work on that. I am authorised to authorise, if you take my meaning, but there can be no shortcuts and we will have to work hard.'

'That's very kind, Sammy, but I think that what you mean is that *I* will have to work hard.'

'No, I really mean *we*. Teaching the proper use of firearms is demanding as I imagine Ellie knows from having seen it done often enough.'

'Yes, indeed.'

They took the train into Charing Cross and then walked the length of Whitehall and on towards Milbank. The coffee shop they had been asked meet Eamonn is was, to say the least, innocuous and hardly the sort of place any of the three might have associated with spies!

Eamonn was already in situ when they entered.

'Solved it yet?' he said, somewhat skittishly.

'You may laugh, but I think we've made real steps forward, even though there is typically disconcerting element in it which we have been encountering elsewhere.'

'Surely you're not implying that there is another bent copper?'

'Possibly an *ex*-copper who is bent though I very much suspect from what Cate and Jo reported when they met him, that it wouldn't surprise me if he had been up to activities not entirely commensurate with his office, shall we say, when he was meant to be doing it.'

'That's not good news,' said Eamon, 'not good news at all.'

'So, what have you got for us, Eamonn?'

'I wanted to give you the information face-to-face rather than in an email or a text. I had been quite unable, however much I searched to find anything relating to the Ace of Spades. In terms of its reference to black men it is a very dated concept but when you made contact and told me about A C E in the export and import business it rang some bells, mainly about the import and distribution of drugs though I have to say we have very little hard information and there's always been a suspicion that the amount that has come to us from the City of London Police has been kept deliberately small. Frankly it's not on our horizon at the present time taken up as we are with concerns of terrorism. The man behind it is called Ace McKenzie, and it seems that it is truly the name he was given when he was born. I believe you know that he spent a short time in prison for tax offences. Apparently, he likes to give the immediate impression that he is rather dull, but those who work with him say he is quite the opposite. I have no proof at all, but I suspect that if you were dealing with this man, you are dealing with a dangerous and rather unpleasant person.'

He handed to Ellie a piece of paper on which were printed addresses, email addresses, bank card numbers and expiry dates, driving licence numbers and other information relating to Ace McKenzie.

'Thank you so much, Eamonn. With this information we can begin to move.'

It was not too far to the latest New Scotland Yardand they were directed into a second basement and the Armoury and shooting range. For the next two hours Sammy worked Chris hard but she knew it was important, and as every authorised firearms officer knew, in advance you can never know how important it might be.

Country Life

Jo made Ellie quite envious as she described their first couple of days working in the Welsh/English border. Even in what was the "bleak mid-winter" there was something so beautiful to see each day. The three of them were staying in Kate's flat in Hereford where they had discovered that Bobi was a talented cook and Cate an unrelenting slavedriver, even though for the effort there was little to show for it, but today they were crossing the border into Powys.

'I have to say,' said Jo as they drove down towards Builth Wells, 'that if I had to choose where to be murdered, it would be here rather than in Boston. The countryside is so lovely and the people so few – it's a perfect combination.'

'I daresay that when we've finished our work as a team,' said Cate, 'Dani would be more than open to the possibility of a transfer – for both you and Ellie, but murders apart, my fear would be that you would soon get bored and wish to be back in London again.'

'Surely there are parts of West Mercia that are not like that,' objected Bobi. 'The nearer you are to Birmingham, the nearer you are to crime and we are now investigating one of the worst imaginable.'

'Obviously I can't entirely deny the truth of what you say, and as I mentioned at breakfast this morning, I have a particular anxiety with what we are going to have to look at, which is above all else the relationship between the village policeman and the widow – very Agatha Christie.

'H'm.' added Jo. 'She's not very good at betraying the value and worth of village policeman – they're mostly idiots on bicycles, so she can make the contrast, say with Inspector Slack.'

'We will have to see then, which bicycle he has been riding, if you take my meaning. I have arranged for us to see him first. I imagine he is going to be extremely defensive. He asked me if he should call his Federation Rep or a solicitor. I said that this is an investigation into a serious crime not an investigation into his policing and that therefore the Rep could not attend in any case, but if he wanted a solicitor then that would be perfectly fine but needed to know that the solicitor who dealt with the will of Tony Hendry was already known to me. Do you think it's odd that he would want a solicitor – a sign of guilt perhaps?'

'I rather think that if I had received a phone call informing me that Superintendent Cate Greene was on her way to interview me, I would probably request at least three solicitors to be present.'

'I think I will take that as a compliment, Jo,'

'Just a reminder then. Meeting us at the police station will be PC Cherry Roberts, who will be coming down from Welshpool and who was the FLO at the time of the murder and accompanied the daughter, Poppy, who identified the body in Hereford. You've read the files, Bobi, so you know the direction to take. Jo and I will attend to Sgt Ronnie Bowie. Later on we shall see what has emerged before we turn our attention to Danny, the widow, and Gordon the son who has inherited everything. We ought also to find time to speak to Poppy. Where they are now, I imagine we will discover from Sgt Bowie.'

Arriving in Builth Wells they parked and entered the small police station where a small interview room had been set aside for the meeting with Sgt Bowie, and an even smaller room for Bobi's meeting with Cherry Roberts.

It is well known that police marriages are often fragile, one of the reasons for which is that police officers can find themselves emotionally close to those with whom they are working, and quite often that emotion spills over into a relationship which can quite easily bring about the collapse of a marriage. Bobi could hardly believe how simply gorgeous Cherry Anderson was.

'You were the FLO to the Hardy family?'

'Yes, Sarge.'

'Have you done it before?'

'This was my fifth occasion.'

'I imagine it's very demanding in terms of dealing with highly emotional people but also it must play havoc with your home life as you just have to give up all your time to the task in hand.'

'A lot of police work is spent dealing with highly emotional people and I'm not sure how much worse being an FLO is, compared say, with attending a road traffic accident where there has been a fatality. As for home life, I have the great advantage of being single.'

'If you don't mind me saying you're a very attractive young woman and I can't really see you not having young men interested in you.'

'There have been some but once they know you are a police officer the majority become uneasy and don't want to touch you with a barge pole.'

'So tell me about the Hendry's. Did they play Happy Families, for example?'

'Most definitely not. There was a great deal of animosity between them, and this was greatly increased when the details of Tony's will became known meaning that Danny and Poppy had now no longer anywhere to live and very little income as Gordon made it abundantly clear that not only would all the chickens have to go but everything else, by which he clearly meant them, had to follow suit. To be honest it gave the impression that he didn't give a shit about any of them, though especially his father and the massive business Tony had built up. In terms of motive, he had the most to gain.'

'I take it you didn't like him.'

'No. His sister, Poppy, became very clingy. I went with her to Hereford mortuary to do the identification but I felt that in some way she was lacking maturity and solidity even when she tried to give the impression of being tough. How she will cope, God only knows. And then there was Danny. For her age she is an attractive lady and Sgt Bowie interested. I imagine she expected to inherit everything and would almost certainly have kept things very much as they were. Her shock on discovering that she was getting nothing and would now have nowhere to live, seemed to me to be real I don't think she was putting it on.'

'Tell me then more about the relationship between Danny and Sgt Bowie.'

'He was around so much that I almost suggested that he take over my role as well as his own. Having, in effect, two family liaison officers present, it seemed to me to be rather over-egging the pudding.'

'Did you say this to him?'

'Like you, he is a sergeant and I had to assume he knew what he was doing.'

'Are you clear that there was something going on between him and Danny?'

'Is the Pope a Catholic?'

'What was the reaction of Sgt Bowie to the reading of the will?'

'It was quite interesting. His immediate response was shock and concern for Danny, with a burst of outrage but then I couldn't help wondering whether these outpourings had merely served to conceal his own disappointment. It was certainly odd that once that bombshell had exploded, I never saw him back at the house up to the time when I left two days later. But whether it was a motive for murder, I cannot possibly say.'

'Is he a good copper?'

'I have no idea. I work in Welshpool which is quite a way away.'

'I know what the rules are with regard to a FLO completing the task and not maintaining contact, though I'm not daft enough to imagine that it doesn't happen, but have you had any continuing involvement with the family?'

She shook her head.

'Poppy has telephoned me on a few occasions, and I follow the guidance on this. I listen and make the right noises but have never agreed to meet.'

'I have nothing further to ask. I hope you think it's been worth while driving down from Welshpool to be here, but I certainly think it's been worthwhile to come from Hereford and meet you, and I hope we meet again.'

They stood and shook hands.

Both Cate and Jo thought that Sgt Bowie smiled too much, as if he was trying far too hard to show that he had nothing to conceal.

'When we last met, Sergeant, I was an Inspector. Sadly, I have now been raised to the dizzy heights of Superintendent which is as much a wonder to me as it is an amazement to my colleagues, and not least among them your own DCI Gwilym Jones to whom I spoke last night and informed him that we were coming to have a chat with you. He said he would join us and I told him he would not. After all there's no point in having power if you don't sometimes use it. Anyway, this morning I want you to be interviewed by my colleague here, DI Enright. She has read everything produced including your own report and is therefore in a position to ask pertinent questions. Okay?'

'Yes, ma'am, and this is my solicitor, Mrs Butler.'

'What was your reaction to the discovery of the contents of the will of Tony Hendry?'

'I was greatly shocked, both for Danny but also her daughter Poppy. Danny is a strong and independent person, quite capable of looking after herself and making important decisions but I'm not sure that Poppy is, so when we learned that everything was to go to Gordon I was shocked for them. As for me there was no personal loss because I had no investment in it anyway. I wasn't expecting anything in the will.'

'As you know, Sgt Bowie, this is not an investigation by Professional Standards, so your answer to the next question is purely in relation to the questions surrounding the death of Tony Hendry. Please will you tell us the nature of your relationship with Danny Hendry?'

He turned and spoke quietly to his solicitor.

'I do not see how this has any bearing on the matter in hand, so I will say "No Comment".'

'Please think carefully again about the answer you have just given. What was the nature of your relationship with Danny Hendry?'

He was silent for about 10 seconds.

'I visited the farm regularly because Tony attracted negative voices and protests and I was concerned for their security, far more than Tony should have been himself. He was so very cocksure and quite obviously loved the fuss he generated. He was never happier than when there was a protest and the television cameras were at the gate of the farm. Increasingly Danny hated it, and though I realise it won't help my case, I think she came to hate him too. I suppose I became part of her support structure. Poppy couldn't do that and whilst Gordon came in to work each day, often he did not call into the house to see his mother. Danny told me the things she might have said to a counsellor even though she would never have countenanced that. I'm sure you both know the feeling as police officers that when you are interviewing someone, perhaps someone who has done something terrible, you can feel strangely close to them as they reveal the secrets of their hearts. That's how it was between Danny and me. And it led inevitably to bed.'

'Thank you for telling us that,' said Jo. 'However, I must ask you again how you felt when you learned the contents of the will?'

'Ah! Now we are getting to the nub of the issue. Isn't that right. Inspector?'

Jo did not reply.

'What you are thinking, and it doesn't take much to work it out, DI Enright, is that I was having a relationship with Danny because I was hoping she would inherit a great deal of money and land, and I would then leave my wife and family, in order to share in the bounty coming from Tony's death. However, I was devastated to discover she was getting nothing and went away thinking "well that was a waste of time". And even more, you are wondering whether I was thinking "that was a waste of a murder".'

'How much of Danny have you seen since the time when the

will was revealed?'

'I haven't seen as much of her as I should have wished.'

'And precisely how much is that?'

'Twice at most.'

'Doesn't it strike you as odd as it does me, that having been present so much prior to the discovery of the will, and after all we are talking about someone with whom you have had a relationship over quite a long period, including a sexual relationship which you have admitted, you now more or less ignored her and when we see her later, I shall ask if she feels rejected by you and why she thinks that might be?'

'It's clear to me, as a fellow police officer with considerably more experience than yourself though by being a woman you have been able to climb further up the greasy pole than some others have, you see in my behaviour indications of a motive gone wrong, but there never was such a motive and I never committed such a crime. Perhaps you do and perhaps you don't, know that relationships, however close, can be blown apart by the sort of experience Danny has gone through, by which I mean not just the death of her husband, but the fact that she has now been forced out of house and home, and been brought almost to penury by her appalling son, who believe me, has also inherited the very worst tendencies of his father.'

'So, when we see Danny later, what will her account sound like?'

'I have no idea what she will say. People say all sorts of things.'

'In the past, when your relationship was at its height, you regularly visited her at the farm. Now, you are wanting us to believe that having only seen her twice at most, to use your phrase, she has more or less told you to stay away, that the former relationship is no more, and that she is the instigator of the break between you? How does that make you feel? Hurt, angry, bitter? We none of us like being rejected in any context, but to be rejected in love is usually regarded as the most painful form of being cast aside. So, how do you feel about that?'

'As you say, when a relationship breaks up, it's painful.'

'Sergeant, you don't come over to me as someone who has been in much pain about this.'

'Well, we are all different.'

'When you were in the midst of your relationship with Danny, when you were in bed together, was your wife in any way aware of your philandering?'

'I don't believe so.'

'And since it ended, have you told her about it?'

'No.'

'Had Danny not now cast you aside in the way that you have intimated, had you been giving thought as to where that relationship might be heading? For example, were you thinking of divorce, abandoning your wife and children and beginning a new life, which might include marriage, to Danny as a chicken farmer?'

'I don't think that the relationship was as advanced as to include that sort of thinking.'

'And it never crossed your mind and you never saw yourselves living in the farmhouse and running one of the largest livestock businesses in Powys? That thought never occurred to you, even once?'

'You overlook the fact that our relationship predated the murder of Tony. Whilst he was alive, that thought could never have been there.'

'And what about in that small window of time between the murder and the disclosure of the will which I imagine you had not foreseen any more than any other, in that small space did the thought occur?'

'I was too taken up with trying to care for the family to give thought to that sort of thing.'

'Despite the presence of a family liaison officer appointed for that purpose.'

'I think I knew them better than she did.'

'There is, Sgt Bowie, considerable reason to doubt that and from the words of your own mouth let alone anything they themselves may have said. You have been highly dismissive of both Poppy and Gordon. The only person you gave time to was

Danny and then you suddenly stopped, all of which was noted by the appointed FLO. I am not at all sure that your account of the ending of the relationship is altogether to be trusted and I think it is quite possible we may need to question you further, after we have spoken to Danny herself and to Poppy, who noted your comings and goings and spoke of them to PC Anderson. Now, let us go back a little and consider how well you know the village of Clyro.'

At this point the solicitor interrupted.

'I think my client needs a break and in view, Inspector, of the fact that you have changed the topic of discussion, it would seem appropriate for us to have that break now.'

'I will defer to my superior officer.

'Fifteen minutes only,' said Cate, unsmiling.

The sergeant and his solicitor rose and left the room and almost at once Bobi came in and took their place.

'This is outrageous,' said Cate. 'Where are *our* drinks?'

'On their way. I persuaded PC Anderson to show me the highlights of the town and they have a little coffee place and she's getting them now.'

'And your conversation with her?'

'Confirmed everything we've been thinking about Danny and Bowie, including his sudden absence after the will had been disclosed.'

'That just proves he might be a total shit, but not necessarily a murderer,' said Jo.

'Which is exactly where we have reached with him too,' added Cate.

'She and I also did some internet investigation and found that more 60 million chickens are slaughtered every year in Wales and that obtaining chicken heads is a doddle. Most butchers don't have them on display these days but will have them for making soup. You can't buy as few as fifteen from an abattoir; abattoirs only deal with wholesalers.'

The door opened and in came Cherry with a tray.

'Good morning, ma'am. Fresh coffee.'

'Thank you, Constable,' replied Cate. 'How do you find doing

FLO duty?'

'It all depends on circumstance, ma'am. If it's built around a missing child, it can be pretty grim because the pain is so intense and you have to work extremely hard at controlling your own fears for the sake of the family.'

'But this one?'

'Not like anything I trained for. I would describe it as a house of animosity controlled, though often from afar, by Tony Hendry, with the proviso that I think he hated them all as much as they hated him.'

'And the possibility of one of them being the perpetrator?'

'Neither Poppy nor Danny would have been capable of it. Gordon, as the one who benefited from it, had the strongest motive. The other person, the one in the other room at this moment, also had the motive, but I cannot accept that a police officer could have done such a thing.'

Cate nodded her head.

'Thank you for that and thank you for bringing the coffee. Make sure Sergeant Jones pays you!'

'It's my treat, ma'am.'

She smiled at them, and Jo noticed she slightly widened her eyes at Bobi and left. Jo returned the smile.

Cate asked Bobi to send in the sergeant and his solicitor. Bobi remained outside and Jo steadied herself for further questioning.

'Is this going to take a long time?' began the solicitor. 'This is a working day for my client and important police duties are inevitably being neglected.'

'I'm sure he knows,' replied Cate, 'that I am unlikely to report him for neglecting any!'

She glanced at Jo.

'Before we paused, I asked you how well you know the village of Clyro?'

'It's in my area so I go there regularly. From time to time there are visitors who don't necessarily observe the parking regulations, so wrapped up are they in the Rev Francis Kilvert, who in the 19th century was the vicar and people, I gather, still read his diaries as masterpiece descriptions of that period.'

'If you are often there, would you say you know the backroads well?'

'I believe so.'

'What shift were you on when Tony Henry was abducted?'

'I was on early but I can't imagine you wouldn't already have found that out.'

Your wife would sbe able to confirm that you were at home with her during the evening and the night of Henry's death.'

'She doesn't keep a diary and therefore if you simply throw a date at her, I imagine she wouldn't have the first idea, but except on the nights when I'm on a night shift, it is my custom to spend the night with her. She will confirm that.'

'How then do you explain to her the periods you spend away from the marital home, not engaged in police work, but time you spend with Danny?'

He looked at his solicitor and they shared some words.

'No comment.'

'From which I can assume you did this in the time when you were meant to be working. Yes?'

'No comment.'

'We are here solely to try and discover who committed a murder. Whether Professional Standards will want to have a discussion with you will not be decided by us though we shall be obliged to send them a report. But tell me, do you think you are a good police officer and worthy of the three stripes you wear on your arm, and I ask that in the context of your reluctance to answer my questions to which you were unwilling to comment?'

'I fully realise it doesn't look good, and it began simply through my care for a family I knew well in the town before it became more complex but that's a quite different thing from murder.'

Jo sat back in her chair and smiled at Sgt Bowie.

'I think we share that point of view, Sergeant. I imagine that like me you have heard of the doctrine of Original Sin. Apparently, it means that there are no superior or inferior people, and that we are all alike. Some of us fail disastrously and our prisons are full of such people, though many as you and I know, get away with far too much, but every single one of us is capable of screwing things up. Does this make any sense to you?'

'Yes, I would agree. The issue for us as police officers is to try and put a stop to as much harm and damage being done when people fail or screw up, as you put it.'

'I can see no further purpose in asking you questions about the murder. With the permission of Superintendent Greene, you may go.'

Bowie and his solicitor left the room and Bobi took their place.

'I've found somewhere for lunch,' he said.

'Good, I'm starving. After lunch, Bobi, go and see the sergeant's wife, whilst I talk to Danni, and you, Jo, should go and see Gordon.'

In Town Tonight

Ellie received a phone call from Eamonn, at just about the worst time in terms of her cooking, but she sat down on the kitchen stool and listened intently.

'I hadn't mentioned anything to you, Ellie, because I didn't want to build your hopes up, but if you remember from Boston we were told that Ace provided drugs for Barry using a parcel delivery service which he thought might be DPD or another. Well, it wasn't them and it took me simply ages to find my way into the well protected systems of some of the others. So, I began looking elsewhere and was completely flummoxed by one company because their protection was even greater than DPD. I then had to get help in the form of my boss, the pregnant Kim. It took her less than 10 minutes to get into a system that I had failed to manage in four hours. I wish I knew how she did it. What we found there was a regular parcel delivered to Barry, contents unspecified, but in quite a large box which smelt of coffee, the implications of which will not be lost on you, disguising as it does the smell of drugs from even the best spaniel. This was the consignment that went to Boston. However, we now know exactly where it was collected from. It's a basic mistake of the lazy. We wouldn't know any of this if they had taken it to a collection centre, but instead it was collected from a private house belonging to none other than Ace McKenzie. And here is the best news of all. Word has obviously not yet reached London of Barry's arrest and there is another scheduled collection and delivery, and the collection is due between 8 o'clock and 9 o'clock in the morning. Good news or what?'

'Eamonn, for that you should receive the OBE. It doesn't give us much time to set it up but set it up I will. Keep checking it please, let me know if there is any change.'

As her conversation was ending, Ellie heard the bell ring and she moved over to press the button to let Sammy and Chris inside. As she was completing her cooking told them Eamonn's news and that they needed to give urgent thought to the morning.

'But first we've got to eat, especially as I have laboured over a hot stove to produce it, and whilst we're eating, Inspector Burton, given that this is your territory and not mine, I need you to come up with a plan so that I can request the appropriate resources as I don't think we should attempt to deal with this by ourselves.'

'Certainly not. We shall need a fully armed response unit and I think it would be best if the three of us play no part in it. When I was doing this work full-time, I wouldn't have thanked someone coming from outside and telling me how to do it, but for that reason we need to be clear what we want them to do. They must be accurately briefed. But I have to say I'm truly amazed that they are using a private house for collection. It just doesn't make sense. By the way, DS Halton should soon be an authorised firearms officer. I just need to complete the paperwork.'

'Well done, Chris. I'm sorry you won't get the chance to put it into practice tomorrow.'

'I'm not, for if there's one thing Sammy has taught me more than anything else tonight, it is that if you carry a gun, you are more likely, as a police officer, to be met with a gun.'

Whilst Sammy and Chris finished their supper, Ellie was already on the phone and was instructed to come to the HQ of SCO19 within half an hour.

'Sammy, I need you with me, even if only to tell me when to shut up.'

They took a cab and at this time of night the traffic was light and they were there well in time. The Commander greeted them warmly.

'Welcome to Specialist Firearms Command, Detective Chief Inspector, and a special welcome to you, Sammy.'

'You two know each other?'

'We certainly do. We meet two or three times a year to discuss matters of mutual concern and to drink more than is good for us.'

'I assume from the fact that you are here, it means you have changed jobs.'

'Yes, temporarily. I'm part of the special squad put together by ACPO to investigate the four brutal murders with factors in common. This one is the one that set us off – a brutal murder of a paedophile bishop in his 80s, whose body was found in a mortuary.'

'That's quite a good place for a dead body.'

'But not in the way that he got there.'

'I gather you asked another member of your team, someone called Eamonn, to send me an outline of what you want of us, which is to intercept a collection of a haul of drugs and to arrest all parties. Is that it?'

'Yes,' replied Ellie.

'Are you wanting to take part, Sammy?'

'No, it will be nice to see how the experts do it.'

'Well, it's straightforward. Once the vehicle has arrived to collect the goods, we shut off both ends of the street. A team will cover the back of the house. Once we gain sight of the goods, we shall move in. Does that sound about right?'

'It does,' said Ellie. 'We are especially on the lookout for a man called Ace Mackenzie who doesn't yet know that the man to whom he is sending the consignment, is on remand awaiting trial in Lincoln Jail for murder.'

'It's not a name that means anything to me but that would only be likely if our paths had previously crossed. What about City? Do they know him?'

'It's a sensitive question.'

'In which case I don't want to know. Before we leave, can we just look at the map and see where it might a good idea for you to be positioned.'

By the time they got back to Lewisham, Ellie knew it was too late to call Hereford, but texted her love even though she had no doubts that Jo being Jo, she would be fast asleep.

The houses in the road were large and detached, some with electronic gates to enhance security though not in the case of the Mackenzie household. However, it did have large bushes at the front to allow adequate privacy. Parked in the drive was a Mercedes S-Class Saloon showing, or at least wanting to give the impression, that business was good. They were in the agreed position, some 200 metres away from the house in good time. They knew that there would be no sign of SCO19 until the carrier arrived and stopped at the house. They themselves were rather conspicuous – three people sitting in a car – so Sammy suggested that he and Chris went for a walk, leaving Ellie to listen to music on the car radio and to make a good show of reading what was in fact yesterday's Guardian.

'Three people sitting in a car doing nothing is suspicious,' said Sammy. 'Almost certainly someone will have noted our registration number and reported it to the police. Very often we acquire important leads that way. The people living in this road are no doubt very security conscious and it wouldn't surprise me if Ellie doesn't receive a visit from a patrol car to check her out, especially being black.'

'And me being brown,' said Chris, 'which you overlooked.'

'Sorry, Chris.'

'You need say no more, Sammy. Besides which I would have thought that even more suspicious than the presence of Ellie and me, is the fact that she's reading *The Guardian*. This, I am sure, is a strictly *Telegraph* road, or at the very least *The Times.*'

Ellie herself had anticipated the possibility of a visit from a local patrol car and so was not at all surprised when one came and parked in front of her, out of which came a young officer.

'Would you mind getting out of your vehicle, madam?' he began.

'I certainly would,' she replied, and held up for him to see her police warrant card, 'and as you can see it's not madam, but ma'am, constable. Any minute now you will get in the way of an SCO19 operation, and they will not be pleased, nor will I. Thank you for doing your job, but it is vital that you leave at once.'

'Yes, ma'am.'

He and his colleague in the car did so and waved as they passed her, which Ellie thought was very polite, so she waved back. Just before 8 o'clock the walkers returned and said nothing.

Ten minutes later there was a radio flash, just one word spoken "Indigo", indicating that the vehicle had been sighted a mile away, but still there was nothing to see. Then, a minute later Ellie saw the delivery vehicle approaching and knew that the road would already have been blocked at both ends and the rear of the property covered. The van stopped and the driver emerged and opened the back of his van and carried something in towards the house. And then it happened. Apparently from out of nowhere three vehicles appeared and stopped at the house, one blocking the delivery vehicle, out of each emerged at a rate of knots five police officers armed with assault rifles shouting their identity. It was all over in seconds and then another two vehicles arrived to transport prisoners (if there were any) to Lewisham. People emerged from their house to see what might be happening. Three people were led out in handcuffs, including the delivery vehicle driver, and Ellie could see that all three were black.

'What will happen now?' asked Chris.

'The house and garden will be sealed off and a Forensic team will go in. We, in the meantime, will head for base. Did they do well?' Ellie asked Chris.

'Textbook, I would say.'

The new fingerprint technology saved fingers getting inky, but more importantly gave results almost immediately, so when Chris went in to sit with the driver she was already armed with his name and record.

'A duty solicitor will be available soon, if you wish.'

He shrugged.

'You are Winston Boyce of Amber Road, N12, and you left prison about 6 months ago after serving 3 years of a 6-year sentence for supplying H and Coke. Yes?'

'Why do you ask when you know?'

'What were you doing this morning when you were arrested?'

'An ordinary collection. It's on my log sheet, printed out at the depot, and you can check with them.'

'Is it a regular call.'

'We have a team of drivers and any one of them makes the call. I've been twice before since I left the nick. We don't have our own regular customers.'

'You carried a box in – was that a delivery?'

'Yeah, and I was due to collect one to take on an East Coast run today as far up as far as Hull. I stay overnight, sleeping in my vehicle and then collect more parcels on the way back.'

'When you were inside, did you ever come across a man called Barry Kisbee?'

'Yeah, and I would have been seeing him later today as that was where the parcel I was meant to collect was due to go.'

'And what about Horace Lumb?'

'Are you joking me?'

'Go on.'

'You've got Horace Lumb, aka Ace Mackenzie, somewhere else in this building. That's who I was collecting from.'

'Did you know that in advance?'

'Course I did. As I said I've been there twice before.'

'And have you met him on any other occasions since you left prison?'

'Why the fuck would I want to do that? He's a nasty piece of work and I was pretty pissed off when I got in this morning and saw my log.'

'Do you know what was in the two boxes?'

'No. A declaration is made by the customer online, but we never see that. I have no idea and no interest. There are so many that I simply couldn't care less. I just deliver them.'

'And does Mackenzie/Lumb have other collections?'

'Oh yeah, all over the place. From his home like today and from his warehouse in Shoreditch.'

'Have you done any of them?

'Of course, we all have, but happily I never see him there when I collect.'

'Has it occurred to you he might be using your company to distribute drugs?'

'Look, miss, I've gone straight since getting out. My mum made me promise and I've kept to the promise. I have no intention of returning to jail, not now, not ever. I know I am telling the truth. There is no way my firm would accept illegal substances, and neither would I.'

'Ok. Winston. I need to talk with my guv'nor. After that we can see what's best for you.'

She stood and left the room, being replaced by a PC, who stood against a wall in silence. Chris found Sammy along the corridor lost in thought.

'Excuse me, sir, can you spare a few minutes to talk about the van driver, Winston Boyce?'

'Of course. I hope you've had better luck than me. The law protects the wife from saying anything incriminating about the husband if she has no wish to do so, and trust me, Chris, she has no wish to do say. I will have to let her go. So what of your man?'

She told him of their conversation.

'Ok. He has to make a statement. When it's done, show it to me or Ellie and we should be able to let him get on with his delivery round.'

Ellie had been forced to wait for the arrival of Ace's solicitor whom she thought a very shifty character. She was joined by Sammy who at once informed him of his rights and placed him under oath. The tape-recorder made its customary drone before Ellie announced the names of those present and confirmed with the prisoner his name and address.

'I'm known as Ace, not Horace, and I'm Mackenzie, not Lumb.'

'Are these legal changes by deed poll, or your own aliases?'

'My own.'

'Well, I must address you by your legal name, but I agree to it being shortened to Ace.'

'Thank you.'

'You arranged for a parcel to be collected from your home this morning. Isn't that rather unusual when you have a parcel warehouse in Shoreditch?'

'If I've got a single then it it's quite normal. My warehouse manager asks me to take it home to be picked up from there and I simply chuck it onto the back seat.'

'Do you look at these parcels you take home or wonder what they might contain?'

'We are in the business of exports and imports so all the time we are handling many parcels of various sizes each day. What's inside they have to declare to customs, but once my men see the green sticker has been stamped, they just get on with moving it on.'

'Today's parcel bore no green sticker?'

'That just means it hasn't come from abroad but that somebody here in the country was wanting us to deal with it. It happens quite a bit.'

'And presumably you will have a record of the origin of every parcel you handle. A paper or an electric record?'

'Everything's done by computer now.'

'Good. We are seeking a warrant to take a closer look at your business, but do you have confidence that everything will be in order?'

'There's no reason not to think so. My staff are very good.'

'Good. Incidentally, the box you were having collected was opened by forensic officers at your home and was found to contain a large quantity of heroin and cocaine enveloped in ground coffee beans. It was in your hands and you were intending to pass it on, and you will be charged with possession and distribution.'

'But that's ridiculous. How was I to know what was in it?'

'Actually Ace, I am uninterested in that parcel, and you will no doubt be relieved to know that any charges relating to this morning will be handed over to the City of London force.'

Both Ellie and Sammy noticed that his face immediately relaxed.

Sammy now took over the questioning.

'We *are* interested to know whether some names are familiar to you: Andrew Robinson, Warren Roland, Mick Ellam and Liz Ellam.'

He shook his head.

'Sorry, can't help.'

'You don't know any of them?'

'That's such a pity, Ace, because it could have made such a difference to the next few years of your life in that although DCI Middlewood indicated we might pass the earlier charges on to City, it might be necessary to let the Met handle them instead, as it was their officers who arrested you. A second sentence for possession and supplying would be considerably longer than before.'

Ace whispered something to his solicitor who whispered back.

'Just tell me those names again, as I might not have heard you properly the first time. My hearing isn't always good.'

'Andrew Robinson, Warren Roland, Mick Ellam and Liz Ellam.'

'Mick Ellam was a copper with the City of London, a DS if I remember right, but not a copper you could use in a slot machine, if you take my meaning. Bad eyesight too – if he had encouragement.'

'And did you know Liz?'

'As did many. She had an insatiable sexual appetite but especially for black men whose dongs, she claimed, were bigger than Mick's. She liked him doing shift work.'

'And what of Robinson and Roland?'

'Total bastards. They run an extensive protection racket across south London – shops, pubs, anything that can be an earner, and it's rumoured that non-payers get 24 hours' grace and that's all. Their men specialise in arson and rape, but they themselves never get involved in direct action – of course.'

'By the way, Ace, I forgot to mention earlier that your former fellow inmate Barry Kisbee, to whom you were due to be sending a parcel of consignment of coffee today is currently in Lincoln prison awaiting trial on a charge of murder, so I guess the order is cancelled.'

'Ah well, I never know what's in the parcel.'

'I shall end the interview now and I am proposing that we release you under investigation, which means that at any time within the next 28 days we may interview you again. Do you understand?'

Chris was in Ellie's normal office reading the paper.

'Well?'

'We've got what we need in terms of a lot of information about the Ellams, and more than an introduction to the wonderful world of Robinson and Roland, and their henchmen,' said Ellie. 'My hunch, and I don't know about you, Sammy, is that the murder of Sherriff might well have been a setup inaugurated by Mick Ellam – perhaps he was owed a few by Robinson and Roland. Where and how it was done we cannot yet know but I'm pretty sure Liz Ellam would have been the one to prepare the body for moving and the information about how and when to get it into the mortuary.'

'Yes, I agree, though inevitably until we get to Roland and Robinson themselves, some of that is guesswork.'

'In terms of how we proceed, the time has come to summon the others to join us. Do you both agree?'

'Yes,' they replied in unison.

Diversion

They had arranged to meet in The Strand Café after their respective interviews. Bobi reported that Mrs Bowie was not what he had expected as the wife of an adulterous husband, but bright and bonny, well-dressed and full of life. She confirmed that he was in bed with her on the night of the abduction as he was every night when not on a night shift. She had said it was the day shifts that worried her most in that she suspected him of abusing his position to engage in extra-marital activities, including but not necessarily exclusively, with Danny until he had realised that far from being a source of income to him, she was now as poor as a church mouse. Bobi had asked why she put up with it and she replied that it was a nice house in a lovely place and great for bringing up their kids. Those two children were her priority now.

'Did it all ring true?' asked Cate.

'Oh yes though it would be lovely for her to meet someone new and enable her to feel special, which I suspect she is. Sadly, Bowie seems to have an uncontrollable itch between his legs.'

Cate described her interview with Danny who was extremely bitter towards just about everyone but especially towards her son, Gordon, and Ronnie Bowie, who had messed about with her, getting what he wanted and promising her a bright future together, until the fateful moment when the content of the will was disclosed, since which time he had disappeared from her life.

'It was exactly as we thought, though at one point, and before the murder, he had suggested a divorce whereby she would get half the proceeds of the business and they could set up a life together.'

'What a shit that man is,' said Jo. 'What can we do about him?'

'Professional Standards – it will all be in my report, and given what we know and I shall say, I cannot see him escaping gross misconduct and dismissal without notice.'

'Good.'

'And now tell us about your visit to Gordon.'

Before Jo had chance to begin, Cate's phone rang. She listened intently, and then replied quite simply: 'Book us two rooms. I'm assuming you'll provide the third.'

She put the phone down.

'We're going to London as a matter of urgency. That was Ellie, and we need to leave now. Unless there is something even more urgent emerging from your interview, Jo, you can tell us in the car.'

The sat nav directed them south to Newport via the Brecon Beacons and on towards the M4, and estimated it would take four and a quarter hours, lengthened by a necessary loo and food stop.

'Gordon's partner, Alyson, who's quite a bit younger than him, volunteered the information that she and Gordon had known the content of Tony's will for at least a year,' said Jo, 'and Gordon confirmed this after returning from a loo visit. They both admitted that it was a dysfunctional family and choosing to live with Alyson provided Gordon with the means of breaking free. They had discussed what they would do with the farm should Tony die and agreed that they would get rid of it completely, together with the houses and land.

'She provided him with an alibi for the night Hendry disappeared but all in all I felt either totally conned by them or a degree of respect. I did ask about contacts with animal rights groups which they found amusing. This was because they originally met on the hills hunting foxes with one of the farmers' packs that hunt on foot and which they enjoy. Animal rights activists they are not keen on. Despite hunting foxes being against the law, the Police were usually in attendance to make sure law and order was observed by the antis, and thereby ensuring that the illegal hunting could go ahead without interference from those opposed to it. I replied that because I am a police officer, it was a good thing he couldn't possibly tell me about fox hunting continuing!

'It was Alyson and not Gordon who showed me out and in fact she walked me to the garden gate and I had the distinct impression she wanted to say something to me without him hearing, and I was right. She said he had told her about the number III on Tony's back and that it suggested that this was the work of a serial killer.'

'How the hell did he know about that. It had not been released to the public.'

'A theory is beginning to develop in my mind, Cate as I begin to piece things together, but let me go at my own pace. At least I'm going home tonight.'

The numbers present at the briefing on the following morning included not only the whole Leamington team, but members of Vice and Serious Crime. Chief Superintendent Charnley chaired the happening but asked Ellie, who was known to everyone present, to begin the proceedings with a full account of everything so far. The "blind eye" turned to Ace passed by unquestioned as everyone understood such things were sometimes necessary in day-to-day policing even if those in more exalted Whitehall circles failed completely to understand.

When Ellie had concluded her long account, Charnley once again took over.

'Vice and Serious Crime have just two targets in mind: Robinson and Roland, and have been doing so for some time. The murder of the bishop matters only insofar as it might lead to them, but not otherwise. Superintendent Greene and her team have the murder as their own principal concern and though you're thereby spending my budget, I can't think it's a good thing to have two police forces operating in the same area chasing the same villains, so I suggest, Cate, that you and your team have two days to come up with something or then leave it to us.'

'That would sound sensible were it nor the fact that ACPO detailed us with solving the four murders.'

'You've got pretty close with this one, ma'am,' said one of the men from Serious Crime.

Cate turned to Charnley.

'I'll consult my guys but we'll go with the two days, guv.'

The team went out for a coffee in Renée's Kitchen opposite St Stephen's Church.

'I couldn't help noticing, Cate, as I walked here earlier,' said Bobi, that just up the road here, there's another church labelled "Unique Salvation Ministries". Should we start there?'

They all laughed.

'Look, everyone, if I had turned down two days, Charnley might have withdrawn us completely, so please put your minds in gear as we walk back to the flat and have some ideas, please, even if it's only to say that you think we *should* give up and leave it to them.'

Once in the flat Cate began.

'Ok. What thoughts has anyone got, and I mean everyone?'

'Charnley's quite right,' said Sammy. 'It's ridiculous running two forces on the same case, but what's even more ridiculous is the fact that they've been working at this much longer than we have and in just a very short time we're further on than they are. So, I recommend we stay a little longer and finish the job and we might succeed because the baddies don't know us – and besides which, we're good.'

'None of us are going to disagree with that, Sammy,' said Ellie, 'though they know one of us, and that's me. This is my manor, remember.'

'But that's just crazy, Ellie,' said Jo. 'We shall still need someone to make the coffee and provide the food.'

They fell about in laughter.

'However, I have some information with which you might make a start,' continued the newly-appointed chef. 'Whilst you lot were driving down yesterday I paid a call on my old friend Boomer, who's a sort of uncle to me, runs a gym for black lads who might otherwise get into trouble, and a source of useful gossip about the underworld.

'This was my second visit in a couple of days and I'm delighted to say that the boys enjoyed seeing me again. Boomer was more wary, at first. He had given us Ace on my first visit and I wanted to try him out on the Ellams, Robinson and Roland. It took a few moments of sweet-talking to get him to open up, but eventually he did.

'He confirmed what Ace gave us about Ellam being on the take from him and, probably, others in his time in the City Force, and I didn't push him for names as it's nothing to do with us. Liz Ellam he described as a scrubber, which we already knew. Most interesting of all, however, was that Mick Ellam was more than happy for Robinson and Roland to have free and frequent access to Liz if they so wished, and that they owed him something big from his time across the river. Far from being in their hand, it was the other way about. They owed him big time, though he couldn't or wouldn't say what that was all about.'

'Cate,' began Jo, 'I wonder whether we might begin with the weakest link – Liz Ellam, by herself. I can't believe she doesn't know what her slimeball of a husband is up to, just as it would appear everyone south of the river knows what she is up to. I assume she takes payment and we might advise her that she is thereby running a brothel even if she's the only functionary and that they are living off immoral earnings, and this would make a wonderful headline in the Standard: "Brothel run by ex-copper's wife". If we can convince her this is for real, it might provide something useful, not least because we're not from Vice and have nothing else dependent on it.'

'Yes. She knows you and me from a previous visit, so, Chris, how would you feel about going to see her and arranging a threesome with Bobi?' asked Cate.

'As Sir Thomas Beecham said I'll "try everything once, except incest and morris dancing",' she replied to general merriment.

'Ellie, I'm sorry that you can't stay here cooking, but I need you to arrange to meet Eamonn in the MI5 coffee shop as he's sent a message saying he has something important for us, but not whether it concerned here or Wales.'

'No problem.'

'Jo, I want you to go to Vice and see what they have on the gay scene and especially relating to Peter Sherriff and other clergy they are keeping an eye on who might have been his associates.'

'Yes.'

'Sammy, dear heart, you and I are going pay a visit north of the river to see the Commander in charge of Security and Ops in the City Force. We're due there soon so let's get going, people.'

'One final thing, boss,' said Bobi. 'Just how I am I expected to spend the day with Chris, engaging in sexual frenzy, without mentioning to her that you've booked her in for an evening's morris dancing class tonight?'

With a measure of laughter each departed for their allotted task.

Liz Ellam was in her mid-50s, still remarkably attractive for her age and apparent occupation. She opened the door and looked at Chris.

'I only do men, sweetheart, and in any case I'm not very good at sharing but I wouldn't throw you overboard,' the latter comment directed at Bobi.

'Can't I come in and wait?' said Chris, with a perfectly straight face.

'I don't think so, though my husband will be in later if you'd care to come back in two hours or so. He's still pretty good.'

'Well, I'll give it some thought, but in the meantime he's Detective Inspector Bobi Jones and I am DS Chris Halton, and we'll come in anyway.'

Her face was a picture of horror.

'Not without a warrant you won't.'

'Have you something to hide?' asked Bobi.

'No, but I want my husband here and if you come back with a warrant he'll be here by then.'

She stepped back and closed the door firmly.

'Sorry, Bobi, it's clothes on all day for you!'

'So it would seem. Let's go to the car and see if we can ask Cate what we should do.'

Cate had already set off so they spoke to Chief Superintendent Charnley who told them to get to Greenwich Magistrates Court on Blackheath Rd. Bobi knew the form and being of Inspector rank knew there should be no difficulty, especially as Charnley was phoning ahead. Chris would have to accompany him and make notes in her service pocketbook of any questions and answers. When they got there, they were expected and it took very little time before they were on their way again.

'Drugs, illegal movies and deriving income from immoral activity?' said Chris as she looked at it. That described my average weekend in Boston, with the exceptions of the drugs, the illegal movies and anything even approaching immoral activity – more's the pity.'

They were soon back and as they approached front door, this time they were faced with Mick Ellam who did not have a welcoming face.

'Mr Ellam? I have here a magistrates warrant to enter ...'

'I know what it says, tosser. I also know that unless you arrest her, you will not speak to my wife without me being present. Do you understand?'

Neither Bobi nor Chris spoke but continued to walk to the door. There was a moment's standoff before Ellam gave way and let them in. Liz sat on the sofa, smoking, saying nothing.

Although uninvited to do so, the two officers sat.

'So, what is it you want this time?' said Ellam.

'Why, immediately after the last visit of police officers did you make calls to Warren Roland and Andrew Robinson?'

'I was due to call them both on a small matter of business earlier but your two goons made me run late, so as soon as they'd gone, I picked up the phone and got through.'

'What was the small matter of business?'

'That has nothing to do with you.'

'Ah, but you see I know that it has. I know you issued warnings that we were on the trail of the bishop killer.'

'You're guessing. You can't possibly know that unless you had a Home Office Licence to tap my phone and if you used that info in court and hadn't had a licence the judge would probably end the proceedings then and there.'

'Yes,' said Bobi calmly, 'I think we know that but thank you for confirming the content of your calls.'

'We were also somewhat concerned about you, Mrs Ellam.' said Chris.

'About me?'

'It seems that you accept payment in return for the pleasure you provide on quite a large scale, which means that as a brothel owner you are living off immoral earnings.'

'You disgusting filthy bitch,' said Mick standing and then began to move towards Chris, who in less than the blink of an eye stood waiting. He put his hands out intending to throttle her, half expecting Bobi to stand and stop him, but he didn't move. All Mick said he remembered afterwards was a slight swivel on Chris's part and that was it, before Liz was leaning over him.

'What the hell happened?'

'The bitch kicked you in the face.'

'On the cheek,' said Chris, who was sitting down again, 'which is why you fell in the direction you did. Do get up. The only thing that's hurting is your pride, you silly man.'

He pulled himself and resumed his seat, but still glaring at her.

'That was assault.'

'Not at all. It was a classic defensive move in taekwondo made to protect myself and, as you realise, it worked.'

'DS Halton is a black belt,' said Bobi by way of explanation.

'So, as I was saying, Mrs Ellam, you face possible exposure, and our warrant allows us to search your home for possible DVDs and videos which are illegal in the United Kingdom, one of which I can see now on the shelf behind your television plus any illegal substances we come across. A move on your husband's part to assault me, captured, I believe on my Inspector's camera, is unlikely to assist your cause.'

'So, what is it you want?' said Ellam.

'None of the things DS Halton has just mentioned, nor even a conspiracy to murder which might well be added to your wife's charge sheet, for having provided information on getting a body into the mortuary of The Hospice and making sure that the last office was done properly in the house style you knew so well.'

'I ask again, what is it you want?' said Ellam.

'I'll tell you, but there's one thing I'm not interested in, unless I'm forced to be, and that is a conviction of any sort against a former DS in the City Force, unless he was responsible for the murder of the Rt Revd Peter Sherriff, which is our sole concern.'

'And I was not, though it didn't surprise me that someone had caught up with him, the nasty perv.'

'"Caught up with" implies someone from the past rather than the present,' interposed Chris. 'Is that what you're suggesting?'

'Have you got a black belt in interrogation as well?' said Ellam. 'Well, I'll tell you what I know. Some years ago, and Liz will tell you exactly how many, she had a conversation at The Hospice with the relative of a patient there to die.'

'He was a nice man, gentle and kind but with pain in his eyes not just about his mother's death,' continued Liz. 'It turned out he was a vicar, and one morning for my coffee break I went and sat with him in the room set aside for visitors, and he told me something of his story. It turned out that many years before, when just a lad in a church choir, some vicar or other from London had come to the village where he lived and, with other vicars present, some participating and others watching, buggered choir boys laid on by the vicar of that parish. I was struck dumb. He mentioned the name of the vicar who'd done these things but I forgot it and I didn't even mention it to you, Mick, did I?'

'No.'

'Then, before Mick left the force, you happened to mention that there were two bishops who had been drawn to your attention for messing about with boys. I was sickened by it. One of them was moved before his offences could be exposed. The other was outside your area, the Bishop of Kennington, and when you told me his name, I almost collapsed: Sherriff, because that was the name the poor vicar I had spoken with earlier had told me about.'

'I won't pretend,' said Ellam, 'that it didn't occur to me to want to go and see him and beat his fucking brains out and cut his balls off, but I did nothing.'

'It was about six months ago that Mick and me went on holiday to the West Country, Devon and Cornwall, which we both enjoy much more than Spain. We stopped to do some shopping in Honiton and went into a supermarket, and as sometimes happens in life, who should I bump into but that vicar I had known at the Hospice, the Revd Alan Isherwood, who was also doing some shopping. Very kindly he invited us for some lunch at his bungalow in a nearby village called Yatcombe, or something like it.'

'Yarcombe,' said her husband

'That's it,' confirmed Liz.

'Actually the conversation threatened to get a little bit out of hand,' said Mick 'when he began talking about growing desire for revenge on a man who had in so many ways ruined his life by what had happened back then, and I steered it round to trying to persuade him to use the law against him.

'He said it seemed a waste of time as there was an apparent shield around this man. The Church didn't want another scandal and Sherriff also had a measure of fame as an organist who had played publicly on both sides of the Atlantic. Even the media didn't want to touch it, not least he suspected, because everyone was now doubly cautious because of the total catastrophe with the guy called 'Nick'. Everyone, but the police especially had burned their hands on that.'

'Anyway,' said Liz, 'we had a nice lunch and needed to be on our way. It turned out that his wife had been a nurse in the dim and distant past and I made the great mistake of giving her our address, not expecting that our paths would ever cross again. And three weeks later, there he was on our doorstep.'

'By then,' said Ellam, 'he had decided what he wanted to do but sought a little guidance. He asked me how he could get hold of a gun and someone to help him and his wife with the physical stuff. He remembered from the time of his mother's dying something of the routine at the Hospice and indicated that he thought it might be funny to leave a body in a mortuary.

'I told him that in terms of providing a gun I couldn't help nor could I participate in whatever he had in mind. He then stunned me by coming out with the names of Warren Roland and Andy Robinson, and said he'd been given them for the payment of a monkey to a guy they had come across in a pub in Peckham and asked me to confirm that they were real and might be willing to help him. I told him that I knew of them from my days on the force but knew nothing about them now. And I can't help it if you don't believe what Liz and me are saying, and if I was in your shoes I'm pretty sure I wouldn't, but it is true, I did not direct them to Warren and Andy, and neither Liz nor I had any further involvement with Alan Isherwood from that day to this.'

Bobi and Chris had been listening intently and remained silent once Ellam had finished, their faces impassive. Eventually the silence was broken by Bobi.

'Implying a bishop was murdered by a priest is a serious accusation. You and I, Mick have had bosses we didn't like, but mostly have managed not to kill them, however much we might have liked to do so. But for a man of God to kill another is quite an accusation.'

'That's true, guv,' said Chris, 'but this is more a case of the abused desperate enough after terrible years doing what he felt he just had to do to the abuser, or at least that is what is the rationale for what we have heard. Do you agree, Mr Ellam? Mrs Ellam?'

Both nodded their agreement.

'We're not going to undertake any search of the house, you'll be pleased and even, perhaps, relieved, to know,' said Bobi, 'but get rid of that DVD over there. If it's here next time, you will be charged. And as for you, Liz, you don't know what you've missed in not wanting a threesome with Chris and me.'

'After seeing her in action with Mick, I think I chose wisely.'

The detectives left with no further words and said little on the way back to Ellie's flat, each deep in thought.

Yarcombe Again

Ellie was back from meeting Eamonn and clearly wanting to share his information but picked up signals that she ought first to listen to Bobi and Chris.

'There's something I have to show you, Ellie – something I recorded on my phone that happened when we went to see the Ellams.'

'Don't you dare,' said Chris.

'Quiet, sergeant.'

Bobi held up the phone and showed Ellie the video.

'That is phenomenal. Oh, how I wish I had been there, and the speed of your reaction was incredible. Did he recover?'

'Oh yeah,' said Chris nonchalantly, 'it was nothing more than a gentle push on his cheek, but the shock floored him more than the kick.'

'How did he react?'

'He was speechless. Oh, it was great,' said Bobi.

'Why did he attack you in the first place?'

'That came about because Chris intimated that we were intending to arrest his wife for running a brothel and living off immoral earnings, which by the way happens to be true. This was too much for him, though she had already told us when we got there that although she only did men, her husband might be up to attending to Chris.'

'I don't know what it is about detectives who train in Boston, but they do seem to be quite extraordinary. First there was Jo the super sleuth and now Chris who fights them off with her feet. It must be all those vegetables, but now you've started you'd better tell me about the rest of your visit.'

They told the full story of the meeting, first from memory, and then when it came to the detail about Alan Isherwood, from Chris's pocketbook. It took some time to tell the story and it took some time for the story to sink in, Ellie having known Isherwood from her visit with Martin to Yarcombe right at the beginning of this involvement with the four murders.

'How much of this did you believe?' asked Ellie.

'We haven't spoken much about that since we left the house,' said Bobi, 'but I'm clear that when it comes to the matter of the involvement of Roland and Robinson, both Mick and Liz were avoiding any sense of their own complicity, but my own feeling was that substantially what they were saying is true. I can't see how they could have made up the part played by Alan Isherwood, or even known about him.'

'I agree with Bobi' said Chris. 'That part sounded authentic to me. If Mrs Isherwood has indeed in the past been a nurse then I can't imagine that doing a last office has changed much. I would guess that a regular visitor over a long period to The Hospice would have provided an enquiring mind with the sort of information they would need to get a body into the mortuary at a time when no one would notice. It does fit and conveniently extricates Liz from our thinking, but it's going to mean a visit to the West Country to sort these things out. But might it not also give our friends in Serious Crime a way into Roland and Robinson, if they did indeed provide him with a weapon?'

'Possibly,' said Ellie, 'though in this life things never normally work out as simply as that. It's much more likely that he will not name anyone, and frankly I wouldn't blame him. But yes, it does mean another trip down the A303, though coincidentally, that may enable us to kill two birds with one stone though I should wait until Cate's back before I pass on the info from Eamonn, but you two have done brilliantly. Very well done. Fancy a luscious and unhealthy burger to celebrate with?'

No words were necessary in reply.

The others were not at all pleased that they had missed out on the impromptu visit to the burger bar but somewhat mollified by the quite astonishing news that it looked like Bobi and Chris had solved the murder, and even more that it did not seem to have been done by a policeman, and therefore took comfort in watching for themselves the video of Chris in action!

For the moment, Ellie was holding back Eamonn's info, to hear what the other three had been doing. Jo had had a thoroughly entertaining morning with the boys and girls from Vice and they had taken her around showing her the sites and the sounds of south London and all the unpleasant things they had to deal with. She said she hadn't laughed quite as much for a very long time but could report nothing back on Peter Sherriff, largely because the issue of gay priests in south London was so widespread. Out and about they had stopped for coffee in what turned out to be a brothel with a group of girls the members of the squad seem to know very well indeed. To her absolute delight one of the girls had propositioned her, and it had made her day.

Cate and Sammy had met the head of security and ops in no lesser place than the Guildhall in the City of London which was a treat but where the force was based. They were given a full insight into the sort of work they did and met one of their number who was a financial wizard, necessary for the sort of crime that went on which would be wholly beyond the capacity of ordinary minds to understand. They had not mentioned any former members by name, though indicated that there was one they had come across who seem to have done far better in life than his salary as a police officer might have allowed. The commander said she was hardly surprised and that it was on-going problem she was determined to deal with, root and branch. Then they mentioned their involvement with Ace McKenzie, and that although he was almost certainly up to no good, that had not been their concern and what they had received from him was extremely important as they moved towards the solving of a murder. Cate had said she trusted McKenzie about as far as she could pick him up and throw him, but that the commander and her team should keep a close eye on him and especially on those on those officers he dealt with in her force.

'Well,' said Ellie, 'I went to the coffee shop though the only spy

I met was Eamonn. Apparently at a high level, and you will understand why it could only be made at that level, they had information which might relate to the murder of Tony Hendry.

We as the police force, and the security services, embed individuals, male and female, inside various groups, infiltrating often over a long period, so that important intelligence may be gained. It must be perilous activity and I guess we've all heard those stories where sometimes people embed too far in the attempt to be fully and completely accepted near to those who make the important decisions. I was given next to no information other than that one of these agents became privy to a conversation in which the name of Hendry was mentioned. This was an extreme animal rights group, or at least that's their public face if they must have one, but which seems to cover up a considerable degree of anarchy. I was told that they have become highly efficient at attaching themselves like a virus to other groups when it suits them and many of them had found their way into political pressure groups.

'When the name of Hendry had been mentioned, someone had, almost in passing, said that he had been taken care of. It was vital that the agent said nothing, asked nothing, and never referred to it again to any group member, including those who had been present. Whether the agent was a man or a woman, Eamonn was not told. It's hoped that we can build on a small piece of information and work towards a conclusion. This means we can turn our attention away from Builth Wells, at least for the time being, and begin to look elsewhere.'

'That's important as far as it goes,' said Cate, 'but it doesn't take us very far. It seems to exclude Builth Wells but the rest of the country's huge and where would we begin to look?'

'I think I can understand your exasperation about the nature of the search, Cate,' said Jo, 'and I'm not saying this, and I'm pretty sure you know that I wouldn't say it just because Ellie is reporting this to us, but I think this gives us quite a lot to work on, and quite a bit to let go of in order to do that. It looks like we're going to be able to close this part of our task and return to dear old Royal Leamington Spa, and it may be that this is going to be the most difficult part with only a small team, but I think we should get back to the Midlands and get on with it.'

'I hope that you and Ellie know how much I trust you both to operate at your best together and apart without allowing other things to interfere, so I know full well, Jo, when you say something is as it is because you have thought about it for yourself, worked it out and passed it on without needing to run it before Ellie. You're quite right and what a day it has been for us. I'm only sorry Martin isn't with us for, after all, it was he and Ellie who started things here in the first place. This is a fantastic team and already I'm anxious about what's going to happen when we solve the fourth murder and we inevitably must break up, but we'll cross that bridge when we get to it. So well done everyone today, but especially to Bobi and Chris, and I'm thinking of making you, Chris, my personal protection officer. Now, please, anyone – food!

On their way back to the flat, Cate and Ellie chatted quietly together apart from the rest and between them developed a strategy for the coming day which Cate outlined when they arrived.

'Ellie and I been trying to think through what should happen next. We may be facing the most difficult phase of our work – discovering within which group there are concealed killers. MI5 could have made it easier of course by indicating which group it was, but that runs the risk of compromising their agent, so we have to work on a number of groups and let word spread among them that we are hunting the killer of Tony Hendry.

'So, tomorrow bright and early, Ellie and Bobi will head off for Yarcombe, hopefully to arrest Isherwood and his wife, and in the process see what info we might gain from them that can be of use to those here in the Met. I don't want anything mentioning to anyone about this until they are there which will be at about noon, or dear Dirty Dave will probably send the cavalry down the A303 and get in their way. Jo, I want you to return to Vice, with whom you have shared a great deal today, but this time taking Sammy with you, as well as paying a visit to Serious Crime, and let them know that we think we've cracked the case, thanking them for their help (even though they didn't), and that if anything comes from the arrest and our interrogation, we 'll happily pass this on to them. Best not say who it is just yet, but they'll be all over them like a rash once we have returned to the Midlands.

'That leaves our black belt and me. We'll tie up the loose ends here and then go back to Leamington Spa. I suggest that Ellie and Bobi spend tomorrow night here, but when you're done tomorrow, Jo and Sammy, just set off and we'll see you tomorrow evening and, who knows, might even manage a curry together. Ok?'

'She's bloody good at her job,' whispered Sammy to Jo.

'Oh yes. It'll be a race between her and Ellie to see who next gets to wear the Commissioner's hat, though of course she may be hampered by the fact that, as far as I know, she's not a lesbian.'

Sammy could not contain his laugh and all looked round.

'Tell us then,' said Cate.

'Ah, nothing, ma'am.'

'When you use that word, Jo, I'm immediately suspicious.'

Four of them decided they would go for a drink in the Lewisham Tavern where Belmont Rd joined the High St, but Ellie and Jo opted for an evening in their home together – just the two of them, until of course they were joined by the two lodgers.

'So tell me, my darling,' said Ellie as they snuggled up together on the sofa, what was your joke about?'

'Sammy and I were comparing you and Cate as to which would make Commissioner first. I said Cate stood no chance, not being a lesbian, as far as I know, or words to that effect.'

'H'm, it's a good question, but we both know that it takes one to know one and I haven't had even the slightest vibe – have you?'

'Nothing other than noticing how close she is to Chris.'

'Technically, Chris is her bagman, so that's not altogether surprising and they have a love of poetry in common, but you may be right. What about you? Do you fancy Chris?'

'Ellie, I can honestly say, and with every ounce of my being, that I spent hardly any time at all fancying anyone, boy or girl, man or woman, until the day I first met you in Boston. I didn't suddenly think "Oh my God, I'm a lesbian", I just knew that in every way I adored you and wanted to be with you always, and no one else, and when you came to Norwich my mum said to me not just how lovely they thought you were, but they could see that I had discovered the person of my life, and it filled them with such joy, and by the way, I rang her earlier and they're longing to see us again.'

'This is bad news, Jo, my darling.'

'Bad? Why?'

'There's a programme I wanted to watch a bit later, but after that confession of your love, there's little chance of my seeing it now!'

'Oh, I don't know. Twice in an evening and night is not yet beyond me. How about you?'

'I'm willing to give it a go.'

Ellie and Bobi were advised by Cate to travel with blue lights in a marked car, with Ellie alerting forces to their presence. She had also asked Avon and Somerset Police to check that the Isherwoods were resident and to be ready to answer a few more questions by officers from London in late morning. She said she didn't think backup would be needed but it was likely that the two residents would be taken to London for further questioning. It was important protocol but the thought that this was someone's else's problem delighted them in Bristol.

Bobi's handling of the car impressed Ellie and it seemed to take less time than it had on her previous visit but they stopped at the same garage to fill up and went to the café at the rear to get some food, probably the last until evening. The lady who ran the café remembered Ellie.

'How lovely to see you again. And with a different man this time! So, what can I get you?'

'If I remember correctly you were charging a paltry £100 for a sandwich and a drink each when we came before, so give him the bill,' said Ellie.

'Well, as I say to my husband as he gets ready for bed "nothing ventured, nothing gained" – but a fat lot of good it does me.'

She and Ellie chatted, Bobi feeling totally out of his depth in such female conversation, but it was he who brought proceedings to a close.

'I'm looking forward to your next call,' said the lady (whom Ellie had discovered was called Rebecca).

'Me too, though I should just let you know that the next time it might be with my real partner – and she's a beautiful woman.'

Expecting Rebecca to be shocked, it was Ellie who was amazed when she replied, 'Do you know, I've thought about that myself. I have a friend called Susie that I dream about and long for. And the sight of you makes me tremble too. Are these feelings wrong?'

Ellie reached into her coat pocket and produced a card.

'This is my mobile number. I'll be back at base by tomorrow evening. If at any time you wanted to chat, I'd be delighted.

Rebecca looked at the card and then took hold of Ellie's hand.

'Thank you. Ellie, thank you very much indeed.'

'And to answer your question, how could feelings so wonderful be wrong?' said Ellie as she waved farewell.

Yarcombe was close and the first thing they noticed was a marked car at the bottom of the road in which the Isherwoods lived. Bobbi stopped and Ellie got out, showing her warrant card.

'I take it they're in.'

'And expecting you, ma'am. Do you know which one it is?'

'Yes, I've been before. Are your instructions to leave now?'

'No, ma'am, we've been told to do what you tell us.'

'Ok, then. We believe they were involved in a crime involving a firearm and both my colleague and I are armed just in case, but I'm perfectly certain this is a precaution that will be unnecessary. All the same, if you park behind us and keep your window open and Radio 1 off, you will hear any discharge of a weapon and summon help. Under no circumstances are you to enter the building unless I or my colleague, Detective Inspector Jones, asks you to. Ok?

'Yes, ma'am.'

Ellie returned to her car.

The two men in the other car looked at one another.

'I wouldn't mind giving her one,' said the first.

'You're not kidding, but remember she's wearing a gun,' came the reply from the other.

Alan Isherwood had been looking for their car, opened the front door and awaited their arrival.

'Please come in. The head of my theological college always used to ask those arriving if they needed to brush their hair – such an odd euphemism, but if you do, it's through that door there.'

Bobi took advantage of the euphemism.

'So, we meet again. Somehow or other I thought you might have worked it out before now, but I expect you have a lot of work on.'

'Yes, I've been part of a task force based in Royal Leamington Spa concerned with crimes that seemed to be closely related and I only returned to London and your case two days ago.'

'In which case, I must congratulate you.'

Bobi entered the room at much the same time as Sonia Isherwood did and both sat down.

'I'm sure you will understand that most of the questioning will take place under the aegis of the Metropolitan Police in London, and that is where we shall take you today, but Inspector Jones has some questions of his own, mostly of a professional nature.'

'That's perfectly fine. I shall plead guilty and I have no regrets whatsoever. That man for nothing more than his own sexual satisfaction destroyed my life whilst he enjoyed only honour and prestige. He was 82 and might have died soon anyway but this was the right thing to do. Because I died inwardly a long time ago, the consequences of my actions are neither here nor there to me.'

'I have known about it for many years', said Sonia. 'Alan told me when we were both much younger and my own feelings of animosity towards Sherriff grew almost in direct proportion to the effects I could see in Alan's life. When we finally got married after his earlier calamities, there was a sort of understanding between us that we had to do something about him, but didn't know what it might be.'

'We tried the church authorities at Lambeth,' said Alan, 'but they just ignored us and seemed more concerned with protecting the supposed good name of the Church. We did become aware, however, that I was not alone, that there are literally hundreds of victims of clerical abuse. Nor did the newspapers or television seem interested, which amazed me. So, there was no alternative, and we decided to kill him as he had killed me.'

'Alan,' said Ellie, 'You do not have to say anything. But, it may harm your defence if you do not mention when questioned something which you later rely on in court. Anything you do say may be given in evidence.'

'I fully understand.'

'I must repeat the caution for you too, Sonia: You do not have to say anything, but it may harm your defence if you do not mention when questioned something which you later rely on in court. Anything you do say may be given in evidence.'

'Like Alan, we have known you would come back, so we're ready.'

'I need ask you a very important question before we can leave. Is there a firearm in your house?' asked Bobi.

'No. I sought a gun in London and returned it after I used it. He was in agony after I had castrated him so I shot him through his forehead. The man with us who set it up and took the body away then did something most odd which I thought unnecessary and hammered something onto his back which turned out to be a playing card. It made a horrible noise.'

I prepared the body for moving,' Sonia said, 'and having once been a nurse performed the last office. We helped transfer the body into a black van which drove off. We rinsed the floor to clear away the blood and got ready to come home.'

'Where were you when it took place?'

'It was in what I think they call a 'lock-up' – something somewhat larger than a garage but without windows. We were driven there and collected afterwards and taken back to where our car was parked.'

'Do you have any idea where it was?'

'I don't know London and I think the driver was intent on us not knowing.'

'Once you are in London again, you might be shown photographs to see if you recognise anyone?'

'I'm certain we won't be able to. You see, Chief Inspector, I don't want anyone else blamed in any way for what was my, our, choice.'

'So how did you set it up in the first place?'

'Through a contact, someone I once met when I was a part-time prison chaplain. He owed me a favour and I gave him £1,000, which he called a "monkey". The other means was £20,000 which of course would be of no use to us once we had done the deed, so we paid up.'

'Whose idea was it to use The Hospice?'

Alan smiled.

'My mother was a patient and died there, so I learned how the place functioned and had been in the mortuary. It wasn't just a joke – I had serious intent, an enacted parable on Jesus's words: "Leave the dead to bury the dead". I am nevertheless sorry for any nuisance my silliness might have caused.'

Ellie went outside and told the officers it was safe for them to go and that they would be taking the prisoners now.

Alan and Sonia had prepared for the journey and brought warm coats and some food, enough to share with Ellie and Bobi. Before getting them into the car she called Cate and informed her, and then informed the Custody Sergeant at Lewisham that they were now leaving and had two prisoners for them, both of whom had been cautioned and admitted the crime. Only then were Alan and Sonia allowed to leave the house, without hand restraints of any kind and take their place in the rear seats of the car, something Alan said was most exciting. This time it was Ellie who drove.

'Right,' she said. 'Blue lights all the way, if you, Inspector, will make the necessary calls.'

'Yes, ma'am.'

Two police officers and two self-confessed murderers, one a priest of the established Church, laughed together.

Paperwork

Cate informed her boss of the third result and said that she and DS Halton would be in Leamington Spa shortly.

'Ah, please make a diversion and come here first, both of you. Can DS Halton hear this?'

'Yes, ma'am,' said Chris.

'Please come with Cate.'

'Ma'am.'

'Is it far out of our way?' asked Chris.

'It all depends on the M42, but if it's clear it will be less than an hour to Worcester.'

'Have you any idea what it's about?'

'None at all. Don't be anxious. I really trust Dani and so should you.'

'Cate, there's something I think I should mention. I was going to wait until we got back to the hotel with going to see the boss, perhaps I should say it now.'

'Go on then.'

'Early this morning I went for a walk in the park in Lewisham with Jo. She had asked me last night. She said she was troubled by something and wanted to talk it over with me before everyone else laughed it out of court.'

'Trust me, Chris, no one would laugh any idea of Jo's out of court.'

'She said that as you told us last night about the information that had come from MI5, she simply didn't think it was the whole story, not just that they were keeping something back, which all accept the must sometimes do and as we do, but something more fundamental, and that furthermore, she said that from the way you spoke about it, you shared her reservations though neither of you brought them out into the open. She is convinced that although some sort of animal group may be involved, and she used the word "may" with what I can only call a measure of disdain, she thinks that you share her view that this is primarily a local crime after all.'

'And what did you say?'

'Only that I don't have the knowledge of place and people that you two have and that when we are back in Leamington tonight she should seek you out. I also got my nose slightly bitten off, because I suggested she share this with Ellie. She replied that there was no possibility of that as it is you who commands this team and no one else. I was a bit confused at that point as I thought they were very close.'

'They are, very close indeed, but Jo would never break the command structure even it was nothing more than a hunch she was more than willing to mention to you. Mentioning something downwards is fine, but mentioning something upwards, even to your bed partner is a different matter altogether.'

'And is she right?'

'Do you think we will escape the rain, sergeant?'

'Possibly, ma'am, possibly.'

Jo and Sammy had completed their tasks with Vice and Serious Crime in good time before heading east and picking up the M25 and choosing the clockwise route. Soon they passed an accident on the anti-clockwise carriageway and a very long queue back as far as the junction for the M23. Emergency service vehicles were in good number and they continued, thanking their lucky stars that it wasn't on their side.

Following her early morning monologue with Chris who had listened patiently but having little idea what she was going on about, Jo continued to go over in her mind everything she could recall from Builth Wells and all about Tony Hendry.

'You're being very quiet,' said Sammy.

'I imagine that like you I'm pretty tired. A good night's sleep will help.'

It was a blatant lie because her mind was working hard and she was energised by her thoughts.'

Arriving back at the hotel, they were surprised to find themselves the only ones there.

Cate and Chris were arriving at Hindlip Hall in Worcester, the home of the West Mercia Police Force.

'People of my rank never normally get to meet the very top brass and especially on their own territory,' said Chris.

'Don't fret. Look who you stood up to yesterday.'

'Yes, but I can hardly face kick an ACC.'

Cate thought this hilariously funny. The ACC, Dani to some, was in an easy chair in her room and the secretary showed Cate and Chris to other such chairs. Cate desperately tried to work out the implications of this – whether it was good or very bad news that can only be dispensed to those sitting comfortably.

'Good afternoon, you two. I apologise for dragging you out of your way but I wanted to talk something through with you. First and foremost, I want to congratulate you, Chris, for bringing about the transformation of the investigation in south London by means of your left foot.'

'Oh.'

'I can assure you there is no need to be shy about it. When the video was sent through to me, and I learned that this really was the turning point in turning on the tap of information which has enabled two arrests to be made today, with confessions, I showed it to the Chief Constable and he thought it was brilliant. I think I could see that you didn't exactly whack him one so much as it gave him such a shock that he tumbled over and somehow or other caused him to spill the beans. The chief and I are seriously giving thought to the possibility that some officers might care to learn the elements of taekwondo. I've seen it on television at the Olympics but realise that in essence it's a defensive method, so when all this murder business is sorted, which at your present rate of progress will probably be tomorrow, I want you to come back here and meet with the chief and myself and give a realistic assessment of how we might use it. I gather you are a black belt which is the very top. Would that allow you teach officers some of the basic aspects which could help them when facing assault?'

'I'm not a qualified teacher ma'am though I could unquestionably find someone who is, and although I have achieved a certain level, that's not saying as being able to make it available to others.'

'Yes, I understand what you're saying but I still think we should use you, not as your main work, to encourage the troops by showing them how they might benefit from this. How easily could you become a teacher?'

'I am a sixth degree black belt which means that I already have the title of Master and under instruction from a ninth degree grandmaster I could probably do what you are asking, ma'am, provided that anyone wishing to go beyond the basics realised that I would have to pass them on to someone else. Otherwise I would be very happy to help as best I can, ma'am, and I'm more than willing to come and meet with you and the Chief Constable when you feel it is appropriate.'

'Good. Now the second matter. The time has come, sergeant, for you to prepare for the national inspector's exam. This is a matter of urgency, not just for you, not just for Cate, but above all for Hereford and West Mercia. Before I get moved to Devon and Cornwall or the Outer Hebrides, I am determined to ensure that the very best women officers are in positions commensurate with their abilities, so realistically how soon would you be willing to do it?'

'I think if I'd still been in Boston, ma'am, it would have been another 10 years before they let me do it, and I'm certainly not taking anything for granted, but if you asked me to go downstairs now and take the exam, I'm pretty confident I would pass.'

'I fear it's a bit late today, but I'll set it up and let you know, but we must get on with it. Do you agree, Cate?

'I certainly do and I'm beginning to consider the possibility that we should make raids on detective constables in Boston every year and liberate them, because the two we have in our team are simply exceptional.'

'I'd like you to stay, Chris, to hear what Cate and I have to deal with now. When we spoke last night, and when you also sent me a certain video, you mentioned that your MI5 man had passed on to you information that had come from one of their agents in the field who obviously cannot be identified but belongs to a radical animal rights group, and that the word was that someone in the group had mentioned that Tony Hendry had been taken care of by the group. You've now had a few hours to think about that so I wondered where you think you will go from here.'

Cate looked at Chris.

'You have my permission to pass on to our Assistant Chief Constable what you told me on our way here.'

Chris reported the concern of Jo as she had received them in their early morning walk in the park, and her comment that not only did she have these concerns but she felt Superintendent Greene might have them too, unspoken though they had been.

'Can you speak them now?' asked Dani.

'I don't think I'm being deliberately obtuse, ma'am, but I feel that I must talk to Jo and ensure we are thinking alike before I should give utterance to my unease.'

'That's a perfectly acceptable reply, Cate. I would rather hear more fully from you and wonder woman Jo tomorrow, by telephone if need be, rather than dragging you both over here again, than that you felt you had to just say something to please me. That, Chris, is superb good practice. You're very lucky to have Cate as your boss, as we are to have her in the Force. But I do want to have a serious conversation with Jo about her future, but let's get this murder out of the way first. I was looking at her file earlier and discovered she had passed both her Sergeant's and Inspector's exam without telling anyone, while still in Boston. You will warn me if she is secretly taking her ACC exam, won't you? Oh, did you know that the inspector in Boston you didn't charge in Boston had died?'

'I heard on the Boston grapevine, ma'am,' said Chris, 'and told the others.'

Just over an hour later, Cate and Chris were back in the hotel in Leamington Spa and delighted to find Sammy and Jo in the bar.

'Hello troops! I can't speak for Chris, but I'm desperate for a shower and change of clothes, but I'd be more than happy to come down and find you two still there as I definitely could murder a drink.'

When she turned round Chris had already gone. Jo and Sammy were giving consideration to their futures and the sort of work they would want to move into after they had finished this particular task.

'It must be pretty disorientating for you, Jo, having left Boston and gone to Lewisham, then coming here and working in Scotland, in Boston again, in Lewisham again and heaven knows where as we address the final task.'

'You're absolutely right in one sense and I'm certainly not wildly keen on being quite so far from my mum and dad, to whom I'm very close and who live in Norwich, but the most important thing in my life, as I'm sure you have gathered, is Ellie. If she arrives back tomorrow and say she's been appointed to a new position as a police adviser in North Korea, I would willingly go with her.'

'But everybody knows, Jo, what an outstanding police officer you are. It's not flattery. You seem to have the most perfect sort of mind for the work of a detective. You make the mental leaps most of us wouldn't dare to make, or even think of in the first place. I hardly know you, but you must trust your intuition to a level that most of us could not do. I think you have a great future and my deepest hope is that this feature can be fully shared with Ellie. I don't know many officers who could sleep together every night and not engage in the sort of pillow talk containing information, often very important information, that was not shared because of the command structure. Frankly, that amazes me.'

'In which case you must blame my mum and dad. They brought me up to think that with some exceptions obviously, few things were so important that they had to be dealt with here and now and could not wait for the right time and place. They practised it and that's where I learned it. I think patience is not something you are or are not born with, but something to be learned, to be acquired. Sometimes you and I will hear someone say "I'm not a patient person" but I want to say back to them, that they should learn to be.'

'Are you not impatient for Ellie's return?'

'Don't get me wrong. Of course I wish she was here with me now, but she will be here tomorrow and that's not far off, and brings with it the added bonus of my being able to read in bed.'

Ellie and Bobi had handed over Sonia and Alan to the Lewisham police Custody Sergeant. Bobi handed over the tapes he had recorded of their confessions and subsequent conversations in the car, to Chief Superintendent Charnley, whilst Ellie typed out her full report, which the Chief printed out and read.

'What can I say, Ellie, other than that how much I look forward to having you back here one you've solved the final crime in the group. We've missed you. From what you say, the chances of getting anything further out of these two as to the identities of any others involved is nil. That is a shame because it might have opened up something on Robinson and Roland who will have pocketed the £20,000 between them and arranged for the weapon used to visit the bottom of the Thames. All the same, we'll have a go and see if I can persuade them that more lives might be saved by giving us that information. Are you going back to the Midlands tonight when the roads will be clear or in the morning?'

'I think we're both exhausted, guv, so traffic or no traffic, we'll go tomorrow.

'Ok. I'll see you soon, Ellie, and great to meet you, Sammy. Thank you for what you've done.'

As they walked back to Ellie's flat, she suddenly said, 'An hour's sleep, a shower, a pizza, and we'll be there before ten o'clock without having to get up and start again in the morning.'

Sammy turned and grinned.

'You're on.'

Reading in bed proved not as successful as Jo had hoped in that when as quietly as possible Ellie used her keycard and opened the door, she was greeted by the sight of her beloved Jo fast asleep with the light on and a book lying open on top of her chest. She smiled and tried to continue to be as quiet as a mouse but couldn't resist a kiss which brought the response of two arms enfolding her.

'I did wonder...' said Jo.

'Wild horses wouldn't have held me in Lewisham, so when I made the suggestion, Sammy jumped at it too. So here, my darling, I am.'

'That's wonderful, though you look exhausted and I promise to leave you alone when you get in here alongside me.'

'Spoil sport, but for once I will agree.'

There was delight and surprise when everyone gathered for breakfast and even more when Derrick Blowes came too.

'I wish I could stay,' he said, 'but I have boring office work to attend to. However I want to offer my congratulations at clearing up number 3. What a team.'

'At least stay and have a coffee and a croissant, sir,' said Chris, unused to the presence a large DCC at the table with her.

'Ok I will, but if any word gets back to my wife about this, you'll all be back on traffic duty by the end of the week.'

'At our present rate of progress, that might be all that is left for us to do,' said Cate.

'Yes, you have turned out to be quite a remarkable group of people, though word has reached me of the use of blue lights all over the place.'

'Only when authorised by me, Derrick,' replied Cate.

'That's what I told those who got in touch to tell me – that it was authorised by 'me Derrick', not you.'

Once Derrick had left, Cate announced that everyone could now have a whole week off which they had more than deserved, but it would begin only after they had a debriefing meeting at 10:00 in the office. It was vital everyone could hear the reports of yesterday's activities and begin preliminary thought on what was to come next. Then the holidays would begin. Cate had however indicated to Jo that she should remain and have another cup of coffee.

'Chris told me of your concerns, and your concern for what you feel might also be my concerns. So out with it.'

'I think I may be on to the perpetrator but I would have to test something out first. The thing about lies is that usually they are just too smooth, but when Ellie reported back from Eamonn and you told us what the MI5 agent had reported, somehow it didn't ring true that the murder had been done by one of the animal rights groups no matter what a shit they thought Tony Hendry to be. I feel, and I think you feel the same, that this is a local job but done deliberately to lead us astray, and if we go chasing after the animal people, they will have won and we shall never solve it.'

'And the liars? Do you know who they might be?'

'Oh yes, but I just need a little more evidence for which I may have to go fox hunting.'

'And why do I think you're not going to tell me?'

'I'm telling no one, if you take my meaning.'

'Ellie?'

'If I'm not telling you, ma'am, I'm not telling anyone. But you will be the first to know when I've gathered what I need. I might also have enough info to know which group the MI5 agent is working in. They took part, I suspect, but only in the ambush in Clyro, and in total ignorance of what was to follow.'

'You do know know fox hunting is banned, so for Christ's sake don't get arrested.'

'I'll do my best.'

Ok – I guess I have no choice.

'You have, Cate, and I'm completely serious about this. If you order me to tell you everything, I will obey, and if you instruct me not to go, I won't – I hope you know that – but I think it might be worth it.'

'You're on safe ground, Jo, because you know I trust you, which reminds me, when all this is done with, Dani wants you to go and see her.'

'Ok.'

'One other thing, Jo, be careful. Tony Hendry died a terrible death and someone might do it again, if need be.'

'I won't be alone. I've seen the video, and I'm taking with me someone who can really fight, even it is only with her feet.'

'What about Ellie?'

'She's going to Norwich to stay with my mum and dad 'til I get there. Don't say anything to the others, please, but late last night she asked me a question and I said yes.'

'And why does she think you're staying behind?'

'The basis of our relationship is absolute trust. I'm staying behind for a further day or so – that's all she wants to know.'

'Am I allowed to say a quiet congratulations to her and to you?'

'That would be lovely. Thank you.'

The meeting when it came was mostly a matter of formally sharing what everyone informally had learned at breakfast but before heading away for a week's rest, Cate wanted to stress that although the team had done remarkably well so far, there was still one horrific murder left unsolved. They all knew that there had been input from MI5 via Eamonn, but she said that other possibilities needed to be explored when they returned next week, focussing once again on it being a local job, but now they could forget about it and she looked forward to seeing them once again for a curry one week on.

Ellie was staying one more night before heading over to Norwich.

'You'll be going to see your future parents-in-law I gather. It's just wonderful for you both. Much, much happiness, Ellie.'

She kissed her cheek.

'Thank you, Cate. I can hardly believe it.'

'One word, however. I saw Dani yesterday and she asked me to tell your fiancée that she wants to see her when we've finished. I only told her this morning and though I know you don't ever discuss work, this is different and you might both want to think things through.'

'Thanks, Cate. You're a star.

On the Hills

When it's an illegal activity, even one that everyone knows is happening, there is no publicity as such, and Jo thought it unlikely that the North Wales Police would provide her with the information she sought as to where the particular hunt in question would be meeting on Saturday, so on the Friday morning she and Chris set off for Colwyn Bay where the North Wales Police had their headquarters. On the previous afternoon she had arranged to meet the officer responsible for rural policing.

The scenic route, avoiding the M6 took them through some lovely countryside. Cate had advised that they take a marked car as it would at least lend credibility with the force they were visiting. Chris was driving and Jo's phone rang when they were close to Telford, still in England. It was the officer Jo had spoken to on the previous afternoon.

'I thought that if I rang it might prevent you doing unnecessary miles, ma'am, and I wondered if you could divert and meet me in Welshpool at the station? If you still want to visit the kennels of the Waen Foxhounds, it's close by and I could take you.'

'That sounds a great idea, thank you, constable. See you in about an hour, I would guess'

As Jo thought about it, this might be quite serendipitous. She altered the sat nav and saw that it would only take three quarters of an hour, unless of course they got behind a tractor (though this possibility was not included on the police sat nav system).

'It would be good to see PC Helen Anderson, who had been FLO after the murder, and Poppy, the daughter of Tony and

Danny Hendry is also living there.

'And I don't know about you, Chris but I could do with some food and drink.'

'Me too. Will you want me in on everything?'

'Of course.'

'The ACC wants me to do my inspector exams as soon as possible and to give basic lessons in taekwondo.'

'That's terrific. Cate's told me she wants to see me when all this over. And do you know, if we'd still been back in Boston I would be a DC yet, and you a PC. Poor old Connor. I do hope there aren't too many female angels or devils wherever he's gone.'

'When I began I was full of enthusiasm and ever so keen. That he made me a DC when you left amazed me, but you're quite right it would not have been a case of onwards and upwards. I've heard he's come to a final end at Boston Crem.'

'A fate I wouldn't wish on my worst enemy.'

Chris turned into the yard of the police station and parked the car. Almost at once a broad and bearded constable emerged from the rear of the building and walked towards them. Both Jo and Chris took out their warrant cards to confirm who they were.

'Welcome to Welshpool, ma'am.'

'Oh. Please, drop the title, I'm Jo and this is Chris.'

'And I'm Neil. Would Jo and Chris welcome some nourishment as we talk?'

'I thought you'd never ask.'

'There's the River Fish Restaurant if you could manage good fish and chips or ...'

'Stop', said Jo. 'No need for more options.'

'It's a five or six minute walk.'

'No problem. Well Neil, let me tell you something of what we're doing here. We're members of a team set up to solve four interrelated murders, or at least that's what they seemed to be at the beginning. We've managed three of them but the fourth took place in or near Builth Wells.'

'Yes, I remember.'

'Having the fire station next to the police station must be

sometimes annoying for residents,' said Jo. as they passed both buildings. There is a sort of involvement which obviously I can't go into, with the Waen Foxhounds, which I gather still hunt.'

'Under extremely strict control, just to kill foxes, not exactly to hunt them over distances. Most are shot.'

'That, I'm afraid, is lost on me. What I need to know is something a couple of people whose names I have, but I'm hoping you can tell me which side they are on – the hunters or the saboteurs, of which I imagine you get quite a few. We can't go to the meet tomorrow because two people there might recognise me and it's important I try to get the information without that happening.

'Ok, fish and chips it is, but we'll have to change the subject until we're out again, and instead I'd be really interested to hear about work, Neil.'

'Yeah, me too,' added Chris.

Once back at the police station, Jo wanted to get straight to work.

'Neil, I want to raid your mind and the resources of your computers regarding the happenings of the Waen Foxhounds. Tell me about the place of Gordon Hendry and his partner, Alyson.'

'That's easy and it totally fits in with his decision to close the chicken farm when he took over.'

'What do you mean?'

'Gordon has been a regular member of the antis since the hunting ban came into operation, and I think I'm right in saying that they met here when she came with students from her uni.'

'Which?'

'Keele. She was the organiser of the anti-hunt brigade. Nasty piece of work. I have some video if you want see it.'

'Thank you.'

The computer images were clear and all too audible, showing Gordon and Alyson at the centre of the action, shouting obscenities at the hunting people and the police alike.

'Were they ever arrested for this sort of behaviour?'

'Well, it was difficult. The hunting ban was in operation when this video was recorded. Anyone arrested might have ended up in court and our complicity with the hunt would have been exposed, and believe you me that woman was more than capable of exploiting everything that came her way.'

'The hunters don't strike me as all that pleasant.'

'They're almost all farmers and can give as good as they get.'

'So why do you let it continue?'

'We don't. How could we when it's against the law. But it goes on and the farmers say that if it is policed over-rigorously they will have no choice but to use poison and traps to control the foxes that kill their lambs, both of which are terrible. So, we just check up on public order offences.'

'And is it the same everywhere?'

'In the hills and forests of North Wales and in the Cumbrian Lakes. I now believe many of the protesters couldn't give a shit about animals and just come for a fight.'

'Neil, thank you very much indeed and we'll let you get back to work.'

'Well, I hope it's been of help.'

'Oh, it has, believe you me.'

Jo's phone rang.

'It's Cate, so let's get going,' she said to Chris.

'Yes, Cate?'

'Where are you?'

'Just leaving Welshpool police station and I truly believe we've cracked it.'

'That doesn't matter, Jo. Please listen. Dani's just called to tell me that Ellie's in hospital.'

'What?'

'Please listen, Jo. She was involved in an RTC with a tractor on the A14, and taken to Addenbrookes in Cambridge by helicopter. She's in theatre now and is described as poorly. Dani has arranged for a police helicopter to collect and deliver you and I'll let her know where you are.'

'There's an aerodrome here. I saw it on the map. The Mid-Wales Airport.'

'Ok, get there and wait. Chris will have to go back by herself.

Jo was numb with shock and could barely find the words to let Chris know what was happening.

'In the car. Come on,' said Chris, opening the door and shepherding Jo inside.

Neil was looking concerned and came over from the station door.

'Trouble?'

'Her fiancée's been involved in an RTC and is in the operating theatre in Cambridge. They only got engaged yesterday.'

'Holy Jesus,' said Neil. 'Are you taking her there? It's hell of a long way.'

'No, the ACC is sending a helicopter to the airport here.'

'Thank God for that. Do you know the way? It's only about two miles away.'

'I'll be fine, Neil. Thanks for everything.'

'Promise you'll let me know.'

'I will.'

Blue lights and siren on, Chris raced away in search of the airport. Jo was on the phone to her mum and dad, and they said they would leave at once and meet up with her there.

Chris parked the car as near she could get to the small flight control box and went out to speak to the two people operating it.

'We're expecting a police helicopter.'

'Yes, we've got it on radar. About ten minutes I would say,' said one of the people.

'It will pick up and depart immediately.'

'In which case you're parked in the right place.'

Chris returned to the car and heard Jo's phone ring as she did so.

'Jo, it's Dani here. The helicopter will take you direct to Addenbrookes, arguably the very best hospital in the country. We're all rooting for Ellie and you. Please keep me informed. I'll text you my home phone number. Don't for a moment hesitate to call at any time day or night. One other thing, congratulations on your engagement. You're going to have many uncomfortable days ahead, but I hope you will also have many years of joy together.'

'Oh, for heaven's sake, Dani, now you've made me start crying.'

'Ah well, that means there's been some good in my call.'

Jo had learned already that Dani always ended her calls abruptly without the formalities of "bye", and so in her tears she also smiled.

'Chris, before you set off back, is there any chance you could call on Cherry Anderson? Neil will let you know where she might be, and even Poppy Hendry who lives here somewhere. Cherry would have reported it if there had been something she hadn't previously mentioned but see her if you can. And ask Poppy about her sister-in-law.'

'Ok, boss. Leave it to me and now forget all about it and just concentrate on getting to be with Ellie and give her a kiss from me. Here's your carriage coming now.'

She had never been in a helicopter before and the first thing that struck her was the noise. Even wearing the headset it was difficult to hear what the pilot said to her, but the noise had one considerable advantage – it prevented her thinking too much. The pilot had said that he hoped to have her at the hospital in about 45 minutes depending on air traffic control at Stansted but as they drew nearer, she thought she heard him say that he was transmitting an emergency squawk which gave them priority access. Jo had not the faintest idea what a squawk was, but she was glad the pilot had one!

He circled the hospital which she could see clearly below her and made for the helipad. The pilot pointed to a police officer waiting for her.

'There's your contact, ma'am. Good luck to you and DCI Middlewood.

'Thank you so much, guys, you're been brilliant.'

Jo emerged and ran towards the officer.

'Hi, ma'am. I'll take to the Major Trauma Centre. It really is state of the art, and the Chief Inspector will get the very best care possible.'

'Thank you. Is it far?'

'No. It has to be near the helipad for obvious reasons.'

They entered the building and the officer led her through to what was obviously a new Unit. She rang the bell and after a brief wait that seemed endless, a nurse opened the door.

'I'm Jo Enright, the fiancée of Ellie Midwood whom I think you are caring for here.'

'Detective Inspector Enright? Come in.'

Jo turned and thanked the officer.

Inside it was bright with everything seemingly new and although she had expected a lot of noise and hurly-burly, it was remarkably quiet and peaceful apart from the machines around most beds which blinked and beeped.

'So', said the nurse, 'which do you want first – the good news or the even better news?'

Jo's sigh of relief must have been audible across the ward.

'Ellie's back from theatre and one of the consultants will come and tell you how she is in depth, but I think it's safe for me to say that although she may have to have a break from crime and driving police cars, by next Summer she'll be as good as new, although she may have a spot of bother going through the x-ray machines at the airport as Mr Challoner will explain. I'll take you to her and she has a special visitor at the moment called Peter, who pops in here from time to time, but mostly spends his time as Bishop of Ely. He's just sitting with her, holding her hand and, if I know him, speaking poetry to her from memory.'

Jo was shocked by the sight of Ellie. There was a cradle protecting her legs and it was clear that she also had a damaged arm which was plastered and in a sling. Her face showed signs that something had hit it but there was no blood. The man on the other side of the bed stood. Jo could see his purple shirt and cross and she judged him to be in his late-60s, but he had an angelic face.

'Please don't go. I'd like you to stay,' she said, and then she went up to Ellie and kissed her lips. 'Oh my darling, you're going to be ok. I'm here and I'm yours forever.'

'I take it you are Jo', said the bishop. 'I was waiting for you to arrive, just sitting with this beautiful lady, holding her hand and speaking some of my favourite poetry – not religious by the way.

I try not to inflict that on anyone, though if they want that, I do my best to find the chaplain, as he's much more religious than me.'

'But you're a bishop.'

'But that's not necessarily anything to do with religion. I deal above all in beauty and love which is where I find God. I blow hot and cold about religion, and mostly cold,' he said, with a smile and a raise of his eyebrows.

'I've recently met with a couple of bishops in a formal interview and I thought them dishonest, to be frank.'

'I won't ask who,' he said, with a gentle grin. 'The church into which I was ordained more than 40 years ago has changed, mostly for the worst, and people no longer care about it, which I understand because I'm not sure I do either. So, some adopt a hard line because they think it will appeal. I'm glad I shall be retiring before too long and can give myself wholly to poetry and beauty.'

'How often do you come here?'

'As often as I can. The staff know that I don't get in the way. Your Ellie and the others have all been close to death and they teach me what's important and what's not. Ellie is my teacher.'

'What you say about beauty and love is refreshing. I spend too much of my time with their opposites, with the ugliness of some people's hearts and, this morning for example, facing up to the hatred of a man who chose to murder his father.'

'In which case, Jo, if I may call you that, what a wonder that it is the likes of you and Ellie who seek to counter such negative energy. Please never lose the vitality and love I can see in you as you do this work, and struggle against the cynicism that has become endemic in our world now. Sermon over, I will leave you two together as I'm sure when Ellie comes round you will have so much love to share.'

'Peter, before you go, can I ask something of you I have never asked anyone before. Might you be able to bless my darling Ellie?'

The bishop smiled and moved up towards Ellie and very gently laid his hands on her forehead and, for a brief, moment, seemed lost to the world. Once again, much to her chagrin, Jo felt tears rolling down her cheeks. Peter reached into his pocket and handed her a card.

'Let me know,' he said, and left them.

The consultant approached.

'Hello, Jo, I'm Alec Challoner and I received Ellie when she came in and operated on her. I try never to say to anyone that they've been lucky, because if they'd been really lucky, the calamity wouldn't have occurred, but in this instance it was fortunate that Ellie was in a car with all the best safety equipment with airbags appearing from every which way, because they saved her life. I gather a tractor pulled out suddenly from a field as she was approaching. Anyway, that is a matter for others to deal with.

'She will take some time to heal but she will, physically. Psychologically, after such an accident it can take a lot longer, but the best cure for that is patience, love and laughter. She doesn't need to be here much longer as everything I can see on all those machines is good, so we'll move her to the orthopaedic ward shortly where she'll have a room to herself. Senior police officers are not always welcome to every patient on an open ward.

'Ellie has a broken left femur and I've put in a metal plate. It's not a very complicated plate but it will mean she can rely on that leg in the future. Her right foot got somewhat mangled and one of my registrars dealt with that at the same time as I was doing the femur. It looked good when she'd finished. The collar round her neck is by way of keeping her head and neck straight but there's no damage we could see, but her right collar bone was broken and so also was her radius in the left arm. Happily, and again it's the wrong word, all her breaks were clean. Not everyone in this place gets away with a crash so lightly.'

'Thank you so much, doctor, for developing your skills to such an extent that you can do these things and more. Will you be seeing her again?'

'No, I'm here in this unit full-time and I don't even have an out-patients clinic, but doctors on the ward will take good care of her. I saw you with Bishop Peter. He likes to come in and just sits with patients and relatives. He doesn't dispense religion in any way. He just is. He says, and I agree, that church and religion put him off God, but he has the exact opposite effect on me, which probably is to define him as a saint.'

Whilst Ellie was being transferred, Jo's mum and dad arrived, and by some miracle found one other. With Ellie being received onto the ward, Jo, her mum and dad went to see what the cafeteria had to offer, most of the time walking hand in hand with Jo in tears, something they had not seen for many years.

The food of course was simply dreadful but it filled a space.

'Jo, it's going to be ok eventually. Besides which you need some time to plan for the wedding, said her mum.'

'How did you know about that?'

'Just before Ellie set off she called us and said she couldn't keep the secret that you were engaged a minute longer. Congratulations. We are absolutely thrilled, and now she's going to have time on her hand to work at the details and arrangements. You, of course, will have to work.'

'Mum, how can you say such a thing! I want to be with her to look after and care for her.'

'Joanna,' said her mum, always an ominous sound, 'where do you think Ellie is going to live other than with us? We love her and we shall do everything to care for her. You'll always be welcome to come, of course.'

'Gee thanks, mum.'

'Your mum's right,' said her dad. 'Ellie is part of our family and it's for us, her family to make sure she gets back to fulness of health.'

'Oh no,' said Jo, 'I'm starting to cry again.'

They made their way up to the ward and introduced themselves to the staff.

'We've settled her in but she's unlikely to come round this evening because of the anaesthetic in her system which had to be strong to protect against the intense pain she would otherwise experience,' said the ward sister.

'Propofol?' asked Jo.

'That's used to make them unconscious, but I gather Ellie was pretty much out of it when the helicopter got her here, on which subject I gather you also came by helicopter from North Wales.'

'Yes, I was just two miles from the Welshpool airport.'

'That must have been exciting. You are welcome to sit with Ellie, but first, Inspector, can I borrow you to get some information about Ellie.'

'No, I'm sorry. Anyone who calls me anything but Jo, will get nothing from me.'

'Ok, Jo, can you come with me?'

'I'd be delighted to do so.'

Mr and Mrs Enright went into the room and tried hard not to show their shock at the sight of the sleeping Ellie, and for a few moments held each other in support.'

Cambridge

'Eleanor Rose Middlewood. Age 35. Born in England of deceased Guyanese parents. Next of kin: her partner and fiancée, that's me, Jo Louise Enright, also of Norwich. Occupation: Detective Chief Inspector of the Metropolitan Police.'

'Ooh, how long have you been engaged?'

'Since last night. She asked me and I said yes.'

'Well, let's hope,' said the sister, 'that the first 24 hours of your married life are not quite so challenging.'

'Sister, you see patients in this sort of state quite often I imagine and Mr Challoner expressed confidence that she will make a full recovery. Do you agree with his prognosis?'

'He's arguably one of the best trauma doctors in the world and trust me, he sees people far worse than Ellie is now, and it's indicative of his confidence that she's here with us. I gather she was driving a sophisticated car with air bags not just in front but also at the sides. She hasn't fractured her skull and there's no sign of internal bleeding. No one, not even Mr Challoner, and believe it or not, that includes me, can predict every change that might occur to a patient following a trauma, but I think Ellie's chances of making a full recovery by the summer are very high indeed.'

'Thank you.'

'Now this a little awkward, Jo, and a little unpleasant, but you might be the person to help us sort it. The thing is we have had a spate of thefts from the lockers beside patient's beds. Small amounts of money, a couple of mobiles – that sort of annoying thing, plus bits of equipment.'

'You ought to be asking the Cambridgeshire police to deal with it.'

'We've tried and they sent a uniformed constable still wet behind the ears and he wandered through the ward speaking to those who had lost stuff and left saying he would log it.'

'That would be the right procedure given that the amounts stolen were mostly very small in comparison with other robberies, as I'm sure you will realise, but I'll give it some thought. When she wakes up, I'll mention it to Ellie and see if she has any ideas what we might do.'

'Thanks, Jo. Yes, it is small fry, but upsetting for us all, patients and staff alike. Now, you go and join your parents.'

'Am I allowed to stay overnight?'

'I'm afraid not. That's only possible for relatives of those in extremis, besides which you've had quite a day yourself and need some sleep. You're welcome to call after 6:00 in the morning and find out how she is and being in a side room you can slip in and out easily, but please take extra care in what you're doing, especially when driving, as you'd be surprised how often people have accidents when their minds are miles away.'

After checking on Ellie again, Jo had phone calls to make, first to Dani who expressed enormous relief at the news.

'Thanks for the helicopter, Dani. Noisy devils, aren't they, but ever so quick.'

'I was just glad to be able to help, Jo. Now take all the time off you need. Cate tells me that you now have the evidence you need to make an arrest and I've suggested she drives over to see you and enables this to be sorted. I look forward to hearing all about it. Give my love to Ellie when it's possible.'

'Thank you, Dani. I owe you one.'

'Good. I shan't forget that.'

Next, she phoned Cate.

'What a relief. I've been worried sick. She will recover outwardly, but it's the inner Ellie that needs you now, so you are to take off all the time you want. If we lose you for months to gain years, it will be worth it.

'The boss wants me to come and see you so we can get the Tony Hendry case closed – some holiday this is turning out to be.

I have to go and collect Chris from Leamington first, but we can then come to Cambridge together and share the driving and stay the night somewhere. By Sunday Ellie might be back with us and I might get the chance to see her, but you and I might be able to manage some time together for you to give me what I need. Would that be ok?'

'It sounds a really good idea. Just let me know when and where.'

Marian and Sidney, Jo's parents had booked two rooms at the very expensive Clayton Hotel in the city and after more than an hour together sitting with Ellie, they persuaded their reluctant daughter to go with them to the car and then to the hotel. They each kissed Ellie, and Jo almost once again collapsed in tears when she heard her dad say "God bless, dearest daughter" after kissing Ellie.

Far from what she might have expected, Jo slept well and it was not until seven o'clock that she was able to call the ward and say who she was calling about.

'Good morning. I'm the ward staff nurse in charge. Inspector Midwood woke up at about four o'clock, a little surprised to find herself here. She's on a drip delivering round the clock pain control and has had some water to drink. She keeps asking for you so I'm sure the sooner you can get here the better.'

'Thank you staff nurse. I'm on my way.'

Sidney was already up and drove her out to the hospital, promising to return with her mum later. Jo took the stairs fearing being stuck in the lift for hours, and then steadied herself, getting her breath back before entering Ellie's room. They looked at one another and said nothing at first, before Jo slowly moved towards Ellie and gently at first, and then more firmly, kissed and was kissed.

'You'd better not touch me,' said Ellie, 'sad though it to say so, I might just scream.'

'Is the pain bad? I thought it was under control through the drip.'

'It is, most of the time if I'm lying still, but the slightest move hurts. But tell me what damage I've done. Nobody's told me yet.'

'A broken femur, a crushed foot, a broken collar bone and a broken radius in the lower arm. The surgeon who operated in the Trauma Centre thought you were saved by the range of air bags in the car and said you will make a complete and full recovery by the Summer.'

'That long!'

'Darling, had it not been for the protection afforded by the car you might have been very much worse. So, you're on an ordinary orthopaedic ward and not still in the Trauma Centre. Furthermore, Dani's told me to take off as long as I need. And we're moving to Norwich. Mum and dad, who were here last night and will be in later are so looking forward to having you with them. He didn't know I could hear him, but when he kissed you last night, my dad called you his "dearest daughter".'

'Do you mind that?'

'Only if in getting married to you it becomes incest.'

'Oh, Jo, please try not to make me laugh. But you were in Wales yesterday. How did you get here?'

'Dani provided a helicopter.'

'Wow. I'm jealous.'

'You shouldn't be as that's how they brought you in.'

'Really?'

'Yes. By the way, Cate's coming later today. She desperately wants to see you and also wants me to give her the missing pieces from the Hendry murder so she can make an arrest, but I am not going to talk about work and in any case I can't tell you until I've told her.'

Ellie smiled.

'You had a very special visitor yesterday after you'd returned from theatre. He was sitting with you, holding your hand and reciting poetry gently to you.'

'Who on earth was that?'

'He's called Peter Walter, and he's the Bishop of Ely, a wonderful man, almost a saint, I should think, who more than made up for those two slimy gits I saw at the beginning. He wants updates on your progress. I thought he was fabulous and I asked him to give you a blessing which he did with hands on your forehead.'

'Thank you, my love. And hey, look who's here.'

Jo turned and into the room came her mum and dad, overjoyed to see Ellie awake, if still groggy and regularly drifting off to sleep. The day staff came on and the new staff nurse in charge urged Ellie's visitors to leave her be for a couple of hours to give the staff the requisite time to attend to her and invited them to return after lunch for the afternoon visiting. Needless to say, they withdrew only reluctantly but fully understood why.

Even by 2:00 pm Ellie remained very sleepy and although Jo remained the full hour and a half, there was barely any conversation. The sister from the previous day was now on duty and reassured Jo and her parents that her doctors were pleased with Ellie's progress,

'I did say getting fully better would take the best part of six months, but it's going to be slow going, not just in terms of broken bones that will heal, not just in psychological terms for which she will be dependent on you and your parents, but first in recovering from the trauma of the accident. We know so much more about how following such a happening the body loses the capacity to react normally. Some people lose their voice for a while, others shake uncontrollably or have major toilet problems. We can help a little with medication, but the main treatment is observation and patience. And that is why, Mr Challoner has sent a message that you strictly limit your visiting because Ellie needs time to recover the body's inner equilibrium and the best way is for her to spend time alone. I know it sounds unkind but it isn't. We see it working time after time.'

'Thank you so much for saying that. Not only does it help to know but I can see that makes sense.'

'You will have to trust me that it is worse for you than for Ellie.'

'Well, yes.'

Jo took her mum and dad for a cup of tea in the cafeteria to explain what the sister had said. They found it as difficult as had

Jo, as their every instinct was to be with Ellie, but eventually could see the sense in it, given that the staff of Addenbrookes knew more about trauma than almost anyone else in the country.

Gazing out of the window, Jo saw a police car arrive, from which emerged Cate and Chris. She rose and went out to meet them.

'Cate, Chris, thank you so much for coming,' she said and gave each a hug. 'Please come and get some refreshment first and foremost. It's not great but it is food.'

She introduced them to Marian and Sidney, who said they would leave them and go back to see Ellie briefly before returning to their hotel. Cate tried in vain to stop them. As Cate and Chris ate and drink, it enabled Jo to tell them everything that had happened since a tractor had pulled out in front of Ellie through to the latest information about the effects of trauma.

'I assume you're staying overnight so would it be best if we could meet in the morning and go through all that Chris and I unearthed (that's a fox hunting pun, by the way) in Wales. By the looks of you, a good night's sleep would be a sound investment. But first come and say a quick hello to Ellie, if she's awake.'

Later in the evening, remembering that Eamonn probably had heard nothing about Ellie, she gave him a quick call and to ask a small favour which was he more than happy to give.

They met in Jo's hotel on the following morning after breakfast, and after giving them the lowdown on Ellie's condition following Jo's call to the ward, she began her report on the trip she and Chris had made to Wales.

'Gordon owes his alibi entirely to Alyson, but it turns out that both are liars. Far from being the keen supporters of hunting, as they told me, they are fact prominent anti-hunt protesters or saboteurs. Chris and I saw film of them, as well as a few stills, and highly offensive their language and activities were too. There is however something more, and although you may say I'm jumping to conclusions, I got the impression from talking with her and then realising she was spinning a web of lies so cleverly, that she may well not just be the leader of that group of animal rights activists, but also the agent embedded there by MI5. The reason I say that is because someone involved in the killing knew about the Roman numerals and presumed that this would divert us from the local to the national, as happened in Boston and Comrie too. They were copycat killings not serial.'

'I went to see PC Anderson after you left by helicopter. She had nothing of much use, though she's a nice woman, but then you asked me to see Poppy. I grant you that she's still vicious on the subject of her brother, but it was as nothing to what she said about Alyson. She said Alyson had pushed Gordon into marriage but also became the family member closest to Tony, and thinks it was she who persuaded him to change his will in favour of Gordon, so it wasn't Sgt Bowie but Alyson who was hoping to get her hands on the money.'

'That's interesting, but at this stage nothing more than the surmise of someone in the throes of bitterness,' said Cate. 'Do you think Alyson was involved in the killing of Tony, Jo?'

'We've never been able to account for the fact that Tony left his car by the side of the road freely, clearly intending to return to it because he chose not to lock it. Might that be because he was summoned by someone he recognised in need of assistance? Alyson is certainly the obvious person he would stop to help. And Gordon and Alyson knew when he was due back in the middle of the night because Gordon was present when he rang to inform Danny. I think that a visit to the files of Keele University is overdue, but I'm not sure this can be undertaken by Eamonn.'

'Why not? Surely he's the best person to do that,' said Cate.

'We've been given partial information by Eamonn because he's under orders from above in MI5. If Alyson is who I think she is, he will have to clear it with his bosses and they may shut him down completely.'

'Oh God, I'd never even considered that possibility. What do we do? You're here, and yet you're also the one we need to complete this and if we can't use Eamonn, who can we use?'

'I rang Eamonn last night at home, to let him know about Ellie, for which he was very grateful and profoundly upset. He also provided me with the phone number of someone who might be able to help trace information about Alyson which I think we need before she is questioned. So, I am going up to town to see this person tomorrow.'

'Joanna Enright, what are you up to?'

Jo smiled.

'Don't worry, boss, and as for being here when we need to complete this, you heard what I had to say about the necessity of Ellie requiring little or no distraction in the immediate aftermath of trauma, so this is a time which I can still use before taking a longer period of break and working with Ellie on her recovery and then having to face up to Dani.'

'I have a sneaking feeling that when you come back you will be the new ACC, having forced Dani out. But in the meantime, *Acting* Detective Inspector, how shall we deal with things now? It always used to be the senior officer who made the decisions.'

Jo was determined not to be distracted.

'After my meeting I'll get the train to Worcester Shrub Hill and change to Hereford, and with luck I should be able to manage to find a room at either the Three Counties or the Premier Inn.'

'Yes, that's a great idea, Jo. I tell you what may be even better is if you get a train to Penzance, change and come back. I think what's happened to Ellie has addled your brain. So listen to me and this will be an order. Tomorrow morning Chris and I will drive to London, and when you have finished your business (whatever it might be), we'll collect you and we'll drive to Hereford with you. An order.'

Jo grinned at her boss.

'Yes, ma'am, and thank you, Cate.'

'Can we go and see Ellie?'

'Of course. Can you come about 2:30? I can't promise anything and she may continue to sleep but please come and be with us. Mum and dad will pop out for a cup of tea. By the way, the ward sister has asked some advice about a series of thefts from the ward. I said it was a matter for the Cambridgeshire police but she said they'd been useless, so I thought I might mention it to the person I'm seeing tomorrow and see what ideas might arise.'

'I got it wrong, Jo. You won't come back as ACC at all; you'll

be the Chief Constable.'
They laughed.

They left after breakfast. In one of her more lucid moments
Ellie had told Jo to go and complete the task and then return
ready for the task that lay ahead of them. Meanwhile she had
said, she had her mum and dad to look after her, and Jo knew
Ellie was speaking of Marian and Sidney as her own parents.

The house they sought was in Barnet, North London, just
inside the M25. Being in a marked car, albeit marked with the
insignia of the Warwickshire Constabulary, Jo insisted being
dropped at some distance from the house and she walked up the
pleasant road with its detached houses but not one as grand as
that inhabited by Ace Mackenzie. Jo smiled at the thought that
crime obviously pays better than the Security Services.
    The door was opened by a very pregnant and very pretty lady.
'You must be Inspector Jo.'
'And you must be Major Kim.'
'Hi. Come in please. I've just made some coffee. I'm sorry you
won't get to meet my wife, Sharon. She works for *The Times* and
sometimes even has to go in, and today is one of those days.
She's wonderful and you're missing a treat, and within this
expanding bump is our baby.'
'That is wonderful in itself and I long to hear all about that as
my fiancée and I hope we might follow in your footsteps. At the
moment she's in bed, and likely to be there for quite some time.
She's a Detective Chief Inspector and she asked me to marry her
on Thursday evening. Unfortunately, on Friday whilst going to
our home in Norwich a tractor pulled out in front of her and she
is now in quite a few pieces in Addenbrookes having been
transported by helicopter and treated in the Major Trauma Unit. I
have been told she is still in a state of profound shock and will
take a lot of caring for, but that she will make a full recovery in
about six months' time.'
'Where I work, we sometimes have people suffering from
major trauma, and it can take ages for them to recover, but with

your love beside her, how can she go wrong, but I'm sure that's not the reason you have come to see me. Eamonn said it was at one level quite straightforward, but if *he* was do what you intend asking, it might be countermanding an instruction. Am I right?'

With regular sips of coffee, Jo told Kim the whole story of the four murders, and that three had been solved and that one was outstanding though she now knew who had done it. The only issue remaining was who, if anyone was an accomplice to murder.

'Can I assume you have someone in mind?

'Yes. She is called Alyson Hill and is an alleged alumna of Keele University. Might you be able to find out if she is?'

'Oh yes, that's perfectly straightforward, and I can't think why Eamonn felt that helping in that would be a problem. Such lists are always open. Come into my work room.'

The computer set-up was astounding. There were three large monitors on the desk and many other pieces of equipment attached. Kim sat in her chair and rapidly typed in various passwords, before Jo saw the Keele University logo appear.

'How do you spell Alyson?'

'With a Y.'

As soon as she had typed the name, a red frame appeared around the screen flashing an alert.

'Ah,' said Kim. 'I see now why Eamonn couldn't answer your question, and he knew it in advance.'

'Is it a big problem?'

'I'll answer that in a moment. First let me report that there has never been an Alyson Hill, spelled that way, at Keele University. Three others who spell it in the customary way, have been there, but not in your timeframe. The warning light indicates that highly privileged information may be disclosed if I go further and override the warning. I shall be breaching the Official Secrets Act if I do so.'

'I see. The information you have given me about that name and the University is very important and almost certainly will suffice, but, Kim, perhaps if you close the system down now, I could ask you a couple of quite general questions about the people you work for.'

'Ok, but you know my limits.'

'Yes, and I respect them and you.'

Kim typed and the screen cleared.

'We already know because Eamonn was cleared to tell us, that an agent of the service embedded in an animals liberation group had reported that the group acknowledged involvement in one of the murders. No more than that was given even though your superiors must know which group but they won't compromise their agent, which I understand.'

'That's bound to be so as some agents embed for long periods of time and put themselves at great personal risk.'

'Are they allowed to participate in illegal activities in order to collect intelligence and prove thereby that they are truly one of the members of the group?'

'That's not easy to answer. As you may know, police officers embedded with groups have been known to father children even though back home they have a wife and family. I suspect your own lawyers would be better placed to help you than I can. I don't know how well tested it has been in the courts, but as I say, agents operate taking considerable risks. Some groups are not frightened of the use of violence.'

'Kim, you have been a great help, if not quite as much as I might have hoped for, but your constraints are real.'

'Remember too, Jo, that though on maternity leave, I am still a serving member of the armed forces. That doubles the constraints. Were I to turn whistleblower I would be court-martialled.'

Jo pointed to a photograph on the desk.

'Your wedding day?'

'Yes.'

'Sharon is very beautiful.'

'Believe it or not she once had a husband, though only for six weeks.'

'Ellie too had a husband. Here on my camera I have some photos.'

'Some black women are simply gorgeous and Ellie is clearly

one of them.'

'You might not think so if you saw her now after the accident.'

'She will recover. I want to give you something Sharon has written about the lesbian route to childbirth – how we did it and others have. She's a fantastic writer and it goes into important detail.'

She handed the booklet to Jo.

'Thanks, Kim. What is it by the way?'

'A girl.'

'How exciting.'

'Would you like to keep in touch? I would.'

'Yes.'

They exchanged information.

'One more thing ...' said Jo, and told her about the pilfering going on in Addenbrookes.

'I might have just the thing,' said Kim.

Hereford Again

In the car, Cate and Chris were talking avidly about Elizabeth Jennings, a great but wholly underrated poet they both loved and who wrote most of her many hundreds of poems sitting in cafés in Oxford. So engrossed were they, the opening of the car door made them both jump.

'Fat lot of good you two would be on a stake-out,' said Jo, once inside.

'We were engrossed in Elizabeth Jennings, if you must know,' said Cate.

'I thought you must be,' teased Jo.

'So, how did you get on?'

'Alyson Hill was never a registered student at Keele University, and when Kim put her name into the MI5 computer, the screen flashed red and she could go no further as she is an army major and would be court-martialled for disclosing anything further, but the name of the person producing such a warning light indicates that Alyson Hill is the work name of an agent of the Security Service, which leaves us in a quandary. If she participated in the conspiracy to murder or was even an accessory, what is our legal position?'

'It's quite clear, Jo. If she is found guilty of either charge or both, she will be sentenced accordingly. The licence to kill belongs only in the fantasy world of James Bond. If we have the evidence, we arrest her.'

Moments later they were back on their way to the M25 and, to Jo's surprise, the M40 to Leamington.

'To their horror, I've summoned Eamonn, Sammy and Bobi

356

back from their holidays. We need their wisdom and experience for this.'

Jo called through to Addenbrookes and spoke to her mum, who reported that there seemed to be a real change for the better in the patient who said she was longing for Jo's return, but knew she had to finish the job first. They have also made the first tentative conversations about the possibility of eventually moving Ellie to the Norfolk and Norwich Hospital.

'If you see the ward sister, tell her that I may have answer to the problem on the ward she mentioned to me.'

'What's that?' asked Cate.

'Kim is one of the great inventors and I asked if she had any ideas about a way of stopping pilfering on the ward and she have me a small packet of devices, one of which will go into each locker and are highly sensitive to movement which is recorded on the equally tiny control box. It will show when someone touches the locker who shouldn't. She said it was variant of a device with which she caught out an Islamist group planning a bombing campaign as they sat in an Indian Restaurant.'

Chris, driving still, and Cate, looked at one another and shook their heads in astonishment. When Cate next looked back at Jo, she was fast asleep, always manifesting an amazing capacity to sleep wherever and whatever was going on.

Once everyone was gathered, and that included Dani and Derrick, Cate opened up the matter of strategy.

'Not for the first time, we are in this position thanks to the efforts of Jo, whose trip to North Wales yielded much fruit, and another to London earlier today to confirm what was taking shape in her mind, not to mention handling the awful injuries sustained by Ellie, but which did allow her, thanks to you ma'am, a helicopter ride.

'You all now know the situation we face. Gordon Hendry lives with someone calling herself Alyson Hill, which is her work name as an undercover agent with the North Wales Animal Liberation Front. I suggest we continue to regard these people as highly dangerous some, of whom may have access to shotguns and knives, as well as pepper and other forms of sprays which they use against hounds and may not do us a lot of good either. Sammy, advise, please.'

'The essence of what we do has to be surprise and to ensure no communications are made to other members of the group,' said Sammy. 'Assuming that we are intending to enter Gordon's house and to take into custody any and all present, we shall also need a forensic team to follow us. Where will they be taken?'

'Hereford,' said Dani. 'Leave that to me. They are not going to Welshpool and I think Jo and Chris would endorse that.'

Both nodded, and Chris added that it was much too small a police station, and that in any case both targets were familiar with it having sometimes been taken there after arrest for public order offences.

'There is one loose end that still concerns me.' said Jo. 'The Roman Numeral III cut into the back of Tony Hendry. Where did they get that from? At that time, it was still being held back from the Press and the only source for both Boston and Comrie was Holmes 3, which implicated police officers in disseminating that info. We have not yet linked this to Sgt Bowie in Builth Wells and having now been suspended pending a hearing with Professional Standards mostly on the basis of our investigation he is unlikely to want to co-operate, so ma'am, if that is so, we need authority from Powys Police to sequester his computers and examine his hard discs and Eamonn will be able to tell us whether or not he knew about the numbers. That doesn't prove he passed that information on, but if it is there, it makes him the most likely source.'

'Once again, leave to that me,' said Dani, with a look at Derrick who nodded.

'Eamonn,' said Cate 'I want you and Bobi to visit Bowie tomorrow and find everything out. Sammy, go and do a recce in advance of our going into action on the following morning.'

'Yes, of course, boss.'

'Tomorrow is ladies' rest day though we shall travel to Hereford in the late afternoon to prepare for the interrogations. I've made a booking for you three gents at the Kilverts Inn and Hotel in the glorious book town of Hay-on-Wye, and I hope you will take the opportunity to educate yourselves, and, with the exception of Eamonn, uniforms, guys, on the morning of the raid.'

'As it's our team leading this, I think we have to insist on it being our backup team not the Welsh,' said Derrick.

'Finally', said Cate, 'Jo tells me that for the first time tonight since the accident, Ellie has eaten something, which is terrific news.'

After everyone had expressed their satisfaction, Cate invited all present for a curry, and all responded positively.

Jo was correct. Despite initially denying any knowledge of the Holmes 3 information, Eamonn, there and then in the house showed his colleagues and Bowie himself that he had been on the Holmes 3 page containing that information several times before the murder of Tony Hendry.

'The contents of Holmes 3 are confidential. There is no way I would ever pass on that information to anyone other than to a fellow officer.'

'I am afraid, Sgt Bowie, ' said Bobi, 'that your record of truth telling is not too special, given the information that our team has found it necessary to hand on to the hearing to be held by Professional Standards. Your behaviour throughout suggests a distinct motive for involvement in the murder of Tony Hendry and because you are the only person possessing the information about the number III if, as you say you did not pass it on to anyone else, Ronald Bowie, I am arresting you on suspicion of complicity in the murder of Tony Hendry, you do not have to say anything, but, it may harm your defence if you do not mention when questioned something which you later rely on in court. Anything you do say may be given in evidence.'

He was speechless and after being handcuffed was taken by Sammy, who had just got back from Gordon's house to the police station in Builth Wells, where a constable on temporary attachment found the first person he had to lock up was his predecessor.

Bobi went outside and sat on a bench not far from the window of the cell where Bowie was being held, and called Cate.

'Bobi?'

'I'm sorry to trouble you, ma'am.'

'I hear what you're saying.'

'DI Enright was correct. After denying that he had been on Holmes 3 before the murder of Tony Hendry, we discovered on the hard disc a record of visits to the web page containing the information of the numbers, which he then admitted, and we have bagged the computer. Subsequently he has denied passing on this information to anyone else, so we must assume that being the only one to have access to that information, ma'am, he made use of it at the time of Hendry's death to cause it to be cut into his back, which because of the haemorrhaging indicates it was done whilst he was still alive. I have therefore arrested and cautioned him and he is being help at the Builth Wells police station awaiting your instructions.'

'Can he hear what you are saying, Bobi.'

'A van sent from Hereford, ma'am? Yes, that would be ideal.'

'Say it then, Bobi.'

'I'm pretty sure, if he did but know it, his own cause here and now, not to mention a good word from us to Professional Standards, would be advanced if we have information from him that enable us to bring this investigation to a close. Otherwise it's looking pretty bad for him.'

'Let me know, Bobi and if you need that van, I'll make sure it will come.'

'Thank you, ma'am.'

Bobi went back into the police station.

'A van will collect the prisoner and take him to Hereford. Do you know the form when holding a prisoner? If you have to enter the cell, you must ask him first to stand well clear of the door and place any drink on the floor. No contact is allowed and he may be a sergeant but the only person you obey is me or my colleague, DI Burton.'

'Yes, sarge.'

Bobi had reached the door when he heard Bowie shout that he wished to make a statement. He walked to the cell door.

'Do you wish this to be done in the presence of a solicitor?'
'No.'
'In which case you must wait until I find DI Burton as we need a senior officer present. Be patient and I will hunt him down.'

He went outside and found him drinking coffee and chatting with Eamonn in the car. It was fortuitous that they were together because Eamonn was carrying with him a portable double cassette recorder he had thought just might come in useful. The three of them came to the interview room and Eamonn set up and tested the equipment and left whilst Bowie was brought. Sammy went through the official formulae necessary to recording an interview.

'I have been informed by Detective Sergeant Jones that you wish to make a statement in order to assist enquiries into the murder of Tony Hendry. For the benefit of the tape can you please confirm that you are making this statement of your own free will and are under no duress to do so.'

'I am making this statement of my own free will and under no duress.'

Sammy opened his hands, thereby inviting Bowie to go on.

'I access the Holmes 3 website regularly, as I believe it is incumbent upon all police officers regularly to do so. It was there that I saw the reference in the instances of the murders in London and Lincolnshire to the apparent use of Roman Numerals on the bodies of the victims. About a week before the death of Tony Hendry, I was leaving the house where I had been having a cup of tea, and only a cup of tea, with Danny Hendry, when Gordon Hendry approached me.

'He doesn't like me, primarily because he thought, correctly as it happened, that I was having a relationship with his mother, though he was always uneasy in his dealings with me, presumably in case I knew about his involvements with the Maen hunt as a protester. He became aggressive and told me to stay away from his mother. I told him to retain his anger for use with his animal thugs, and then I did a stupid thing, because I was losing my control completely, and told him that the next time he attacked one of the hunters he should scrawl III on his back before he killed them as someone had already used I and II. I admit it was a stupid thing to do but I didn't for one moment think he would even remember what I had said, let alone either pass it on to others or ever make use of it himself.'

'In your opinion, setting aside for the moment the possibility that you liked him as little as he liked you and you might even now wish to see the proceeds of the will of his father pass to someone else, did you think Gordon capable of an act of brutal murder.'

'He had motive, means and opportunity and I imagine North Wales Police could tell you about the anger and violent behaviour he shows when protesting against hunting, and that bitch of a woman he lives with too. Indeed of the two I would actually say she was the more likely one to kill.'

'Can you confirm for the tape that you are referring to Alyson Hill?'

'Yes. Trust me, sir, you don't know what she's like. She's an animal herself.'

'Sergeant Bowie, have you anything further to add to your statement?'

'Only to say, sir, that what I have said in this statement is completely true. If it is of assistance in solving the crime, I hope that my co-operation might be made known to Professional Standards.'

'I shall now turn off the tape and a copy will be bagged in your presence and signed by us both and made available to any legal representative you may require.'

Bobi called for the van from Hereford, and Sammy called Cate who was now on her way to Hereford with Chris and Jo.

'Bowie admitted informing Gordon about the number III and whilst he believes him capable of murder, he suggests that the truly violent one is Alyson Hill.'

'Oh God, I hope not. That really will be letting the fox into the hen house.'

'Very funny, but I know what you mean.'

'All set for morning?'

'No problem.'

The early morning wake-up call experienced by Gordon and Alyson was a rude awakening. Suddenly to find your bedroom replete with men in body armour and face masks, each of them carrying a large weapon, can be no one's idea of fun. Their loud protests continued all the way downstairs into their sitting room. An unlicensed shotgun was discovered in a cupboard complete with a box of cartridges. Both were handcuffed and Sammy informed them why they were being arrested and placed them under oath. They were then led outside to waiting cars which took them separately off to Hereford police station. Sammy waited until the house was secured and tape put up forbidding entry to a crime scene. The only people who seemed to enjoy the excitement of it all were the neighbours.

In Hereford, Cate had decided that Gordon would be interviewed by Jo and Bobi, whilst she and Sammy would take on Alyson. Solicitors had to be provided which delayed matters but eventually Gordon was brought into the interview room.

'At the present time Mr Hendry,' began Jo, 'your alibi for the night in which your father was abducted before being brutally murdered comes only from Alyson Hill, maintaining that you were together in bed and probably asleep. Is that correct?'

'Yes.'

'And vice versa, you would say the same of her.'

He nodded and was told to speak his reply for the benefit of the tape.

'Why did you lie about your supposed love of fox hunting on the hills with Maen hunt?'

'Because what Alyson and I do on Saturdays and Sundays has nothing to do with my father's death. Why should I have to tell you?'

'Because we were bound to find out that far from being lovers of fox hunting you and Alyson use considerable violence to oppose it, violence to people and violence to the hounds by means of pepper and other forms of spray, which is hardly consonant with an alleged love of animals, as is working with thousands of chickens in cages for many years and deriving an income from that.'

'Anything that may have been reported to you by the North Wales Police should be ignored as biased and indicative of whose side they are on.'

And that is?'

'The cruel hunting bastards.'

'Am I also therefore to ignore what I have seen for myself in the videos recorded by them over a considerable period showing you and Alyson engaging in breaches of the peace, fighting and using violence against animals in the back of a pickup?'

'If you could see instead, the terrible things done to foxes by the dogs and the use of terriers to bring them out from their earths, you wouldn't complain about a little bit of pepper.'

'Foxes live in the wild; your chickens lived tightly packed in cages, a point made by whoever killed him by stuffing his corpse into a cage. When that was made known to you, what was your reaction?'

'I had no reaction.'

'And what about the other manifestations of brutality: the slitting of his throat from ear to ear, the stuffing of chicken heads into his throat and the deep cuts made into his back. What was your reaction to these?'

He did not respond other than a facial indication of not caring. For the benefit of the tape this recorded by Bobi.

'Would you agree with me, Mr Hendry, that whoever abducted and killed your father must have known that he was returning from Oxford late that evening, and that this was known only to you, your mother and your sister when your father telephoned when you were all taking your morning break. Let's apply Occam's razor. Do you think it likely that your sister Poppy would have passed this on to someone likely to be wanting to kill your father?'

'No. Anyone who knows her would regard that as ridiculous.'

'Your father's mobile phone record shows that he did not make another call. So that leaves us with you and your mother or did you return home later that day and mention the intention of your father to come back during the night to Alyson Hill?'

'Probably. You'll have to ask her.'

'Trust me. We shall.'

'Did you leave the house that evening, perhaps to go for a drink or for some other reason?'

'No, we stayed in and would have gone to bed at about 10:00 pm.'

'You had known for some time the contents of your father's will?'

'Yes.'

'What do you think might have been your father's motives in disclosing this to you and did you raise objections to the way he was intending to leave nothing at all to your mother or your sister.'

'You never knew my father. He did not argue once he had made up his mind.'

'In fact, you didn't like your father. Maybe in fact, you hated him. Is that right?'

'I had hated him for years, despised him from deep inside myself. When you mentioned the things done to him, I couldn't care less. He was a vile and horrible man, and I was and am glad that he's dead. But saying all that is not the same as saying that I killed him, because I did not, though a big part of me wishes that I had and envies whoever did so.'

'The third member of the group that knew of the timing of his return, was your mother, Danny Hendry. Was she hovering by the roadside at midnight in Clyro waiting for him?'

'No. But she didn't need to because she passed the information on to Sgt Ronnie Bowie, her lover.'

'Was this by carrier pigeon, Mr Hendry, because we have checked the telephone record of the farmhouse landline and her mobile and the mobile of Sgt Bowie and the landline at his home, and no such call was made?'

'She didn't need to, she probably told him in her bed.'

'On that day there was no contact between your mother and Sgt Bowie, because we have at least a dozen witnesses confirming that he was on a course all day at the Police Training Centre in

Bridgend.'

Well, of course they would vouch for him – I'm sure they're all masons.'

'Absolutely correct, Mr Hendry, apart, that is from the seven women officers on the course and Sgt Bowie, who is not a mason either. Now, do tell us about the Roman Numeral III and why it was savagely cut with a knife into your father's back?

'I have no idea and didn't know it had been.'

'I am suspending the interview. We have 36 hours from the moment of your arrest, unless the magistrate grants an extension, before we need release you. You will therefore be returned to your holding cell and return if and when we need to continue the interview.'

Jo and Sammy stood, the latter stopping the tape and taking out the solicitor's copy which they both signed after it was placed in a sealed bag.

No Comment

Gordon had looked uncomfortable throughout his interview, whereas when Alyson and her solicitor entered the interview room, she looked totally at ease and smug.

After the official introductions for the tape, Cate was about to ask the first question when Alyson asked for a pen and a piece of paper on which she wrote and passed it to Cate. On it was written a single word in alternative upper and lower case letters: LeMoN. At once Cate guessed it was form of codeword to be used by an agent of the Security Services if the police ever came into contact with them.

'If this is to be authenticated I have to have the name that goes with it.'

Cate could see she was thinking hard.

'Without that, your piece of paper means nothing, and in any case, as I suspect you know, you're finished here. Your name, please.'

'Rebecca Hopwood.'

'I need to suspend the interview for a short while as I need to seek confirmation of the name you have provided. There is no reason for you to move.'

Outside she asked Eamonn to confirm the name. In turn he telephoned Kim. She came back moments later.

'No.'

Cate disliked being messed about at any time of the day or night and immediately called Dani and explained. It took her ten minutes before she called back. 'Olivia Keelan.'

Cate returned, the recorder was turned back on.

'I do not take anyone messing about with our work lightly, and so, in addition to any other charges you may face, Miss Keelan, I shall be recommending that wasting police time will be added to them. Is that clear?'

Keelan shrugged.

'So what? You know that I shall be exempt from all charges.'

'It's true that there will be no charges for lying that you were at Keele, or that you loved hunting, and that the issues of your behaviour as a member of the particular animals rights group will not be pursued, but there are some crimes not included in that exemption, the principle one being conspiracy to murder, aiding and abetting another or others in the act of murder, and of course murder itself.'

'In which case you should let me go now.'

'You provided Gordon Hendry with an alibi that was quite false for on the night that Tony Hendry was abducted, neither of you were in bed. That lie will be included in our request to the CPS that you be charged with conspiracy to murder.'

'You made a special point of informing DI Enright, away from earshot of Hendry, that he had told you about the significance of the Roman Numeral III, and that there was a serial killer on the loose in the country. Why did you do that?'

'Because I thought your officer should have that piece of information, because I was beginning to consider the possibility that Gordon might have had some part in Tony's murder.'

'It also meant that you were privy to the information. Did you mention it to anyone else?'

'No.'

'Whose idea was it that you should give the appearance of being in distress in Clyro as Tony approached?'

'Gordon said that if he saw it was me, he would stop, and the intention was to fill his car with chicken heads, lock him in a cage and leave him there 'til morning. A classic sort of protest.'

'But that never happened, so what part did you play in what followed?'

'None. I came home.'

'And who did you leave behind with Gordon?'

'A couple of lads from the animal group.'

'Whose names are?'

Her solicitor spoke in her ear.'

'No comment.'

'You departed, presumably having been seen and recognised by Tony so that when morning came he would easily identify you to the police, and that went also for Gordon, but in fact morning never came for him. Do you have any idea how he was transported away from Clyro, or where to?'

'No comment.'

'I am suspending the interview to give time for refreshment.'

'My client has provided you with an instruction in code from the Security Services and you now have her name. In view of the concordat between the police and the Security Services, she should be released. If you will not, I will approach a Judge to instruct you to release her.'

'That concordat remains a possibility after all interviews have been completed to our satisfaction, and until that time your client will remain in her holding cell. End of.'

Cate left Bobi to complete the formalities with the tape and a uniformed officer came in, handcuffed Keelan and took her away, followed by her solicitor.

When Cate returned to her office, Chris, there with Jo and Bobi. had some news following the work of the forensic team in the house at Builth Wells.

'Ma'am, the forensic team found considerable quantities of illegal drugs under a floorboard, under a carpet in the sitting room, including Heroin, Coke and Weed. Alongside it was a bottle of opaque white liquid from which the label had been removed and a few needles and hypodermic syringes.'

'Are there any fingerprints?'

'No.'

'Pity. Take the bottle, Chris, to a company called Tactical Advance just outside the the city, and when you get there make sure you do not hand the bottle to anyone but Dr Corey Wilson, who will be expecting you. He will take it for analysis.'

'Ok.'

'I'll be with you in a moment,' said Cate to Jo and Bobi, who were now being joined by Sammy.'

She took out her phone.

'I need to speak to Dr Corey Wilson, please ... That is your problem, not mine ... Tell him it's Detective Superintendent Greene at Hereford Police Station and it is urgent ... No, it can't wait until he calls back ... Tell him it's an urgent murder enquiry and he must take the call now – please.'

The three members of her team loved the "please" and grinned at one another.

'Corey, hello. This could not be more urgent. On its way to you now is a bottle of an opaque white liquid. A clock is ticking as we hold two persons, and I need to know what the liquid is. I cannot tell you what I think it is, of course, as you are an independent expert and my forensic labs would take too long ... Corey, you are a star, and as a reward you can take me out to dinner very soon, though no sex at the end of it. Ok?'

'"No sex at the end of it", Cate?' said Sammy.

'Corey's gay. He will get the joke,' she replied. 'So, guys, who did it? Gordon or Olivia?'

'Who the hell is Olivia?' asked Jo, somewhat confused.

'She is the latest incarnation of the one already identifying today as Alyson Hill, Rebecca Hopwood, and now Olivia Keelan, the final name being confirmed by your friend Kim from MI5. Keelan is claiming total immunity having produced a magic word for me. Here it is: LeMoN. Her solicitor claims that under the terms of the concordat agreed between police and the security services, she should be released immediately to protect her identity. I have said that under the terms of the concordat, no member of the security services has a licence to kill, and the investigation we are carrying out is to determine whether she has either carried that out or is complicit in the murder.

'She freely informed us, because I implied I knew, that she was the lure to bring Tony Hendry to a stop in Clyro, and to my mind that already makes her complicit in whatever followed. She said there were two others from the animal rights group who helped in what followed but insists it was only intended as a prank.

Needless to say, she didn't give their names. But perhaps Gordon might be persuaded to disclose them, Jo?'

'I've noted it down.'

'Bobi, can you find Eamonn?'

'Of course, he's bound to be in your communications centre.'

'And what about Gordon?' continued Cate.

'Hated his father from the depth of his being but insists he did not kill him. Denies knowing about the III and was more than happy to blame his mother and Sgt Bowie for passing on the information of Tony's return until I pointed out the impossibility of this.'

'Does he show any indication of the true identity of Alyson Hill?'

'None.'

'It will be interesting to see how he reacts. If we find ourselves running out of time, bring up the drug find and we shall be able to hold them on a charge of possessing and supplying Class A drugs.'

The door opened and in came Bobi and Eamonn.

'Eamonn, you have been brilliant throughout these investigations, and we couldn't have managed without you, and thanks especially for enabling us to discover the real name of your agent. My first question is, would an agent functioning in this way, know how to administer a drug such as Propofol as part of his or her training?'

'No chance – none at all, and the Security Services ombudsman would never allow it.'

'So, how might an agent learn how to use it?'

'Only by previous experience before joining the service. Even if she or he had a relationship with an anaesthetist, I can't see a doctor instructing someone, can you?'

'I think we all understand that there is nothing more we are going to get out of MI5 about her past record, so I am not going to ask you to do that, not least because I know you would be bound to refuse by virtue of the Official Secrets Act. However, would you be able to a search of lists of registered doctors and nurses, and even, if possible, check med schools for anyone who might have dropped out?'

'Med schools don't keep lists of drop-outs but starter lists can be compared with lists of graduates. Anymore?'

'Sorry if it's not enough, Eamonn. We'll try harder next time.'

Even Eamonn joined in the laughter. He departed and was at once replaced by Chris bearing sandwiches and drinks.

'Oh fabulous,' said Cate. 'Working with you, Chris, is clearly going to be a good experience. But much more important than anything we've been dealing with is how Ellie is doing.'

'I spoke to her on the phone this morning and told her how we were doing, and she sends her love. After the weekend Adenbrookes have agreed to her transfer to Norwich and when I told Dani earlier, she would arrange for a police ambulance helicopter based at Culdrose to move her, which is so kind.

'She did however tell me a story which at first I thought was hallucinatory, all about a woman who runs a café near Honiton whom she's met when visiting Yarcombe. A middle-aged but still very attractive lady, according to Ellie, which to my mind shows she's beginning to heal, came out to her whilst she was supplying her and Bobi sandwiches and drinks, and Ellie, having turned herself into a lesbian counselling service, told her to ring when she needed to do so. Well, now she has, and has left her husband and moved in with someone called Susie. Ellie explained her own situation and the lady, apparently called Yvonne, has said that next week she'll call me! I'm out of my depth.'

By now the whole team was laughing.

The door opened and in came Eamonn, smiling and looking pleased with himself, but before saying anything he tore open a packet of sandwiches, removed one and took a bite. Everyone looked at him and put his lunch down and pulled out of his pocket a piece of paper.

'Staff Sergeant Olivia Mary Keelan, graduated as a nurse with the Royal Army Medical Corps seven years ago, before leaving to take up other work in the army which the RAMC lists do not mention.'

'I think we can work that out,' said Cate. 'All we need now is to hear from Corey.'

The team continued to eat in silence, each of them thinking and considering the possibility that this could be the last day of their work together. Cate and Jo knew only too well the burden that they faced in the afternoon of bringing it to a proper conclusion.

Kate's phone rang as they were about to break up and get ready.

'Hi Corey.'

'Cate, I am rather surprised that you had this substance which presumably was in the possession of one of your miscreants and I have never been asked to identify it before. The first clue, which you missed, was on the base of the bottle in the glass itself. Paper labelling is wholly insufficient for dangerous drugs, so that told me what it was meant to contain. A spectrograph confirmed what it is: to you, Diprivan; to me, as a former hospital doctor, Propofol, a short acting powerful anaesthetic applied intravenously.'

'Corey thank you, and ok, I will pay for the dinner.'

Cate had turned on the speaker so everyone had heard it.

At Last

'Mr Hendry, how much do you know about Staff Sergeant Olivia Keelan?' began Jo.

'Nothing, as far as I know. I've never heard of her.'

'And yet, when police officers rudely awakened you this morning they found you in bed with her, and you insist you know nothing about her.'

'Is this some sort of trick? I was in bed with Alyson Hill as I have been each night for more than a year and a half.'

'In which case, please tell me how much you know about Alyson Hill?'

'We met, as you know, when her group of protesters from Keele University, where she was a student, joined up with ours protesting at illegal hunts in North Wales.'

'What sort of protester was she? Did she just stand and wave a banner or was she more active than that?'

'She was a natural encourager of others and led by example as we endeavoured to stop the illegal killing of foxes by being torn apart by dogs.'

'I've seen some of the videos made by the police and she certainly was a leader, perhaps *the* leader with a wonderful turn of phrase when hurling obscenities at hunters and police alike.'

'They deserved them.'

'When not protesting, what did she do?'

'I assume was doing her student work.'

'Were you invited to her graduation ceremony?'

'No, she said it was a load of crap and nonsense and wasn't attending herself.'

'When did you tell her that as well as running with the fox, you also ran with the hounds?'

'What on earth do you mean?'

'That you were a chicken farmer keeping your animals in conditions generally regarded as unacceptable.'

'She was appalled of course as increasingly I had become.'

'Did it occur to either of you to find a way of putting a stop to it?'

He did not answer.

'Mr Hendry?' asked Jo.

'We did talk about it from time to time, though after my father informed that he was leaving everything in his will to me, I remember Alyson saying that if he died, we could be rid of it all, but she did not say anything to the effect that we should bring that about.'

'What did Alyson do when you were working?'

'She was writing a book on our works of protest.'

'Is it good? Can I get it from Amazon?'

'It's not finished yet.'

'But you've read some of it surely.'

'She said she would only let me read the finished product.'

'Did you ever see her engaged in writing?'

'No, she only wrote when I was out.'

'I would like to return to the lie with which you concluded our morning session. You said you knew nothing about the Roman Numeral III which was brutally cut into your father's bare back with a knife whilst he was still alive, whereas in fact you did know about it because you were informed about during a heated argument outside your mother's farmhouse with Sgt Bowie. He has made a statement admitting that he told you about it. Cast your memory back and see if you can recall the event and his words.'

'It was a heated encounter and I can't remember anything he said.'

'I see.'

'You may remember that I came to visit the pair of you at your home. Miss Hill informed me as I was leaving, that you had informed her of the Roman Numeral III and its significance. So, I must ask again, do you now remember hearing about this at the time of your altercation with Sgt Bowie?'

'Yes.'

'And you reported this to Alyson.'

'Yes.'

'Do tell me, Mr Hendry, what you feel about and for Alyson Hill?'

'I love her and I admire her even if sometimes she can be quite scary.'

'And how much do you know about her family.'

'She has no contact with any of them and so never speaks of them.'

'In which case let us return to Staff Sergeant Olivia Keelan, with whom, as I said earlier, you were in bed this morning at the time of your arrest. You might be interested to know that the woman you have known as Alyson Hill not only has never been a student at Keele University, but trained as a soldier and then a nurse in the Royal Army Medical Corps before transferring to the Security Services or MI5, if you prefer. She volunteered for a mission as a mole in the animal rights movement, reporting everything she learned with names, including yours, to her case officer. Technically she has been a singleton, an agent working alone.

'However, she also had a sideline, unless it was you. Under a floorboard in your sitting room under the carpet, forensic officers found a considerable cache of heroin, cocaine and marijuana, far more than would be regarded as likely to be for personal use, more than suggesting that someone in your house was supplying others with these drugs.'

'This is all ridiculous. Alyson would never do that. You're making it all up to frame me. I've never done drugs, I would never supply them to others and I did not kill my father.'

'Staff Sergeant Keelan has fully disclosed her identity and is presently seeking immunity under the terms of a concordat worked out between the Security Services and the police. She denies any involvement in your father's death and says that this was done by you, together with two members of the animal rights group.'

'But it wasn't me, it was her. All she could talk about was the money we would make from the sale of the farm and a different sort of life we would be able to afford to live. I had no idea about the drugs – I promise. I told her about my dad's plans to return late and she was meeting up with Kenny Baker and Mick Scanlon to plan the following Saturday's protest where she had an idea which needed their help. I waited up but fell asleep in my chair and only woke about 2:30am when Alyson came in, full of herself. It only struck me in the morning that I was sure she was wearing different clothes to those she went out in.'

'Did she explain why she was out so late?'

'What? Alyson give an account of anything she'd done? I would have been wasting my breath.'

'What do you think happened to the clothes she went out in?'

'I've no idea.'

When did you come to the realisation of what had happened, that Alyson had killed your father?'

'I don't think I ever let myself think it. I assumed it was Kenny Baker and Mick Scanlon who'd done it. They're wild animals themselves and live in Welshpool. Baker is unemployed but might be with Scanlon, a gardener at Powis Castle. Perhaps Alyson was paying them in drugs.'

'Once again, Mr Hendry, I am suspending this interview. I should forewarn you that having spoken with my superior officers, we may decide to apply to the Crown Prosecution Service to charge you with a number of offences, of which you will be fully informed. However, you have been helpful to our enquiries and I thank you for that and it may be helpful to you as I'm sure your solicitor will point out.'

Jo informed Cate of what she had just been told and she in turn made immediate contact with the North Wales Police informing them of the presence in Welshpool of two men wanted immediately suspected of murder. She said they would possibly be dangerous and recommended searches of their homes as it was likely they had caches of Class A drugs which they were supplying to others. She gave their names and locations.

Jo and Bobi then briefed Cate on the interview with Hendry and his belief that Alyson was responsible for the murder of his father, and then recounted Gordon's account of the night in which Hendry had been abducted and his apparent ignorance of the drugs under the floor and the book she was supposedly writing. Cate returned to the Interview Room, but this time taking Jo with her as well as Sammy.

The solicitor said that his client was now requesting a solicitor from the Security Services who would free her from this farrago.

'No,' said Cate.

'What do you mean "no".'

'What I say: no. Now, let's press on.'

'The regulations according to the Police and Criminal Evidence Act are clear. Anyone arrested can ask for a solicitor of their choice and my client has made her request.'

'As her solicitor you should know better. Those who have been arrested may be held for 36 hours, then charged or released. A well-known ploy is for someone to ask for a different solicitor to use up time. In this instance it would not be possible for a solicitor from London to be here before morning which would conveniently leave your client fewer hours before being charged or released. Where this is suspected of being a deliberate ploy, an officer of the rank of Superintendent or higher, may allow the application for a new solicitor, but insist on the present interview continuing. This is the second attempt made by your client to avoid the possibility of being charged with an offence. A solicitor from London can be applied for, but as Superintendent I can and insist that we continue now.

'Staff Sergeant Keelan, how much did you imagine the farm and buildings would be likely to bring on the open market, approximately?'

'I have no idea.'

'You didn't for example discuss it with your friends Kenny Baker and Mick Scanlon?'

'I have no idea who you are talking about.'

Jo noticed that she suddenly seemed more nervous.

'They were members of your rent-a-mob group attending meetings of the Maen Hunt of which videos were taken showing you in a leadership, no, *the* leadership position. Your language, by the way, was appalling and I'm sure your mother would blush, though perhaps you picked it up caring for soldiers when you were training to be a Registered nurse. Those two gentlemen will soon be brought here to help us with our enquiries. They will first be asked who their supplier was, not just for the personal use, but for further supply down the line. I'm clear that the considerable quantity of H, Coke and Weed, found under your floorboards by our forensic team who took up your carpet is where they were supplied from.'

Keelan remained silent.

'That they are not the pleasantest of people suited you well. At the meets they were happy to be as offensive as you demanded, partly because that is how they are anyway, and partly because they knew they would be well rewarded. Have you anything to say?'

'No comment.'

I now want to turn to something else found beneath your floorboards. It was a bottle from which the label had been removed, containing a white opaque liquid. Can you tell me please what it was.'

'It must have belonged to Gordon. It had no label and I put it there for safe keeping.'

'But you maintain you did not know what it was.'

'Yes. I was a nurse not a chemist.'

'How long in your training did you serve in theatres?'

'Not long.'

'Were you aware that manufacturers of dangerous drugs have a fail-safe identification method should a label become detached or deliberately removed?'

'No.'

'It's built into the glass on the bottom in the form of a code, hence when our expert witness received it this morning, he knew at once what it was likely to be, something confirmed by spectrograph. So have a guess, go on, say what you think it might have been?'

'I have no idea.'

'Ooh, Staff Sergeant, I think you are a fibber, because you know exactly what it was, after all you placed it there for safe keeping, you took it out when you went out to meet your Welshpool friends, as you told Gordon you were doing, and you used one of the accompanying hypodermic syringes to deliver the drug intravenously, but you hadn't thought about was the fact he died too soon for it to be out of his system and the post-mortem found significant amounts. Do you recognise the scenario?'

'No comment.'

'I am, as you know perfectly well, speaking of Diprivan, also known as Propofol, used by anaesthetists across the world because it renders a patient unconscious in seconds. It has to be applied intravenously, as you know, and would have no effect if injected into a muscle, so requires someone to do that who is suitably skilled as you are. Would you like to comment?'

'None of what you have said makes me a murderer. Propofol doesn't kill and as I understand it, Hendry did not die of any kind of drug overdose.'

'Yes, you're quite right. In itself it does not make you a murderer, but I have never suggested that you were. The precise details and timetable will, I am sure, emerge from our later conversations with Baker and Scanlon, but before you left them to return home to Gordon, whom you found asleep in his chair, you took part in the killing of Tony Hendry, even if you didn't yourself slash his throat, but I am certain that it was you, prior to the moment of his death, cut the three stripes into his back making the Roman Numeral III, or else you'll be telling me next that one of them is a Latin scholar. You waited until he was dead and loaded his corpse into a cage before changing your clothes and going back to Builth Wells. I imagine that any fox might think itself quite well off compared with Tony Hendry though of course you didn't care tuppence about the fate of foxes. It is most likely, and we shall know more very soon, that the cage was transported by one of the men in a van and brought to Brilley later and unloaded. And the reason why they would do this for you lay under your floorboards and it's even quite possible that they were stoned when it came to doing the killing.'

'You're scum, do you know that?'

'Well thank you for that review. Olivia Mary Keelan, I shall now make contact with the Crown Prosecution Service requesting their permission to charge you with the murder of Tony Hendry. I rather think you'll find you are disowned by the Security Services and likely to face a Court Martial by the army. I am now ending this interview. You will be taken to a holding cell for now, and once charged, will be taken before magistrates.'

Cate stood. Sammy removed the copy of the tape for the solicitor and a uniformed officer handcuffed her and took her out.

'Get Gordon back, Jo, and release him under investigation. I don't think he had any part in the murder and he can hardly be charged with being a fool, which he is. Tell him that we may summon him again within a fortnight for further questioning. I shall see Bowie now and inform him that he too is being released under investigation, but that all that emerged will be forwarded to Professional Standards, when he meets with them next week. Then Jo, I want to see you in my office – alone.'

Both Gordon and Bowie emerged from their respective interview rooms a lot lighter-headed than they had entered them. Their solicitors took their leave, and the two men decided that they would take a taxi back to Builth Wells together, though they barely spoke on the way back. On arrival, Gordon lifted the carpet and saw where Alyson had hidden her store of goodies. What a fool he had been. He knew he was not the first and would not be the last to be made a total fool of by a woman but at this precise moment it didn't help much.

Ronnie Bowie found an empty house, with wife and children gone and a note saying she was seeking a divorce and custody of the children. He knew he would be out of work very soon. What a fool he had been.

Kenny Baker and Mick Scanlon knew the form and both had records for ABH and GBH and had served time in prison. Their solicitors advised them to come clean and say that whatever they had done, none of which they could recall, was done under the influence of the drugs supplied to them by Alyson Hill. They had been stoned. They admitted their complicity in the abduction of Tony Hendry which yhey had been told by Alyson was intended as a joke. She had promised them a considerable amount of both H and Coke, plus a lot of weed if she helped set it up. They had to hold him whilst they watched her inject something into what was clearly a vein in his neck. They had then helped her carry him to the nearby Clyro Brook, where for reasons they never understood she took a knife and made three deep cuts in his back which caused him enormous pain but by this time he was incapable of making noise because she had stuffed his mouth with chicken heads. She then took the knife and cut his throat from one ear to the other and said something like "Let's see how he likes it". There was a lot of blood but she made sure it drained into the brook. Scanlon had been asked to bring a large cage which he had stolen from the local kennels, and she made them push the body into it. The cage they took to Brilley Village Hall on their way back to Welshpool and wasn't discovered for a further 24 hours.

With slight variations, their stories tallied and they remained at the police station until charged, appeared before the magistrates and were remanded in custody prior, to long spells in prison.

DCI

Jo, however, missed this final episode and was on her way to Worcester where she had been invited by the ACC to have supper and to stay the night. She spoke to Ellie on the hands-free and told her all about everything.

'Cate said she wanted to see me in her office. It was to tell me where I was going to staying overnight. I think she was jealous.'

'Of course, because you have solved all these cases, and Dani and Cate know that. I am so proud of you, but once this evening is over, promise you will forget everything and give yourself wholly to me, and to our mum and dad. They have been wonderful.'

'Why not? You're their daughter.'

'Let me know how the evening goes before you go to bed.'

It was a relaxing evening and most of the time it was just Dani and Jo chatting and laughing but Jo knew that sometime something was going to be said. It came.

'How on earth can I, and the whole country, thank you for what you have done, Jo? You will say it was a team effort, and as always there is truth in that, but this was mostly brought about your quite remarkable skills as a detective.

'This afternoon I had a long conversation about you with the Chief Constable. We both know that now the Leamington Spa squad has completed its work, everyone must return to their previous work and for you that would be to the Met, who just might let you turn your *acting* into an *actual* DI, though I wouldn't bet on it.

'I'm sure you know the way some officers feel about rapid promotions but our graduate schemes are producing some very good senior officers. You haven't come via that route and I know there isn't a single member of your team who doesn't know what you have done in solving these crimes, which means that any position you may hold is on merit.

'Cate tells me that even if you don't like them and think they may be being made mistakenly, that you obey orders. Is that right?'

'I might indicate why I think an order may be mistaken, but as a police officer I obey an order when given by a senior officer.'

'Would that include an order in the course of work given by Ellie?'

'Of course. She has more experience of policing than I have, and I welcome any opportunity I to learn more from her and indeed from anyone. When we are working and she recognises that I've got something wrong, knowing that I can rely on her to tell me, regardless of our relationship, it is essential that I can rely on her as my superior and more experienced officer to guide me and put me right.'

She gave Dani a little grin.

'And I'm sure that's exactly how it is between you and the Chief Constable.'

Dani returned the grin.

'Well, Jo, in this instance, it's not Ellie or Cate issuing an order, but yours truly. But first, can you tell me something honestly? Did you cheat when you took the National Inspector's Exam, I mean, really cheat? For example, did you manage to get hold of a copy in advance, or use a hidden earpiece in which some utterly corrupt Chief Constable dictated what you should write?'

Jo pursed her lips, and suddenly realised when she looked at Dani that she was quite an attractive woman or had she had too much to drink.

'Go on. I'm willing to play the game.'

'It's no game though, is it, Jo? You chieved the highest score recorded since the form of the exam was changed. So why the fuck, and please excuse my French, have you allowed yourself to be held back so long? The problem in Boston was not that poor man who's just died, but you. As a woman you've got to fight. Apart from the orders I am about to give, in future if anyone gives you a stupid order, whether Ellie, Cate or for that matter Cressida Dick herself, you must, absolutely must, challenge it, fight it. I hope I have made myself understood.'

Jo burst out laughing.

'Oh, I know. I know what you're saying and, even worse, I know you're right. I hope, however late in the day, I'm learning to do things differently. Look at the amazing role models I've got – Ellie, Cate but above all, you. It's not enough to have a quick mind if you're a woman, you also have to possess a determination, and, if need be, a willingness to fight a little dirty when dealing with male colleagues.'

'This is music to my ears, Jo, so ... and this is the centrepiece of why I wanted you here tonight. Take off all the time you need as you assist Ellie as she recovers, both mentally and physically, though after what you have been doing in the past months, you also need a period of rest and recuperation. Then, when you've had enough of all that, and I suspect it won't be too long, you will discover that you have left the Met and will be taking up a brand new appointment as the DCI heading the Midlands Police Intelligence Unit covering West Mercia, West Midlands and Warwickshire, though a lot of your work will probably be centred on West Midlands.

'Before you begin, I want you to go to spend a month with the Security Services and see what you can learn from them. Ok? Obviously, you can't say Yes straight away and you will need to talk to Ellie, though I have a senior job in mind for her too if she wants to remain in the Police. So don't rush your decision. Just let me know by breakfast. Another glass of wine? My husband will be back soon. It's rather embarrassing having to admit it, but he's a Rotarian and it's been one of their nights.'

Over the toast and marmalade, with the minimum of fuss, having talked it over with Ellie late into the hospital night, she accepted Dani's offer.

Dani smiled.

'I'm sorry, Jo, I'd forgotten I'd suggested that you sleep on it. I just took it for granted.'

This time it was Jo who smiled.

'By the way, Cate tells me that things have rounded off quite well. The two men from Welshpool, Baker and Scanlon, have been charged with conspiracy and complicity in the murder of Tony Hendrybut will no doubt claim diminished responsibility and that Keelan got them stoned. Our erstwhile MI5 agent herself, Staff Sergeant Olivia Keelan has been charged with murder, and she faces a trial in the ordinary courts, but it is likely to cause quite a stink in parliament and you should not be surprised to hear on the news in the next couple of days of the resignation of the head of MI5, Sir Robert Browning. Staff Sergeant Keelan hasn't done the Security Services any favours at all, nor the army for that matter. My hope is that he will be replaced by Colonel Martha Sinclair, an extremely hardened but quite delightful black woman who at present is his deputy. The winners, ironically, are likely to be the lawbreakers of the Maen fox hunt who can continue their illegal activities with the police turning a blind eye, and now without the worst protesters and troublemakers, unless Gordon Hendry decides to go alone, which somehow or other I rather think he won't.

'When I initially pushed ACPO to set up the team I really believed a year's funding totally inadequate to the task, but I hadn't reckoned on you behaving like a foxhound, putting your nose to the ground and running all four to earth quite so quickly. They are very pleased with you, having saved them quite so much money.'

As she thought about this conversation on her way to Cambridge via Leamington Spa (for what she hoped was the last time) after breakfast, she kept breaking into fits of laughter. Dani was arguably the most irritating person in the Police Force, but also one of the best. She was a person of vision and almost certainly would not be an ACC much longer but soon have her own Police Force as Chief Constable. Lucky the force that acquired her – and good luck to them too. She also had an odd feeling that late last night Dani had hinted that they might spend the night together, but maybe she had drunk too much to have remembered that aright, or maybe as her mentor, Sigmund Freud, might have said, it was what she hoped she had said. Either way she had slept alone.

Ellie had been perfectly clear about Jo's decision when she had told her before getting into bed (alone) on the previous evening: she must accept the appointment even if Ellie decided to be a stay-at-home wife and not return to active service – "Two DCIs in the same kitchen would never work" she had insisted.

She called her on the hands-free phone in the car.

'Great news, Jo. The helicopter is coming for me tomorrow.'

'Mum and dad will be over the moon.'

'I would love us to have a baby, Ellie.'

'Jo, we live in the 21st century. It's not a problem, though it would have to be me who became pregnant given your new job, so perhaps not this week.'

'As long as it is my egg within you, I shan't mind.'

'I'll remind you of that.'

'We shall have to find a man though. I wonder if the Bishop of Ely would help! I should be more than happy for his genes to be in our son or daughter.'

'Should I ask him or you?'

They both laughed.

'It's quite an important question though. My white egg would need a black sperm. I presume you can specify something like that. Now I must concentrate on my driving and avoid hidden tractors as my police driver training taught me at least to do.'

'You can't see but I'm sticking my tongue out at you for being such a clever clogs.'

'M'm, well, for all sorts of reasons I'm glad that wondrous part of you was not injured. By the way, any advance on the pilfering on the ward?'

'It was a patient, I'm sorry to say, and thanks to you he was caught in the act.'

'No thanks to me. It was Kim at MI5.'

'Look Jo, I think you should drive straight home to Norwich and not come via here, now I know I'm being moved tomorrow. I shall miss you today once again, but it's easier for you and we will see one another tomorrow instead.'

'If you're sure about the helicopter, I will.'

'I love you, Jo.'

'Ellie, the words don't exist to tell you how much I love you and we are going to have the most wonderful rest and holiday. No more murders and no more mortuaries – well, at least for now!

Printed in Great Britain
by Amazon

41837074R00215